THE LEGAL THRILLER HAS BEEN
REBORN FOR A NEW GENERATION WITH
THE "FRESH VOICE" (Robert Dugoni) OF

## ALLISON LEOTTA

The former federal sex-crimes prosecutor scores
"a recipe for success: a vulnerable tenacious
heroine, surprising twists and turns, and equal
parts romance and danger" (*Library Journal*,
starred review) in her acclaimed novels.

### Praise for

*DISCRETION*

"A first-rate thriller. Leotta nails the trifecta of fiction:
plot, pace, and character."

—David Baldacci

"A realistic legal thriller that's as fun to read as it is fascinating."

—Lisa Scottoline

"An assured and authentic voice, and a highly entertaining
storyteller."

—George Pelecanos

"Smart and sexy . . . rock-solid plotting . . . top-notch."

—John Lescroart

"Beautifully crafted and frighteningly real."

—Douglas Preston

"Allison Leotta is by far one of the finest new thriller writers today. Chock-full of twists and turns, *Discretion* will have you on the edge of your seat."

—*Strand Magazine*

## SPEAK OF THE DEVIL

### Named Best Book of the Month by Apple and featured in the iBookstore

"Sexy and brutal . . . convincing and authoritative. . . . This is an author who knows what she's talking about."
—*Seattle Post-Intelligencer* (Editor's Choice)

"Suspenseful . . . exciting."

—*Publishers Weekly*

"Vivid, explosive."

—*RT Book Reviews* (4 stars)

"Absolutely a must-read!"

—*Fresh Fiction*

"Chilling and deftly done."

—Catherine Coulter

"Allison Leotta doesn't just write about this world. She lives in it and works in it. That's why *Speak of the Devil* comes to life in the most haunting and best way."

—Brad Meltzer

"Taut and fast-paced . . . intelligent, probing, and clear-eyed. Part morality tale, part riveting drama, and very, very good."

—*The Washington Independent Review of Books*

"Leotta is on fire in the literary world."

—*Deadline Detroit*

*LAW OF ATTRACTION*

*Named One of the Best Legal Thrillers of 2010 by
Suspense Magazine*

"Riveting. . . . Leotta joins the big leagues with pros like Lisa Scottoline and Linda Fairstein."
—*Library Journal* (starred review)

"A racy legal thriller . . . taking on a still-taboo subject."
—*The Washington Post*

"Intense and realistic. . . . Leotta is an up-and-coming literary giant."
—*Suspense Magazine*

"Realistic, gritty, and filled with twists and turns. . . . A great read."
—Alan M. Dershowitz

"Suspenseful . . . strikes all the right chords. . . . Impressive."
—*Mystery Scene Magazine*

"Sexy, fast-paced. . . . Reminiscent of Linda Fairstein."
—*City Pulse*

"A riveting page-turner. . . . Leotta turns her experiences into visceral prose."
—*Washington City Paper*

"A great ride . . . a shocking end. . . . A stunning debut indicating a bright future."
—Robert Dugoni

# ALLISON LEOTTA

# DISCRETION

POCKET BOOKS

*New York   London   Toronto   Sydney   New Delhi*

Pocket Books
A Division of Simon & Schuster, Inc.
1230 Avenue of the Americas
New York, NY 10020

This book is a work of fiction. Any references to historical events, real people, or real places are used fictitiously. Other names, characters, places, and events are products of the author's imagination, and any resemblance to actual events or places or persons, living or dead, is entirely coincidental.

First Pocket Books paperback edition April 2015

POCKET and colophon are registered trademarks of Simon & Schuster, Inc.

For information about special discounts for bulk purchases, please contact Simon & Schuster Special Sales at 1-866-506-1949 or business@simonandschuster.com.

The Simon & Schuster Speakers Bureau can bring authors to your live event. For more information or to book an event, contact the Simon & Schuster Speakers Bureau at 1-866-248-3049 or visit our website at www.simonspeakers.com.

Manufactured in the United States of America

10  9  8  7  6  5  4  3  2  1

ISBN 978-1-4767-9371-9
ISBN 978-1-4516-4486-9 (ebook)

*For my grandmother Bertl Reis
who taught me to keep asking questions*

# Sunday

# 1

Even now, Caroline got nervous before every big job—and this was bigger than most. She knew how to smile past smirking hotel concierges and apartment-building doormen who deliberately looked the other way. The key was looking confident. But committing a crime in the U.S. Capitol was a different experience altogether.

She tried to radiate authority as she strode up the marble steps to the Capitol's Senate carriage entrance. It helped that she was dolled up like a successful K Street lobbyist: ivory St. John suit, Manolo heels, hair painstakingly highlighted just the right shade of blond. Two men coming out of the portico murmured hello to her, and she smiled as if she greeted congressional staffers all the time. One staffer turned to watch her pass. His glance was appreciative but not shocked; she was young and beautiful, but she looked like she belonged in this world of high-octane political deal-making. Good.

She stepped out of the muggy August twilight and into the air-conditioned cool of the security vestibule. To calm herself, she concentrated on the feeling of lace garters skimming her thighs. This was one of the riskiest moments, so she arranged her face into its brightest smile.

"Hello." She greeted the two Capitol Police officers with cool professionalism. "I have an appointment with Congressman Lionel."

Her heart beat like hummingbird wings as she

handed her ID to the officer sitting behind the counter. The guard just smiled as he cross-checked the ID against a paper on his clipboard. He scribbled something down and handed back her ID, along with a rectangular sticker that said VISITOR in red. "Just stick that on your suit, ma'am. Your escort will be right down."

Caroline pressed the sticker onto her jacket as the second guard sent her Fendi bag through the X-ray machine. When she was on the other side of the metal detector, she took her purse off the belt—and exhaled.

She stood in the quiet entranceway, sensing the officers checking out her legs. The hallway was 1800s chic: mosaic floor, arched ceiling, black iron candelabras casting a golden glow on flesh-colored walls. She'd heard that the Capitol was one of the most haunted buildings in D.C., and she imagined the ghost of John Quincy Adams swirling through the corridor. Was it always so empty? This was a private back entrance reserved for congressmen, staffers, and VIP visitors who'd been pre-cleared. And it was almost eight P.M. on a Sunday. Most employees were home. Still, she wished it were busier.

A gangly young man rounded the corner. He wore an ill-fitting suit and sneakers, along with a smudge of tinted Clearasil on his temple. An intern. "Ms. McBride?"

"Yes." Inwardly, she cringed at the sound of her real name, but she was an expert at keeping a serene face no matter what was in her head. Besides, the kid was harmless, in the way that only a young man wearing his first suit can be. His sleeves were too short, exposing two inches of pale, freckled wrists. He reminded Caroline of her little brother, whom she adored.

"I'm Chester! Congressman Lionel's intern! I can take you up to his office!"

"Thank you." She walked with him down the corridor.

"So what are you here to see the Congressman about?"

"Constituent services." She smoothly changed tacks. "What do you do for the Congressman?"

Men—whatever their age—were always happy to talk about themselves. The intern enthusiastically described the process for answering congressional correspondence. "We can send sixty different form letters, depending on what a constituent asked about!"

He stopped for a breath as they entered the most beautiful corridor Caroline had ever seen. The hallway itself was a work of art.

"These are the Brumidi Corridors," Chester said in an excited stage whisper. "Originally painted in the eighteen hundreds. Most tourists don't get to see them."

Every inch of wall and arched ceiling was covered in elaborate paintings of American history. Chester pointed to the figures of men sculpted into the railings of a bronze staircase. "The Founding Fathers." He waved at a lunette painting above a wooden door. "The Goddess of War." Despite herself, Caroline was impressed.

The clack of her heels echoed off the walls as they walked into a circular chamber, as large and ornate as a cathedral. She remembered coming here ten years ago, on a seventh-grade field trip. This was the Rotunda, the ceremonial heart of the Capitol. She recognized some of the iconic canvases: the *Declaration of Independence,* the *Landing of Columbus.* The domed ceiling, 180 feet above, was covered with *The Apo-theosis of Washington,* a fresco painting of the first President depicted as a god among angels.

"Wow," she whispered.

For the first time that night, Caroline had a real sense of the history of the place. It wasn't some TV backdrop. So much had happened in this building, so many famous people had made world-changing deci-sions here. Who was she to be prancing through? She was a fraud.

Then she noticed the paintings of revolutionary America. Among hundreds of soldiers, explorers, and men in white wigs . . . she saw only four women. Of those, two were naked and on their knees.

She felt better. Some things never changed. She wasn't a fraud—she was a constant.

Chester led her past a sign that said NO VISITORS BEYOND THIS POINT. They went up a series of curved staircases and down some empty white corridors, then stopped in front of an unlabeled door tucked around a corner.

"Here's the Congressman's hideaway!"

She had no idea what a hideaway was.

"His personal office," the intern whispered. "A little oasis. Where he can get away from the hustle-bustle."

There didn't seem to be much hustle-bustle at this hour, but Caroline understood the precaution. Her prior appointments, at the Congressman's regular of-fice in the less glamorous Rayburn Office Building, had caused difficulties. She was glad for the privacy this place afforded.

Chester pushed the door open and gestured for Caro-line to go in. He himself stood outside, as if fearful of crossing the threshold. The door clicked shut behind her.

The hideaway was quiet and unoccupied. It looked more like a sitting room in a nice hotel than an office. The walls were deep maroon; the floors were covered in Oriental rugs; a leather couch faced a white marble fireplace. Pictures of the Congressman in action crowded every horizontal surface. An antique desk in the corner seemed less a place to work than a space for displaying more photos.

A door at the back was open to a wide marble balcony overlooking the National Mall. Caroline's breath caught. The Washington Monument and Lincoln Memorial were framed against a fiery sunset. It was a stunning view, better than a postcard.

A man stood on the balcony, his elbows resting on the railing, his back to her. The sunset threw his figure into dark silhouette.

She smoothed her skirt and ran a manicured hand through her hair. This was the part she liked best. She was good at it—great, to be honest. She had a talent for it like nothing else she'd ever tried. It gave her incredible satisfaction.

She smiled and walked out to meet him.

A woman's scream pierced the stillness of the Capitol grounds.

Officer Jeff Cook was on patrol on the Capitol steps. He'd been a Capitol Police officer for twelve years, but he'd never heard a scream like that around here. He put a hand on his holster and turned toward the sound. His eyes flicked over the scenery until they identified the source of the scream. There—up the hill—the third-floor balcony of the Capitol's south wing. A man and woman locked in a jerky dance. Cook couldn't make out the people, but he knew the geography: That was Congressman Lionel's hide-away.

The couple lurched left, then right. The woman shrieked again.

Then the man shoved her over the edge.

The woman seemed to fall in slow motion, emitting an operatic wail the whole way down. Arms flailed in graceful circles, legs kicked in lazy swings, as she dropped past marble flourishes and arched doorways.

A thud. And silence.

She'd landed on the marble terrace in front of the Capitol. Elegant for walking on, it was a disastrous place to fall. What would that slab of rock do to flesh and bones traveling at the speed of gravity?

Cook squinted back up at the balcony. The man was still up there; he peered over the balcony, then turned and disappeared inside.

Cook ran up the Capitol steps.

# 2

Anna Curtis and twenty other women stood in rows on the wooden floor, looking at their feet, at each other, anywhere but at the woman standing in front of them. The instructor stood in front of a floor-to-ceiling window, waiting with a fading smile. The gym was on the eleventh floor of the prosecutors' office, overlooking the rooftops of Judiciary Square. In the distance, the Capitol towered with smug superiority behind the brutalist concrete slabs of local government buildings. Behind the women, lawyers on stationary bikes and deputy U.S. Marshals on weight machines watched to see what the class would do. Anna felt a growing sympathy for the instructor.

Two weeks ago, an e-mail entitled "Women's Self-Defense" had gone to everyone in the U.S. Attorney's Office:

> Ladies, learn to defend yourselves!
> The USAO gym is excited to announce a special class:
> August 5–9
> 7:00–9:00 P.M.
> Led by Eva Youngblood, founder of
> StrikeBack DC!

A male attorney had replied to all, feigning outrage that men weren't invited. The next day, the gym sent an apologetic follow-up. "To clarify, the StrikeBack class is not just for women. Anyone can be vulnerable and should learn to defend themselves." That sealed it—not a man showed up.

Tonight was the first class. Many students, like Anna, were prosecutors in the Sex Crimes and Domestic Violence section. Others were paralegals, victims' advocates, secretaries, and prosecutors from other sections. Anna figured some were there because they really wanted to learn self-defense, but others just wanted to meet Eva Youngblood in person.

Eva was the wife of City Councilman Dylan Youngblood. The couple appeared regularly in the *Post*'s "Reliable Source" column and the *Washingtonian*'s society pages. They had achieved even more celebrity a few months ago, when Dylan announced he was challenging Congressman Emmett Lionel for D.C.'s lone congressional seat. It was a position of power and influence on a national scale, but the post had particular significance for the men and women of the D.C. U.S. Attorney's Office. The winner would recommend the next U.S. Attorney—their boss. Rumor had it that Dylan's pick would be Jack Bailey, the current homicide chief and his longtime friend. Many in the office planned to vote for Dylan just for that reason.

Anna wanted both—to learn self-defense and meet Eva. She had admired the fierce feminist advocate for a long time and was excited to take a class with her.

Eva didn't look so fierce in person, though. She was smaller than Anna had expected, maybe five-two. She was toned and tanned but seemed tiny before the crowd of silent women. Nothing about her appearance suggested Eva was a local luminary rather than just a thirty-seven-year-old aerobics instructor.

Anna looked around at the class, hoping someone

would volunteer. Her fellow prosecutors were some of the toughest women she'd ever met. They faced the city's most violent men on a daily basis. Yet despite their enthusiasm for the class and their willingness to sign a packet of waivers and consent forms, no one was stepping up. The instructor's smile faded.

Anna's sympathy kicked into high gear. Even for a woman like Eva, it must be hard to stand up in front of a group like this. And this was Anna's home turf. She felt a sort of good-citizen responsibility for things to go smoothly. She couldn't sit here while the woman floundered.

Anna stepped forward. "I'll be the guinea pig."

Eva's smile returned as she gestured for Anna to join her on the mat at the front of the class. As Anna stood next to the instructor, she felt Amazonian. She could look right over Eva's head and see herself reflected in the mirror. They were an odd couple. Eva was tiny, muscular, and dark-haired, wearing bright new Lululemon gym clothes. Anna was tall, lanky, and blond, in a faded blue tank top and black yoga pants so well loved they were fraying at the hem. Eva's face had the expertly made-up look of the "after" picture of a makeover. Anna, whose pre-class primping involved pulling her hair into a ponytail and applying ChapStick, was closer to the "before."

"What's your name?" Eva asked.

"Anna Curtis."

"Thanks for helping with our first lesson in self-defense."

The instructor smiled and held out her hand. When Anna took it, Eva's fingers closed tightly around Anna's palm. The instructor yanked Anna toward her, pivoted, and flipped Anna onto the ground. Anna's back hit the mat with a thwack.

The class buzzed with exclamations and laughter. "Wow!"

"How'd she do that? Anna's like six inches taller!"

"Anna, are you okay?" That was her best friend, Grace.

Anna blinked up at the fluorescent panels. Her flash of anger was eclipsed by a desire to learn that move.

Eva's voice cut through the racket, loud enough to reach the Nautilus machines at the back of the gym. "That's your first and most important lesson, ladies." She strode in front of Anna on the mat. "Never let your guard down!"

Anna didn't mind being the butt of a joke, but she could give as good as she got. And the opening was too perfect. She swept her foot out at Eva's ankle, knocking the instructor's feet out from under her. Eva tumbled to the mat with a yelp.

Throughout the gym, weights froze midlift; elliptical machines halted midstride.

The two women's heads were level, a few inches above the floor. Anna grinned at the instructor. "Nice to meet you?"

Eva seemed to consider her options, then returned the smile. "Nice to meet you, too."

They got to their feet, and Eva stuck out her hand again. Anna made a show of exaggerated suspicion, then braced herself and took Eva's hand. It was just a handshake this time.

"So there you go!" Eva said, turning back to the class. "Another demonstration of why you should never let your guard down!"

The students applauded. StairMasters whirred again;

weights continued their up-and-down trajectories. Anna trotted back to her place with the other women in the class. Her friend Grace, an elegant black woman in pink capris, said, "You're a natural on your back, kiddo." Anna smiled and rolled her neck in an attempt to get the kinks out.

Eva launched into an impassioned speech. "Too many women's lives are ruled by fear. By taking this class, you'll get confidence, independence, and the ability to stand up for yourself when you need to."

Anna was skeptical that throwing students to the floor would inspire a feeling of confidence, but she hoped the instructor was right. As a prosecutor of sex crimes, Anna felt particularly vulnerable. Last year, a man she was prosecuting forced his way into her home, where they'd struggled until the police arrived. Since then, Anna had been looking over her shoulder every time she walked down the street. She hated feeling that way. She'd become a prosecutor in order to escape the sense of powerlessness she'd had as a child. She needed to feel in control again. She needed to be able to kick some ass.

Eva had them all sit in a circle and then asked each woman to say why she'd signed up for the class. Anna was surprised to hear her colleagues talk about abuse they'd suffered as children or as girlfriends. They all worked together, helping victims of similar incidents, but rarely talked about what they'd experienced themselves.

Anna knew she shouldn't have been surprised. She rarely talked about the darkness in her own childhood. She hadn't planned to tonight, either. But after everyone else had shared their most private experiences, it felt cowardly to hedge when it was her turn.

"My father used to beat up my mom," Anna said. "It's probably the reason I became a prosecutor."

Grace patted her back, and the other women murmured support. Anna looked at the circle of sympathetic faces. The exercise had been cathartic for everyone.

Eva herself didn't share anything. Anna wondered whether the instructor had some trauma of her own that had led her to become a women's self-defense guru.

Eva stood up and started the first lesson. Anna expected to punch some foam pillows, but they spent the next hour learning about verbal deescalation—the art of defusing tense interactions with words. They practiced talking their way out of difficult situations with dates, coworkers, and strangers. It was less of a workout than Anna had expected, but a good idea. Many attacks started with verbal parrying.

"Okay, ladies!" Eva called. "I'm going to teach you one series of moves tonight. You know the most common injury from a bar fight? Broken fingers, from punching with a closed fist. Hit with the heel of your palm, and you won't hurt yourself—and you won't hold back because you're scared of hurting yourself."

She showed them how to strike an attacker's nose with the heel of a hand. The key was twisting from the torso, creating torque power from the core. Then she showed them how to grab an attacker by his shoulder, pull him close, and deliver a debilitating groin kick.

"It seems counterintuitive," Eva said, "but you have to go *through* your attacker. Don't run away until he's disabled. Pull him tight to your chest, so he can't get away when you kick his groin. He'll bend over in pain, and you follow up with a knee to his head."

Eva had them practice on each other. Anna buddied up with Grace. To practice the groin kick, Grace pressed Anna against her, so they were chest to chest and hip to hip.

"You should've at least bought me a drink first," Anna whispered.

They cracked up.

"I'll buy you a drink tonight." Grace loosened her grip on Anna's shoulders. "A bunch of us are going to Rosa Mexicano after this."

Anna shook her head with regret. The women from their section always had a great time swapping war stories over pomegranate margaritas. Sex-offense work was tough, and raucous happy hours were cheaper than therapy.

"I can't," Anna said. "I promised to pick up dinner on the way home tonight."

"He's got you on a tight leash, huh?" Grace was the only person who knew Anna had a boyfriend.

"No." Anna bristled. "We just have plans."

But there was a kernel of truth in Grace's statement. The last time Anna came home at midnight with margaritas on her breath, her boyfriend had not been happy. He didn't like her to go out drinking when he had to be home with his daughter. Anna didn't want to mess up this relationship, so she hadn't gone out in a while.

Anna softened her tone. "Have a margarita for me."

"That's what you said last time everyone went out," Grace chided gently. "And the time before that."

Anna was surprised that her absence had been noted. She didn't want to be one of those women who disappeared when she got a new boyfriend.

Eva came over and eyed them disapprovingly. Anna

and Grace were holding each other like two sixth-graders at a dance, hands on each other's shoulders, standing an arm's length apart.

"What are you waiting for?" Eva asked Grace. "If this were an attack, your assailant would've dragged you to an alley by now."

"Right." Grace pulled Anna against her again and performed a mock groin kick.

Anna bent over in pretend agony just as a musical ringtone went off. The theme song from *COPS*: "Bad boys, bad boys, whatcha gonna do? Whatcha gonna do when they come for you?" The entire class looked to the wall, where a dozen identical BlackBerries were lined up.

"It's mine," Anna said, slipping out of Grace's grasp and trotting over.

"Coward!" Grace called.

Anna picked up her phone. She used that ringtone only for calls from her boss, the chief of the Sex Crimes and Domestic Violence unit. But Carla Martinez was in South Carolina, teaching a course at the National Advocacy Center. Why would she be calling at almost nine o'clock at night?

"Hi, Carla?"

"Anna, hello." Carla's voice was harried but relieved. "I've been trying to reach you. I left you a message."

"I'm sorry, I'm at the gym." The locker room was right next to the National Security section, where the lead-lined walls interfered with cell signals.

"How quickly can you get to the Capitol Building?" Carla asked.

Anna walked over to the tall window. She could see the top of the Capitol dome, eight blocks away.

"I can be there in ten minutes." So much for dinner plans.

"Great. I'll explain while you're on your way. Get there as quickly as possible." Carla cleared her throat. "Preferably before Jack Bailey shows up."

# 3

Anna thought the Capitol illuminated at night was the single most impressive sight in a city full of impressive sights. Tonight, however, the landmark was trussed up like any other crime scene. Yellow police tape cordoned off the white marble steps, and a haphazard layer of TV vans and police cruisers jammed the street.

The night air retained the scent of baked asphalt and the sultry heat of the August afternoon. Anna was flushed from speed-walking over, but she tried to appear calm and official as she squeezed through the bystanders. She was glad she'd changed out of her yoga clothes and into a spare black pantsuit she kept in her office. She held up her U.S. Attorney's Office credentials, and an officer lifted the yellow tape. As she ducked under, a few reporters shouted questions at her back. She was not at liberty to answer them, even if she had the answers. She kept walking.

The Capitol sat atop one of the biggest hills in the city, and the landscaping around it was like a wedding cake, all white, scalloped, and multitiered. A fountain separated two sets of marble steps. She jogged up the closest one.

She reached the top just in time to see Jack Bailey crest the other set of stairs. Jack was a tall African-American man with a clean-shaven head and light green eyes. His work ethic and courtroom skills had propelled him up the ranks in the U.S. Attorney's Office. Now, at only thirty-seven, he was the chief of the

Homicide section, one of the most coveted positions in the largest U.S. Attorney's Office in the country. He usually favored dark suits, but tonight he wore jeans and a navy T-shirt with the Department of Justice seal on the pocket. He'd been called here from home.

So much for Carla's hope that Anna get here first. Anna felt a rush of happiness to see Jack, though she was careful to project only the polite smile of a colleague. She greeted him in her most formal voice. "Hello, Jack."

Jack laughed and shook his head when he saw her. "Hello, Anna. Did Carla send you to stake a claim to this case?"

"I was supposed to get here before you."

An MPD officer passed them and chuckled. "No fighting, you two. Flip a coin or something." The ongoing turf war between Homicide and Sex Crimes was a joke to everyone outside the two sections.

Anna and Jack walked to the Capitol's long rectangular south wing, where dozens of officers clustered on the brightly lit marble terrace. She saw uniforms from the Metropolitan Police Department, Capitol Police, Park Police, Secret Service, and a few agencies she didn't recognize. D.C. had more separate police forces than any other American city.

She and Jack navigated through the outer layer of police personnel. The closer they got to the center, the quieter the people were. There was an open space in the middle of the crowd, like the eye of a hurricane. Anna wended her way into it.

A woman lay on her side on the white marble terrace, her arms splayed one way, legs bent the other. A pool of dark blood spread under her blond hair. Her ivory skirt was hiked above her waist, revealing ivory

garters. Ivory lace panties were bunched around her
right knee. The panties had been ripped off her left leg
and hung in tatters. The way her knees were angled,
her bottom was bared to the onlookers. Anna wished
she could cover the woman with a blanket.

"They have to wait for the medicolegal investigator," Jack said quietly. "They can't move the body until
she's been pronounced dead."

Anna nodded. On the woman's neck hung a delicate white-gold necklace with the name Sasha scrolled
in cursive. Odd, Anna thought. One of the few facts
Carla had been able to tell her was that the victim had
checked in to the Capitol with a Georgetown student
ID under the name of Caroline McBride.

The young woman's face was turned to the side.
She had alabaster skin and the finely carved profile of
a Greek statue. She was about the same age, hair color,
and build as Anna's little sister, Jody. Or Anna herself.

Anna looked up at the balcony from which the
woman had fallen. A Metropolitan Police Department
officer was standing on it, looking down at the woman's body. A few feet from Anna, an MPD crime-scene
technician was taking photos of something glimmering
near the woman's head. A grayish-red dollop. Anna
gagged and turned away, realizing it was a piece of the
woman's brain.

She'd handled some gruesome cases: injuries in-
flicted with razor blades, bullets, boiling oil. Sex of-
fenses committed on the most vulnerable victims. But
this was the first time she'd seen a murder victim at
the scene. The muggy night seemed to press down on
her; she felt unbearably hot and claustrophobic.

Anna pushed her way back through the crowd. She
made it to the railing at the edge of the terrace in time

to retch over the side. She prayed she wasn't contaminating the crime scene—and that no one was watching. When her convulsions stopped, she kept gripping the rail. Her legs were rubbery and her throat was raw, but mostly, she was mortified.

The view ahead was beautiful. The Washington Monument shone like a beacon against the black sky, and beyond it, the Lincoln Memorial was a steady white square. Anna dug in her purse for one of the tissues she always carried; they were essential in a job where witnesses routinely broke into tears. Now that she needed one herself, she was out. She searched for a crumpled Starbucks napkin, a CVS receipt, *anything*. Her hands shook.

"Anna." Jack stood beside her, offering a folded handkerchief.

"Thank you."

As he placed the handkerchief in her palm, he gently squeezed her hand. She closed her eyes and concentrated on his cool grip. It steadied her. She took a deep breath and reluctantly pulled her hand away. She blotted her cheeks and wiped her mouth with his handkerchief. The cloth smelled of fresh peppermint.

"God, I'm so embarrassed," she whispered. "Is anyone laughing at me?"

"No." His deep voice brokered no argument. "Everyone does that at their first homicide scene."

She doubted that was true, but at least it was comforting. Her hands stopped shaking enough for her to find a Life Saver in her purse. She sucked on the mint and willed her stomach to settle down. She checked her lapels to make sure she hadn't spattered herself. She seemed clean.

"Okay, let's do this." She turned back to the terrace

and stuffed Jack's handkerchief into her purse so she could wash it before returning it. Jack nodded, and they walked to an MPD officer standing at an arched marble entranceway.

"Hi, Frank," Jack said. "Can you show us where our victim fell from?"

"Jack, hey!" The officer was obviously delighted to see him. Jack had a loyal following among law enforcement. "Follow me."

The officer led them through the arched entrance into the Capitol. They walked past a security vestibule and through a rabbit's den of narrow white corridors. Compared to the mugginess outside, the intense air-conditioning in the building felt like the inside of a meat locker. Anna shivered.

The officer pointed up a curving staircase. "Two flights up to the third floor. Turn left, the door's on your right."

Jack thanked him, and the officer went back the way he'd come. Anna followed Jack up the empty stairwell. When they got to the second-floor landing, Jack stopped and turned to her. He lay a hand on her cheek. "You okay, sweetheart?" he whispered.

For a moment, she leaned into his touch. She still felt queasy from the sight of the young woman on the terrace. Part of her wanted to rest her head on his chest and let his solid form blot out what she'd seen. But anyone might see them. She pulled his hand away from her cheek. "I'm fine," she said.

"You're pale." He reached for her.

She stepped back quickly and raised a hand. "Not here," she whispered fiercely. No one besides Grace knew they were dating, and Anna intended to keep it that way.

Jack sighed as he turned back to the stairs. "At least that put some color back into your cheeks."

They walked up the final flight of steps in silence. At the top, she pointed to a dark globe implanted in the ceiling.

"Pull the video?" she said.

Jack nodded. "McGee's on it. He's waiting for us."

They rounded a corner and walked down the hallway until they came to a crowded vestibule in front of a single door. Anna could see even more activity inside the sumptuous office beyond the door—Capitol Police officers securing it as a crime scene.

In the vestibule was Tavon McGee, a huge, dark-skinned homicide detective from the Metropolitan Police Department. Anna had worked with him on her biggest case, a domestic-violence prosecution that led to a homicide. McGee loved flashy suits, chili cheese fries, and a good joke. He was also very good at his job.

The detective stood next to a beautiful dark-haired woman in a pantsuit. Anna saw the gold badge clipped to the front of her belt and the slight bulge of her suit jacket over a firearm at her side. Some kind of federal agent.

McGee and the female agent were interviewing an older African-American man who sported a mane of salt-and-pepper hair, a dark suit, and a gold lapel pin with the House of Representatives crest. Anna instantly recognized him: Emmett Lionel, the District's Delegate to Congress for the last thirty-one years. Because D.C. wasn't a state, Lionel didn't have a vote in national matters. Technically, he was a "Delegate" rather than a full-blown "Congressman," but everyone used the honorific. He was the city's most powerful local politician.

Detective McGee greeted Jack and Anna's arrival with a gap-toothed grin. He excused himself from the Congressman, pocketed his little notebook, and walked over, putting his huge hands on both prosecutors' shoulders. "The cavalry has arrived!" The homicide detective wore a beige five-button suit, a black shirt, and a tie with stripes of beige, black, and purple. A black fedora sat at a cocky angle on his head. McGee pointed his thumb at Congressman Lionel and shook his head in disbelief. "You know whose office this is? The Lion's! He spoke at my Police Academy graduation twenty-two years ago."

Jack nodded. "What's he saying?"

"He was at some kinda reception downstairs, doesn't know how a girl came to fall from his balcony. But he was found coming down the stairway near his hideaway by a Capitol Police officer running up to check it out."

A booming voice interrupted. "Congressman Lionel!"

All heads turned to see a tall, dark-suited man striding up the hallway. Anna recognized Daniel Davenport, although she'd never met him. Every lawyer in D.C. had seen his silver hair and imperious gray eyes on the cover of bar journals and inside newspapers. At a thousand dollars an hour, Davenport had represented CEOs and elected officials in the country's most notorious white-collar criminal cases. It was said that in thirty years, none of his clients had gone to jail—and his cases more often ended with the prosecutors facing charges for misconduct. If they got anything wrong tonight, Anna knew, Davenport would hammer them.

Davenport walked between Congressman Lionel

and the female agent and whispered something in
Lionel's ear. Lionel took a step away from the agent
and pointed to two men in suits who were being interviewed by MPD officers.

"Stanley. Brett. Come here," Davenport commanded.
The two men looked nervously from him to the police
officers questioning them. "Right now!" The men complied like puppies being called to their owner.

Jack walked toward Davenport, with Anna and
McGee flanking him.

"Hello, Daniel," Jack said. "Nice to see you. What's
going on here?"

"Good evening, Jack. I represent the Congressman.
He and his staff would love to answer these officers'
questions, but I simply can't allow that until I know
more about what's happened."

"You don't represent the staffers," Jack said, inclin-
ing his head toward the men in suits.

"The Congressman's office will be paying for their
representation. I think you'll find they will not consent
to be interviewed outside the presence of their lawyers."

"They can speak for themselves." Jack turned to the
men, who stood a few feet behind Davenport. Both
appeared to be in their forties but had little else in
common.

The shorter staffer stepped forward. He was African-American, fat, and bowlegged, with a chest puffed
out with the pompousness of a miniature bulldog. His
shirt was rumpled, and a spot that looked like ketchup
marred his tie. He put his hands on his hips. "I'm
Stanley Potter, Congressman Lionel's Chief of Staff.
As Mr. Davenport said, we'll be happy to cooperate—
once we've had a chance to talk to our lawyers."

Potter elbowed the taller white man standing next to him. The man said, "Brett Vale, Legislative Director. Ditto what Stanley said." If Potter was a bulldog, Vale was a greyhound. Good-looking in a wonkish way, with a sharp face and the leanness of a daily runner. He wore an impeccably pressed gray suit and had slicked his prematurely gray hair back against his head. Stylish silver glasses framed blue eyes so light they seemed almost transparent.

The Congressman himself didn't say anything. His lawyer must have told him to keep his mouth shut. He stood there with his hands in his pockets, looking distinguished and contemplative. But Anna could see the sweat beading his salt-and-pepper hairline despite the arctic air-conditioning. She was disappointed in him. It was his right not to talk to the police, but she expected better from a public official.

"You have their contact information, and here's mine." Davenport handed Jack his business card. "I'd ask that you let these men go home."

"Go home! They're suspects in a criminal case," said the female agent. She'd come over to stand next to Jack.

The Chief of Staff puffed up his chest even further. The Legislative Director regarded her with icy disdain. The Congressman looked sick. Davenport took a step forward so that he was standing between them and the agent.

"That's precisely the reason they won't consent to be interviewed," Davenport said. "Unless you're arresting them for something, you've got no grounds to keep them here. And I'm sorry, but you are who?"

"Samantha Randazzo. FBI, Violent Crime squad." The agent put her hands on her hips, which drew back her jacket and exposed the Glock holstered behind her badge. She was in her early thirties, slim and athletic. Her heels were a little higher—and her black pantsuit a little tighter—than the average cop's. Curly black hair spiraled past her shoulders. She turned to Jack. "Any grounds to arrest them as material witnesses?"

Anna shook her head and saw Jack doing the same. It would be convenient to haul everybody into the police station and force them to answer questions, but that wasn't how the system worked. Without probable cause to believe that one of the men had committed a crime, or proof that they had material evidence and would flee to avoid testifying, there was no legal basis to detain them. The police could take the names of everyone in the building, but they couldn't keep them locked in.

Jack turned to the Congressman and his staffers. "You're not under arrest. But Detective McGee will give you subpoenas to appear in the grand jury tomorrow."

"Too soon," Davenport said. "They'll need time to meet with counsel to decide whether to waive any Fifth Amendment privileges."

He knew exactly what to say to delay things, Anna noted with equal parts admiration and annoyance.

"Tuesday, then," Jack said. He looked at the men in suits. "Two days is enough. If you leave town while you're under subpoena, I'll send the U.S. Marshals to collect you."

The Congressman and his two staffers nodded. But Davenport wasn't finished. He pointed to the police officers in the hideaway. "Now we need to prevent these overeager officers from violating the Constitution and compromising their own investigation. Please tell these well-meaning men and women that the Speech or Debate Clause requires them to leave my client's office."

"They're securing a crime scene," Jack said. "There could be more victims in there, or even the assailant."

"There are half a dozen officers in there," Davenport said. "Even they would have found another victim by now. They've swept the office, so there are no exigent circumstances. Now they're merely intruding on my client's constitutional rights."

"Those are just Capitol Police," McGee said. "We still need to process this as a homicide scene."

"No," Davenport said. "You've read the *Jefferson* case? I can see you haven't. Suffice it to say that any items you seize from my client's legislative office will be suppressed, and if those officers don't leave right now, you all risk being sanctioned."

Everyone in the U.S. Attorney's Office had heard the basics of the *Jefferson* case—the FBI had found ninety thousand dollars in a congressman's home freezer, but because of the Speech or Debate Clause, they weren't allowed to search his office. The specifics of this esoteric corner of the Constitution were the province of federal political-corruption prosecutors. Anna was certain that in thirteen years of murder cases, Jack had never run across the issue. He looked worried, an expression Anna rarely saw on the confident Homicide chief's face.

Anna's youth was actually an advantage here. As a student at Harvard Law School, she'd studied the *Jefferson* decision. She knew Davenport was right. "Can I talk to you for a minute?" she asked Jack.

Davenport looked surprised that the young pup was interrupting the big dogs. But Jack nodded to

Anna and motioned for McGee and Samantha to join
them. The four of them went around the corner and
stood in a huddle.

"He has a point," Anna said softly. "There's only
been one search of a congressman's office in all of
American history—and the appeals court held it to be
illegal. The Speech or Debate Clause protects legislators from interference by the Executive Branch, even
when looking for evidence of a crime."

McGee looked incredulous. "You mean a congressman can kill somebody just as long as he does it in his
office?"

"No, he doesn't get a pass. He can be prosecuted,
but not with evidence arising from his legislative
activity. It's about separation of powers between the
branches of government. In *Jefferson*, the FBI walled
off the prosecution team from the search team, but the
Court of Appeals still held the search to be illegal. If
we search his office and disturb his legislative papers,
anything we find could be suppressed."

"What if there's blood or fingerprints on his papers?" Samantha demanded.

Anna turned to McGee. "Will blood or fingerprints
degrade overnight?"

"No."

"Let's call the judge in chambers," Anna said. "We
can apply for a warrant tonight. Even if the judge
wants to hold a hearing, we could probably be in
court before seven tomorrow morning."

McGee frowned but nodded. He wasn't happy
about the delay, but he'd defer to Anna on the legal
issue.

But Samantha looked furious. "There's no reason
to wait. Throwing someone from a balcony is not a

legislative act. Any judge will let us go in there and process the crime scene."

The strength of the agent's reaction made Anna pause. Was she being too cautious because of the scandal she'd gone through last year? She hoped not. "I think you're right," she said. "But it's worth waiting a few hours to make sure we can keep the evidence we find."

"The killer could be gone in eight hours," Samantha snapped.

Anna narrowed her eyes. This agent was getting on her nerves.

"All right." Jack stepped between the two women and held up his hands. "We'll do this with a warrant and a judge's signature. I'll call the judge in chambers. She'll probably let Davenport file something and hold a hearing in the morning. Meanwhile, we'll post MPD officers outside the office."

Anna nodded. "I can brief the Speech or Debate Clause for the warrant application."

"Don't work all night," Jack said. "You need some sleep if you're going to argue this tomorrow."

"You're letting *her* argue the motion?" Samantha asked Jack.

"I don't know the Speech or Debate Clause," Jack said, "and Anna does. She'll get the warrant, and the police will be back in there to do a search by mid-morning."

"If not"—Samantha glared at Anna—"we'll know who to blame."

# 4

Nicole laughed like it was the funniest thing she'd ever heard. It allowed her to tip back her head, exposing the curve of her neck and pushing her breasts farther out of her little black dress. She squirmed as if in uncontrollable delight on Tom's lap—or was it Tim? Oh well, it hardly mattered. What mattered was that she could feel his erection straining desperately through his pants. He was ready to go.

She glanced toward the doors leading to the bedrooms. Both were closed, so she'd have to wait her turn. Not exactly a hardship. She lifted two champagne flutes from the coffee table and handed one to Tom (or Tim), who took it with a wondrous smile. He looked like a kid who'd received a pony *and* a shiny red bicycle for his birthday. She clinked her glass against his. "Cheers."

She savored the Cristal, letting the tiny bubbles linger on her tongue. She didn't get to party like this much nowadays. They sat on a couch in an opulent suite at the Willard. More Cristal cooled in buckets on the sideboard. The men were well dressed, well groomed, and well behaved. Auto execs from Detroit or something like that. So what if they were a little bland and round in the middle? This was the best gig she'd had in a while.

Belinda danced between two men by the bar as Sinatra crooned from the speakers. The women would've preferred Jay-Z, but they knew their audience. The middle-aged men weren't natural dancers but were happy for an excuse to run their hands over the beautiful woman. Belinda was a gorgeous Chinese-American woman with dark hair floating past her shoulder blades. She wore a dress that shimmered like it was made of liquid mercury. One guy held Belinda's hips; the other stroked her ass. Nicole caught Belinda's eyes and lifted her glass in salute. "Thank you," Nicole mouthed. Belinda was the one who'd included her in the party.

Belinda smiled, then leaned back to kiss the man behind her. The man in front skimmed his hands up her torso and caressed her nipples through her shimmery dress. She murmured like she was loving it. The men glanced at each other over Belinda's head. They were wondering how far this could go. Nicole knew. If they continued to show interest in the arrangement, Belinda would lead them both to a bedroom and take one in her mouth while the other took her from behind. The men would go back to Michigan thinking they were sexual conquistadors, boldly exploring uncharted lands.

They had no idea.

Nicole glanced at Bill, the lobbyist lounging in a leather chair. He appeared satisfied, and that was what mattered. He was picking up the tab. Thank God for lobbyists. The auto execs might not even realize the girls were escorts, although they'd have to be pretty dense. But Bill was a pro, and he was trying to land their company as a client. If he succeeded, they would pay Bill exorbitant fees so he could use every means at his disposal—including girls like Nicole—to persuade certain politicians to pass laws allowing higher emissions, fewer miles per gallon, that sort of thing. Nicole wondered if anything would get done in Washington without professionals like her to lubricate the joints of power.

Bill pulled a smart silver case from his breast pocket and set it up on the coffee table. A mirror, a razor, a heap of white powder. He cut the powder into generous lines, rolled a crisp twenty into a straw, and called to the dancing threesome. The two men and Belinda each had a bump, then Bill pushed the mirror toward Nicole. She wanted a line so bad her eyes itched.

She loved the white stuff. She loved it so much that last week she'd blown her nose and found a chunk of bloody cartilage in the tissue. After she was done freaking out, she'd called a friend, who told her not to worry, it happened to everybody. It was her septum, the internal wall that separated her two nostrils. Too much cocaine had eaten it away. There was nothing she could do about it, but she couldn't snort anymore.

So she'd started freebasing.

In fact, she'd smoked a rock in the ladies' room of the Willard's lobby right before coming up here. She obviously couldn't freebase at a party like this; it'd be like riding a donkey at a polo match. Her midwestern clients might not draw the subtle but important distinction between freebasing and smoking crack. Crack was for ghetto dwellers only; freebasing was a perfectly acceptable part of the high life. She knew they looked pretty much the same.

Nicole shook her head at Bill. "No thanks, sweetie." Ironically, she felt all prim and proper declining the coke. She felt like the girl in an afternoon special who just said no, the goody-goody A-student, the all-American golden girl.

She felt like Caroline.

Bill shrugged and hoovered a line himself.

One of the bedroom doors opened, and a girl walked out with another dazed exec. Nicole snuggled closer to Tim (or Tom), pressing her thighs into his erection and stroking his thinning hair. She grazed his ear with her lips and whispered, "I want to show you something." Her eyes flicked toward the bedroom door. His eyes followed.

Desire and fear fought a battle on his face. His thumb instinctively tapped his wedding band, and he was perfectly still for a moment. Then he chugged the rest of his champagne and nodded. Chalk one up for desire. She led him by the hand into the bedroom. One of the other men hooted. Nicole shut and locked the door.

A flat-screen TV, muted, provided the only illumination. Good. You wanted the room dark enough to hide imperfections but light enough to allow the visuals that would move things along. The girl before her had remade the bed, so the room looked fresh and new. Nicole had to hand it to Belinda. She ran a tight freelance operation.

Nicole sidled up to the exec. "You're so hot," she murmured, smiling through the lie. She kissed his neck, pungent with the scent of cigar smoke, red meat, and Scotch. The men had apparently gone to a steak house before this. She removed his clothes with skillful efficiency, gently nipping the parts that she was baring. He was naked in under two minutes, pale and pudgy as the Pillsbury Doughboy. That was par for the course.

She turned and gathered her long brown hair on top of her head. "Can you get this for me, honey?" He fumbled with the zipper on her back. When he finally got it, she let the dress fall to the ground. He inhaled sharply, which she appreciated. She worked hard to have a body that caused that reaction.

With the dress off, Nicole wore black stilettos, a black bra and thong, a long string of pearls, and a delicate white-gold necklace with the name Bethany in cursive. She'd been told to return the necklace when she was fired, but fuck that. She'd earned it.

She arched her back and rubbed her buttocks against him. He was erect as a double-A battery. Good. Some women wanted size or stamina, but in Nicole's profession, the smaller and quicker, the better. You didn't want to get sore, and you didn't want to have to work for hours, grinding and licking and ooh-babying, to close the deal. She turned, ran bloodred fingernails down his squishy chest, and pushed him onto the bed.

In other circumstances, she might have lingered over him more. The goal of every escort was to secure steady clients. Each new trick presented unknown challenges and dangers. There was less risk and better compensation if you could get a steady book of business. Regular customers were good. Getting set up in an apartment was better. Marriage was the ultimate goal. Girls who actually married johns were legends, often talked about and much analyzed, but with their true stories warped by time and exaggeration. Nicole knew that marrying a client was as rare as winning the lottery, but that didn't stop her from buying tickets and hoping.

She knew she had a limited shelf life. Today, at twenty-two years old, she could command up to five thousand a night, although circumstances had forced her to take much less lately. That kind of cash wouldn't even be a possibility in her thirties. Tick-tock. Nicole was constantly on the lookout for Prince Charming or, if his white horse didn't gallop over the horizon right quick, Prince Charming Enough.

Tom (or Tim) wasn't that guy. Married men could be fabulous clients: undemanding, apologetic, grateful. But he was from out of town, so he wouldn't be a regular. And there was no way this midlevel auto exec had enough money to keep a girl the way Nicole wanted to be kept. She didn't need to make him feel like he couldn't live without her. He just needed to have a good time and tell Bill. Quick and easy would do.

She pushed him back against the pillows and unclasped her lacy bra.

"My, my, my." He sighed, cupping one of her bare breasts. "You are a beautiful little girl."

Something about the way he said it reminded her of Larry. She hadn't planned to, but she leaned down and kissed his doughy mouth. She wanted to show him how good she was. She took the string of pearls off her neck: this was her specialty.

Caroline was always going on about "the girlfriend experience." Unless you were willing to service the fetishes, the girlfriend experience was where the money was made these days. It was about more than sex. You had to make the client feel like he was having the best date of his life. Chat, laugh, really listen. Act as if he were the most interesting person you'd ever met. Give the impression that being with him was the place you'd most like to be on earth, even if you weren't getting a wad of cash to do it.

That was why Caroline was so damn successful. She wasn't that much prettier than Nicole. She just had a way of connecting with people, making them feel happy and wanted. For a while, Nicole had tried to compete with that, but it wasn't her thing. Instead, she'd mastered a few technical flourishes that kept her in the game.

She focused on the sliver of his body that was the core of her business and wrapped her string of pearls around it, starting at the bottom and winding around until everything but the head was wrapped in luminescent beads. He watched with wide eyes. "Don't worry," she giggled. Grasping the cylinder of pearls, she stroked up and down the shaft. Simultaneously, she took the head in her mouth. Clients told her this was a sensation unlike any other.

She watched the man's face as her tongue traced his circumference. His eyes rolled back in his head; his mouth gaped like a carp; his hands grasped the sheets in a death grip. He either loved this or he was having a heart attack. "God, you're good," he gasped. Okay, he loved it. She increased the tempo and pressure. To be honest, Nicole thought this was a cheap trick. But something about the pearls convinced clients they were getting a high-class service. As an act, it was actually easier than many options.

The man's soft belly pressed against her forehead as he writhed. She breathed through her nose, wondered how long it would take, and angled herself so she could watch the TV as she worked. It was tuned to the news.

A reporter stood in front of the U.S. Capitol, surrounded by flashing police cruisers and yellow tape. He spoke gravely into his microphone. Nicole couldn't hear what he was saying, but she read the banner across the bottom of the screen: WOMAN FALLS FROM OFFICE OF CONG. EMMETT LIONEL (D-DC) AT U.S. CAPITOL.

Nicole stopped what she was doing. She sat up and stared at the TV, wiping a string of saliva from her mouth.

"Don't stop," the man gasped. He tried to pull her head back down, but she ducked out of his grasp.

"Where's the remote?" she demanded.

He looked disoriented. She clambered off the bed and ran to the TV. It was one of those smooth, flat rectangles that didn't seem to have any buttons. She searched frantically around the room. Finally, she found the remote control in the nightstand drawer. She turned up the volume.

". . . police have not yet released the identity of the woman who died after plummeting from the third-floor balcony of Congressman Emmett Lionel's hideaway at around eight P.M. tonight. Congressman Lionel's office has no comment at this time."

Nicole stared at the TV in horror.

"Please, honey, I'm so close." The man reached for her, panting like he was in pain. He looked ridiculous, naked with only her pearls covering his member.

She grabbed the cordless hotel phone and ran into the bathroom, slamming the door shut. Standing by the marble Jacuzzi, she punched in Caroline's number and prayed for an answer. It rang, then went to voice mail. She tried again. This time it went straight to voice mail.

"Are you okay?" Tim (or Tom) banged on the door. "Hey, what's going on?"

Nicole sank down on the edge of the tub. She tried to think of someone she could call, anyone who could help her, advise her, or just tell her everything was going to be all right. There was no one. She pulled her knees tight to her bare chest and hugged herself. She was shaking.

What had she done?

# 5

Anna had been at the U.S. Attorney's Office for almost two years, which in USAO time made her a relatively senior prosecutor. She had her own office on the tenth floor, a step up from the little room she'd shared with Grace in the beginning. Compared to the offices of law firms, it was shabby—tired blue carpet, scuffed walls, a row of battered filing cabinets. But it was hers. Behind her desk, a window overlooked the homeless shelter at 2nd and D streets. A few blocks behind the shelter, the U.S. Capitol glowed white against the black sky.

She'd perked up her office with plants on the windowsill and colorful Romare Bearden posters on the walls. An array of colorful toys lined her desk: a squishy yellow stress ball, painted turtles with bobbing heads, a game where you tried to catch little plastic fish with a little plastic rod. Children liked to hold something when talking about difficult subjects. During countless interviews, Anna had watched the stress ball being squeezed by little hands as their owner described what Mommy's new boyfriend had done.

Anna grabbed a Clif Bar—she still hadn't had dinner—and hurried down the hall toward the red exit sign. She walked down two flights of stairs and emerged into the Law Library. It was quiet except for the hum and blink of fluorescent lights. Most legal research was done online, from lawyers' desks, these days. But sex-crime prosecutors used this library more than anyone else in the office.

Two computers sat against the far wall—the only computers in the office that weren't blocked from viewing sexually explicit websites. In Anna's line of work, she frequently had to go to such sites. A few idiotic federal employees had surfed porn from their work computers, and now the whole federal government was blocked with filtering software.

She logged on to the network and went to www.TrickAdviser.com. She'd been to this site for a few cases. It was the nation's leading customer ratings site for prostitution, and she'd convinced the office to pay for a VIP membership. It had proved invaluable in a number of investigations. Anna didn't prosecute prostitution itself but had handled many cases where prostitutes were raped or assaulted. From ten-dollar prostitutes to thousand-dollar escorts, the sex trade was a dangerous business.

If she'd been gathering evidence to use in a later prosecution, she would have partnered with a police officer so he could testify about it later. But right now she just wanted to check out an idea.

The home page popped up. Today it was a picture of a young woman wearing only a string thong, lying on her stomach on satin sheets, arching up and looking at the camera through her eyelashes. Her breasts were bare; her buttocks made a heart-shaped silhouette behind her head. She was the "featured provider" of the week.

A loud thump behind her made Anna flinch. She looked back. A janitor was pushing a big garbage can through the library door.

"Oh, hey, Marcus," Anna said.

Marcus stared at her computer and froze. "Um, I'll come back later."

The janitor clanked the garbage can against the doorjamb and tripped in his haste to back himself out of there. She suppressed a laugh and turned back to the screen.

TrickAdviser.com was like a sleazy *Consumer Reports* for the high-end sex trade. Men who frequented escorts used the website to describe their experiences and rate the women on a scale from 1 to 10. They could also check out what other people had said about different women. Users took it seriously, leaving incredibly detailed descriptions of their sessions. The women who were rated took it even more seriously. It was a matter of compensation. If a woman got consistently good ratings, she could charge more for her services. If she got bad ratings, it could destroy her career. High rollers would only hire women who got the best reviews on TrickAdviser.

Anna ran a search for escorts in D.C. named Sasha—the name she'd seen on the necklace around Caroline McBride's neck. A professional girl wouldn't be listed under her real name. TrickAdviser listed four Sashas in D.C. Their profiles had no photographs, only text. But there was one whose vital statistics seemed to match the woman who'd fallen from the Capitol tonight.

## SASHA

### General Information
City: Washington, D.C.
Agency: Discretion
Phone: n/a
Website: n/a
E-mail: n/a
In/out: Outcall

Delivered as promised: Yes
On time: Yes
Porn star: No

## Appearance
Build: Skinny
Ethnicity: White
Age: 21–25
Height: 5'6"
Transsexual: No
Breast size: 35–36
Breast cup: C
Implants: No
Breast appearance: Youthful
Hair color: Blond
Hair type: Straight
Hair length: Below shoulders
Piercings: None
Bikini line: Shaved
Tattoos: Egyptian eye, lower back

| SERVICE | LENGTH | PRICE |
|---|---|---|
| Escort Outcall | one night | $5,000 |
| Long-Term Rental | one month | $100,000 |

## REVIEWS

| DATE | REVIEWER | APPEARANCE | PERFORMANCE |
|---|---|---|---|
| 8/12 | DupontDD | 10-One in a lifetime | 10-One in a lifetime |
| 8/12 | lc518 | 10-One in a lifetime | 10-One in a lifetime . |

| 7/12 | beenthere-donethat | 10-One in a lifetime | 10-One in a lifetime |
| 7/12 | rambo | 9-Model material | 10-One in a lifetime |
| 7/12 | AKclub | 10-One in a lifetime | 9-I forgot it was a service |
| 6/12 | ccc | 10-One in a lifetime | 10-One in a lifetime |
| 5/12 | belowthe-belt | 10-One in a lifetime | 10-One in a lifetime |
| 5/12 | DaveT | 9-Model material | 9-I forgot it was a service |

*Page 1 of 1, 2, 3, 4, 5, 6*                    *Next Page*

There was a section called "Services Offered" which listed a variety of sex acts and combinations of people the prostitute might service. They ranged from the traditional to the I-didn't-know-that-was-possible. Sasha was a "yes" for everything. She did it all.

Anna had cringed when she first read these profiles, where women were reduced to a sheet of specs like a car for sale. She'd wondered whether all men thought of women this way. She had long since gotten over that sensitivity. Now she read the macro with an eye toward finding evidence.

Anna had never seen a profile like this. The consecutive 10s were rare. And Sasha's prices were off the charts. A nightly fee of five thousand dollars was the highest Anna had ever seen in D.C., although top New York escorts charged that much. The monthly option was also something new. Most prostitutes had hourly or nightly sessions.

From an investigative standpoint, the most notable thing about Sasha's profile was that it didn't include a phone number, e-mail, or website for her agency. Despite the obvious illegality, most reviews posted that information. How would a potential john get an appointment with Sasha? How did this agency, Discretion, work?

Anna ran a quick search, ranking all of the D.C. escorts by price. When she saw the results, she picked up the phone and dialed Jack.

"Bailey," he answered.

"Hey, it's Anna. I assume you ordered a sex kit on the victim?"

"Sure. The medicolegal investigator just got here. The body will be transported to the ME's office soon."

"Good," Anna said. "Can you ask them to check on something? See if there's an Egyptian-eye tattoo on the victim's lower back."

"Will do. Why?"

"I'm on TrickAdviser. I think our victim is the most expensive call girl in D.C."

# 6

Jack hoped that Anna was wrong. He stood on the Capitol terrace with his cell phone pressed to his ear, watching the medicolegal investigator probe the victim where she lay. The crowd had thinned, since McGee had shooed away nonessential personnel. The perimeter around the body was now staked out with yellow tape, and two large portable lights were set up, adding a stark glare to the scene. In the middle of the bright, empty marble circle, the MLI knelt next to the woman's body, taking her temperature by pressing an electronic thermometer to the forehead.

Jack knew that if the dead woman were an expensive prostitute, the public interest and media coverage would multiply. And every extra ounce of publicity made his investigation more difficult. Crank calls; rumors and speculation; fake witnesses concocting stories to get attention; real witnesses clamming up to avoid it. Elected prosecutors sometimes pounced on high-publicity cases, which raised their profile with the electorate. Federal prosecutors, who were appointed, had less to gain from publicity. Personally, Jack just wanted a clean case. He wanted to find out who had done this and hold that person responsible. If the woman were an escort, he wouldn't be able to turn around without bumping into *The National Enquirer*.

Still, if Anna said something was true, it probably was. One of the things he loved about her was how bright and intuitive she was. He cupped his hand over his phone so the officers wouldn't hear their conversation. You never knew who might leak something to the press.

"What is TrickAdviser?" he asked. "And why do you think our victim was a call girl?"

As Anna explained, Jack watched the MLI work. Checking for rigor mortis, the stiffness of the body; and livor mortis, its color. This would help determine when and how the woman died. In many cases, that was a mystery. Jack once prosecuted a mother who killed her three children, then left the bodies to disintegrate in their beds for several months. The remains were barely recognizable as people. It was a human nightmare and also a forensics nightmare. The Medical Examiner—D.C.'s coroner—could only speculate on the cause and time of death for those victims.

Here, however, the authorities knew exactly how and when the victim had died. The guards at the senate carriage entrance had written down the time she'd checked in. The Capitol Police officer who'd seen her fall had noted the time. The authorities knew the how, when, and where. They just needed to find out the who and why.

The most useful thing the Medical Examiner would do was run a sex kit. They would swab the victim's orifices with long Q-tip-like implements, take samples from her panties and under her fingernails, and comb her body for foreign hairs and fibers. If there was any foreign DNA on her, it could be of tremendous evidentiary value. Semen lasted only seventy-two hours before it degraded to the point where no DNA profile could be determined, so the ME would do it as soon as her body arrived at the morgue. But for now Jack had a simpler question.

He ducked under the yellow police tape and walked

over to the medicolegal investigator. He placed a hand on the young man's shoulder.

"Can I take a look at her lower back?" Jack asked.

The man nodded. The victim was on her side, where she'd landed. With gloved hands, the MLI pulled her suit jacket up and her skirt waistband down, revealing the small of her back.

In the center, where her flesh undulated around her lower spine, was a black-and-white Egyptian-eye tattoo. Whatever protection it was supposed to provide hadn't worked.

Like the sky above, the house was dark at one A.M. Detective Tavon McGee stood on the front porch of the modest split-level house and braced himself. In a job full of heart-wrenching tasks, this was one of the hardest. He exhaled through pursed lips and rang the doorbell. After a moment, a light in an upstairs window went on. McGee could hear shuffling at the front door and a frightened female voice on the other side.

"Who is it?"

"Metropolitan Police Department."

A curtain was pulled back, and a middle-aged woman stared at him from behind the glass. The curtain dropped back into place. "A big black man," murmured the female voice. Now a boy, maybe fifteen years old, came to the window. Must be her son. McGee held his MPD badge closer to the windowpane.

Columbia was a quiet bedroom community in Maryland, halfway between D.C. and Baltimore. McGee expected they didn't get many police visits to this neatly mowed patch of suburbia. He held his badge steadily, giving the homeowners plenty of time to check it out.

More shuffling, lights, soft voices. Finally, the door swung open. The boy wore checkered pajamas and stood a step in front of his mother, as if to protect her. The woman wore a terry-cloth bathrobe and an expression of dread. McGee had seen that look on hundreds of parents' faces when he'd made similar house calls. Everyone knew that a midnight visit from the police meant something had gone horribly wrong.

"Good evening. I'm Detective Tavon McGee, with MPD's Major Case unit. Are you Donna McBride?" The woman nodded, confirming the information he'd gotten from a police database. "May I come in?"

She stared at the hole where his two front teeth used to be. In D.C., the gummy gap added street cred. Here, it made him more of an anomaly. She hesitated, then led him into the living room, a soft plateau of beige wall-to-wall carpeting. A family picture hung on the wall above them: a younger version of the woman, with a husband at her side, each holding a towheaded child. Caroline McBride, perhaps fifteen years ago, and her younger brother. McGee wondered what had happened to the father. He took off his fedora and suggested the woman and the boy sit down. They did, in tandem, on a blue couch.

He remained standing and took a deep breath. He was about to create a moment that would forever mark their lives into two clear sections. Before and after. There was only one way to do it: as directly as possible, without dragging out the information, and leaving no room for uncertainty.

"I'm afraid I have some bad news, ma'am. Your daughter, Caroline McBride, was killed tonight."

The woman moaned and collapsed into her son's

shoulder. The boy put his arm around his mother and stared at the carpeting as she sobbed.

McGee had seen every different way people could respond to this, the worst of all possible news. It ranged from hysterics to absolute calm. He'd seen family members roll on the floor, scream, or punch holes through walls. He'd seen parents shake their heads and say, "I knew this day was coming." In those cases, the victim had been lost to the streets for a long time. This wasn't one of those families.

The mother keened, "My baby, my baby, my baby."

It was the sound of a breaking heart.

McGee waited while the woman cried. He waited a long time, hating the next thing he'd have to tell her: that she'd have to come to the District tomorrow to identify her daughter's remains.

# 7

Anna directed the cab to the yellow Victorian on a quiet street in Takoma Park, an oak-lined neighborhood in Maryland just over the D.C. line. She didn't usually indulge in taxi rides, but the Metro didn't run at two-thirty A.M. on weeknights. Stepping from the cab felt like entering a rain forest, the air was so muggy and filled with the chirping of insects. A few lightning bugs floated up from the ground and glowed as she tiptoed through the garden of roses and wild peppermint. She walked up the steps onto the wide front porch.

The house was dark except for a light in the living room window. Anna put her key in the door quietly, trying not to wake anyone. In the foyer, she slipped off her shoes and set her bag next to a *Princess and the Frog* backpack.

She followed the light into the living room. Jack sat on the couch in his navy DOJ T-shirt and jeans. At first, she thought he was reading by the light of the Tiffany dragonfly lamp. His head was tipped down toward some documents on his lap, and his reading glasses were perched on his nose. The lamp's stained glass threw patches of colorful light onto his brown hands. When Anna got closer, she noticed his eyes fluttering in REM sleep under his eyelids. Poor guy.

She sank down next to him. Despite her protests, he always waited up for her. His daughter, Olivia, woke up every morning around six, and he would be exhausted. But once he made up his mind to do something, Anna could rarely persuade him otherwise.

She glanced at the papers on his lap: Westlaw printouts of cases dealing with the Speech or Debate Clause. There was something touching about the fact that he'd been trying to catch up on the subject. She'd spent the last three hours researching and writing the government's memorandum to accompany her search-warrant application. Anna expected that the rest of the case would be handled by a more senior prosecutor, someone in the Homicide section. There was no chance the Sex Crimes section would wrestle the case away, with a dead victim and Jack's presence at the murder scene. Arguing the issue tomorrow would be her last chance to contribute to the investigation.

Jack made a low grumbling noise and jerked his arms. Another nightmare. He would never say what they were about. She cupped his cheek and kissed his temple. He startled awake, his face morphing from ferocious to embarrassed. He focused his green eyes on her. "What time is it?" he asked. "Are you just getting home?"

"Two-thirty. Yes."

He took off his reading glasses, set them on the side table, and put an arm around her. She molded herself into the curve of his torso. She'd wanted to do that all night, even when she stepped away from him in the stairwell. She hated to admit it—she liked to think of herself as independent and self-sufficient. But what she really craved every day was to be skin to skin with Jack.

"I don't like you working this late," he said. His lips brushed her temple as he spoke.

"I know."

"You'll have to do a better job of listening to me if we're going to work together on this case."

"Hm?"

"I spoke to Carla. She's happy to lend you to this investigation. I'd love to have you around."

She sat back and looked at him in surprise. He would normally fight to keep a Sex Crimes prosecutor *off* his investigation.

"I don't want to get this case just because we're dating," she said.

"You have sex-offense expertise. I could use that on this case."

One part of Anna wanted to jump at the chance to stay on the case. She'd had a rocky start at the U.S. Attorney's Office, when she'd dated a public defender who had ended up on the opposite side of a homicide case. After the ensuing scandal, she felt a deep need to show that she could run a major investigation smoothly and professionally. A case of this significance was exactly the type of challenge she'd been hoping for. It was a chance to earn the respect of her colleagues.

But there were dangers to working that closely with Jack. Although he was in the office leadership and had ten years more experience than Anna, he normally didn't supervise her; she reported to Carla. Jack was on a different floor, working on different cases. But if they worked the case together, he would clearly be the boss. It would be difficult to be equals in their personal relationship while she was his subordinate at the office.

For an instant, she wondered if he was deliberately trying to create that power dynamic. *You'll have to do a better job of listening to me,* he'd said.

Jack must have sensed her hesitation. "I'm asking you to work on this case because I need you."

Anna studied his face. His eyes were sincere. She felt small for harboring unkind thoughts. She took his hand, held it palm up, and traced its lines. After a long streak of bad-boy boyfriends, Jack was the first really good man she'd ever fallen for. They'd been dating for five months and were at the end of the euphoric stage and the beginning of the how-is-this-really-going-to-work-on-an-everyday-basis stage. Unlike her usual dating MO, her attraction to Jack had deepened gradually, as she got to know him. He was kind, generous, and strong, a great father, an incredible lawyer. She didn't want to mess this up. She knew that refusing the case would hurt his feelings.

There was also the issue of keeping their relationship a secret. The flip side of Anna's need to prove herself in the office by doing good work was her need *not* to be the center of another gossip frenzy about her personal life.

"People will see us together," she said. "They'll talk."

"Let them. That's the other thing I wanted to talk to you about. Let's stop hiding. It's time." He gently squeezed her hand and nodded to the coffee table, where a small blue vase held a bunch of lavender sprigs from his garden. "I'd like to be able to send flowers to where you spend your days."

When they'd first started dating, he'd sent a dozen roses to her office: eleven pink and one red. His note read, "In every bunch, one stands out. You're the one." Anna hid the flowers under her desk so no one would ask who sent them. When she brought them home that night, she thanked Jack, then asked him not to send her flowers at the office. Now he made bouquets from the flowers in his garden and gave them to her at his house.

"I love the flowers you give me here," she said. "And I'm not ready to go public."

"I don't mean take out an ad in the *Post*. Just tell a few close friends. Let it be known that we're dating. Stop the ridiculous cloak-and-dagger stuff. I've been saying this for a while now."

Anna shook her head. Jack didn't understand. If a police officer saw him kissing her in a stairwell, that would just add to his status. She, on the other hand, would permanently shift from being a prosecutor to a pinup. It was hard enough, as a young woman, to be taken seriously. Anna was still stinging from the scandal last year. She couldn't be ground zero of another gossip explosion.

"I can't, Jack. I need to prove myself as a prosecutor."

"Does that mean you can't date? You're a lawyer, not a nun."

"If people knew we were dating, they'd see me as the little hussy sleeping with the boss."

"No, Anna. This is the real thing, not some cheap affair. We shouldn't sneak around like it's something to be ashamed of. People will be happy for us."

"They won't. You'll be a stud. I'll be 'sleeping her way to the top.' I'll be completely trivialized."

"I think it's a mistake." Jack sighed. "But I know how important it is to you. We'll keep it under wraps. Will you work the case with me?"

The fact was, Anna really wanted the case. The stakes were high. If the case went well, it could make her career; but if it went badly, it would be a public humiliation. But there was a larger reason she wanted the case. She couldn't get the image of Caroline Mc-Bride out of her head. She felt a visceral need to find out who had killed the young woman and bring that person to justice. Despite all her reservations, she couldn't turn it down.

She smiled at him. "I'm in."

"Great." The smile he returned was steady and warm. "We make a good team."

Anna was relieved that the negotiation was over. Debates were an inescapable part of a two-lawyer relationship. Often, she and Jack enjoyed them. But she didn't want to debate whether to keep their relationship secret. It was too important; she couldn't appreciate the verbal tug-of-war. And tonight, more than usual, she needed the comfort of his body, not the challenge of his intellect. She took his hand and led him up the stairs.

They passed Olivia's room, dark and quiet. Her door was cracked, and Anna could see the little girl was asleep, her thumb resting on the pillow near her open mouth. An orange tabby named Raffles was curled at Olivia's feet. The cat was Anna's—she'd adopted the stray a couple of years ago. Now that Anna was spending so much time at Jack's house, he'd invited the cat to move in. Olivia had been pleased about this development, if nothing else. Raffles raised his head and meowed to Anna, then let his orange eyes slide shut again.

Anna's gaze lingered, as it always did, on a framed picture hanging in the hallway by Olivia's room. A studio portrait of Jack and his late wife, Nina Flores, holding the infant Olivia between them. They were a beautiful family. Jack's wife had been a police officer, killed in the line of duty four years ago. He rarely spoke about it. But Nina's presence was everywhere in the house.

Unlike Jack's spartan office, his bedroom was decorated with cheer and warmth. The walls were cherry red, the bed was covered in a colorful quilt, and the golden oak floors were softened with a sisal rug. Anna guessed his wife had been responsible for the decor. In this room, though, there were no pictures of her.

Anna locked the door and turned to Jack with a smile. She pulled his T-shirt over his head, appreciating the sight of his bare chest in the moonlight. Wearing just jeans, he reminded Anna of the guy from the Old Spice commercial. She pushed him back onto the bed. He let her, cooperating with a widening grin. He watched as she pulled off her suit and shirt and threw them on a chair.

She pushed him back onto the pillows, straddled his waist, and savored the sight of him beneath her, all sinewy muscles and dark copper skin. He seemed to appreciate his view, too, skimming his hands over her thighs as their eyes met. She lowered her face until it was an inch from his. His breath was tinged with the peppermint that grew outside the house.

His lips were soft, his hands confident as they traveled the length of her back. Her whole body warmed and melted. She felt his breathing quicken and his heartbeat accelerate with hers. The rest of their clothes were quickly shucked aside. She stretched herself out on top of him, ran her hands down his body, and guided him inside her. There was no place in the world she'd rather be.

Her mind had been racing all day, processing tragedy and law and strategy and politics. All of that was eclipsed by the sensation of his long body beneath her. She let the analytical side of her brain give way to blissful emotion, the sweet release of feeling without thought.

# Monday

# 8

Mornings were trickier than nights at Jack's house. At night, Anna and Jack were just a couple, the simplest group in human relations. In the morning, Olivia woke up. Then it was clear that Anna was an addendum to a pre-made family, an addition whose status was uncertain and not necessarily welcome.

Jack's kitchen was cheerful and sunny, with a colorful tiled backsplash, large windows overlooking a big backyard, and a fridge covered in first-grade artwork. It was a pleasant place to make breakfast, but recently, it had become a battleground of sorts as Anna tried to win the heart and mind of the local population: Jack's six-year-old daughter.

Anna was standing over a pan of scrambled eggs when Olivia came downstairs. The little girl looked adorable, dressed in a purple T-shirt and khaki shorts embroidered with flowers. She had caramel skin and her father's green eyes. Her wavy black hair was pulled back into two neat pigtails.

"Good morning!" Anna said. "I made you breakfast."

Olivia glared into the frying pan. "I hate scrambled eggs."

Anna had seen the girl devour a cheddar omelette last weekend. "Hm. How about I add cheese?"

"Yuck."

"I could toast you a waffle?"

"No, thanks."

"Okay, you name it."

"I'll wait for my daddy to make me breakfast."

Anna kept the smile pasted on her face. She felt a sudden longing for the peace of her own apartment, where she could just listen to Matt Lauer bantering with Ann Curry as she got ready for work. Anna loved curling up with Jack at night. But she wished she had a clue how to win over his stubborn first-grader in the morning.

Things hadn't always been tense between her and Olivia. When Anna was someone who stopped by occasionally, Olivia seemed to love her. But as Anna's relationship with Jack grew from friendship to romance, Olivia withdrew. The little girl understood that there was someone who was becoming almost as important to her father as she was. She didn't like it.

Anna wondered if her transition into the Bailey family had been too fast. The first time she spent the night, Anna snuck in and out of the house so Olivia wouldn't know she'd slept over. If Anna had a daughter of her own, she wouldn't want the child to see new men staying the night. But Jack insisted on frankness in his family. If Anna was staying over, he said, Olivia had a right to know. Anna was surprised that he wanted to integrate her so quickly into Olivia's life. Although Anna loved Jack, she wasn't confident that the relationship would be permanent. Her own childhood had taught her to be skeptical about long-term romance. She hadn't found the words to broach that with him. It seemed too cruel to say: "Are you sure you want me to stay over? Because Olivia will be confused if and when we break up."

Anna wanted things to work out with Jack, but she hedged her bets. A month ago, he'd asked her to move in. The offer was, in some ways, a technicality, since she spent most nights here. She demurred and kept her apartment in the city. The rent was ridiculous, especially for a place she didn't use. But it was like keeping a life raft strapped to the side of a yacht.

Anna looked at the pan of eggs, then back at Olivia. She could hear Jack upstairs in the shower. They would need to leave for court soon. There was no time for him to make a whole separate breakfast for Olivia after he got dressed. Anna had never thought that winning over a first-grader would be so challenging. She wished her own mother were alive to give her pointers.

"Tell you what," Anna said. "We can make anything you want. And you can make something for your dad, too. We'll surprise him."

Olivia was fascinated by kitchen gadgets but not allowed to cook on her own. She narrowed her eyes, considering what was more important: defying Anna or using the toaster.

"Okay," Olivia said.

Anna watched as the little girl toasted three slices of bread and grabbed ingredients from the fridge and cabinets. Olivia covered the toast with peanut butter, then bologna, then honey, then crushed some Fruity Pebbles on top. "For crunch."

Anna considered, then decided against trying to guide the creation. You had to pick your fights.

"Your breakfast," Olivia said, handing Anna one of the gooey slices of toast.

Was that a peace offering? The toast looked disgusting, but Anna couldn't turn down the chance to make the little girl happy. She took a bite. Her teeth sank through the layers of sugared cereal, honey, bologna, peanut butter, then toast. Each clung to the roof of her mouth, adding a new layer of horrible. After chewing for a long time, Anna managed to swallow the bite and suck the gooey bits from between her teeth.

"Delicious," she pronounced.

"Have some more," Olivia said, sliding into her chair at the kitchen table.

Anna put the concoctions on three plates and sat down at the table. She stared at the toast, and the toast seemed to stare back at her, mocking her with glittering honey dripping off floppy pink lunch meat. All she wanted was a granola bar. Olivia sat next to her, watching expectantly. Anna took a swig of coffee, braced herself, and took a bite, then another. With a concerted effort to override her tastebuds, Anna ate the entire piece.

When she was done, Anna smiled at Olivia. "Thanks for my breakfast!" She looked at the colorful blob still sitting on the little girl's plate. "Aren't you going to eat yours?"

"Of course not. It looks terrible. I'll just have a granola bar."

Olivia trotted out of the room just as Jack came in. He surveyed the mess and grinned at Anna. "For a woman who's so formidable in court, you certainly are a pushover with Olivia."

"The difference is, I want Olivia to like me."

He kissed her lightly on the lips, but he didn't claim that—somewhere deep inside, perhaps—Olivia really did like her. Anna appreciated that Jack was honest.

"Why don't we stay at my place tonight?" Anna ventured.

He shook his head. "You know how hard it is to find an overnight sitter."

Anna nodded. Jack was ten years older; he had a child, a mortgage, a firmly established schedule. She wished there was a way to integrate him into *her* life, but there was always a reason why it didn't work. If Anna wanted to be in this relationship, she had to become part of his life.

"You look gorgeous," he said, running gentle fingers through her hair. She usually wore it in a ponytail but had blown it out this morning. It looked sleek and professional, tucked behind her ears and falling just below her shoulders. She wore her best black pantsuit and a double-stranded necklace of big silver links. Usually, the necklace felt too dressy, but today she hoped it gave her an air of gravitas. She was nervous about the hearing. Looking the part helped her feel the part.

"Thanks." She glanced at him appreciatively. He struck a tall, impressive figure in his charcoal-gray suit. His smoothly shaved head lent a hint of street tough to his otherwise Brooks Brothers aura. She remembered how intimidating he seemed when they first met a year and a half ago. "You're not too shabby yourself."

Jack smiled and grabbed a couple of granola bars from the cupboard. He offered one to Anna, but she shook her head, feeling a bit green from Olivia's toast. She threw some cat food into Raffles's bowl. The tabby streaked into the room and purred as Anna scratched behind his ears. He'd put on a lot of weight since his days as a bony neighborhood stray. Anna liked seeing his striped orange fur plumped up with feline paunch.

Olivia came back into the kitchen, wearing her Crocs and the *Princess and the Frog* backpack. She held a sprig of peppermint from the garden. Jack knelt down so she could put the mint inside his suit jacket, next to his handkerchief. This was their daily ritual. He liked to chew the leaves throughout the day.

Anna would leave now and take the Metro to work. Jack would wait until Olivia's nanny, Luisa, came to take over. Anna preferred arriving separately at the office anyway.

"Now clear your plates from the table," he said to Olivia. "And give Anna a hug goodbye."

Anna shook her head subtly at Jack. The more he pushed Olivia toward her, the more the little girl pulled away. But he smiled with tender confidence. He was accustomed to being in charge and determined to orchestrate the relationship his way.

Olivia rolled her eyes, brought a plate to the sink, and reluctantly patted Anna on the back. Anna's arms went up to embrace the little girl, but Olivia ducked away.

Anna hoped she'd have a more receptive audience in the courthouse.

Ninety minutes later, Anna and Jack walked into a courtroom in D.C.'s federal District Court. They wore dark suits, towed wheeled briefcases, and kept a respectable distance between them. They were two serious prosecutors heading into battle. Anna hoped no one could guess that a few hours ago, they'd been making love.

She tried not to feel overwhelmed by the courtroom. It was designed to impress, with soaring ceilings, marble floors, and a huge bench from which the judge could peer down at the players. A giant metal medallion of an eagle was mounted on the wall above the judge's bench. This wasn't where Anna, as a sex-crimes prosecutor, usually tried cases; the vast majority of her cases belonged in D.C. Superior Court, the local courthouse next door. But because the crime had taken place at the U.S. Capitol, the prosecutors had the option of bringing it in federal court. They'd jumped on it. Federal courthouses were less crowded, federal facilities were nicer, federal judges had more time to think about cases. The lawyers who practiced in federal court had a more genteel reputation. Nevertheless, Anna knew this was going to be a street fight as fierce as any in Superior Court.

Daniel Davenport sat at the defense table, surrounded by a team of suits, eight in total. Junior partners, associates, and paralegals, Anna guessed. She and Jack were starting off at a disadvantage.

Jack looked unfazed. He nodded at the defense lawyers and said good morning as he passed them. She did the same.

Aside from Davenport's lawyers, the courtroom was surprisingly empty. The hearing had been docketed as an emergency late last night; it hadn't gone through the computer system that reporters and court followers checked.

The Congressman and his staffers were nowhere to be seen. Davenport's job was to handle this as discreetly as possible, with the least possible impact on the Congressman himself.

As Anna and Jack set up at the prosecution table, one of Davenport's junior associates came over and handed her a binder, thick with defense motions that Davenport's team had drafted overnight and filed minutes ago. Anna didn't think she was imagining the smug look on the guy's face. At the same time, she could feel his envy. He looked about her age, but he was relegated to writing motions, while she would be arguing before the judge. It might be years before he said anything in court. Being a law-firm lawyer was nothing like the image on TV—it was a job spent almost entirely sitting in front of a computer, writing memoranda or clicking through scans of corporate documents. But this junior associate could console himself with his $180,000 salary, over three times what Anna made as a second-year AUSA.

Anna opened the binder. As she and Jack read the motions, she was careful to keep her head several inches away from his, even though it was harder to read that way. She didn't want anyone to think they looked too cozy together.

The defense had moved to deny the search warrant on the grounds that there was no probable cause to search Lionel's office; to deny the warrant or restrict the search based on the Speech or Debate Clause; and to gag the prosecutors and seal the courtroom. The voluminous defense motions were detailed, well researched, specific, and persuasive. And they had done it all in one night! She was more than a little intimidated.

"Psst! Anna!"

She glanced behind her. Grace sat in the front row; she signaled for Anna to step out of the courtroom. Anna joined her in the small anteroom outside the courtroom door. There, Grace spun her around. "What's on your suit, girl?"

Anna looked over her shoulder. There was a gooey brown, pink, and green lump on the back of her left shoulder. "Yikes. Peanut butter and Fruity Pebbles."

Grace pulled a wet wipe from her purse. The best

prosecutors, like Boy Scouts, came prepared. She scrubbed the back of Anna's suit.

"Don't worry," Grace said. "Lynn came to court yesterday looking all nice from the front but with a line of her baby's spit-up dripping down her back. The hazards of a working mom, right? You just skipped a decade and went right to sugared cereal."

Anna nodded and smiled, but her mind stuck on the phrase "working mom." That wasn't her. She had no idea how to be that. She wasn't sure she was ready to learn.

"Jack made Olivia hug me goodbye," Anna said. "I guess she didn't appreciate that."

"She's a modern girl, doesn't like to be told what to do." Grace blotted Anna's shoulder with a dry napkin. "So she's not falling for your charms, huh?"

Anna shook her head.

"Hang in there. No one can resist you for long." Grace came around and studied Anna critically. "Gorgeous. Now go knock those high-priced hired guns on their asses."

"Thanks, Grace."

They hurried back to the courtroom, and Anna took her seat again at counsel table. She smiled at Jack, trying to convey competence, cool, and the impression that everything was under control. No peanut butter here.

He gave her an encouraging smile in return. His light green eyes, next to his brown skin, reminded her of spring leaves on a strong tree.

Ten minutes later, the side door opened and the judge strode out. "Remain seated," she said as she took the bench. Despite the command, everyone momentarily lifted their butts a few inches from their chairs.

Judge Lydia Redwood was a tiny black woman with silver hair pulled back into a neat bun. She had perfectly straight posture and, although she was in her sixties, a face as smooth and radiant as her pearl earrings. Whenever Anna sat in her courtroom, she wanted to ask what moisturizer she used. Anna thought Redwood was a mixed draw. The woman was whip-smart and meticulous in her legal reasoning. But she also had a history with Emmett Lionel. Like the U.S. Attorney, D.C. judges were appointed by the President, but great deference was given to the recommendations of D.C.'s Congressional Delegate. For the past thirty-one years, that had been Emmett Lionel. He'd recommended Judge Redwood for the seat she now held. The judge literally owed her career to him.

"Counsel, please identify yourselves for the record," the judge said.

Anna stood up. "Anna Curtis, along with Jack Bailey, for the United States."

Anna got a thrill every time she identified herself as a lawyer on behalf of the USA. Her job was not just to win cases but to seek justice. Most lawyers were duty-bound to the narrow interests of individual clients, not free to aim for the result they believed was fair. Anna had a luxury most lawyers didn't have—her job was to do the right thing.

"Daniel Davenport of Wilbur and Cooperman, here on behalf of Congressman Emmett Lionel, whose office the government seeks to invade." The silver-haired lawyer looked tall and sleek in his tailored suit. His voice was kindly, but with an undertone of passionate indignation, like that of a loving father defending his child.

The judge said, "We're here on the government's

application for a warrant to search Congressman Lionel's congressional offices. The Congressman has filed a number of motions in opposition. I'd like to commend both parties on their thorough research and legal argument." The judge held up a thick binder. "But sometimes, Mr. Davenport, less would be more."

Behind her, Anna heard the courtroom door swinging open. She glanced back and saw a few reporters coming in. Paul Wagner, from FOX 5, and Del Quentin Wilber, who covered crime for the *Washington Post*. The court database might not have this hearing docketed, but these guys had human networks that were higher-speed than most government computers.

The judge said, "I'm denying the Congressman's motions to seal the courtroom and gag the prosecutors. Criminal proceedings are presumptively open to the public, and I see no reason to alter that calculus here. Your arguments are creative, Mr. Davenport, and you can raise them with the Court of Appeals if you so choose."

Anna was glad that the judge was ready to cut to the real arguments. That was both the greatest and most frightening thing about Judge Redwood. She had a low tolerance for bullshit.

"On the merits," Judge Redwood continued, "the government proposes a search of Congressman Lionel's office for evidence related to the death of Caroline McBride. The government hypothesizes that Ms. McBride may have been working in her capacity as an escort at the time of her death. The prosecution seeks to search the Congressman's office and to seize documents as well as computer records, including e-mails, that may show whether Congressman Lionel or any of his staffers arranged for the victim to visit the Congressman's office."

The judge looked up from her papers. "I commend the government for getting a search warrant before going in to search. With a case this sensitive, and law so novel, it was wise to get a judge's approval first. It shows me that the government is acting in good faith. Which will go a long way as this case progresses."

Jack met Anna's eyes and smiled. She felt a rush of relief as she was vindicated for her caution the night before.

"I'll hear argument now," the judge said.

As Anna stood up, she could hear more people coming into the courtroom. Word had gotten out. She tried to ignore the sounds of seats swinging down, papers rustling, and whispers.

"As set forth in the affidavit," Anna said, "there is probable cause to believe than an assault occurred last night and that we may find evidence of that crime in Congressman Lionel's office. The victim had an appointment to visit the Congressman, which we understand required e-mails to the Capitol Police. Records of such e-mails should be on one or more computers in the Congressman's offices. The government also seeks documents relating to the agency for which the victim worked and any prior instances in which she interacted with the Congressman or his staff."

The judge nodded impatiently. "I've read the papers, Counselor. Despite the defense's efforts, I agree that there is probable cause. But the issue is the extent to which the Speech or Debate Clause of the Constitution protects the Congressman's office from being searched. What of that?"

"The Speech or Debate Clause is meant to protect

legislators from Executive-Branch interference into their decision-making," Anna said. "But the Clause covers only legitimate legislative activity. Assaulting a visitor to the Capitol is not a legislative act."

"Not yet," the judge said.

"The government seeks three types of evidence. First, basic forensics: processing the hideaway for things like blood, semen, and fingerprints—"

"Mr. Davenport?" the judge interrupted.

Davenport stood up. "If police officers are allowed to search the Congressman's office, they might find papers and notes relating to his decision-making. Obviously, forensics need to be done. But the *Jefferson* case ruled that the legislator should be afforded the first chance to go through his office, to minimize Executive intrusion into the Legislative process. Congressman Lionel is willing to retain private forensics investigators who can conduct the search and report their results to the police. Then there will be no interference with his decision-making process."

"The Founding Fathers didn't intend for a suspect in a murder case to dust for his own prints at the scene," Anna said. "That's our job. The *Jefferson* case didn't consider a circumstance where the office itself is the scene of a violent crime. Blood, semen, or DNA is not going to reveal secrets of the legislative process."

"I agree," the judge said. "The Metropolitan Police Department may go into the Congressman's hideaway and process it just as they would any crime scene. But the officers are not to read or seize any papers."

Anna could hear the reporters scribbling in their notebooks. It wasn't lost on them that she had publicly implied that Congressman Lionel was a murder suspect. But there was no avoiding it—she needed the judge to understand why the search was so important.

Anna turned back to the judge. "The second category of items is the Congressman's computer records. The FBI can mirror—that is, copy—the hard drive on the computers in the Congressman's offices. We don't have to take the computers themselves. Then we can run specific word searches on the computers, such as the victim's name. We'll only look at the documents that match, minimizing the legislative materials that will be viewed. The Court of Appeals approved this approach in the *Jefferson* case."

Davenport objected, but he didn't have the law on his side. The judge ruled in favor of the prosecutors. "The government has acted in good faith thus far, and I trust they will continue to do so." No legislative material would be revealed by a search for the term "Caroline McBride." For other search terms, like "Discretion," resulting documents would be reviewed by the court before the prosecutors got them.

"The third category are the papers in Congressman Lionel's hideaway," Anna said. "And the issue really boils down to who gets to conduct the search first: the Congressman or the police? Despite what the court said in *Jefferson,* we think the process set out in our memorandum is reasonable." She knew this was a long shot. The case law was distinguishable, but it wasn't in her favor.

Davenport stood again. "The law on this is very clear. We get to review anything that law enforcement wants to search, first. Your Honor can double-check the items we say are legislative, but the prosecution simply cannot search them. Ever. Only items that have no relation to the legislative process can be seen by the police."

"Mr. Davenport's process could take weeks," Anna said, "even months, before we would get evidence we are entitled to. Your Honor knows how important the first forty-eight hours are in a homicide investigation. *Jefferson* was a public corruption case without the same exigencies as a homicide case. We propose to set up a filter team, of police officers unaffiliated with the prosecution, to take the first look at the papers in the Congressman's office. Documents that relate solely to legislative acts will be returned to the Congressman. Those that do not, and which might relate to the crime, will be immediately turned over to the prosecution. Anything ambiguous will be submitted to Your Honor for review."

Davenport said, "Your Honor, the government suggests the same process rejected by the D.C. Circuit in *Jefferson*. Congressman Lionel is shocked and saddened that a woman died by falling from a balcony attached to his office. But I am equally shocked and saddened that a government lawyer would use that tragic death to propose a process that has been found to be unconstitutional."

"How important is this, Ms. Curtis?" the judge asked. "This isn't a bribery case, or a pay-to-play scheme, where evidence of the crime would more likely be written. What do you expect to find in the Congressman's papers?"

"There could be notes related to the victim or where she worked. An appointment in a calendar. A business card from the escort agency. Written reference to the agency's location or phone number."

The judge leaned back in her chair and studied the ceiling. Then she returned to her usual straight-backed posture and shook her head. "I appreciate your arguments, Ms. Curtis. A homicide case is a different creature than a public corruption investigation. But I'm not going to disagree with the *Jefferson* case. The Congressman may take the first pass through the items to be searched and pull out any legislative materials."

"Thank you, Your Honor," Davenport said.

It was a blow, but not unexpected. Lionel's people could significantly delay when Anna got to see incriminating documents by claiming they related to his "legislative process." The judge would double-check their work, but she wouldn't necessarily know what to look for, and her review could take weeks, depending on the volume of materials Lionel dumped on her. Anna wouldn't even have a chance to argue that the papers weren't legislative—she'd never even see them. This was a huge disadvantage in investigating a sitting congressman. If Lionel were a car salesman, they'd be able to search everything in his office right now.

"There's one final matter," Davenport said. "I've learned that the prosecutors requested the Capitol Police to pull the security videotape throughout the Capitol from last night. We move to squash that request."

"On what grounds?" the judge asked.

"Again, Speech or Debate. The security videos capture the movement and meetings of 435 members of the House, five nonvoting delegates like Congressman Lionel, and a hundred senators, not to mention their staffs. They reflect meetings with constituents, lobbyists, and members of the press. The videos reveal who attended meetings with whom, and for how long, in the U.S. Capitol itself. These are core legislative acts that cannot be exposed to the Executive Branch."

Anna was alarmed. "Those videotapes are essential to the homicide investigation," she said. "The whole case might be solved with them. And the meeting in Congressman Lionel's hideaway last night was hardly legislative in nature." She felt the same anger she had last night, when all of the Congressman's staffers refused to talk to them. It offended her sense of public service that an elected official would impede a criminal investigation, even an investigation of himself.

"Whatever meeting preceded the young lady's death could easily have been related to legislative activity," Davenport countered. "I understand that the young lady was a constituent."

"Most of what's depicted on the videotape will be legislative activity," Judge Redwood said, nodding. "The tapes would allow the Executive Branch to see the inner workings of the Legislature. Meetings with constituents and lobbyists and the press. Exactly what the Speech or Debate Clause is meant to prevent."

The judge looked troubled. It was a sticky constitutional issue involving two major players: Congress versus the Department of Justice. Her decision would set a groundbreaking new rule in constitutional law and would be Monday-morning-quarterbacked by every legal analyst on cable TV.

"I'm not going to decide this now," she said. "This motion comes as a surprise, and I want to give the government a chance to brief the issue. I would also like to hear from the general counsel to the House of Representatives, to find out his position on the matter. We'll reconvene in four days, on Friday, for argument." The judge looked at Anna. "Unless the government decides to drop the issue. I think Mr. Davenport has the better of this argument. My decision may not be something the government wants on the books."

The proceeding was adjourned.

Anna sat back. She felt sandbagged by Davenport's move to keep the videos from them. And the judge's signal was not a good one for the prosecution. A ruling against them here would subsequently make it much harder for any future prosecutors to get videotapes from Congress.

Anna turned to Jack. "I'm sorry about the videotapes."

"Welcome to Homicide. Don't expect anything in this case to be easy."

# 9

Anna understood the drill: Keep your head down, keep walking, and keep saying, "No comment." She knew some of the reporters and liked them. But line prosecutors in the U.S. Attorney's Office weren't allowed to talk to the press about cases. If she stopped to chat, the journalists would try to eke some nugget of information out of her—and they were good at it. So she kept walking out of the courtroom, even as she said, "Hi, Del. I loved *Rawhide Down*. No comment, sorry."

Jack just shook his head at them. They knew him well enough not to even try. If a public statement were to be made, the head of the office would make it, or issue a written press release.

As Jack and Anna walked out the glass doors at the front of the boxy concrete courthouse, the steamy August air condensed onto her air-conditioned cheeks. She hardly noticed. She was distracted by a fleet of news vans parked on Indiana Avenue. She recognized local channels like FOX 5 and WTOP but also saw logos for CNN and MSNBC. The story was national. An army of photographers waited by the curb. Their line of tripods reminded her of a row of aliens in Space Invaders.

Anna was surprised to see a woman holding a printout with Anna's picture on it. Anna recognized the article from Above the Law, a popular legal website that had covered her scandal the year before. "Here!" the woman shouted to the line of tripods. The cameras pivoted like synchronized swimmers

toward Anna and Jack. She realized why the woman
had printed out the article. The reporters wanted a
shot of the prosecution team leaving the courthouse—
cameras weren't allowed inside—but they didn't
know what the prosecutors looked like, so they'd
Googled Anna and found the picture. She hated that
such a low point in her life was still her primary
cyber-image. If this case turned out well, maybe
newer, better articles about her would bump the old
ones into obscurity.

After a few seconds on the prosecutors, the cameras
pointed back to the front door. The shot they really
wanted was the Congressman exiting the courthouse.
Which was exactly why he hadn't shown up today.

Anna was glad to leave the press behind; she was
always afraid she'd trip and fall right in front of the
cameras. A block away from the courthouse, she and
Jack ducked into the Firehook bakery and ordered a
couple of iced coffees. As was their custom, they both
tried to pay. As was his custom, the barista smiled at
Anna and took Jack's cash. Completing the ritual,
Anna stuck her money in the tip jar. "Thank you," the
barista said in a cheerful Jamaican accent.

As they turned to leave, a beautiful dark-haired
woman stood up from a table. Anna recognized the
FBI agent from last night, Samantha Randazzo. The
agent tossed her dark curls over her shoulder and
walked toward Anna and Jack. How did the agent
make a simple gray pantsuit look so sexy? And how
did she chase suspects in those heels? Maybe FBI
agents didn't have the same kind of foot chases that
MPD did.

"Sam." Jack greeted Samantha with a smile. "How'd
you track us down here?"

"If I couldn't find my prosecutor, I wouldn't be much of an investigator."

"Glad we got FBI's finest on the case," Jack said. "And I'm glad to see you and MPD playing together nicely."

"It's not every day there's a murder at the Capitol," Samantha said. "My SAC wasn't going to let this one go."

Anna wasn't as delighted as Jack about the woman's assistance. But she smiled at the FBI agent. "Glad to have you aboard."

"Congrats on the ruling," Sam said. Before Anna could respond, Sam continued, "I told you any judge would let us search the hideaway. If we'd gone in there last night, we would already have the evidence now."

"No," Anna said. "Any document might have been suppressed, and just by reading them, we'd have violated the Constitution. Now we can collect our evidence and be sure we'll be allowed to use it."

"We'll be lucky if anything is still there."

"Enough," Jack said. "I know we didn't do this fast enough for you, Sam, but we did it the right way. McGee and his team are headed there right now, so we'll have the forensics soon enough."

Samantha nodded and closed her mouth. Jack's deep voice conveyed authority—agents accepted what he said, even if they disagreed with it. Anna always admired his style when she saw him in action, but she wondered if she'd ever have that kind of gravitas.

The U.S. Attorney's Office was an eleven-story glass and concrete box occupying a city block. A few people congratulated them as they walked in, but the lobby was mostly empty. It was just after nine A.M., and many prosecutors were in court. They rode the

elevator to the ninth floor and headed to Jack's office.
When they reached his door, his secretary jumped up
from her cubicle. Vanetta was a plump black woman
with graying dreadlocks and an easy smile. The smell
of fresh-baked chocolate-chip cookies always surrounded her. She wore a long flowery skirt, a turquoise
blouse, and a many-stranded necklace that clicked
cheerfully when she moved. She pulled Jack over to
her computer. "You're on TV!" she said.

Anna, Jack, and Samantha crowded around Vanetta's desk. A CNN video streamed on the computer
screen, showing Anna and Jack walking out of the
courthouse minutes earlier. "You two look beautiful!"
Vanetta said, squeezing Anna's arm. Anna wondered
if Vanetta suspected their romance. But her smile was
genuine and innocent. Anna smiled gratefully in return. The next shot was of Daniel Davenport and his
team exiting the courthouse in a pin-striped clump.
The reporters shouted questions, but Davenport just
nodded without answering. He was like Jack that way.
These were not lawyers prone to dramatic showdowns
on the courthouse steps.

A voice-over said, "Although Congressman Lionel
had no statement, his challenger in the Democratic
primary had plenty to say."

The picture cut to the Wilson Building, an elegant
columned structure that housed the City Council.
Councilman Dylan Youngblood stood on the marble
steps behind a podium with a cluster of microphones
arranged before him like a metal bouquet. He was a
trim, handsome man with sandy hair just turning gray
at the temples. Now that Anna had met his wife, she
was curious about him as a person as well as a political figure. He and Eva must make a gorgeous couple.

As he spoke, Youngblood looked right at the cameras in a way that made Anna feel like he was talking directly to her. He had that TV magic. He said, "What I want to know is, why did Congressman Lionel oppose the search of his office? What is he trying to hide? A young woman is dead—why won't he cooperate?"

It was inevitable that the homicide investigation would become intertwined with the upcoming primary election; Anna was just surprised by how quickly it had happened. She supposed Youngblood didn't have time to waste. He was trailing Lionel in the polls, but only by a few points. And the Democratic primary, in mid-September, was only six weeks away. In D.C., where 75 percent of the population was registered Democratic, the primary *was* the election.

It was a sign of the changing demographics of the city that a white man even had a shot at taking down Emmett Lionel. Lionel had ruled D.C. for thirty-one years with hardly a real challenge. Perhaps he had been resting on his laurels for the past few years, taking his position and his electorate for granted. But the city was changing. Lionel was sixty-four years old and a technophobe, proud of the fact that he had no idea how to tweet. Youngblood was thirty-eight, sponsored technology initiatives, and carried a BlackBerry everywhere he went. He was famous for replying to every constituent e-mail himself. There was a feeling that D.C. needed to step into the twenty-first century.

Youngblood spoke into the cameras. "My opponent has the constitutional right to remain silent. All criminals have that right." Anna was surprised at Youngblood's choice of words. It was all *citizens,* not all criminals, that the Constitution protected. Youngblood was going to milk this for all it was worth. "But that's not the kind of leadership our city deserves. If he wants to hide behind the Fifth Amendment, that's his prerogative. But that doesn't mean the people of D.C. have to elect a man who won't cooperate with the investigation of a murder in his office. This is serious. It's not about some SUV the taxpayer paid too much for. A woman is dead! The investigation is being run by Jack Bailey, one of the best prosecutors in the city. I've known Jack for many years, and I'm confident he'll get justice in this case. Bailey ought to be U.S. Attorney. And my opponent ought to cooperate with him."

Anna cringed at the statement. It wasn't the substance of what he said. Youngblood was right: Jack would be an excellent U.S. Attorney. In a city full of lawyers from somewhere else, Jack had been born in D.C. and raised in one of its toughest neighborhoods. He was not only a great lawyer but one who deeply understood the District, its people, and their needs.

But Youngblood shouldn't have endorsed Jack like that. She wondered if the Councilman understood the problem he'd just created. Now the case was personal for Jack. If he ended up indicting Lionel, some people would say that he'd done it to help Youngblood and snag the U.S. Attorney position for himself. Was it a conflict of interest for Jack to try the case now? She glanced at him.

"I hate politics," he said.

Vanetta's phone rang. She answered it, then turned to Jack with a sad smile. "Donna McBride is here."

Donna McBride was an attractive woman in her late forties, with dark blond hair and a shell-shocked expression. She sat in a guest chair in front of Jack's desk; Anna and Sam sat beside her.

Jack's office was one of the nicest in the building, a large corner space overlooking the beautiful redbrick Building Museum across the street. Next to his credenza stood an American flag, a sign of high station in government decor. Jack himself looked calm and authoritative behind his desk. But it was Anna whom the mother kept glancing at. Anna glanced down at her suit to see if there was still some peanut butter there; she didn't see any.

Donna's eyes were rimmed with red, and her cheeks were almost as pale as her daughter's had been, pressed against the marble terrace last night. Caroline's mother explained that she had gone to the Medical Examiner's office this morning and identified her daughter's body. Anna couldn't imagine a more painful experience. But Donna brushed away their attempts at condolences. She didn't want platitudes. She wanted answers.

"I need to know how she ended up there," Donna said. Her words sounded thin, like she was having difficulty pushing them out of her tight throat. "What happened?"

"Your daughter was pushed from a balcony at the U.S. Capitol at around eight P.M. last night," Jack said. "She died from injuries sustained from the fall."

"I can read that in the newspaper. Who did it? Why was she there?"

Jack was silent for a moment. Anna knew their information was going to devastate this woman. But it was better for her to hear it here than through the inevitable news story.

"There's no good way to tell you this," Jack said. He explained how Caroline had been found—skirt hiked up, torn panties around her knee. "It appears that your daughter was working as an escort for the past few years. She may have gone to the Capitol last night in that capacity."

The mother cried out as if a part of her had just been amputated. Tears rolled down her face. Jack handed her a box of tissues, then sat quietly and let her digest the news.

"I didn't know," Donna said at last.

"Of course."

"I was so proud of her. When she got in to George-town! And then the scholarship."

"I'm so sorry."

"Who did this to her?"

"We're working on it. Any information you have will help. Did she have any friends who worked in the Capitol?"

"She didn't mention anyone."

"What about a boyfriend?"

"She dated a few boys at Georgetown. No one seriously. I don't think she's seeing anyone now." The woman's voice hitched. "*Was* seeing anyone."

The mother kept answering Jack's questions in a soft, matter-of-fact voice. Anna admired the strength it took to talk to them the morning after her daughter's death. She didn't have to do it—the prosecutors would have waited until she was ready. But the woman wanted to help. It made Anna think of her own mother, who found the courage to leave her abusive husband only after her daughters were threatened. Anna, who'd lost her mother, felt an affinity to this woman, who'd just lost her daughter.

Donna told them that she taught second grade. Her husband—Caroline's father—had been a plumber who died of prostate cancer three years ago. The family had struggled to make ends meet after that. Anna wondered if financial worries had something to do with Caroline's decision to become an escort.

The mother gave them Caroline's cell phone number, social security number, date of birth, address. Sam jotted it all down in a notebook. Donna also signed a form giving the prosecutors permission to enter Caroline's apartment, search it, and take her computer.

"Did Caroline have a roommate?" Anna asked. If anyone would know the daily routine and dark secrets of a college student's life, it would be her roommate.

"Yes." The mother looked like she'd tasted something bad. "Nicole Palowski. That girl was a bad influence."

"How so?"

"She ran with a fast crowd. Out all night partying. A couple times when I visited, I thought she was on drugs."

"Did Caroline ever get into that?"

The mother shook her head. "She was a good girl. Always sunny and happy. She loved people."

Donna shut her eyes like she was trying to block out the nightmare or wake from it. She tightened her hold on the tissue in her hand. Anna could see Donna holding her breath, trying to stop herself from crying. She felt her own tears welling up. She forced them back. It wasn't her place.

When Donna opened her eyes, she glanced at Anna again. "I'm sorry," she said. "You just . . . you look so much like my daughter."

Anna nodded. She'd noticed it, too. She and Caroline were both blond and long-limbed and around the same age.

Although Jack was clearly the one in charge, Donna

spoke to Anna. "Please," she said. "Find out who did this to my daughter."

Anna's eyes locked on the other woman's, and a moment of understanding and shared need passed between them.

"We will," Anna said. She hoped it was a promise she could keep.

# 10

As luxurious as the Congressman's hideaway was, McGee thought, it was a stingy crime scene. He was accustomed to blood and bullet holes, screaming witnesses, a history of beefs between suspect and victim. The Congressman's private office was quiet and neat. No bloodstains on the Persian carpets, nothing in disarray on the fancy antique desk. The white marble fireplace shone as if it had been polished this morning.

Mobile Crime Lab techs were processing the office, looking for any trace clue. One MCL technician used a small handheld vacuum to suck up hairs and fibers, while another dusted surfaces with black powder, looking for fingerprints. She found a few prints on the desk and used clear tape to lift them. All usable prints would be compared to known prints in the police database as well as those of Lionel and his staffers. It was by the book, but McGee thought it was all useless. Lionel and his staff could have been in here hundreds of times for perfectly legitimate reasons. Their fingerprints, hair, or DNA would prove nothing.

McGee focused on the room as a whole, though nothing appeared amiss; there was no sign of a struggle. Still, he took pictures of the office from every angle. Even if he didn't notice anything now, he could refer back to the pictures later.

When he was done inside, McGee went through the open doorway to the balcony. The view was awesome. The techs hadn't processed the balcony for fingerprints yet—the marble railings were still clean and white, with no black powder residue. McGee started taking pictures of the area. On his second click, something on the floor glinted off his flash.

He went to the corner and lowered his 290-pound body, his knees creaking in protest. He pulled a pair of purple latex gloves out of his suit pocket and snapped them on. He picked up the small object and held it to the light, then whistled through the gap in his teeth. He had to tell Anna about this.

# 11

Daniel Davenport didn't usually make house calls. His clients met him on his own pricey turf, a high corner office overlooking other marbled office buildings at the intersection of 11th and G. But Congressman Lionel had insisted. In the middle of his reelection campaign, Lionel couldn't afford a picture of himself walking into a criminal lawyer's office. He wanted to stay out of sight. So the defense attorney made the trip up 16th Street to a posh neighborhood of Tudor-style homes in upper Northwest.

The plan didn't work. Davenport parked on Blagden Avenue amid a forest of satellite trucks. He walked silently past the crowd of reporters, ignoring the shouted questions without even offering a "no comment." The Lionels' mansion had crisp white stucco and dark half-timbering that made it look like a large old English tavern. The landscaping was elaborate and meticulously trimmed. Davenport strode calmly to the side door to avoid the stand of cameramen staking out the front.

A moment later, he was seated in a cushy floral chair in the Lionels' living room, a porcelain cup of coffee in his hand. A picture window provided a peaceful view of the lush green backyard. The room was so large that the baby grand piano in one corner seemed small. A plate of cut fruit and scones sat on the table next to a crystal vase filled with white roses. The defense attorney was uncomfortable. It wasn't just because his chair was too soft. It was the group of people arrayed in the room.

Congressman Lionel paced in front of the picture window. His mane of silvering hair and ferocity had helped earn him the nickname "The Lion of D.C." His agitated pacing around the room was the trait that reminded Davenport of an angry, caged predator now.

Stanley Potter, the portly Chief of Staff, sat on the couch, alternately checking his BlackBerry and eating a scone. Crumbs dropped onto his electronic device. Lionel's wife, Betty, poured coffee from a silver pot into a delicate cup set in front of Potter. He thanked her and took a slurp. A drop splashed onto his rumpled blue shirt, leaving a stain on his round belly. He tried to brush it away, managing only to smear it in.

Lionel's Legislative Director, Brett Vale, sat watching Potter with a look of disgust in his light blue eyes. His fingers pinched the impeccable crease of his gray trousers. The LD was lean as a whip and quiet as a stone. He appeared to be in his mid-forties and already sported a full head of silver hair. Together with his clothes, it gave the impression of someone too old to still be an LD. When Betty offered Vale coffee, he declined with a slight shake of his head.

Lionel's campaign manager, Terrance Williams, stood in a corner, talking agitatedly into the cell phone clamped to his right ear. His index finger was inserted into his left ear, although he was the noisiest thing in the living room. "This is the worst fucking time for Malik to be on vacation," Williams fumed. Malik Cole was Lionel's press secretary, who'd left for a honeymoon in New Zealand three days ago, the day everyone had expected Congress to go into August recess.

Betty set the silver coffeepot on a silver tray and led her husband to the couch. They were a handsome, powerful couple, and they dressed the part even at home. Betty wore a blue crushed-silk skirt suit and had her dark hair swept into a chignon. Lionel wore a navy blue suit. In ten years, Davenport had never seen him without a tie.

Betty and Lionel sat together on the couch, holding hands. The room quieted, all eyes looking at Davenport expectantly.

Davenport couldn't have a client meeting like this. For one thing, he relied on the attorney-client privilege, which kept secret anything said between him and his client. But the privilege didn't cover advice he gave in the presence of his client's wife or staff. Even if Davenport fashioned a joint-defense arrangement that allowed the discussions to remain confidential, he wasn't at all sure he wanted the staffers to hear the advice he would give their boss. He didn't yet know enough. Any of them—in addition to his own client— might have killed that girl.

And Davenport knew that the Congressman couldn't speak frankly in front of his wife. A week from now, Betty might file for divorce. Potter, Vale, Williams—or all of them—might cooperate with the authorities against the Congressman. Davenport had to be prepared for the worst. For this meeting, the entourage had to go.

"Congressman," Davenport began gingerly, "last night when we spoke, I advised you not to discuss this investigation with anyone, including your staff."

"I haven't discussed last night's events with anyone," Lionel replied. "But this is a political problem, not just a legal one. These are my top advisers. I rely on their counsel." Davenport glanced skeptically at Betty, and Lionel reacted. "I have nothing to hide from my wife! I had nothing to do with that woman's death last night."

Betty showed no emotion. There had long been talk of Lionel's womanizing, but she always stood by his side. She was the consummate political wife, supportive and helpful, skillful at turning the subject and, if that failed, steadfast in defending her husband. Perhaps she simply wasn't bothered by her husband's cheating. Or did she blind herself to it?

Potter set down his scone and leaned forward. "We have to talk about it. Any legal strategy has to work with our campaign strategy."

Davenport looked at Potter, speaking softly but sternly. "Although I am not your lawyer, let me give you some friendly advice. Do not talk to each other about the subject of this investigation. I don't care how innocent you all are or how much you're dying to figure out what happened—if you talk to each other about what happened last night, the prosecutor will find out, and he will assume that you're trying to get your stories straight."

Potter blanched. "Can I talk to my wife?"

"If you must. Your conversations with your spouse are privileged. But do not talk to any other family or friends about it. The prosecutors can drag them into the grand jury to find out what you said. Your loved ones will not appreciate that experience, I assure you. If you're smart, you won't discuss what happened last night with anyone except your lawyers."

"We don't have lawyers," Vale said.

"Congressman Lionel has offered to pay your legal bills, provided you hire competent representation. I've arranged for excellent attorneys to represent you all. Obviously, you're free to turn them down and pay for any other lawyer you want. It could cost less, but you should be prepared to spend fifty to a hundred and fifty thousand, assuming you don't go to trial."

In the old days, Davenport's firm would have represented everyone; today's conflict-of-interest rules no longer permitted that. But it was important to Davenport that the staffers be represented by attorneys who would work well with him—optimally, attorneys who would *defer* to him. They would have independent fiduciary duties to their clients, of course, but they would know who was paying their bills. D.C. had dozens of criminal-defense lawyers who made a living from Davenport's referrals. They were excellent defense attorneys, but they rarely advised their clients to cooperate with the government and testify against Davenport's clients. If they did, they could expect their livelihood to dry up.

The staffers nodded. They would accept Davenport's free lawyers.

"Good," growled the Congressman. "The next thing we need to do is draft something to tell the press." He nodded toward the front of his house, where the reporters were camped. "I can't stay in here forever."

"Until we know more about the situation, you should say nothing," Davenport advised. "You have the right to remain silent."

"Plead the Fifth?" Betty said, horrified. "He has nothing to hide!"

This was always tricky ground. Davenport didn't want to tell her all the things her husband might have to hide. That would just alienate the one ally his client needed most of all. "Of course, Betty," he assured her. "But right now anything he says will be misinterpreted."

Davenport looked at the three other men. Any one of them might know exactly what had happened to the girl last night. As much as Davenport wanted to know, he first needed to make sure that the staffers didn't prematurely say anything to law enforcement. "I don't represent the rest of you, but speaking as your friend, I'm sure your lawyers will tell you the same thing. The Constitution protects you from having to talk to the police, and you should rely on that right."

Davenport expected he wouldn't get any resistance from the pudgy Chief of Staff, who was Lionel's top man, devoted to his boss for over twenty years. Potter would take his marching orders. Williams was a hired gun who might give Davenport pushback but would ultimately listen to whatever Lionel told him. Vale worried him, though. He'd been with the Congressman only two years. Long enough to know some secrets but short enough that he had little to lose if his boss went down. Vale had to be treated with care.

"If you agree, your own attorneys will be available to meet with you this afternoon. In the meantime, the office can just say 'no comment' to any press inquiry. You'll say Congressman Lionel regrets the young woman's death, but he cannot comment further due to the ongoing investigation."

"The hell we will!" Potter said. "Congressman, if you plead the Fifth, tomorrow's *Post* will read 'Lionel Pleads the Fifth in Murder Case.' That's as good as a conviction for your campaign."

"We appreciate your advice, Mr. Davenport," Betty added, "but you have to understand our position. The primary is in six weeks, and Youngblood is a real challenge. My husband didn't know this woman. He'll be cleared in the investigation. But if he no-comments his way through it, we'll lose the seat he's held for thirty years."

Davenport shook his head, frustrated. In times like this, he thought wistfully about his decision to turn down medical school in favor of the law. If he were a surgeon, his patients would be anesthetized while he operated on them. A patient never got up during surgery and disputed the doctor's technique. Davenport often wished he could put his criminal-defense clients under sedation while he operated. "The risk to your husband is much greater than just losing his seat," he began.

Lionel stood up, interrupting him. "Daniel, I appreciate your counsel. I'm sure it's the best defense strategy. But 'no comment' is not an option I can take. This office cannot be seen as obstructing a murder investigation." He turned to his staffers, his deep voice slow and deliberate. "If one of you knows something about this woman's death, I would appreciate receiving your resignation immediately." No one responded. "Good. In that case, I will offer the police our full cooperation, within the bounds of my legislative prerogatives."

Davenport closed his eyes for a moment, disappointed, but he could tell the decision was final. "They'll want to interview you right away. I'm not going to let you go into the grand jury."

Lionel nodded and sat down next to his wife. She took his hand again.

"Congressman, I need to speak to you privately now," Davenport said.

Betty kissed her husband's jowls, stood up, and led Potter, Vale, and Williams out of the room. Davenport could hear her herding the staffers to the back porch.

The defense attorney carefully considered his next question. He preferred to spend as much time as possible investigating, figuring out what evidence the government had and what its witnesses might say, before asking a client for his side of the story. Rarely would a client be completely honest in the first conversation. If Davenport didn't have the documents and the knowledge to keep his clients honest, whatever self-serving half-truths or outright lies the client told could hamper Davenport's defense strategy. A client might tell a lie often enough that he came to believe it and was devastated on the stand when it was disproved.

There was no time for that kind of research now. If the Congressman was going to be interviewed, Davenport needed to know what he would say.

"All right, Emmett." Davenport leaned toward his client. "That woman didn't wander into your hideaway and fall off your balcony by herself. What *really* happened last night?"

Vale cut through the Congressman's backyard to avoid the waiting TV cameras, stepping carefully through the grass to avoid scuffing the shine on his shoes. His silver Smart Fortwo coupe was parked half a block away. He held Davenport's handwritten note—the name and address of his assigned attorney. That arrogant son of a bitch. Vale doubted Davenport's hand-picked lawyer would really have his best interests at heart. But he no longer had the savings to afford his own attorney, and he'd be damned if he was going to get a public defender, like some crack dealer.

He slid into his tiny Smart car and started the noiseless engine. It was the smallest car on the road; the wingspan of his arms was longer than its width.

The car was perfect for parking in tight spots no one else could squeeze into. Vale always felt superior to the gas-guzzling monsters circling the blocks, looking for somewhere to park. He was smarter than they were.

He was smarter than most people. That, he knew, was what had held back his career. At his age, he should be a chief of staff. But he couldn't put up with others' mediocrity, so he had a reputation of being hard to get along with. He felt a nagging disappointment that his career had stalled out.

Vale would cooperate with the police investigation, though not for the reasons Congressman Lionel wanted. He didn't care whether the Congressman was reelected. He wasn't going to be a good soldier, like Potter, keeping the Congressman's dirty secrets. The police were going to find someone to blame that girl's death on, and it sure as hell wasn't going to be Brett Vale.

He would give the police exactly what they were looking for. Everything about Emmett Lionel's relationship with that girl. That whore.

# 12

While they'd been meeting with Caroline's mother, Vanetta had turned the conference room next to Jack's office into a "war room." The police paperwork and Davenport's binder of motions were neatly stacked on the conference table. One of the library's unrestricted computers had been rolled into one corner, and a TV tuned to the local news sat in another. Vanetta had even put a box of Jack's favorite snack— peanut-butter crackers—on the credenza.

Anna thought back nostalgically to the war room she'd shared with Jack during the D'marco Davis case. It was during the hours spent together in that room that she'd fallen in love with him.

Jack thanked Vanetta, who beamed at him. Anna shared her own secretary with six other AUSAs; the poor woman was stretched thin. Junior prosecutors like Anna did their own copying, faxing, mailing, phones, and scheduling. As Homicide chief, Jack got a secretary to himself. But Vanetta's thoughtful preparations weren't just a result of Jack's seniority, they were also a sign of how much she liked him.

On the table was a faxed report from the Medical Examiner. Anna skimmed it. It had the results of a sex kit. No vaginal injuries—typical in most sexual assaults. Although juries, conditioned by shows like *CSI*, expected such injuries, they were rare in anatomy that could stretch to fit a baby. Negative for semen, too. That meant the sexual assault hadn't been completed, or the man had worn a condom. Anna passed

the report around to Jack and Samantha, who nodded
with disappointment at the lack of DNA.

Jack turned off the TV and sat at the head of the
conference table. Anna and Sam sat on either side of
him.

"We have to find out everything there is to know
about Caroline McBride, the Congressman, and his
staff," he said. "Anna, start by drafting some subpoenas. Caroline's phone records, student records, credit
reports—those'll lead us to her banks and credit cards.
Find out what kind of money she had and where it
was coming from."

Anna nodded and jotted the to-do list on her legal
pad. When she looked up, she noticed a piece of lint
on Jack's lapel. She reached to pluck it off, then felt
self-conscious about making such a personal gesture.
She turned the movement into what she hoped was
a convincing stretch. But Jack had noticed her intention; he looked down and plucked the lint off himself.
Samantha's eyes flicked curiously between Anna and
Jack. Anna cursed the agent's sharp eyes and her own
mistake. Their secret was going to be harder to hide
than she'd anticipated.

"I'll have my analysts examine whatever records
you get," Sam said to Jack. "And I can run everyone
through ChoicePoint, NCIC, and our internal databases."

"Great," Jack said. "And we need boots on the
ground. I want agents and MPD detectives out there
talking to her friends, teachers, neighbors. If we're
lucky, somebody's heard of this escort agency, Discretion. Anna, what's it say about them on that porn site
you've got the taxpayers paying for?"

"TrickAdviser?" Anna said. "Not much. There's no

contact information for Discretion, and they don't advertise on Backpage or Eros. I'm guessing they get all their business through referrals. But I can tell you who their most prolific client is."

Anna pivoted her chair so she was facing the unrestricted computer and logged on to TrickAdviser. With a few clicks, she got to the profile of "Sasha." She scrolled through as she spoke. "It's the world's oldest profession, but they've adopted modern methods. The first man who reviews an escort creates her profile on TrickAdviser, not the woman or her agency. The guy fills out a macro and inputs all of her vital statistics, says what she's willing to do, how much she charges. So the first reviewer is critical. Agencies can be very particular about who gets that first appointment. Look at Caroline's first review."

Jack and Sam stood behind her. The first review of Sasha was written by someone with the screen name BigBoy89. He had given her a 10 in both the "appearance" and "performance" categories. Anna clicked on his full review.

> General Details: Every once in a while you meet a girl
> so amazing, it makes you wonder why you bother
> with any other providers. Tonight, I met that girl.
> Madeleine told me Sasha was something special,
> and as usual, she didn't exaggerate. Sasha arrived
> at my place on time, and when I opened the door, I
> was knocked out. I expected beauty, given the price,
> but this girl should be a centerfold. Sports Illustrated
> Swimsuit, not Hustler. Nothing fake about her, no
> silicone or spray tan, just all-natural girl-next-door
> beauty. She's exactly what every hobbyist hopes
> for—the chance to bask in a gorgeous creature

> you'd never be able to do in real life. She came into
> my house and greeted me with a passionate DFK. I
> was getting hard already. VIPs, read on . . .

"What's a DFK?" Jack asked.

"Deep French kiss," Anna said. "One of the more innocent acronyms on this site."

"Who are the VIPs?" Sam asked.

"Anyone can look at a limited amount of information. But if you want the really down-and-dirty stuff, you have to be a VIP member. Guys get VIP status by paying or writing reviews. For every review a guy writes, he gets fifteen days of VIP access. Otherwise, it costs a hundred and fifty dollars a year."

"So these guys write up their crimes just to avoid a small fee?" Jack asked.

"No. I think they do it because they get off on it." Anna clicked on the link for the VIP information.

> The Juicy Details: Personally, I could've done her
> right there at the front door, but I knew this was
> her first time out, and I can be intimidating. I took
> her into the living room and we talked for a couple
> minutes. She said she was nervous, but I was
> someone she'd want to get to know outside the
> hobby. I know this is the schtick, guys, but she
> was so convincing, I almost believed her. After a
> few minutes, she's the one who started undressing
> me. I've been with some rookies who you have to
> lead through every step, like training a new horse,
> but this girl was amazing—hot to trot, couldn't
> wait to take my clothes off, I didn't have to use the
> spurs at all. Pretty soon we were both naked, and
> she's got a smoking-hot body. Now, here's where

I would normally give you all the juicy details. But
I gotta tell you, we connected in a way that was
so amazing, I don't want to cheapen it by posting
the details here. Can you believe I'm saying that? I
know some of you will be disappointed. What can I
say? Life isn't fair. Long story short: It was amazing.
Hands down, the best experience I've had with any
provider, ever. And she said it was the best she'd
ever had, too. I think she meant it. Sasha, if you're
reading this, you are phenomenal. Keep it up, and
you'll be a legend.

"This guy is disgusting," Sam said. "And delusional."

"So who's BigBoy89?" Jack asked.

Anna clicked on a link to BigBoy89's page. It contained no personal information but had hyperlinks to all 322 of his reviews. He'd been a member of TrickAdviser for five years. "He seems to be an influential reviewer. But he's not a high roller. Mostly, he writes about two-hundred-dollar-a-night transactions. The only time he reviews thousand-dollar escorts is when he's writing an initial review for a Discretion escort. He must be getting a discount for being their tester."

"Testing what?"

"Women," Anna said. "Most of the high-end escort agencies are run by white women, unlike your typical street pimp. The madams hire the escorts, but they can't really sample their own product, right? So they'll often have a man they trust 'test' a woman before she's hired. The tester tells the madam about the escort's performance and attitude—is she attractive, enthusiastic, sane? If not, the madam won't hire her. If the tester likes her, he'll write a good review, which can launch a career. Testers have a closer relationship with the escort agency than other johns. BigBoy doesn't get the expensive escorts unless he's with a Discretion escort. I'll bet he gets them at a steep discount, maybe even free, in exchange for providing his stamp of approval here on TrickAdviser. He might know a lot about Discretion."

"How quickly can we get BigBoy's real name?" Jack asked.

The last time Anna had tracked down an anonymous guy from a website like this, it had taken two weeks to get compliance from all of the companies involved. "If I push it," she said, "I could probably have this guy's name and address by next week."

"I can have that before lunch," said Samantha.

"Really?" Anna was skeptical.

Sam laughed. "You've never worked with the FBI, have you?"

Jack's BlackBerry buzzed, and he answered it. Anna only heard his part of the conversation.

"Hello—yeah, I saw it—I wish he hadn't mentioned me—there's nothing *to* do about it—fine, I'll be right there." Jack reattached the BlackBerry to his belt. "I'm going to see Marty."

Marty was the acting U.S. Attorney, the temporary boss who would serve until a permanent U.S. Attorney was appointed by the President and confirmed by the Senate. The last U.S. Attorney had left a few weeks earlier to take a lucrative job at a law firm.

"What's it about?" Anna asked.

"Nothing important."

Anna raised her eyebrows. It sounded important. She wondered if it had to do with Youngblood's press conference and his announcement that Jack should be U.S. Attorney. It put the case in a strange position. Perhaps the front office was concerned.

"When I get back, I expect you'll have magically found BigBoy," Jack said.

"I'm on it," Sam said.

"*We're* on it," Anna said.

Jack nodded and walked out.

Anna and Sam set up their laptops on opposite corners of the table in the war room. Anna relaxed a little when Jack left—she no longer had to keep strict tabs on her body language to make sure she was hiding their relationship. She could just concentrate on the investigation.

She banged out a raft of subpoenas. The team of FBI and MPD agents working the case would serve the warrants. Sam tapped away on her computer. They didn't speak to each other.

The silence was interrupted by the phone ringing in the middle of the table. Anna and Sam reached for the green speakerphone button at the same time.

"Hello?" they answered in unison.

"McGee here." The detective's deep voice boomed from the speaker. "The techs are going to finish up a few things in the hideaway, but I'm wrapping up."

"What'd you find?" Anna asked.

"No blood, no semen, no signs of a struggle."

"Anything?"

"You'll like this. I found an engagement ring on the balcony."

"A *real* engagement ring?"

"It ain't a hologram."

"What does it look like?"

"Like a ring. With a diamond on top."

"How big's the rock?"

"Normal size, I guess."

"You're no jewelry connoisseur, are you?"

"My two ex-wives could tell you that."

Anna looked at Samantha, and they laughed.

"I think the ladies need to take a look at that ring," Anna said.

"I'll bring it by tonight, after I log in all the evidence."

"One more thing," Anna said. "We got Caroline's address from her mother—see what you can find." She gave him the information. "And try to find Caroline's roommate, Nicole Palowski. We need to talk to her, probably put her right into the grand jury."

"Sure."

Anna expected that Nicole would have important information. But there was something more. The roommate was likely involved in this dangerous business. Anna had been too late to save Caroline. But maybe she could still help Nicole.

# 13

Nicole opened her eyes and blinked against the piti-less sunshine lasering through cracks in the cur-tains. She was sprawled on top of her covers, still in her little black dress, cheek resting on the long string of pearls. Last night's events came crashing back. She moaned and wished she could slip back into uncon-sciousness.

The only part of her body that moved was her eyes, taking in the room. God, what a mess. Designer clothes and stilettos thrown everywhere. Her dresser was crammed with wadded-up tissues, makeup, a flat-iron, and hairbrushes of varying sizes and purposes. The room smelled dank and musky.

She closed her eyes. She couldn't face the day, not after last night. She couldn't hang around this apart-ment, sitting on Caroline's couch, eating Caroline's food, knowing Caroline was lying in a morgue.

But she needed a hit.

Nicole sat up slowly, then wished she hadn't. The room swayed back and forth, and for a moment she thought she'd vomit. She lifted a hand to her face. She could feel the indentations the necklace had pressed into her cheek. The nausea passed, but her whole body ached, and she felt as if a layer of needles was implanted below the surface of her skin, painful and itchy at once.

She looked to her nightstand. A crumpled cello-phane wrapper sat on top, next to an empty Ambien bottle. In better days, she could've opened the drawer and found a buffet of coke, Special K, MDMA, the occasional baggie of mushrooms, and prescriptions like Ambien, Valium, and Oxycontin. But as her cash had dried up, so had her supply. After running home empty-handed last night, she'd freebased the last of her coke. The searing smoke had burned away her worries in a euphoric surge; it was like great sex, a good-hair day, and Godiva chocolate all rolled into one lip-numbing rush. When the high had worn off, she'd taken her last three Ambiens and fell into a tortured sleep.

Now her nightstand was empty.

Panic began to set in. She picked up the cellophane wrapper, which had a faint white residue. She ran her finger over it, accumulated a sliver of white powder, and rubbed it onto her gums. It gave her a tiny shimmer of relief, but she needed more. Soon.

She picked up her cell phone. Maybe she'd call T-Rex.

On second thought, maybe not. She owed her dealer over ten thousand dollars, and he'd been seriously on her case lately. He wouldn't even give her a little product in return for sex anymore. He could get laid, he said—what he needed from her was money. In his last voice message, he said he'd "peel her wig" if she didn't pay him soon. She didn't know what that meant, and she didn't want to find out. She tossed the phone onto the nightstand.

She stood and caught sight of herself in the full-length mirror. She was a wreck. Hair a rat's nest, mascara smudged on her cheeks, rumpled dress, a couple of chips in her red nails. It took a lot of grooming to keep yourself up to standard. She still had the essentials—slim body, nice face, perky little tits. But lately she'd been slipping. She was getting a bit too bony, and her long brown hair was overprocessed. She'd recently gotten her highlights done at a random bargain place, and the streaks looked more cheap brass than rich gold. Her eyebrows were also wrong, overplucked and a bit crooked. It was amazing the difference good eyebrows could make. She hadn't realized that until she skipped her usual hundred-dollar-a-brow waxing specialist and tried doing it herself.

She would get herself together, she vowed. Earn a few hundred dollars tonight, go back to Christophe Salon, get everything done right. Then she could hire out again for the kind of cash she'd need to pay back T-Rex. Having a plan made her feel better.

She dragged herself to the kitchen, purposely ignoring Caroline's neat, empty bedroom. The drugs canceled out hunger most of the time, but she might feel better if she could force herself to eat something. As she passed through the apartment's living room, she glanced out the window, which was six stories up and had a fabulous view of the National Cathedral across the street. A flash of blue and red down on Massachusetts Avenue caught her eye. She peered out.

A police cruiser and an unmarked Crown Vic pulled into her building's circular drive and parked illegally. Two uniformed cops got out of the squad car, while a huge black man in a ridiculous light blue suit and fedora emerged from the unmarked Crown Vic. They strode up the walk to her apartment building.

Holy shit. She couldn't be here.

Nicole ran into her bedroom and threw on brown cowboy boots and a denim jacket, hoping to make her tiny black dress look like street clothes. The rush of movement made her head feel like it would explode.

She forced herself to think through the pain. *What do you need to do?*

She yanked open her nightstand drawer. There was little left to hide. The cellophane wrapper and a few empty zips went down the toilet. Her glass pipe went into her oversize Hermès bag. What else? The Vaio laptop, her most essential asset. It was the only way she could keep her business going. She stuffed it into the carrying case. She would've raided Caroline's room for money, but Caroline had stopped leaving cash around the apartment.

She slung the bag over her shoulder and rushed into the hallway. As she closed the door behind her, the elevator dinged. She bolted in the other direction. Pushing through the stairwell door, she glanced back. The big guy in the fedora strode toward her apartment with the building manager, the uniforms behind them.

Nicole flew down the concrete steps and emerged into the tony Cathedral Heights neighborhood. She flagged down a passing cab and threw herself into the backseat. As the taxi took off, she rested her head on the seat back.

"Where to, sweetheart?"

She raised her head and opened her mouth, but no words came out. She hadn't spoken to her mother in years, not since their blowup about Larry. Her friends had dwindled recently, too, as she'd burned through their goodwill. Caroline was pretty much the only friend she had left—and look what she'd done to her. Nicole choked back a sob.

The driver looked at her in the rearview mirror as they cruised past the Cathedral. When the silence stretched to the breaking point, she gave him an address. She shouldn't go there—it was just asking for trouble. But it was the only place she could think of.

# 14

"You're right," Sam explained into the phone for the third time that day. "A faxed subpoena isn't valid service. You don't have to respond to it. Technically, I should send a pair of armed FBI agents to serve you in person. At your place of business, in front of your customers and neighbors. And then you'll have to respond in person in front of a D.C. grand jury next Monday. It should only take six or seven hours of your day. But let me make a suggestion. How about we skip the formalities and you e-mail me the information now?"

Anna's attention was split between her computer and listening to Samantha. The agent was getting results.

"Sure, I'll hold." A few seconds later, Sam jotted something down on a legal pad. "I agree, that's a wise choice. Thank you very much for your cooperation." She hung up and grinned at Anna. "TrickAdviser captures its users' IP addresses, probably sells them to other sex sites. That information might be more valuable than the yearly subscriptions."

Sam's fingers flew over her computer, then she made some friendly phone calls to her ISP contacts. When she hung up, Sam looked at Anna triumphantly. "BigBoy89 is Brian Stringer. He posted his most recent reviews from 1312 L Street, Northwest."

"Great!" Anna was impressed that the agent had been able to find him this quickly. "You want me to draft an affidavit for a warrant to seize the computer and we can interview him together?"

"I don't need a chaperone. You do the lawyering, I'll do the interviewing."

"Interviewing witnesses is lawyering. It's not that I don't trust you," Anna lied. She remembered Sam's musing at the Capitol about whether to arrest the congressional staffers as material witnesses. This FBI agent played a lot more aggressively than Anna would, and Anna didn't want to have vital parts of her case suppressed on account of mistakes. "But whatever this guy's story is, I'll want to hear it myself. There's no time for you to do the interview, write it up in a 302, then drag the guy in here for me to interview him again. I usually go with my officers to interview witnesses."

"Look, maybe it's important for you to babysit the MPD, but I'm an FBI agent. I went to law school. I know how to build my case."

"I'm sure you do. But when we're in court, it's my case. I'll have to defend how we did things. I'm coming on the interviews."

Sam didn't respond, just started typing. Anna finished up her subpoenas, then logged on to Facebook. For a prosecutor, social-networking sites were a treasure trove of information. There were a bunch of Caroline McBrides on Facebook, but one showed a profile picture of the woman at the center of this case. Anna clicked on it. Caroline's privacy settings were more restricted than the public setting, so Anna couldn't see much. She'd subpoena Facebook to get the information. For now she sent friend requests to a bunch of Caroline's friends. One of them accepted within a few minutes, allowing Anna to see much of Caroline's profile, apparently set to the friends-of-friends privacy setting.

Caroline had a typical college-student profile: 354 friends, she liked *American Idol* and Lady Gaga, she had posted some pictures of herself and friends at a bar. Anna scrolled through Caroline's daily posts. Campus activities, inside jokes, happy birthdays. Then something more relevant. Three months ago, Caroline had written: "Signing up for StrikeBack self-defense class. Anyone want to join me?" Many people liked that post, and a few responded that they couldn't come. It was the same self-defense class that Anna was taking upstairs with Eva Youngblood.

"Hard at work on FarmVille?" Sam smirked behind her.

"It's Caroline." Anna pointed to the profile. "She took Eva Youngblood's self-defense course."

"And she still got killed? That's not much of a class."

"I'm taking it now. Seems pretty good, actually."

"Buy a dog. That's the best self-defense."

"We should interview Eva and see if Caroline said why she was taking the class."

"Eventually," Sam said. "There are a hundred other things that take priority."

"This could be important. A lot of students take a class like that after a traumatic incident—and a lot of them share that at the first class."

"Okay, Sherlock. We'll get to it. First this." Sam tossed down the affidavit supporting a search-warrant application for BigBoy's computer. Every search warrant request in D.C. had to have a prosecutor's signature before it could be presented to a judge. Anna picked up a pen and read the papers. She typically edited these heavily—officers tended to be action guys, not word guys. But Sam's affidavit was perfect. Anna didn't have to use her pen except to initial the bottom.

The warrant described how the computer's owner was engaged in the crime of soliciting for a lewd and indecent purpose. Then it described the premises in which the computer was located and how Sam had obtained the location. It said that 1312 L Street was a historic landmark registered to an all-men's organization called the Hunt Club.

Anna looked up. "What's the Hunt Club?"

"Once I get this signed by the duty judge," Sam said, "we'll go find out."

# 15

Nicole tried to suppress her envy as she walked up the steps to Belinda's townhouse on O Street. The tree-lined street was just two blocks from the high-end shops and restaurants on M Street, prime Georgetown real estate. Three stories on this cobblestone stretch probably cost over five thousand dollars a month, but Belinda lived here by herself. It was a sign of how well she was doing.

Nicole rang the bell, waited a moment, then rang it two more times. Finally, Belinda opened the door. The beautiful Asian woman never left the house without a full-body armor of couture. Now Belinda wore a T-shirt and boxers, and her long black hair radiated a cloud of static electricity. Nicole had obviously woken her up. Belinda greeted her with naked fury. "What the hell, Nicole?"

"I'm really sorry."

"Yeah, you are! I heard you fell on hard times, but I gave you a chance. And what do you do? Walk out in the middle of a *service*! Right as the guy was about to pop! I've heard of bad sessions, but that sets a new record."

"Did someone finish him off?"

"Oh yeah, *that's* a true girlfriend experience. 'Sorry that chick just flipped out, but let me administer the last few strokes to get you there.' Do you have any idea how pissed Bill was? He was one of my best clients. I ended up giving him the whole night for free, and I still had to pay the other girls. I *lost* two thousand dollars from that booking."

"Caroline died last night."

"What?"

"She's the one who fell at the Capitol."

"Oh my God." Belinda put her hand to her mouth and stared. Finally, she opened the door and stepped back, allowing Nicole in. Belinda led her to the living room, a modern space with shiny wood floors and lavender walls. She sat on the white couch and gestured for Nicole to sit in the zebra-skin chair.

"What happened?" Belinda asked.

"I have no idea," Nicole lied. "She was going to meet a client at the Capitol. Next thing I know, she ends up dead."

"Oh, Nicole, I'm so sorry. I know how close you two were."

"Yeah. Thanks."

"Does Madeleine know?"

"I haven't talked to her in a while. Have you?"

"Madeleine's not exactly my biggest fan, either."

Nicole nodded. That was what had bonded her and Belinda more than anything else, although they'd each reached Madeleine's bad side via different routes. They'd both worked for Discretion, Madeleine's exclusive escort agency. Madeleine had recently fired Nicole. Belinda had recently quit to start her own agency. Madeleine didn't take kindly to competition. The last girl who tried it got a visit from one of Madeleine's enforcers, who stabbed the girl through the hand. Nicole gave Belinda points for the sheer courage of striking out on her own.

"Are you worried about her coming after you?" Nicole asked.

"Yeah. I'm gonna have to do something. Get aggressive."

Nicole nodded absently. She didn't really care how the two rival madams hashed out their differences. She had a more immediate concern. "Can I crash here for a few days?" she asked. "The police asked me to vacate my apartment for a while so they can, like, process the crime scene."

"But your apartment's not the crime scene, right? The Capitol was."

"Yeah, I dunno, whatever. They just needed me out, okay? Can I stay here? Just for a little bit?"

Belinda studied her suspiciously. Nicole was suddenly aware of her rumpled dress, her mussed hair, the bruises that appeared on her legs after a night of partying. She didn't look like the most responsible houseguest. She wished she'd taken a moment in the taxi to wipe the mascara from her cheeks. The only thing she could do now was look anguished. She was, after all, a woman mourning the death of her best friend. And Belinda had always been a sucker for puppy-dog eyes.

"Okay," Belinda said. "Just for tonight."

Nicole exhaled. "Thank you!"

"I need some coffee." Belinda led the way to the sleek modern kitchen at the back of the townhouse. Nicole followed, her eyes skimming the well-appointed interior, identifying small valuable items she could carry away later.

"Do you have any jobs I can help with this week?" Nicole said.

"Don't even ask."

Belinda started making the coffee, and Nicole set up her laptop on the kitchen counter. If Belinda wouldn't hook her up with a job, Nicole needed to set things up for tonight. She logged on to Backpage and paid for another week of running her ad there. Now that the feds had shut down the Adult-Services section of craigslist, most girls advertised on Backpage. Nicole used to scoff at the Backpage girls. Madeleine had taken care of all her bookings, and she never needed anything as gauche as online advertising. But now that Nicole was on her own, this was the only way to do it.

She had a standard advertisement. These things all were in code. "Fresh," "innocent," and "new faces" meant underage girls. "Sophisticated," "experienced," and "mature" meant geezers. Nicole's headline read "College Cutie Will Make Your Dreams Come True." Inside, she gave her age, vital stats, working name, and phone number and posted a body shot of herself stretched out on a couch, wearing a bra and thong. The photo cut off at her chin. She didn't want anyone she knew to recognize her. She'd been asking three hundred an hour, but at that rate, she hadn't gotten many calls. She lowered it to two hundred. She couldn't charge even close to what she used to. Damn TrickAdviser.com.

At first she'd been getting good ratings on TrickAdviser: 8s, 9s, even the occasional 10. Those were in the glory days, three years ago, when she'd first started at Discretion. Back then she'd used drugs recreationally and as part of the job. So many of her dates wanted to party, and sharing was part of the experience. But then the drugs became more of a lifestyle. She'd always known she could walk away at any time—until she couldn't. As she became more addicted, her numbers started to drop. First it was in little increments in the performance category, for things like showing up late or spacing out during conversations. Eventually, her performance really suffered. Sometimes she got so high, in order to get through a hideous date, that she turned into a total zombie and could do little more than lie there. There was even a rating for that: "4— She Just Lay There."

Even worse, her appearance ratings went down. As she lost weight, her breasts shrank from a C cup to an A, a definite liability in the industry. And clients began to comment that her skin was bad. Acne, one client called it. Sores, declared another—the same guy who'd given her the 4 in performance. Even if it was just your skin's reaction to the toxicity of drugs, a word like "sores" could kill your career.

That review killed hers.

When Madeleine let her go, two months ago, the madam had been all business. No shouting or lecturing. No second chances, either. She'd called Nicole to her home in Kalorama and said their business relationship was terminated. Madeleine instructed Nicole to return the white-gold name necklace—the one all Discretion girls wore as part of what Madeleine called their "branding." Nicole had stomped out, refusing to give back the necklace. She wouldn't just hand over her status as a Discretion escort.

But it was over. Necklace or no, Nicole was on her own.

She was lucky that Madeleine hadn't sent an enforcer to collect the necklace. Yet.

Without Discretion's backing, and with her declining ratings, Nicole wasn't getting any more two-thousand-dollar-a-night bookings. She was lucky when she got bookings in the three-hundred-dollar range. She'd tried advertising under a different name, one that didn't have "sores" in the track record, but that was worse. Few men wanted to take a chance on a new girl, and no one would pay high prices for an untested product.

She'd posted a few fake reviews of herself with better numbers and prose, hoping to bury the last few bad ones. Her avatars didn't have a track record on TrickAdviser, so they didn't hold much sway. At least her profile didn't look so disgusting at first glance now.

Tonight she'd try to book as many three-hundred-dollar calls as she could as "Bethany." They'd have to be outcalls—Belinda obviously wasn't going to let her bring incalls to her home. Maybe Nicole could do four or five outcalls if the hotels were near each other. It was physically possible—she'd done it a few times lately—but grueling. It would barely put a dent in what she owed T-Rex, but she'd invest the money in some grooming and build herself up again.

Belinda handed her a mug of coffee and peered over her shoulder at the laptop. "Backpage, huh?"

"Yeah." It was shameful.

"I'm there, too," Belinda said. Nicole looked at her in surprise. "You have to start somewhere. I haven't built up enough word of mouth yet. And after last night . . ."

"I really am sorry."

"I know. Come on, I'll show you the guest room."

After Nicole was settled into the pretty little guest room, Belinda went to take a shower in the master bathroom. Nicole used the opportunity to rifle through the medicine in the linen closet. Belinda didn't use except when she was working, but luckily, she kept her old prescriptions. Nicole found a half-full bottle of Vicodin, some generic codeine, and a bunch of expired Valium. She popped one of each, then stashed the bottles in her bag. She sat on the edge of the bed and waited for the cocktail to take effect. She was scared and tired, but at least she was in a nice house where the cops couldn't find her. For the next few days, anyway.

Despite herself, she thought about Caroline, and the last time they'd seen each other—was it just last night? Caroline, all happy and excited for her appointment with the Congressman; Nicole, knowing the setup her best friend was walking into and giving her no warning. Watching Caroline head out of the apartment in her gorgeous suit and heels like some kind of goddamn princess—and smirking at her back.

Jesus. She was a monster.

The pharmaceuticals began to kick in. Nicole sank back onto the pillows, grateful for the expanding chemical haze that blurred out her thoughts. She just wanted it to obliterate the train wreck that was her life and her self.

# 16

Sam drove an unmarked black Dodge Durango with windows so deeply tinted that the outside world looked like it was undergoing an eclipse. Anna watched Judiciary Square slip by in darkness, although the afternoon sun was shining brightly. The heavy tinting was necessary for an agent like Sam—a white woman driving through certain neighborhoods in D.C. would scream "law enforcement." The tint was so heavy, it was impossible to see the driver from the outside. Sam's big SUV had been seized from a drug case and repurposed for law enforcement. It fit into the neighborhoods she often drove through.

Sam pulled onto New York Avenue, then swung into an alleyway and parked right under a no-parking sign. This was the alley behind Sergio's, a popular Italian restaurant. Not the Hunt Club.

"Why the detour?" Anna asked. She was anxious to interview BigBoy89.

"You can't work on an empty stomach." Sam got out of the car.

It was past one o'clock, and Anna realized she hadn't eaten since Olivia's baloney concoction this morning. She *was* hungry. But she didn't want to waste time on a sit-down restaurant. "Let's get it to go," Anna said, climbing out.

"This'll be as 'to go' as it gets."

Anna followed the agent through the back door into the restaurant and was surprised that it deposited them in the kitchen. Cooks and waitstaff bustled around steaming pots of pasta and sauces. The scent of garlic, fresh-baked bread, and tomato sauce made her mouth water. A slight gray-haired man in a white apron slid a pizza into a woodburning oven with a wooden pole. Sam kissed his cheek.

"Hey, Sammie girl!" The man beamed at her as he rotated another pizza. "Got a roasted chicken for you, right out of the oven."

"Thanks, Dad. Where's Ma?"

"Out front."

"Just tell her I stopped by, okay? I have to run."

A stout woman in a navy dress came through the swinging doors from the dining room, where every table was packed with customers. She made a beeline for Samantha. "Sammie!" she said, throwing her arms around the FBI agent. She had to pull down Sam's head to kiss her. The embrace left a dark red lipstick print on the agent's temple.

"Hi, Ma. I'm just grabbing something to go."

"That's no way to eat! You gotta sit down, take a breath. And you can't just eat plain roasted chicken every day. Get some meat on those bones! You want chicken? I have some nice cutlets. You'll have chicken Parmesan. At a table. There's someone I want you to meet out front anyway. Nice Italian boy, works at the Commerce Department." Sam's mother picked up a white napkin and wiped her lipstick mark off Sam's face.

"I'm on the job, Ma." Sam ducked away and headed to the stainless-steel counter. "I gotta go."

"Always on the job! You'll come by for supper tonight, then."

"Not tonight."

"You gotta eat. And you didn't come last night. You trying to kill your poor father?"

"Fine. I'll swing by and pick up dinner."

"You'll sit down and have a real meal."

"Okay, okay." Sam sighed and started carving the roast chicken on the counter.

Anna couldn't hide her smile as she watched the bossy FBI agent getting bossed. Sam glared at her. Her mother followed the glare to Anna.

"Hello! Are you a friend of Sammie's?"

"She's a prosecutor," Sam called out. "She wants to learn how to interview a witness."

Sam's mother was already putting her arm around Anna, giving her a warm hug. "Nice to meet you! You like chicken Parmesan?"

"Love it."

"To go, Mom. To go."

Sam threw together a roast-chicken sandwich while her mother prepared a chicken Parmesan sub bubbling with melted cheese and covered with red sauce. There was probably a five-hundred-calorie difference between the two sandwiches.

"A prosecutor, huh?" A tall man stood next to Anna, holding a tray of small round patties. He looked like a male version of Samantha, with dark curly hair and great bone structure. He smiled at Anna with big brown eyes, causing her instinctively to raise a hand to smooth her hair. "You keeping my sister out of trouble?"

"Sorry," Anna said, "my job is to get people in more trouble."

"That, she doesn't need." The man laughed. "I'm Tony. Here, try this. Tell me if it needs more salt." He held out his tray.

Anna took one of the brownish-purple patties and bit into it. "Oh my God," she said. "That's amazing. What is it?"

"Eggplant patty."

"Can I have the recipe, or is it a family secret?"

"Maybe we can work something out."

Sam strode over, holding a bulging brown paper bag. "Enough sampling the merchandise," she said to Anna. "Let's go."

"Don't you need to change into a cape or something?" Tony asked his sister as she walked out the door. The entire Randazzo family waved at Anna as she exited.

"Goodbye—thank you!" Anna called. She and Sam got into the car. "Nice family."

"In small doses."

If Anna had a family like that, she would appreciate them. Her mother had died in a car accident when Anna was in college, and she hadn't seen her father since she was twelve. The only family she had was her sister, Jody, who was back home in Michigan. They called each other all the time but only saw each other in person two or three times a year. The idea of having this close-knit family so near brought a sharp stab of envy.

Sam handed Anna a foil-wrapped sub. Anna peeled back the foil, took a bite, and almost groaned at how good the chicken Parmesan was. As Sam unwrapped her own sandwich, the agent's BlackBerry buzzed. Sam unclipped the little phone from her belt, checked it, and frowned at the text message. "Oh, for Christ's sake."

"What?"

"Tony wants your number."

"Oh. Um . . ." He was just her type; a year ago Anna would have been delighted. Now she needed an excuse. "I'm not really on the market now."

"You have a boyfriend?"

"Not . . . really. It's, um—"

"No need to explain." Sam threw the Durango into reverse and screeched back into the alleyway. "It's my fault. I never should have brought you in there." She navigated the city streets with speed and in silence.

The Hunt Club might have been a bucolic English riding club at some point in its existence, but was now completely surrounded by modern city life. The building was a small replica of a nineteenth-century castle, sandwiched between modern concrete and glass office buildings in the business district. With stone walls, stained-glass windows, and multiple round turrets, the Hunt Club looked like a fussy old man squashed between two plus-size supermodels. All of the castle's windows were covered with thick curtains. Although there was significant foot traffic on the sidewalk—office workers heading to coffee breaks or afternoon meetings—no one outside could see what was happening behind those walls.

Anna had Googled the Hunt Club before they left. It was one of the city's most exclusive private social clubs. Anna couldn't find a list of its current members, but in the past century it had reportedly included Presidents, Generals, Supreme Court Justices, and other distinguished men. Never a woman.

Sam pulled the Durango to the curb in front of the club. A black Taurus and a blue Grand Prix pulled up behind them. Six FBI agents got out of the cars.

"I'll call you after we secure the place," Samantha told Anna. The agent twisted around and grabbed a Kevlar vest from the backseat. She pulled it over her torso, fastened the velcro straps, and put an FBI

Windbreaker on top of it. Then she rolled the windows down. The sweltering August heat immediately invaded the car. "This might take a while, so I'll leave the windows down for you."

"What am I, a Labrador Retriever?"

"Of course not. A Lab would be way more useful in securing a building." Samantha hopped out of the Durango and started to walk up to the front door, then stopped and returned to Anna. "Actually, there is something you can do that would be useful."

"Great. What?"

"Don't let the meter maids give me a ticket." Samantha tossed her car keys in through the open window.

Sam joined a group of male agents on the sidewalk and walked up to the door of the Hunt Club. The agents wore matching navy Windbreakers with FBI in large yellow letters across the front and back; Sam's long curly hair covered the upper portion of the letters on the back of her jacket. The Windbreakers made the agents' body armor less conspicuous, and the big letters were supposed to prevent people from mistaking them for intruders and shooting.

There were professional risks to being a lawyer, Anna thought, but they didn't usually include being shot. She sent up a quick prayer for the agents.

As she waited alone, she reconsidered her decision to attend every key interview. Jack had said he didn't want to come; he was happy to let the agents do the legwork and to read their 302s later. It was a more efficient use of a lawyer's time. As Homicide chief, he had twenty lawyers to supervise, maybe three hundred cases to keep tabs on. The most sensitive cases, he would handle himself. He didn't have time to be supervisor, lawyer, and agent. By contrast, Anna had twenty-five other cases on her docket at different stages of investigation or litigation. They could stand to be put on hold for a bit while she focused on this one, which was by far her most important. The case was the most significant of her career. And the truth was, she didn't really trust Samantha to do it right.

Sam scanned the scenery as she walked up to the Hunt Club: no immediate threats. She knew the other agents were doing the same. Five agents and a Computer Analysis Response Team, or CART, examiner would accompany her into the building. Agent Steve Quisenberry would be at her side, taking notes as she asked questions. He was the best agent on the Violent Crime squad. Besides Sam, of course. If there was trouble, they could handle it.

Sam could have let Anna come in with them. She didn't expect any real danger at this old social club. But Sam didn't feel like watching two backs instead of just her own.

She'd been at the Bureau for nine years, since she graduated from law school, and she'd seen her share of young prosecutors come and go. Some remained AUSAs for years, and some left to cash in their credentials at private law firms. They all had one thing in common—they wanted to tell Samantha how to handle her cases. Whether they were right or wrong, they always slowed her down. Samantha wasn't interested in holding the hand of a junior prosecutor climbing up a steep learning curve. Anna wasn't all bad. She was smart and had good ideas. But she interfered. Samantha just wanted to investigate and be left alone.

Sam and Steve walked up the black iron steps to the rowhouse with four other agents behind them. One agent would stay on the front steps to keep people out, and a final agent was posted in the alley around back, on the chance that anyone tried to run out the rear. Samantha rang the bronze door buzzer. If no one answered the door in thirty seconds, agents would knock it down with a steel ram.

Sam started counting. One-one-thousand, two-one-thousand—

The curtain of a second-story window in a turret was pulled back, and a skeletal face peered down at them. The man's sunken eyes took in the agents in their FBI jackets, then scanned the street full of government vehicles. Samantha held up her papers. "FBI. We have a search warrant. Please open the door." The face disappeared behind the curtain, and Samantha kept counting. Six-one-thousand, seven-one-thousand . . .

At twenty-three, the thick black door swung open with a creak. The man who stood there was far younger than the skeleton who'd peered at them from upstairs. White male, medium height, medium build, maybe forty years old. He was bug-eyed, with thinning brown hair and a large mole on the left side of his chin. He wore a blue button-down shirt with khakis.

"May I help you?" he asked.

"FBI." Samantha held up her credentials and the court papers. "We have a warrant to search the premises."

He stepped back and let them in. When the agents were in the foyer, he closed the heavy door. An agent stopped him before he could slide a dead bolt into place.

Inside it was dark, cool, and quiet, a stark change from the summer afternoon. As Sam's eyes adjusted, she kept them on the man who'd let them in. He stood with his hands by his sides, posing no threat. She scanned the room for other people but saw none. This front hall felt like a scene from a different century. It was paneled in dark wood, and the floor was black marble inset with a six-pointed star of gray and white stone. A candlestick telephone sat on an antique chest.

"What's your name, sir?" Samantha asked.

"Brian Stringer."

So this was BigBoy89. What struck Samantha about him was how very *normal* he appeared. The only physically notable thing about him was how skinny he was—his belt seemed to be the only reason his khakis didn't fall to the floor. SkinnyBoy was more like it. He didn't seem like the type who would be a member of a secret gentlemen's club.

"Do you have some identification?" Samantha asked.

"Sure." He fumbled nervously with his wallet.

Agent Quisenberry gently took the wallet from Brian's hands. "Let me help you with that," he said. He began flipping through the wallet.

"I'm Samantha Randazzo. I'm a Special Agent with the FBI. Are there any weapons or sharp objects on your person?"

Brian shook his head.

"We'll have to check to be sure. Please put your hands on the wall and spread your legs."

Brian complied. Samantha nodded for Steve to do the frisk—if she did it, the guy might get off on it. Samantha took the wallet from Steve and flipped through the cards while Steve ran his hands over

Brian's body. One card caught Sam's eye. She pocketed it.

"He's clean," Steve said.

Sam handed Brian a copy of the search warrant. "Who else is in the building?" she asked.

"A few members are having drinks upstairs." Brian's voice was trembling as much as the mole on his chin.

"How many members?"

"Six."

"Are there any weapons on the premises?"

"There's a Samurai sword hanging over the fireplace in the cardroom."

"Good to know. Anything else?"

"No."

"Okay, thanks. We're going upstairs."

"Only members are allowed up there," Brian protested meekly.

Sam pointed to the warrant. "We're allowed anywhere in this building that a computer could be."

Half the agents fanned out through the first floor as the other half followed Samantha. She knew little about the Hunt Club, only what was available in public records and through law enforcement databases. The place was purchased in 1897 and had been under the same ownership—the Hunt Club, Incorporated, a standard 501(c)(7) nonprofit social club—for more than a hundred years. There had been no criminal activity or 911 calls logged from the building. The only police intervention was from sixteen years ago, when an MPD beat officer noticed a lot of men coming and going at a late hour. He'd investigated and found "a bunch of old men playing cards," according to his police report.

They followed Brian past a large room that looked like a sixteenth-century tavern, with heavy beams on the ceiling and a gigantic stone fireplace. An immense table was set with pewter dishes and surrounded by Windsor chairs. Brian led them into a dark hallway, where a wall was covered in caricatures of distinguished-looking men. Sam assumed they were the club members. Most were white, although a few darker faces had made it into the more recent drawings. Samantha recognized drawings of two past Presidents, a CIA director—and both City Councilman Dylan Youngblood and Congressman Emmett Lionel.

"Congressman Lionel is a member?" she asked.

"Yes," Brian said.

"And Dylan Youngblood? Must make for some interesting dinners."

"This primary election is nothing. You should see the campaigns for club president."

Brian led them up the stairs and into a round card-room located in a turret at the front of the house. Samantha didn't believe in government conspiracies, but if conspiracies were going to be hatched, this was where the hatching would be done. The room was lined with leather-bound books and marble busts. Oil paintings covered the walls. Thick curtains blocked out sunlight, and the room was lit with antique sconces. There was the Samurai sword, mounted over a stone fireplace.

Six old men stood in a cluster around one of several card tables. They wore conservative suits and appalled expressions as the team of FBI agents strode in. Among the men, Samantha recognized Blakely Hamilton, the CEO of the Hamilton Group, a global asset management company. Hamilton had sought the

Republican nomination for President two years ago. Though he eventually withdrew from the race, Samantha had voted for him in the primary.

"Hello, gentlemen," Samantha said. "We're from the FBI." She considered, then dismissed, the idea of frisking them. These men might attack them with lawsuits or press releases, but they weren't about to stab anyone. "I need to see some ID, so if you wouldn't mind, please pull out your wallets slowly."

She probably hadn't needed the "slow" part. Their natural speeds seemed to range from careful to glacial. As she wrote down their information, she recognized a federal judge. When she handed back their drivers' licenses, Hamilton stepped forward. At sixty-two, he was one of the younger men in the group.

"I'm the president of this club. What's this all about?"

"We have probable cause to believe the computers in the building are being used to commit and facilitate crimes, sir. We have a warrant to search the premises and take any and all computers on the grounds. We'd be happy to simply mirror their hard drives and let you keep the machines. But I'd ask you to please direct me to all of the computers in this building."

His eyes narrowed. "What crimes?"

"Solicitation for a lewd and indecent purpose. Also known as prostitution," Samantha said. One of the older men gasped and coughed. "You can look at the warrant. And you can all sit down."

The old men posed no danger, she decided, except to themselves from a coronary. Brian handed Hamilton the warrant, and the CEO eyed the paperwork suspiciously. All the members sat except for the federal judge. He began to walk toward the door, muttering, "I can't be here. I have to go."

Sam put a hand on his arm. "I'm sorry, Your Honor. I have to ask you to stay here."

"Am I under arrest?"

"No. But we're executing a search warrant, and we need the scene to be secure. So you need to stay where we can see you. You'll be free to go shortly."

He looked like he wanted to make a run for it. Samantha wondered whether she would have to tackle a federal judge.

"If you want to avoid headlines, sir, you're walking in the wrong direction."

The judge sat down.

Hamilton looked up from the search warrant. "I want to call my lawyer about this."

"That's fine, sir, you're free to do that. But we're not going to wait for him to come here before we conduct our search. Now, you can tell us where the computers are, or you can force us to search every single part of the building where a computer could fit. And you know, computers have gotten so small these days."

Hamilton held up one finger, sat down, and whispered with the judge. They seemed to come to an agreement.

"There are two computers," Hamilton said, coming to his feet again. "One in the general manager's office upstairs. One on the concierge's desk off of the lobby."

"Is the general manager here?"

"Not tonight. But you've met our concierge." Hamilton nodded to Brian. So BigBoy89 was the concierge of the Hunt Club.

The computer examiner, Quisenberry, and a handful of agents went upstairs to secure the premises and mirror the manager's hard drive. Other agents stayed with the men in the cardroom. While the search was being conducted, the agents would try to talk to each club member separately. But Samantha could see where this was going. They would all lawyer up. She wanted to get Brian out of the room before that rubbed off on him. She turned to the concierge. "Can you please show me the computer at your desk?"

He nodded meekly. As he led her down the stairs, Samantha called for Anna to come in.

Anna sat next to Samantha in a small office adjoining the lobby of the Hunt Club. The room was window-less but nicely appointed, with an antique desk, dark-green-on-green-striped walls, and two studded leather chairs. Samantha and Anna sat in the two guest chairs, while Brian sat behind his desk. Anna thought the guy might feel more comfortable, and thus be more likely to talk, in the power position behind his desk. Brian's laptop had been taken by the other FBI agents to mirror its hard drive, but otherwise, his of-fice was intact.

"While we're waiting for the computer examiner to finish up, do you mind if we ask you a few questions?" Samantha began.

"D-do I need a lawyer?"

"Why don't you just listen to the questions," Sa-mantha said, "and then decide if you need a lawyer?"

Good answer. If Anna had been in this guy's position—having hired hundreds of hookers and posted online reviews of them from a computer that the FBI was searching—she would run to a lawyer. Do not pass go, do not collect two hundred dollars. But she didn't have to tell him what she personally would do. Anna was happy to take any information the guy was willing to give them.

"Meanwhile, you're free to leave at any time," Samantha said.

That made the conversation "non-custodial." He wasn't under arrest, so they didn't have to read him his rights. That alone might scare him into clamming up.

"So, how long have you worked here?" Samantha asked.

"Um." He paused, nervous. "Six years."

"You from D.C.?"

"I grew up in Wheaton."

"Is that where you live now?"

"I live in Shaw." He gave them the address.

"How old are you?"

"Forty-one."

Anna knew the point of Sam's questions was to put him at ease, get him talking, and lull him into a rhythm, so that when they got to the real questions, the momentum would keep him going. His hands had stopped shaking, and his voice grew a little stronger.

"How'd you land a job here?" Samantha asked.

"I was a caddy at the Chevy Chase Country Club. I caddied a lot for Judge Seiler, who's a member here. When they had an opening, the judge told me about it."

"How many members are there?" Samantha asked.

"One hundred exactly. The only time they take a new member is when someone dies."

"Seems like a pretty distinguished crew."

"Yeah. But the membership is secret. The only time you'll hear that someone is a member is in an obituary."

He spoke in a soft, nasal voice and looked at his hands, occasionally sneaking peeks at Anna's and Sam's faces. The members of the club might like him, but he was uncomfortable with women. Anna remembered the review he'd written about Caroline: full of ridiculous braggadocio and swagger, as if he were Smoove B from *The Onion*. The only sincere thing in his review was that Caroline had made him believe he was great in bed. Anna had a new appreciation for the skills of an escort who could make this weird little guy feel that way.

"What do the Hunt Club members do here?" Sam asked.

"Have drinks or dinner, play cards, talk. Run the world."

"So what does your job entail?"

"I get the members what they want."

"Like what?"

"Anything. Tickets to *The Lion King* when their grandkids are in town. Reservations at the restaurants you can't get reservations to. I arrange for flowers on their wives' birthdays. If someone wants to take an Alaskan cruise, I find the best deals, and I book the flights."

"Do you also get them hookers?"

"L-listen, I don't want to get anyone in trouble. Myself included."

Sam showed him the card that she had taken from his wallet. It was all black, worn and tattered around the edges. Silver script read, *Discretion: For the gentleman who can afford anything but publicity.* There was a phone number on the back. Sam said, "We'll subpoena the call records for this phone and see everyone who called this number."

"You took that from my wallet! You can't do that. I have rights."

"You handed the wallet to us."

He chewed his thumbnail. "Look, if a member wants companionship for the night, I might refer him to an escort service. Escort services are legal. Whatever they do is between consenting adults."

Anna had heard this kind of justification before. As a legal matter, it was wrong. But now wasn't the time for that debate. She spoke for the first time. "Sir. Do you remember a young woman named Sasha?"

His face softened, and his eyes took on a faraway look, like a man indulging in his favorite fantasy. "Ah . . ."

"She was killed last night," Anna said.

He seemed to sink into his seat. "Oh no."

"Let me tell you something." Anna leaned in toward him. "I don't prosecute prostitution. I've got no interest in whether you hired escorts. I'm investigating the sexual assault and murder of your friend Sasha. And I need your help."

"She was—assaulted, too?" His face was white.

Anna nodded. "We just want to find out who did this to her."

"What do you need from me?"

"She had an appointment last night. We need to find out who that appointment was with. Do you know?"

"No. I didn't set up any appointments for last night."

"Then we need to find Discretion's madam. This will be useful"—Anna held up the business card—"but what's her name?"

Anna was asking the questions now, and Samantha was jotting the answers in her notebook.

"Madeleine Connor." He seemed shell-shocked.

"How long have you known Ms. Connor?"

"I hired her when she was an escort herself, back in the nineties. We became friends. I supported her when she went out on her own."

"And now you hire her escorts?"

"She gives me a discount. I give them good reviews."

"You're BigBoy89?"

He nodded. "My reviews are always honest. I only give a good review if a girl deserves it. If someone's no good, I just don't review her, and Madeleine won't hire her." He seemed proud to have a code of ethics for operating in this illegal world.

"Do you bring escorts here to the Hunt Club? Or do the members?"

"Goodness, no," he squeaked. "That's not what this club is about."

"So what is the relationship between Discretion and the Hunt Club?"

"I just refer members to Madeleine if they ask. It's not that different from suggesting a new restaurant or a good show at the Kennedy Center. My job is to know what they'd like and find it for them."

Women were just another form of entertainment to him, like a concert or a sushi bar.

"Did you refer Emmett Lionel to Discretion?" Anna asked.

Brian's eyes widened to the point where she could see the whites above his irises. She'd been trained to look for this sign—it meant the witness was experiencing a rush of adrenaline, often from fear. "Is Sasha the girl who fell from Congressman Lionel's office?" he asked.

"I can't answer that question," Anna said. "You referred him?"

Brian nodded, his eyes still wide. "About two years ago."

"What other members did you refer to Discretion?"

The door flew open and hit the wall with a bang. Hamilton, the club president, stood there. "The other members and I were wondering if you're okay, Brian."

The concierge nodded.

"We think you might want to get a lawyer before talking to these ladies any further."

"I think I'm okay."

"We *really* think so, Brian."

"Um, all right." He looked apologetically at Anna. "I guess I shouldn't talk to you anymore."

Anna took a subpoena out of her briefcase and handed it to Brian. "Come to the grand jury next week. Bring a lawyer if you want one. In the meantime, it would help if you didn't tell anyone that you've spoken with us or what information you shared."

"Okay," he said.

He seemed sincere, but Anna knew that Hamilton would be calling the shots as soon as they left. And he had different incentives than his concierge. This club didn't even reveal their members' names. What else would they do to protect them?

# 17

An hour later, Anna walked through the ninth floor of the U.S. Attorney's Office, home of the Homicide and Major Crimes sections. It was just one floor below the Sex Crimes section but had a totally different vibe. Sex Crimes had so many female prosecutors that it was nicknamed the Pink-Collar Unit. Homicide was macho—most of the prosecutors were men, as were almost all the homicide detectives. Sex Crimes offices were decorated with plants, pictures, children's drawings, and desk lamps that threw more flattering light than the fluorescents overhead. Homicide offices were decorated with gym bags and crime-scene photos clumped in corners. Sex Crimes prosecutors kept candy bowls on their desks. Homicide prosecutors kept bottles of Scotch in their drawers. The two floors even had different odors. The Sex Crimes section smelled of potpourri, Glade FreshScents, and fruity Body Shop lotions. If the Body Shop tried to bottle the scent of the Homicide section, Anna thought, they might call it Testosterone.

When she got to Jack's office, he looked up from his desk and smiled at her. She sank into a chair. His office had no personal decorations except for a single picture of Olivia, facing him, so witnesses couldn't see it. One of his bookshelves was crammed with awards and plaques he hadn't bothered to hang, gathering dust and barely visible behind pamphlets on DNA testing.

"When are you gonna get some women here in Homicide?" Anna asked. "Your floor would smell better. Look better, too."

"You disapprove of my interior decorating?"

"Seriously, how many of your twenty prosecutors are women? Five?"

He shrugged. "A lot of young women, like you, want to work on crimes targeting women, so they apply to Sex Crimes. And lawyers who are mothers usually try to work in sections where they can control their hours, like Appellate or Special Proceedings."

"You could make Homicide more family-friendly. Offer part-time positions, flexible hours." She smiled at him. "Join the twenty-first century."

"Homicide prosecution isn't a part-time job. A murder happens, we have to respond."

"Carla does it in Sex Crimes. It works. And her employees love her for it."

"Good for Carla. If people want to come to this section, they have to be committed to it."

Anna realized she wasn't the only one from whom Jack demanded total commitment. Jack's Homicide section was so elite that he had a surplus of young lawyers eager to work long hours for him. They wouldn't complain.

He pointed to his computer screen. "Take a look at this—Lionel is about to have a press conference."

"You're kidding!" She leaned forward and peered over his desk. "Think he's gonna confess?"

"Yeah, right. But whatever he says might be interesting. The tech guys are taping it. Tell me what you learned at the Hunt Club."

Anna described the interview with Discretion's tester. "Sam's tracking down the madam. As soon as we find her, we'll get her into the grand jury."

"Good." Jack tapped his desk, a bit of nervous energy she didn't usually see from him. "I don't like you going with the agents on search warrants. If you see anything useful, you could make yourself a necessary witness, and you won't be able to help me prosecute the case. If you don't see anything useful, you're just wasting your time."

"C'mon," she said. "*You* go on plenty of search warrants. So do a lot of the older lawyers in your section. There's always an agent who can testify about whatever I see. Why shouldn't I go?"

"I only go under special circumstances. And you shouldn't do it just because the ungovernables do. The FBI doesn't need another lawyer there. You're not armed or trained." He paused and looked away. "I worry about you."

"Don't." She lowered her voice. "Treat me exactly like any other prosecutor in your section. Pretend I'm Harold Schwarzendruber."

"You're much better-looking than Harold," Jack whispered back.

"Not in the office, I'm not. Take me seriously."

"I do." He grinned. "It's Harold Schwarzendruber I don't take seriously."

Their argument was interrupted by Vanetta yelling from her desk. "Jack, the press conference is on!"

Jack turned to the computer and maximized the streaming video. "I bet he says he can't comment because he doesn't want to 'interfere in our investigation.'"

Anna was happy to turn to something besides their relationship. She sat in a guest chair and watched the live-streaming news. Lionel's press conference was arranged in the usual tableau: The Congressman gripped a podium as if trying to choke it. Betty stood one step behind and to the left, gazing at him serenely, her hands clasped lightly in front of her blue suit. American and D.C. flags formed the backdrop. The Congressman read from a written statement, forcing the words out through a tight grimace.

"I've been honored and humbled to serve the people of the District of Columbia for the last thirty-one years. Together, we've accomplished many great things. Throughout my tenure, I've always prided myself on being straight with the people I represent. And I'm gonna be straight with you now." Lionel cleared his throat, then continued reading. "What happened last night was a tragedy. My wife and I are praying for that young woman's family. My office will cooperate fully with the authorities to get to the bottom of this incident. I'm willing and available to be interviewed, as are my staff. So far"—he said with a shake of his head—"no one has asked me."

"What a load of crap," Anna said. "We asked his lawyer. We can't ask *him;* he's a represented party."

Jack shrugged it off. He was used to the political posturing.

"The Lord knows, I'm not a perfect man," Lionel continued. "I've made some mistakes in my life. I haven't always been the husband that Betty deserved. For this, I am truly sorry."

Over his shoulder, Betty nodded beatifically.

"Poor Betty," Anna said. "If it were me, I'd kill him. I'd stab him right there at the podium. No jury would convict me."

"Ouch." Jack winced. "C'mon, no one's perfect. Men make mistakes."

Anna glanced at him, wondering what mistakes Jack had made that gave him such sympathy. But Lionel was working up steam in his speech.

"Let me be perfectly clear: I had *nothing* to do with what happened to that young woman last night! I want to get to the bottom of this just as much as the police do. I call for a complete and honest investigation." Lionel looked up from his notes for the first time, speaking directly into the camera. His voice, which so far had been subdued, returned to its trademark growl. "And I demand an independent prosecutor. It can be no coincidence that mere weeks before the Democratic primary, this investigation is being pushed by prosecutor Jack Bailey, who is a friend and supporter of my challenger. I will not stand for a political witch hunt!"

Anna glanced at Jack; Lionel was trying to make the case about him. The muscles in Jack's jaw were clenching and unclenching. He was furious.

"I had nothing to do with this woman's death, and I expect to be fully exonerated. In the meantime, I will continue my fight for the people of D.C. Together, we will continue to work to make this the best city in America. God bless you all."

Lionel took Betty's hand, and they walked out a side door together. Whatever mistakes he had made, his wife appeared to have forgiven him. Anna wondered what would happen behind that door. Would she slap him, like *The Good Wife,* or was she really as supportive as she appeared?

Jack picked up the phone.

"Who are you calling?" she asked.

"Daniel Davenport. Apparently, Lionel can't wait for us to interview him."

"Should you really be the one making the call?"

"What, because of that 'independent-prosecutor' bullshit? The defendant always wants to make the case about what the government does instead of the crime he committed. You can't let it distract you."

"But maybe he's got a point. You're a friend of his opponent."

"You think I'm investigating this case to help out my buddy?" Jack put down the phone. "I'm the Homicide chief, and a homicide took place on Lionel's balcony. I investigate it."

"I'm not criticizing you, but it does look . . . funny. Somebody who doesn't know you might *perceive* a conflict of interest. Youngblood is telling people that if he's elected, he'll make you the U.S. Attorney. That could be used against you."

"No, Anna. This is trick number one in the sleazy-defense-attorney playbook—attack the prosecutor. You can't back down. You stand your ground and do your job."

"Davenport isn't sleazy. But he knows what he's doing. He's got a real issue, and he's gonna make the most of it. I'm not saying he's right, but if you're not careful, it could come back and bite you on the—"

"Okay, Anna." Jack held up a hand. "I get your point. But I've made my decision. And it's final." He picked up the phone and smiled at her as he dialed. "You can come to the interview, too. Make sure I don't turn it into a political witch hunt."

She didn't smile back. "I think you're making a mistake."

He ignored her and spoke into the phone. A coal of frustration heated Anna's chest as Jack talked with Davenport. She didn't like being dismissed with a wave of the hand, as if she were a fly buzzing around his ear.

Daniel Davenport made a living turning the tables

on prosecutors. The defense attorney would use Jack's friendship with Lionel's competitor as an element of Lionel's defense. No matter how careful Anna and Jack might be, their case would rely on evidence collection and processing by teams of officers, technicians, and clerical workers, all with different degrees of skill and motivation. Mistakes were inevitable, but Davenport would frame any mistake through the lens of Jack's motive to help Youngblood. Such accusations had the potential not only to sink a case but to do serious damage to Jack's career.

Jack was too stubborn to back down or even talk about it. This could go very badly, Anna thought.

# 18

Nicole bolted upright in Belinda's guest bed. She'd been dreaming that she was falling through darkness. The most terrifying part was not the fear of crashing but the certainty that the abyss had no end.

She'd sweated through her little black dress. The room was dark except for a crack of light coming from under the door. How long had she slept? She checked the time on her cell phone: 8:47 P.M. Shit.

She scrolled through the call log. While she was sleeping, she'd missed three calls from unknown numbers—three potential clients calling in response to her Backpage ad to set up dates for tonight. Falling asleep during the crucial late-afternoon booking time was incredibly bad business. But she'd been so tired and upset, her body had crashed.

Maybe she could still catch some of the guys. She called the first number.

"Hello?" answered a man.

"Hi." She used her breathless, flirty voice. "This is Bethany. You called? I'm sorry I didn't pick up."

"Oh, yeah."

"I'm available tonight if you're still looking to book an appointment."

"I already made other plans."

"I'm sorry it didn't work out today. Maybe next time?"

"Maybe."

Click.

She tried the other numbers. One gave her a similar

response; the other didn't pick up. She cursed her bad luck, her bad timing, her—okay, she'd admit it— stupidity in falling asleep when she should have been fielding calls and setting up dates.

To make matters worse, she was getting the unbearable craving that made it hard to concentrate on anything else. She felt lethargic and low; the whole world appeared gray. Only another hit would provide the intense euphoria that—for a few minutes, at least— would make her feel all right.

She fished through her bag for Belinda's prescription bottles, popped a couple of codeine, and swallowed them dry. The pills made their painful way down her throat. When they hit her stomach, they would make her feel a little better, though they wouldn't satisfy her real craving. She needed the sweet smoke of rocked-up cocaine burning its way into her lungs. And for that, she needed cash.

There was one place where she could always make a quick buck. She wasn't proud of it, but no one would know. The house was quiet—Belinda was out conducting her own business. And none of her friends would be caught dead where Nicole was heading.

Nicole promised herself that this was just a quick fix until she got back on her feet. This wasn't going to be her life—she was just resourceful. She was a survivor.

She couldn't go out like this. Pulling off her sweaty dress, Nicole padded down the hallway in black panties and bra and crept into her friend's room. Belinda's venture must be doing well; her walk-in closet could have starred in a *Sex and the City* movie. Nicole spun a lazy-Susan-like shoe rack and chose a pair of high strappy stilettos. Then she plucked out a slate-gray leather dress with broad zippers slashing diagonally across the front. She checked the label: Hervé Léger. It must have cost over two thousand dollars. She hated to ruin the dress, but Belinda could afford it.

She went to the bathroom and ran the shower. As she waited for the water to heat up, she unclasped her pearl necklace and tucked it regretfully into her bag. This wasn't going to be a string-of-pearls kind of night.

# 19

Anna hurried to the USAO gym, hoping to arrive before Eva Youngblood's self-defense class ended at nine P.M. There was an infinite amount of office work that Anna could be doing on the homicide case; the motion to obtain the congressional videos alone could keep her late every night. She would've skipped the self-defense class entirely, but she wanted to talk to Eva about Caroline. If Anna waited for Samantha to do it, the information might come too late to be of any use.

Jack had long since headed home for Monday "movie night" with Olivia. Anna could picture him tapping away on his laptop as Olivia watched the Disney movie of the week. He'd asked Anna to join them, suggesting she work from home, too. But she demurred. Part of the reason was she knew Olivia didn't want her there. Another part was that it was easier for Anna to do her work at the office—an excuse Jack always respected. But neither reason was the whole truth. The fact was, Anna was still a little annoyed by how quickly Jack had discounted her opinion about a potential conflict of interest. She knew she shouldn't take it personally, but it felt personal. Would he brush her off so cavalierly if they were colleagues with no personal relationship?

When Jack had asked her to be on the case, he'd said he needed her. Those words had meant a lot to her. So far, though, he seemed to put very little weight in her judgment.

As Anna walked into the gym, the students from Eva's class were leaving the floor and heading for the showers. A handful of women carried powder-blue flyers; Anna couldn't see what they said. Blotting her face with a towel, Grace came up to Anna. "Hey, there you are! We thought yesterday's class scared you away!"

"No." Anna laughed. "But this Capitol homicide case is a hot mess. I couldn't get here earlier."

Grace lowered her voice. "How's it working out, doing a case with Jack?"

Anna smiled ruefully. "Some ups and some downs."

"Highlight the ups. The whole office is watching. It's not every day you get to prosecute a congressman for killing a prostitute. There's been some gossip about why Jack put you on the case. You know how people are."

"What are they saying?" Anna said softly.

"Just jealousy." Grace waved dismissively. "Did he put you on the case for your brains or your boobs, that sort of thing. Ignore it. But—try not to screw anything up."

"Wonderful." Anna knew the talk would be worse if her relationship with Jack were public. She changed the subject. "How was Rosa Mexicano?"

"Fun. We missed you."

"Next time," Anna said. "Promise."

"No worries," Grace trilled. "This is make-or-break time for you, my dear. I'll force margaritas on you when it's done."

"Sounds great."

Grace squeezed Anna's shoulder and headed to the locker room. Anna turned to the mats, where Eva was collecting foam pillows. The petite instructor looked like an athletic-gear model, in black pants with fuchsia racing stripes and a tight fuchsia tank top that show-cased her muscular arms. Her dark hair was pulled into a long ponytail. Anna set her gym bag on the floor and went over to the instructor.

"I'm sorry I missed today's class," Anna began. "I have this case—"

"No need to explain," Eva said. "I'm married to a lawyer. I know all plans are tentative." She handed Anna a powder-blue flyer. "Dylan and I are having a fund-raiser Friday night. All my students are invited."

"Oh, thanks," Anna said. She couldn't go to Dylan Youngblood's fund-raiser in the middle of an investigation of his rival. She looked at the flyer. It started at five hundred dollars a head. She held back a laugh. Even if she weren't conflicted out of the party, she was certainly budgeted out of it. She tucked the flyer in her bag. "I actually came tonight because there's something I wanted to ask you about."

"Ask away. But you really should make up today's lesson," Eva said.

"I know. Maybe I'll sign up for the class next time you offer it."

"Don't wait until my next class. Let's do it now."

Anna looked down at her clothes. She was wearing the standard female prosecutor's uniform: a sleek black pantsuit and comfortable pumps.

"You're more likely to get mugged wearing a suit than yoga pants," Eva said. She called out to someone behind Anna. "Barry—one more!"

Suddenly, strong arms grabbed Anna's waist from behind in a tight bear hug. She heard a masculine grunt as he practically lifted her off the ground, dragging her backward.

Anna twisted, thrashed, and battered her fists back

against him, but the guy was wearing some sort of thick padding, and his grip was strong. She only managed to scrape up her own knuckles. His arms squeezed tighter, making it hard for her to breathe. Mock fight or not, Anna's heart started racing. She remembered her father punching her mother, then dragging her across the kitchen by her shirt.

"Stop!" Anna yelled. She hated the note of fear she heard in her voice.

Eva blew the whistle, and the arms released their grip. Anna pulled away and turned to see her attacker. He looked like a sci-fi cousin to one of the huge-headed mascots at a Nationals game. The man wore an enormous foam helmet wrapped in silver duct tape. The helmet's big eyeholes were covered in red mesh netting, giving the impression of an evil space alien. He wore loose blue overalls over massive body padding.

Anna put her hands on her hips as she tried to get her breath back. Eva's surprise assaults were getting on her nerves.

"I wasn't ready," Anna said.

"You won't be ready when it happens for real, either. Watch how it's done."

Eva nodded at the mock attacker. He grabbed the instructor from behind in the same bear hug.

"You plant your feet wide to get a strong stance," Eva explained as she demonstrated. "Use your hands to push his hands down. Then you pivot from your torso, and—" Eva twisted from her waist, thrusting her elbows backward into the mock attacker's head: right, left, right. Even with the foam helmet, the mock attacker was forced to pull back a bit. But he kept his grip around her waist. "Now watch this." Eva stomped down on the guy's padded foot. He reacted as if in real pain. Eva then slammed an arm backward, grabbed his groin cup, and yanked.

"Ow!" The attacker bent over and loosened his hold on Eva. She spun around, hitting him in the head with her elbow again. She was free. She faced the attacker, who appeared to be in Oscar contention for his performance of "injured man."

Eva wasn't through. "If you run away, he'll chase you. You always have to go *through* your attacker." She grabbed his shoulder and pulled him so close, his chest was pressed against hers. She kneed him in the groin, then followed with a swift kick to the same place. He went down on all fours, and Eva finished the exercise with a running knee to the head.

"Now you try," she said to Anna.

They practiced that for ten minutes. Then Eva demonstrated how to get out of a headlock before passing out. "It only takes six seconds for the blood flow to your head to be cut off. And once you're unconscious, it's over."

By the end of the session, Anna felt as tired and bruised as the armored attacker pretended to be. He took off his giant helmet, revealing a medium-sized man with a blue handkerchief tied over red hair. Even with all the padding, he looked exhausted. It must be a tough job. So many blows to the head. Anna wondered what kind of man would voluntarily endure that on a nightly basis. He must have his own issues to work out.

She thanked him as he walked off to the men's locker room. Despite the surprise attack, she was glad to have learned the techniques.

"Thank you, too." Anna turned to Eva. "For staying so late for me."

Eva started to walk toward the locker room. Anna grabbed her gym bag and fell into step.

"You're welcome," Eva said. "Being able to work late is one of the advantages of not having kids. One of the very few."

Anna looked at her instructor curiously. The note of melancholy was surprising. Eva seemed to have the perfect marriage, the perfect life. Anna had seen so many glamorous pictures of Eva in the society pages. Wearing fabulous gowns, standing next to her handsome husband. Traveling to Europe on a trade delegation, smiling in front of the Eiffel Tower. Anna had always wanted to travel and see the world. Maybe once she paid off her ninety thousand dollars in law-school loans.

"Do you have any children?" Eva asked.

*Kinda,* Anna thought, picturing Olivia. "Not yet," she said. "I'm not married. Someday. I have to make sure I'm ready for that kind of commitment."

"Don't wait too long. I always imagined I'd have a big family. But I put it off, and now—too late."

"I'm sorry," Anna said. She wondered whether she should ask more but decided against delving into such a personal issue.

"It's not *your* fault." Eva seemed to shake herself out of the moment. "Anyway, you didn't come to hear my family-planning troubles. What did you want to ask me about?"

"A class you held at your studio about two months ago." Anna pulled out a copy of Caroline's DMV photo and handed it to Eva. It was only a matter of time before the photo began circulating in the press. "Do you remember this woman?"

Eva took the picture as they walked into the locker room. "Yes. I don't remember her name. She took a one-day Women's Basics. Beautiful girl." Eva handed the picture back to Anna and unlocked her locker.

"Did you ask everyone why they took that class?"

"Sure. Every class is tailored to the students' needs." Eva kicked off her shoes.

"Do you remember what Caroline said?" Anna asked.

"Those are personal stories, not gossip."

"She's the woman who was killed falling from Congressman Lionel's balcony. That's what I'm investigating."

Eva sank down onto the bench. "Oh God. That's awful." She suddenly seemed small and fragile. Anna remembered how terrible she herself had felt two years ago, when she lost a trial against a domestic abuser and the battered woman was killed a few months later. Anna had blamed herself for the death—if she'd won that first trial, everything might have been different. She wondered whether Eva was having similar regrets.

"Do you remember whether Caroline said why she was taking the class?" Anna asked again.

Eva nodded slowly. "She had a stalker. Somebody she met at work who wouldn't leave her alone. I don't think she said where she worked. She didn't mention Lionel. I would have remembered that."

"Did she say anything else about who was stalking her?"

"No. It was just a one-day class—you don't get to know the students very well. But I liked her. There was something about the way she spoke, the way she carried herself. I saw a lot of myself in her. I can look up her name in my records, get her address and phone number if that would be helpful."

"Sure, whatever you have, I'd appreciate," Anna

said, although she doubted Eva would provide anything Anna didn't already have. "Do you remember anything else she said?"

"I remember she was scared. There might've been more to the story, but I can't recall. I see so many students. I only remember her at all because her story resonated with me. When I was in grad school, I had some bad experiences with men. It's why I started studying self-defense."

Eva stood up and pulled off her tank top. She wore nothing underneath but seemed comfortable with her partial nudity.

"I know Congressman Lionel is innocent until proven guilty," Eva continued. "But I wouldn't put this past him. Let me tell you, people like that, in politics—once they've got that power, they'll do anything to keep it. That's why we're running against him. I hope you'll come to our fund-raiser on Friday."

Eva pulled off her pants, dropped them to the ground, and walked naked to the showers.

# 20

After Anna left the locker room, she headed down to her own floor. Most of the offices were dark, a federal-government nod toward conserving energy; frequent e-mails reminded workers to turn off the lights when they left. She found Detective McGee sitting in one of the guest chairs in her office. He wore a black suit, a red shirt, and a tie that looked like a checkerboard. His black fedora sat on the guest chair. He was playing with the little plastic fishing game on the edge of her desk, having a hard time steering the tiny plastic fishing pole with his thick fingers.

"You could have a day care in here," McGee said, waving at the collection of children's toys on her desk.

"They're for child victims," Anna explained as she sat down. "Children don't want to look right at you when they're talking about what Uncle Vincent did to them. It helps them open up if they can focus on something else."

"Man, I thought working Homicide was depressing." McGee put down the little fishing pole and reached into the breast pocket of his suit. "I knew you'd still be working."

He pulled out a plastic evidence bag and handed it to Anna. Inside was a white-gold diamond engagement ring—the ring he'd found on Congressman Lionel's balcony. The round diamond looked to be between one and two carats. Anna shifted it in the light, noticing how much it sparkled, even through the plastic bag. She held the bag under her desk lamp and looked closely at the ring. The letters TJB were inscribed inside the band.

She showed the inscription to McGee. He put on a pair of reading glasses and squinted at it. "Huh," he said. "You think those are the initials of the guy popping the question? Or the girl he was giving it to?"

"C'mon, McGee," Anna said. "You lived in D.C. your whole life, and you've been married twice, and you never went to the Tiny Jewel Box? No wonder those women left you."

McGee laughed. "Now, wait a minute. Maybe a detective can't afford your rich-lawyer jewelry stores, but I know how to treat a lady. A diamond from Zales—in a box from Tiffany's!"

Anna laughed, too. "Maybe the store can tell us who bought it." She studied the ring again. "Caroline's family said she wasn't engaged."

"Her college friends said she didn't even have a boyfriend, far as anyone knew," McGee added. "I don't think it was hers."

"It's not the sort of thing that gets misplaced. It must have something to do with her death."

"Maybe the Congressman or one of the staffers is missing it."

"Let's ask tomorrow. But you should probably go to the Tiny Jewel Box. They might be able to identify the ring. If nothing else, maybe they'll give you some empty boxes."

"Now you're talking." McGee flipped through his little notepad and summarized the notes from his day of interviews. "Caroline was poli-sci at Georgetown, average grades, no extracurriculars. Only one thing in her disciplinary file—she and her roommate got kicked out of Darnall Hall freshman year for underage drinking."

"Did she lose her scholarship?" Anna asked, remembering what Caroline's mother had said.

"Never had a scholarship," McGee said. "She paid for college by personal check. Forty thousand, nine hundred and twenty dollars a year."

Anna wasn't surprised that Caroline had lied to her mother about the scholarship. The young woman had found a way to take some of the financial pressure off her family without revealing the source of her newfound wealth.

"Since they got kicked out, Caroline and her roommate lived in—" McGee looked at his notebook. "Alban Towers, a fancy apartment building way too pricey for two college students. On Massachusetts Avenue, a stone's throw from the Cathedral. The roommate's name is Nicole Palowski, like the mother said."

"Did you find her?"

McGee hesitated and looked down at his shoes, a sign that he was embarrassed about something. "The thing is, she might've left right when we came in. I think somebody went down the stairwell as we came out the elevator."

"Wouldn't you be *trying* to talk to the police if your roommate got killed?" Anna asked. "What's she hiding?"

"Yeah," McGee agreed, looking relieved that Anna didn't harp on the witness getting away. He pulled a folded copy of a PD-81 from his jacket pocket. "Here's the inventory from the search of the apartment."

She scanned the seizure inventory. "Photo albums could be useful. Empty zips found in the garbage with cocaine residue. That dovetails with what Caroline's mother said about the roommate using drugs. The autopsy didn't find any drugs in Caroline's system, although cocaine metabolites would only last seventy-two hours." Anna read the next line and looked up at McGee. "What's this? You seized a, quote, drawer of lace underpants and sex toys, unquote?"

"We, uh, we figured it was an escort case, so, uh, maybe that was evidence." He looked down at his shoes and shrugged his big shoulders. "My guys wanted to seize it."

"Don't be embarrassed, you're right. Could be evidence of prostitution. I'll look through the stuff later. What'd you learn about the roommate?"

"Apartment manager complained about her, said she was always bringing guys into the house. Multiple guys per night. It's not that kinda building. He put a stop to it, then she started coming and going at crazy hours, leaving the house around three A.M., coming home around seven in the morning."

"Those are track hours, not escort hours. Let's see if she has a record."

Anna pulled up the RCIS database on her computer and ran a check on Nicole Palowski. There was one hit—but as a victim, not as a defendant. Three years earlier, when Nicole was eighteen, she'd walked into the Second District police substation and reported that her stepfather had molested her multiple times when she was a child. It fit a pattern Anna had seen over and over. More than 75 percent of women working in prostitution had been sexually abused as children. In this case, MPD declined to investigate Nicole's complaint because the incidents took place in Pennsylvania. They told her to call her hometown police department.

Nicole's report was a fairly common one—a college student, away from home for the first time, finds the strength and independence to talk about an assault that happened long ago. But there was frustratingly little that the criminal justice system could do. There was no jurisdiction—no connection to D.C. that would allow local authorities to prosecute the crime. Even for D.C. crimes, it was hard to bring a one-witness case based on a decade-old claim. Without corroborating proof, the office would usually prosecute it as a misdemeanor, which carried a maximum of six months of jail time but could be tried before a seasoned D.C. judge instead of a skeptical D.C. jury. But misdemeanors were subject to a three-year statute of limitations, so old cases too weak to be tried as a felony were barred by the time limit. Anna hoped that MPD at least referred Nicole to a counselor. She might've just been shown the door.

"Between the hours and the coke," Anna said, "you think we should look for Nicole Palowski at the track?"

"It's possible. Even high-end escorts can fall low if they get into drugs."

"I know you're about to go off-duty," Anna said, "but . . . do you think we could swing by the track now?"

McGee sighed mightily. "Only because I like you."

She knew Jack would disapprove of her going to the track. He'd think it wasn't safe enough. But McGee would be with her the whole time. She'd be fine.

Fifteen minutes later, Anna rode in McGee's unmarked Crown Vic while he slowly steered the car up and down K Street, from 10th to 14th streets, Northwest. During the day, the strip of expensive office buildings was home to the prestigious law firms and lobbying shops that made the term "K Street" famous. Late at night, when the lawyers and lobbyists were tucked into their suburban homes in McLean and Bethesda, an older profession did its own billing by the hour along these streets. As McGee cruised, Anna watched a man in an expensive suit step out of a revolving door and slide into a waiting Lincoln Town Car. The Town Car then drove past a woman standing on the corner wearing platform boots and a tube top stretched over massive breasts.

"You know the difference between a D.C. lawyer and a D.C. hooker?" McGee asked. "Five hundred dollars an hour!" He chuckled, then stopped and glanced at Anna. "No offense."

Prostitution was illegal in D.C., but enforcement hardly made a dent. MPD would occasionally run undercover stings rounding up the prostitutes or the johns who hired them. They received a citation and were released, the equivalent of a very serious parking ticket. Johns used to be sent to "John School," a program that taught about things like sexually transmitted diseases and child trafficking, and which had slashed recidivism. The prostitutes used to be eligible for a program called Project Power, which provided drug treatment, counseling, and job training. Both programs had been halted recently because of budget cuts. The occasional roundups sometimes shifted the track's location but never eliminated it for long.

The Sex Crimes section didn't prosecute prostitution; that was handled by another unit. Anna's section saw these women when they were *victims* of sex crimes. Prostitutes were easy targets for violent men. They were unlikely to call the police if someone robbed, assaulted, or raped them. Most

prostitutes didn't trust the system, having been processed by it themselves. And many were runaways
or throwaways—no one would look for them if they
went missing. For that reason, many of the world's
most famous serial killers, like Jack the Ripper, preyed
on prostitutes. Women involved in prostitution were
eighteen times more likely to be murdered than other
women of the same age and race.

When a prostitute did turn to law enforcement,
she would often lie about what she'd been doing that
night and the circumstances that led up to the crime.
Anna had heard many variations on the story of a
woman who left a club at two A.M., accepted a ride
from a friendly stranger, and was raped or robbed instead of being taken home. The story would change in
the second or third telling, as the victim became more
comfortable with the prosecutor and more willing to
say what she had been doing out that night. But the
initial lies made the cases hard to prosecute. Juries
were willing to accept that a victim worked as a prostitute and still convict a man who assaulted her—but
they were reluctant to believe anyone who initially lied
about an incident, regardless of her profession.

Tonight there were about twenty women in various
stages of undress, loitering in two- or three-person
clumps on the street corners. They spanned the full
range of age, race, and attractiveness. Some looked
sick and weak, others hale and hearty. The one thing
they had in common was sky-high heels: stilettos,
gladiator sandals, platform boots. They walked with a
bumptious sway that lawyers, in their sensible pumps,
never achieved.

McGee cruised the street, his eyes skimming the
women. Finally, he seemed to find what he was

looking for. He pointed his chin at a woman wearing a yellow bikini under a dress made of white wide-weave netting. "That lady was a witness in a homicide last year," he said. "I couldn't keep track of her till I arrested her for indecent exposure. She was wearing that same dress, but without the bikini. She got six months' probation, but she had to check in regularly with her probation officer."

McGee parked illegally in front of a fire hydrant, and they got out. The muggy night air smelled of auto exhaust and cheap perfume. The detective walked toward the woman in the net dress, who was posing for the passing traffic in front of a darkened Cosi restaurant.

"Hey, Capri," McGee said.

The woman glanced over at them. She had a thick scar across her neck and kind brown eyes that narrowed when she saw the detective. "Come on, McGee, I ain't done nothing yet."

"I know. We need your help."

Capri put her hands on her hips, cocked a knee, and regarded him skeptically.

"We need to find a girl," McGee said.

"She in trouble?"

"Not with us," Anna said. "But she might be in danger."

"Ain't we all."

McGee showed Capri a DMV photo of Nicole. "Have you seen her?"

"Naw, baby. She don't look familiar."

McGee handed the prostitute his business card. "If you do see her, tell her we'd like to talk to her."

"We can help her," Anna said, scribbling on the back of her own business card and handing it to Capri.

"Okay," Capri said. She tucked both cards into her cleavage and turned to go.

"You don't have to do this," Anna said quickly. She knew it was a futile exercise, but she couldn't leave without offering assistance. "We can arrange job training, emergency shelter, whatever."

Capri looked over her shoulder and gave Anna a broad grin. "Don't have to do *what*, darlin'? I'm just waiting on the bus." She sashayed away.

"C'mon, Mother Teresa." McGee laughed, patting Anna on the shoulder. "We got a lot more women to talk to."

Sam turned her Durango onto Kalorama Circle and gawked at the stately old mansions dotting impeccably landscaped lawns. Although it was dark outside, most of the houses had spotlights hidden in the flower beds, illuminating the fabulous facades. The private homes looked like embassies. Just north of this cul-de-sac was Rock Creek Park; the houses on that side of the street had views of the parkland. Samantha murmured with appreciation. She'd grown up in her parents' apartment over Sergio's and now lived in a one-bedroom condo on H Street, two blocks from the restaurant. She spent a lot of time on HomesDatabase.com, fantasizing about big houses.

Sam glanced at Steve Quisenberry, the agent riding shotgun. "Madeleine Connor's doing pretty well, huh?" she said.

"Yeah." Quisenberry paged through some printouts. "According to ChoicePoint, she bought the place in 1996 for five hundred and nineteen grand. With the rates she's charging, maybe she could still afford to buy it today."

"God, I wish I'd invested in real estate in the nineties. My parents would never have to make another tray of ziti again."

The District's real estate spike began with the Internet boom and correspondingly high law-firm salaries and continued when business-friendly mayors replaced Marion Barry. Once yuppies realized they could live in D.C. and actually have their trash picked up, they swarmed in. Unlike the rest of America, home prices in D.C. hadn't gone down after the bust. Sam guessed that the homes here on Kalorama Circle were worth around three million dollars apiece.

Sam pulled up to the address they'd found for Madeleine Connor. It was a stone mansion with a peaked slate roof and arched doorway. With a stone walk meandering through gold, pink, and purple perennials, it looked like the mansion Hansel and Gretel would have bought if they'd grown up and become lobbyists.

Sam was proud of how quickly she'd found the house. It would've taken her days back when she was a rookie, but advances in technology had practically made her a magician. With a name and state of residence, Samantha could get a photo, date of birth, address, credit history, and property records, among other things. There were two Madeleine Connors in D.C., but Sam hadn't wasted her time on the twelve-year-old in Cleveland Park.

Sam parked a block away. She and Quisenberry walked through the warm night, redolent with the scent of fresh-cut grass. FBI agents didn't interview important subjects alone—there'd be no one to provide corroboration later if the subject denied what was said. The FBI rarely allowed agents to tape-record their interviews. Instead, they took handwritten notes, later typing them into a form FD-302: The nation's most prestigious law-enforcement agency still used last century's detective methods. But a notepad wouldn't malfunction if you dropped it or got it wet, and it couldn't crash or run out of batteries. And it wouldn't record the questions Sam asked or the technique she used to convince a witness to talk.

As they walked toward Madeleine's house, Quisenberry noted the makes, models, and license numbers of the cars parked along the curb. Later, he'd run them through a DMV database to find out who they were registered to. Although the interiors of most houses were dark, the windows of Madeleine's home blazed brightly. This was the middle of the day for an escort agency.

Their research suggested that Madeleine lived alone. A police database confirmed what Brian Stringer had told them—that Madeleine had been an escort herself. She had two misdemeanor arrests for solicitation of prostitution from the early nineties. For one, she got probation before judgment—essentially a get-out-of-jail-free card. For the other, she got two days in jail and a year of probation.

The agents walked up the stone walk to the front door. Through the diamond-shaped glass panes, Samantha could see an opulent living room.

"You got the subpoena?" she asked.

Quisenberry nodded, patting the breast pocket of his suit jacket.

"Don't serve her until I say so," Sam said.

She rang the bell. A moment later, the arched wooden door swung open. The smell of expensive perfume wafted out, and Madeleine Connor stood in the doorway. The light from the house illuminated her long honey-brown hair. She was pretty, though her beauty was now caught in a tug-of-war between age and plastic surgery. Samantha knew that Madeleine was forty-six, but she looked like a thirty-six-year-old whose face was being pulled back by significant g-force. She wore beige linen pants, a sleeveless brown linen shirt, and Tory Burch ballet flats. When she saw the agents, she sighed with an air of resignation.

"You're the police, I assume?"

"FBI," said Samantha as she showed her credentials. "You were expecting us?"

"Of course not," Madeleine said with mock surprise. "What would the FBI want with me?" She didn't wait for a response. "Come inside. I'd rather the neighbors didn't see you here."

Madeleine gestured the agents into the foyer and showed them into the formal living room. The walls were a deep raspberry with dark wood trim; the furniture was antique; the upholstery was flowered damask. A stone fireplace held logs that were too pristine to be real wood. A framed picture of Madeleine, from about twenty-five years ago, sat on a side table. The photograph was artistic and high-quality—perhaps she'd tried modeling before settling on her current business. The home was lightly scented with Madeleine's perfume.

Sam and Quisenberry sat on flowered chairs across from Madeleine, who lounged on the couch. Between them, an antique coffee table held a stack of *Washingtonian* magazines and a copy of the *Washington Post* opened to the headline "Woman Killed in Fall from Congressman Lionel's Balcony."

"Ms. Connor, we're here about Caroline McBride,"

Samantha said. "We're investigating her death and hoping you can help us."

"I doubt I can," said Madeleine. "Although I would like to." Though there was emotion in her voice, her expression was blank—she either had a perfect poker face or too much Botox.

"Were you close to Caroline?" Samantha asked.

"I loved her. But you'll have to address questions to my attorney."

Madeleine handed the agents an ivory business card with her lawyer's name and number.

"Do you know who Caroline met with last night?" Quisenberry tried.

Madeleine stood up and smiled coldly. "I shouldn't have asked you in. Now I must ask that you leave."

She stood, and the agents followed suit. Samantha nodded toward Quisenberry, who handed Madeleine the subpoena.

"This is a court order," Samantha said, "requiring you to appear before the grand jury tomorrow at nine A.M. If you have any questions, you can call the prosecutor, Anna Curtis, whose number is at the bottom."

"My lawyer advised me not to answer any questions," Madeleine said. "I won't come to the grand jury."

"If you're not there at nine o'clock sharp, you'll be arrested. And bring something to do, because there'll probably be a lot of waiting." Samantha held up the lawyer's business card. "If I were you, I'd tell your attorney to call Ms. Curtis right away."

As they walked back through the door, Samantha turned to face Madeleine one last time. "We know the business you're in, but frankly, we don't care about that. What we care about is finding out who killed

Caroline. I expect you care about the same thing. We have to move quickly. Please help us."

Madeleine paused. Finally, she nodded. "I want to help you. But call my lawyer. I need immunity. And then I'll tell you what you need to know."

She shut the door in Sam's face.

# 21

It was close to midnight when Anna opened Jack's front door and tiptoed into the house. Raffles dashed over and rubbed his cheek against Anna's calf. She picked up the orange tabby and stroked under his chin; she was rewarded with a motorboat of loud purrs. Slipping off her shoes, Anna padded to the kitchen. Jack sat on a stool at the counter, reading through some papers. Waiting up for her. She was touched by the gesture.

Perhaps her frustration with Jack earlier in the afternoon hadn't been entirely fair. Regardless of their romantic relationship, he was the chief. Maybe he'd considered her opinion but simply disagreed with it. She didn't have to take that personally. She should give him the benefit of the doubt.

She set Raffles down, put her arms around Jack's waist, and rested her head on his shoulder. He felt solid and warm under her cheek.

"Hello, love," he said, putting down his papers and reaching back to put his hand on her leg.

"Hi." She kissed his neck. "I told you not to wait up."

"I know."

She held him, savoring the feel of his body pressed against hers. He turned to face her. She shifted so she stood between his knees, then pulled his face to hers and kissed him. Putting her mouth on his was the best part of her day. She inhaled the scent of mint.

The house creaked, and they pulled back at the same time. They didn't want Olivia to see them locking lips. All was quiet; it was just the old house shifting. Jack smiled at her.

"I saved some dinner for you." He slid a foil-wrapped plate to her. She pulled off the aluminum foil and found baked chicken, rice and beans, and a tomato salad.

"Nice!" she said. "Don't tell me you made this." Jack was a good cook, but not when he was in the middle of a big case.

"Luisa did." Olivia's nanny sometimes cooked for the family when Jack was busy. Anna had occasionally tried to whip up dinner in the Bailey kitchen, with uniformly disappointing results.

"Thank Luisa for me." Anna sat at the counter and tucked into the rice and beans. "Mm. This is great. I was starving."

He went to the fridge, pulled out a bottle of sparkling water, and poured some into a glass. "What kept you at the office so late?" he asked, setting the glass in front of Anna.

"Thanks." She took a sip. "I was at Eva Young-blood's self-defense class. Learned a few moves, if you want me to demonstrate on you."

"That would be fun." He sat next to her.

"I spoke to Eva. Turns out Caroline took the self-defense class because she had a stalker."

"Hm. Any prior stalking convictions for Lionel or his staffers?"

"No, but that doesn't mean much. Stalkers typically start later in life—late thirties or early forties. They might have a long trail of failed personal relationships but no criminal record. They can be very high-functioning: doctors, lawyers, whatever. They get more violent over time."

Jack shook his head. "Lionel's sixty-four. He's been married for decades. I don't think he's the stalker type. Did you have an officer with you when you spoke to Eva?"

"No, it was after a class."

"Okay." Jack sighed. "Write it up—that's *Brady* evidence, suggesting another possible killer. We'll have to turn it over to Davenport when we bring charges. You were talking to Eva until midnight?"

"No. Then I went to the track to try to find Nicole Palowski."

"Anna! Didn't we *just* talk about dangerous field trips?"

"I was with McGee and we were just talking to some of the women. It's not like I was working the track as an undercover."

Jack's flinch was small but noticeable. She paused with a forkful of chicken midway to her mouth. "What?" she asked.

He slid off the stool and placed his mug in the sink. With his back turned to her, he said, "Nina worked undercover."

Jack hardly ever mentioned Olivia's mother. "Do you want to talk about her?" Anna asked softly. She set the fork down. He turned to her, and she let the silence stretch out. He opened his mouth, and she thought they were about to have a breakthrough.

"No," he said. Despite his entreaties for openness, he kept the secrets he wanted to keep.

As much as she wanted Jack to open up about Nina, she knew it wasn't something she could force. He would tell her when he was ready. She nodded and finished eating her dinner. Jack rinsed her plate and put it in the dishwasher.

"Let's go to bed, sweetheart," he said.

She nodded, and they went upstairs, creeping quietly past Olivia's open bedroom door. The little girl was sound asleep.

"I'm gonna take a bath," Anna whispered as they went into Jack's bedroom.

"Now?"

"I need to wash the track off of me." She smiled at him. "Join me?"

She was rewarded with a crinkling of his eyes.

The bathtub in the master bathroom was a huge claw-foot affair that looked like it had been there since the house was built in the 1890s. Anna poured Neutrogena body oil into the warm water spilling from the tap. The room filled with sweet almond-scented steam.

She unclipped her BlackBerry and set it on the wooden table next to the tub. Jack brought a match to a votive candle in a stained-glass globe; the flame danced, then caught the wick. He turned off the light, and they undressed in the colorful flickering candlelight.

She lowered herself into the warm water and slid forward so he could sit behind her. When he was settled in, he wrapped his arms around her, and she leaned her head back against his chest. She closed her eyes and wished things could always be as easy as this, the simple pleasure of skin against skin.

"I love you," Jack whispered. "I just want to keep you safe."

"I know. I love you, too."

Jack drew her hair to one side and brushed his lips against the side of her neck, sending happy shivers down her spine. Her BlackBerry buzzed with an incoming call.

"You want to get that?" he asked.

"Shut up." Anna laughed. She reached out and pressed the button declining the call. The silence and the feel of Jack's body curving around her were all she wanted right now. She tipped her head back and kissed him. Her breath came quicker, her heart sped up, and she forgot how tired she was.

Making love in a bathtub was overrated, Anna thought, logistically tricky and apt to slosh water all over the floor. But as his hands skimmed up her sides, her objections evaporated into the steam. Somehow, they managed.

Afterward, they sat facing each other in the bath, smiling sleepily. Lulled by the warm water and dim light, her eyelids slowly drifted downward. She crossed her ankles across his abs. He picked up one of her feet and massaged it in the oiled water. As his thumb slid slowly over the arch of her foot, she made a sound close to Raffles's motorboat purr. She could stay like this for hours. Days.

Except that the flicker of candlelight was punctuated every few seconds by the flash of her BlackBerry's LED, calling her like a master to a servant. A message was waiting. Eventually, her conscience overpowered her sense of hedonism. She pulled her foot back and sat up regretfully.

"I better get that," she said.

# 22

If the track had been located in a dangerous part of town, it would've been harder for Nicole to come down here. But surrounded by the expensive office buildings and fancy storefronts of K Street, she didn't feel like she was leaving her world. She was just hanging out during off hours.

Nicole arrived a little after two A.M., when the nightclubs let out and things got busy on weeknights. Although the day had been hot, the night air felt soft and pleasant. She staked out a spot on the corner of 14th and K, the track's western edge. That was the best place for a girl who was here on her own, without the protection of a pimp. The first time she'd come here, she'd stood right in the middle of the action and gotten chased away by some nasty hookers with incredibly foul mouths.

She could see a few other girls a ways down the street, wearing tacky clothes and ridiculous shoes. She would stay a good distance away from them.

*They* were hookers, of course—not her. This was *their* life. She was a Georgetown student. She would leave this all behind and go on to privilege and money, perhaps a colonial in McLean with a horse barn and a closet full of shoes. She was like a sex tourist, or perhaps a wild sociologist, briefly visiting this world and making interesting observations. The fact that she was getting paid for her work here was just a bonus.

A late-model Acura RL pulled up to the curb, and

the driver rolled down the window. He was bald and paunchy, with an expensive tie hanging loosely around the collar of a rumpled white shirt. He appeared harmless. Nicole checked his hand: wedding ring, Breitling watch. Probably a lawyer heading home after a night in the strip clubs on M Street. He hadn't found a stripper willing to take a ride with him, so he'd come here for a sure bet.

She leaned down to his window, giving him a glimpse of her Miracle-Bra'd breasts over the top of her dress. She propped her hands on her thighs, where they would remain hidden from view. The red polish on her nails was chipped in several places, and her cuticles were torn, conveying the aura of decay. "Hi, sweetheart," she cooed. "You looking for a date?"

"Yeah." His speech was slurred. "How much?"

"Are you law enforcement?" She'd heard that police officers had to answer this question truthfully. Maybe that was just a rumor, but she always asked just in case.

"No." He laughed. "Are you?"

"No. A hundred."

"Going rate's fifty."

"I'm better than that," she said, playing with the long zipper that slashed diagonally across the front of the leather dress. "You'll appreciate the difference."

"That may be true, but all I've got is fifty." The smell of pot wafted from his car.

"Fifty," she said, "and some of what you're smoking."

He hit the button unlocking the doors, and she got in. He handed her a joint, and she took a long drag as he steered the car into an alley. She could see another car, half a block ahead of them, where the occupants were doing the same thing she was about to. It was a busy night on the track.

He parked, and she held out her hand. You always got the money up front. He pulled out his wallet and counted his cash. He had only forty-eight dollars.

"I'm sorry, baby." He laughed again. "I told you I was light."

He dug in his console for some coins.

"Stop it," she hissed. "I'm not taking your fucking change."

Furious, she considered getting out. But she'd already done all the real work—waggling herself at passing drivers, negotiating the deal, driving back here. The sex itself was a minor time commitment compared to what it took to set up the transaction. She snatched the bills and stuffed them in a pocket behind one of the zippers on the dress.

She handled him roughly at first, expressing her anger. But then she had to concentrate on getting the job done. It wasn't easy, with the steering wheel blocking her movement, the seats that didn't fully recline, the low roof that made her scrunch down like the Hunchback of Notre Dame. The stick shift jammed painfully into her leg. Nicole closed her eyes and tried to pretend she was at the Willard. But it was no good. Beneath the marijuana smoke, the guy smelled of sweat and bad cologne, and his car smelled of stale french fries.

She was flooded with shame. She wasn't an avant-garde sociologist. She wasn't on her way to a life of horseback riding and shoe shopping in McLean. She was a hooker, getting paid in crumpled one-dollar bills.

She didn't even try to brush away the tears that streamed down her face.

At least there was some serious cash in her purse by five A.M., when the sky started to lighten and the clientele changed from homebound clubbers to work-bound construction workers. Nicole preferred the construction workers, although the negotiations in mixed English and Spanish could be challenging. They were generally cleaner and more respectful than the clubbers, and certainly more sober. Still, by this point, her feet throbbed in Belinda's too-small stilettos, and she was exhausted.

As Nicole climbed out of a pickup truck, she was surprised to see a top-heavy woman approaching her. The woman wore a mesh dress over a yellow bikini. Nicole had seen her around here, but they'd never spoken.

"Hey, I'm Capri," the woman said.

"Hey." Nicole tried not to stare at the thick scar on the woman's neck.

"You got a pimp, sugar?"

"I'm an independent contractor."

"Mm-mm. You need protection out here. My man runs a good house. He wanna talk to you."

Nicole glanced down the street. She could only see women, but she knew the pimps were hidden in the shadows, watching everything. "No, thanks. I'm good."

Capri angled her body so the rest of K Street couldn't see her face. "Police looking for you," she said quietly. She pulled two business cards out of her cleavage and held them out to Nicole.

How did they find her here? No one knew she was working the track. Nicole hesitated, reluctant to touch anything that had been squished between the hooker's breasts, but she took the cards. The first was for MPD Detective Tavon McGee; the second was for Assistant U.S. Attorney Anna Curtis. On the back of the prosecutor's card was hurried female handwriting.

> Nicole—
> I can help you. Call me.
> —Anna

Sure, help send her to jail. Nicole stuffed the cards into one of the zippered pockets of the dress. She had no intention of calling either number.

"Thanks for the heads-up," Nicole said.

"God bless."

Nicole turned back to the corner of 14th and K and was surprised to see a lanky black man standing there. He wore shiny black pants, a black button-down shirt, a belt with a huge rectangular rhinestone buckle, and gold Gucci sunglasses, although the sun had yet to rise.

"Hey, ho." The man leered. He had gold edging on his front teeth. She backed away from him—right into another man.

"Where you think you going, bitch?" the second man said.

As she turned, more men emerged from the shadows. Before she could run, she was surrounded.

"You can't be out here on you own."

"You ain't about your business, ho!"

"We don't tolerate no renegades out here."

Nicole spun around, looking for a way out. She'd heard of a pimp circle, and she knew it was a risk she took, operating on her own out here. But she'd worked the track a handful of times and had come to believe they'd leave her alone.

"You gotta pick one of us."

"That's the rules of the game."

"Choose up."

The men closed in. She felt their hands on her hair, stroking her arms, tugging at her dress. "Please," she said, her voice cracking as it came out of her throat. "Please, I just—"

"You just nothing, bitch."

An open palm struck her across the cheek, knocking her head sideways. She gasped, then tried to run, but she was easily pushed back into the circle. More hands slapped her, grabbed her dress, pulled her hair. Terrified, she squatted on the ground, using her arms to protect her face. They kept hitting her. She wondered if she was going to die like this.

A voice boomed over the other men's. "Step off!"

The pimps looked to the source of the command, then backed away. "Shit, man, we didn't know," one muttered. They rolled away, disappearing back into the shadows.

Crouched on the ground, Nicole gasped for breath hysterically. "Oh my God, thank you!"

Strong arms lifted her from behind. Before she could turn to see her savior, she felt the hard nub of a gun pressed into her lower back. The man shoved her toward a black Escalade idling at the curb.

"Please don't hurt me," she whimpered.

"Shut the fuck up, bitch. You're in a world of hurt."

Rough hands threw her into the backseat, and the door slammed shut. Her head whipped back as the car screeched off.

# Tuesday

# 23

As the sky lightened from black to gray, Anna sat at Jack's kitchen table, typing on her laptop and drinking her second cup of strong coffee. She still wore her pajamas and glasses, and her hair was in a bed-mussed ponytail. Raffles lay curled on the table next to the computer, chin on his paws, watching her with sleepy orange eyes.

The message on her BlackBerry last night had been from Jane Thomasson, Madeleine Connor's attorney. Madeleine was willing to identify the client who had made an appointment with Caroline at the Capitol—if she received immunity for running an escort service.

That was fine with Anna. She was far more interested in finding out who killed Caroline than prosecuting one of the hundreds of escort services operating in the D.C. area. Jack agreed. One luxury of being a prosecutor was the authority to decide which crimes to charge and which to overlook. That decision-making power, known as prosecutorial discretion, was unique to prosecutors, a luxury private lawyers didn't enjoy. But it wasn't just Jack's call. They had to persuade a small army of DOJ managers to approve the immunity, too.

Before Anna had gone to sleep, she'd spoken to Thomasson, then e-mailed a DOJ form and memorandum to the acting U.S. Attorney, Marty Zinn. She'd gone to bed a little after midnight, then woken at five-thirty A.M. to the chime of an e-mail—from Marty, approving her immunity request. If Jack was on board,

Marty said, so was he. Now that she had her office's approval, she was typing up a memo to get authorization from the Department of Justice, which oversaw every U.S. Attorney's Office.

Anna was sleep-deprived and weary of red tape but excited for the break in the case. By the time she finished the DOJ memo, the sun had risen and the birds were singing at full volume. She could hear Jack and Olivia puttering around upstairs. She e-mailed the memo, lowered her forehead so Raffles could give her a fuzzy headbutt, and went upstairs to get ready for one of the biggest days of her legal career.

Jack was in Olivia's room, sitting on the bed behind the little girl, combing her hair into two neat braids. Anna stood in the doorway and watched wistfully. Jack had learned to do this after his wife died. His big hands braiding Olivia's hair was one of the most tender things Anna had ever seen. She tried to envision her own father doing her hair, but it was beyond the powers of her imagination.

She remembered a token she'd gotten for Olivia. She went to Jack's bedroom, dug through her purse, found the CVS bag, and brought it back to Olivia's bedroom.

"Hey, maybe you can use these." Anna handed Olivia a package of *Princess and the Frog* barrettes.

Olivia's face lit up with delight. Then she scowled. "They're for babies." She thrust them back at Anna.

"Olivia!" Jack scolded. "Say thank you."

Olivia sighed dramatically. "Thank you."

"You're welcome." Anna tried to smile. "I'll leave them here in case you change your mind."

She set the package on Olivia's dresser and went to take a shower. As the hot water pounded her shoulders, she tried to attribute the knot in her chest to too much caffeine. But she knew it was from Olivia's continued rejection.

Anna remembered the first man who'd tried to date her mother: an insurance salesman named Fred. It was two years after Anna's mother had finally left her father; Anna had been twelve or thirteen. Fred seemed like a decent enough man, but Anna and her sister didn't like the idea of a newcomer. A male presence upset the peaceful all-female equilibrium they'd finally achieved. Anna and Jody had mocked and undermined Fred at every opportunity. Eventually, he gave up. It was years before their mother tried dating again. At the time, it seemed like a victory. Now Anna wished she could tell her mother she was sorry.

She got out of the shower, dried off, and put on a sleeveless pink shell and a black skirt suit. She normally wore pants, but today was a big day. She spent a few minutes primping in the mirror. There were soft blue circles under her eyes from lack of sleep. But with a little concealer and a touch of mascara, she looked presentable enough.

By the time she came downstairs, Jack and his daughter were out in the backyard, looking for the best sprigs of mint. Anna looked out the kitchen window at Jack's garden. He was kneeling down, his arm around Olivia's waist, pointing at something in the dirt. In addition to the mint, which grew like a weed, the garden brimmed with basil, oregano, lavender, tomatoes, green beans, carrots, and zucchini. Jack had grown up in Anacostia, a poor urban neighborhood. But his mother had always kept a vegetable garden. He often spoke warmly about digging in the soil with her. Veda Bailey had been a legal secretary, devoted to her only child. Jack's father had never been in the picture, and Jack was determined to do a better job himself. After Veda died, he created this garden in his own backyard so he could share gardening with Olivia. The little girl loved it. Now Olivia reached down and picked up the thing Jack had been pointing at.

Anna turned and grabbed a granola bar from the cupboard. She wouldn't attempt cooking breakfast today. Unwrapping the granola bar, she went to the kitchen table and clicked on her laptop. There was a new message. She sat down and opened it.

A DOJ attorney had already e-mailed her the immunity authorization. The speed of that turnaround might have set a record. That was one advantage of a high-profile case. People were paying attention; her requests jumped to the front of the line.

Madeleine Connor would be granted use and derivative-use immunity. Nothing she said about running an escort service would be used against her. This immunity would trump her Fifth Amendment privilege. There was no right not to incriminate yourself if the government promised not to use the statements against you.

Anna had one final step. Last night she'd drafted a motion seeking a court order compelling Madeleine's testimony. Now she filed the motion electronically with Judge Redwood. If the judge issued the order, the prosecutors could require Connor to testify in the grand jury. Anna hoped Judge Redwood would sign the order upon arriving in chambers. For now Anna packed up her laptop and put the madam's testimony out of her mind. She had to focus on the next most important thing: their interview with Congressman Lionel.

Olivia ran into the kitchen, cupping her hands around a hidden treasure. Jack was still outside, putting away a hose. "I have something for you," Olivia told Anna. "Hold out your hand."

Anna did. The girl dropped a fat earthworm into Anna's palm. It squirmed and writhed, leaving a dirty trail of slime on her skin. Olivia watched with wicked glee. But Anna had played with her share of earthworms as a kid; she wasn't fazed.

"Cool," Anna said. "That means it's a healthy garden, right?"

"Yeah." Olivia seemed disappointed that she hadn't elicited a shriek. She plucked the night crawler back from Anna and ran it outside, where she set the creature down in the dirt. Anna sighed as she went to the sink to wash her hands.

Anna felt strange as she boarded the Red Line train with Jack; they usually traveled to work separately. Jack sat in one of the double seats facing the front of the subway car. She hesitated, thinking it would look too intimate if they sat together, so she chose a seat across the aisle. A moment of hurt flashed across his face, and she felt heartless. When they changed to the Green Line at Fort Totten, she sat next to him and hoped that no one she knew would see her sitting thigh to thigh with the homicide chief.

They got off at L'Enfant Plaza. Although it was only eight-fifteen, the day was already uncomfortably hot. They walked into the Starbucks on 3rd Street, where Samantha and three more FBI agents were waiting in a dark-suited circle around a small table. Jack ordered two iced coffees, and he and Anna sat down with the agents.

Sam pulled two pages from a folder. She grinned and slid them across the table to Jack. "You'll want to ask the Congressman about this."

Anna peered over his arm and read the paper. "Wow!" She looked up at Samantha. "The computer guys found these in Lionel's e-mail account?"

"Yep. In his deleted items."

"Great," Jack said. "Any other e-mails with Caroline's name? Or Sasha or Discretion?" They spoke in low voices although this corner was empty.

"Not yet," Samantha said. "But it'll take a while to search through everything."

McGee ambled up, holding a foamy pink Frappuccino that matched his shirt and tie. Behind him were three other MPD homicide detectives, all wearing five-button suits with bright coordinating shirts, ties, and pocket squares. "You all waiting for us?" McGee asked, coyly slurping his Frappuccino.

Together, the ten-person team walked to Lionel's office. The Congressman and his staff had insisted they would plead the Fifth rather than testify in the grand jury. Grand jury testimony was under oath, went for as long as the prosecutors wanted to keep them there, and was done without counsel present. But the Congressman had agreed to be interviewed with his attorney, in his own office. He could tell his constituents that he was cooperating, but his lawyer could call off the interview if it started to go downhill.

Capitol Hill was dotted with massive federal buildings that housed the offices of members of Congress. Although the politicians went to the Capitol to vote, they did their work and housed their D.C. staffers in the sprawling office buildings surrounding the Capitol. The architecture of the congressional buildings varied:

Russell and Cannon had been built at the turn of the century and were fronted with classical marble columns and filled with arched colonnades and rotundas. Hart was the most modern, in the blockish Cold War style. All had underground tunnels connecting them to the Capitol.

Congressman Lionel's office was in the Rayburn House Office Building, one of the less glamorous structures. Rayburn was built in the 1960s but designed to blend with the more historic buildings. The result was a mash-up of neo-classical Greek architecture and sprawling Cold War box. The entrance had marble columns that resembled the Supreme Court, stuck in the middle of an enormous white office building in the shape of an H.

Streams of young people in khakis or sundresses flowed into the congressional office building. It was the August recess, so the junior staffers wore snappy-casual. The few members of Congress still in town would arrive later in the morning; most members were back in their home districts, with their families and constituents.

The Capitol Police officers at the entrance to the Rayburn Building allowed the MPD officers and FBI agents—and their guns—to pass through the screeching metal detectors, but Anna and Jack had to put their bags through the X-ray machine. As Anna was wanded by an officer, she understood that the location was a power play by Lionel. Usually, AUSAs conducted witness interviews on their own turf. But Lionel didn't have to talk to them at all. He could call the shots in terms of where they met. Walking the long gray and white marble hallway, past American and state flags designating the entrance to every

representative's office, Anna felt the power of the legislature surrounding her on all sides.

They rode an elevator to the second floor and followed the signs to room 2136, Lionel's suite. As the
prosecution team turned a corner, they almost collided
with a stanchion of reporters and photographers en-
camped outside the office. Jack, Anna, and the officers
kept their heads down and walked silently past the
shouted questions and flash photographs. At the end
of the line, Detective McGee turned back and gave the
cameras a broad, gummy grin.

The team crowded into Lionel's waiting room,
where two women sat at two desks. The older one
had a nameplate that said Jamiya Henderson. Anna
had read some articles about Lionel and knew Jamiya
was his scheduler, the person in charge of running
his calendar and one of his oldest and most trusted
employees. At the other desk was a pretty, young
receptionist, most likely a staff assistant right out of
college. Both women regarded the investigators with
silent suspicion.

As the door to the hallway closed, muffling the
sounds of the press, Daniel Davenport emerged from
another room. The silver-haired lawyer regarded the
troops filling up the small reception area. "Good
morning, Jack. You've made your show for the press."
He pointed toward the door. "But there's no need for
half a dozen armed men to conduct these interviews."

"Good morning, Daniel," Jack said. "I've got four
interview teams here. We'll conduct simultaneous interviews."

"No." Davenport shook his head. "I intend to be at
each interview."

"That's not how we're doing it. You can obviously

sit with your client while we interview him, but I can't let you be present for the other interviews."

"Then we're at an impasse."

Anna watched the two lawyers like a spectator at a tennis match. Physically they were well matched, both tall and imposing, although Davenport had the trim, patrician demeanor of someone who would win a regatta, while Jack, with his broad chest and shaved head, looked like he'd have the advantage in a fist-fight. Davenport had put Jack in a tough spot again. The prosecutors would never get the unvarnished truth from staffers if the boss's lawyer were sitting in the room. On the other hand, she didn't want to lose the opportunity to interview the Congressman entirely.

"We're not at an impasse," Jack said coolly. "These are voluntary interviews. The Congressman said he was going to cooperate fully with the investigation. If he's changed his mind, so be it. He either cooperates or he doesn't."

Davenport paused, then pursed his lips. "I'll ask Congressman Lionel what he wants to do." He went back into the adjoining room.

When Davenport was out of earshot, the team mumbled their two cents. Some of the officers approved of Jack's hard line; others thought it was too much of a gamble, that they should take whatever interviews they could get. Jack and McGee bent their heads together and whispered. Anna walked a slow circle around the reception area, checking out the enormous color photographs of Lionel on all the walls. He looked like a joyful, caring grandfather as he shook hands, cut ribbons, and greeted constituents. She didn't expect to see that side of him today. She noticed all the photos had a signature at the bottom of the matting: *B. Vale*.

"Are those pictures by Brett Vale, the LD?" Anna asked the scheduler.

The older woman seemed to consider the question and decide it harmless. "Yes. He has quite an eye, don't you think?"

"Very impressive."

After fifteen minutes, Davenport returned, looking unhappy but resigned.

"Very well," he said. "But the Congressman can only spare an hour. I hope you'll understand that he is taking time out of a very busy day to help you."

Jack had won this round. Now came the hard part.

# 24

In some ways, Lionel's office suite was less impressive than the chambers of judges in the local courthouse. In addition to the reception area, it held only three rooms. The Congressman and his Chief of Staff had their own offices; the rest of his staffers shared a bullpen-like office. Anna and Jack needed a moment to figure out the logistics for simultaneous interviews in the limited space.

They weren't interviewing all of Lionel's employees. Several had gone home for the August recess. Malik Jones, the press secretary, was on vacation in New Zealand. Terrance Williams, the campaign manager, was out working on the campaign. But even with the skeleton staff left, they didn't have enough space for everyone.

They decided Jack, Samantha, and an MPD officer would take the Congressman into his office. Anna, McGee, and an FBI agent would interview the LD in the emptied-out bullpen. Teams of one MPD officer and one FBI agent would interview the Chief of Staff in his own office, and the lower-level staffers in the reception area. The rest of Lionel's staff would wait in a committee room next door. Anna was reminded of something a law professor once told her: 80 percent of practicing law was logistics.

"Good luck," Anna whispered to Jack.

He nodded wordlessly and turned to instruct the team. He was in the zone.

• • •

Emmett Lionel sat behind an enormous wooden desk, scowling down at his hands. Jack's eyes skimmed the office as he and his team walked in. Behind the desk was a large window overlooking the Capitol and a credenza holding photos of Lionel with his wife, children, and grandchildren. Flanking the window were glass-fronted china cabinets showcasing political souvenirs. A side table held a computer that was turned off. Across the room sat a black leather couch, a small conference table, and a six-foot-tall wooden sculpture of intricately carved African animals. Photos of the Congressman in action hung on the walls, interspersed with plaques and certificates. It was the office of a man who'd spent his life doling out and collecting political favors.

When Lionel's eyes landed on Jack, his face morphed into pure fury. He stood up from his chair and jabbed his index finger at Jack. "I am not talking to that man!"

Jack sighed. Hadn't they just been through this? "You agreed to be interviewed by the U.S. Attorney's Office, sir. I'm the Assistant U.S. Attorney handling this case."

"I demanded an independent prosecutor!"

"Shall I call off the interview?" Jack said.

"This is a sham!" Lionel glared at Jack. "You want me hanged so your friend Youngblood can have my seat."

"Let me assure you, Congressman, that my only goal is to follow the evidence. A woman fell from *your* balcony. It's my job to investigate it." Jack could hardly believe the man's self-righteousness. A woman had been killed, and Lionel was acting like he was the target of a trumped-up political smear campaign. But

Jack kept his tone mild. "We appreciate your 'cooperation.'"

"I *am* cooperating! But you have an army of lawyers here. Give me someone else."

"With all due respect, sir, you don't get to choose who asks the questions. You can choose to answer them or not."

The Congressman looked to Davenport, who just shook his head, as if to say, "You chose this course."

Lionel sank resignedly into his chair. "Fine."

Davenport introduced a young associate, who sat on the couch. Jack, Samantha, and the MPD officer sat in guest chairs before Lionel's desk. Davenport pulled up a chair and sat next to Lionel, as if he could protect his client through sheer proximity.

Lionel's Chief of Staff, Stanley Potter, answered Agent Quisenberry's questions but with little detail. His hands patted his round belly as he said he couldn't remember the answers to many of the questions. He ate a king-size Snickers bar between answers, dropping chocolate crumbs on his shirt. His lawyer sat silently next to him, seemingly content with his client's say-nothing tap dance. After a few minutes, Quisenberry concluded that Potter believed his boss was guilty and needed cover.

Potter claimed that all the staffers had access to the Congressman's hideaway. The keys were kept in the scheduler's desk, and the drawers were never locked. He claimed not to recognize a photograph of Caroline and never to have heard of the Congressman using escorts.

Potter recalled the events of Sunday night. "The Congressman and I had a dinner meeting at the

Monocle with people involved in the redevelopment of the Anacostia River. I was staffing the Congressman, but he didn't need me; he knows all about the issue. My job was really just to get him out of there in time to stop by the stakeholders' meeting back at the Capitol."

"What's a stakeholders' meeting?"

"Generally, it's a meeting hosted by organizations with an interest in a bill. A chance for them to check in with the members, and the members to show their faces and get credit. In this case, it was basically a cocktail reception. Food and drinks. To butter them up, really. The energy bill came out of the conference committee on Friday, and the vote was Monday. You heard about that, right? Most contentious issue this session. No one was happy about the timing of when that conference report dropped. It was the last day of the session—August recess was supposed to start last Friday. Everyone had vacations planned, and that made the session drag out over the weekend. Any proposed bill has to be posted on the Internet for three days before there's a vote. So the House just stayed in session over the weekend to do a bunch of uncontroversial suspension votes and wrap things up while they waited for Monday so they could vote and get out of there."

Potter seemed much more relaxed—and informative—prattling on about congressional procedures than talking about the dicier subject of his boss's extracurricular activities. Quisenberry steered him back on track. "So what time did you leave the Monocle?"

"Um. I broke him free about six-forty-five, and we headed back to the Capitol. We got to the stakeholders' meeting around seven-fifteen. The Congressman was there, eating and drinking, the whole time. Next thing I knew, the police were calling."

Agent Quisenberry cocked his head. "In the middle of a party, you know where one man is the whole time?"

"He's the boss. Part of my job is to keep him moving and to interrupt whenever someone is monopolizing him."

"So you were by his side the whole time?"

"Pretty much."

"You know there are video cameras throughout the Capitol, right?"

Potter shifted his paunch. "Of course."

"Because when we get the video, we'll be able to see exactly when either of you left the party."

*If* they got the video, Quisenberry thought. He knew Davenport might be able to keep it away from the prosecutors forever. But the threat was getting to Potter.

"Maybe we *did* get separated for a while," Potter said, blinking rapidly. "I couldn't say for sure."

Anna had done her research before coming here. Brett Vale had worked his way up the Hill hierarchy, never staying with any one politician for longer than a few years. He'd been a Staff Assistant, then a Legislative Correspondent, then a Legislative Assistant, to Congressmen from Tennessee, Ohio, Nevada, and Illinois, before Lionel hired him as Legislative Director. He was a reputed whiz at combing through the fine print of proposed bills. As LD, he was one of Lionel's more trusted aides, though not his wingman. Anna thought that might make Vale the most likely both to know something and to be willing to talk about it. By contrast, Chief of Staff Potter had served with the Congressman for over twenty years. With so much invested in Lionel's career, Potter was likely to keep his boss's secrets.

Anna walked into the bullpen with MPD Detective McGee and FBI Agent Wanda Fields behind her. The big office was crammed with six desks. Stacks of papers, binders, and newspapers seemed to be everywhere. A large flat-screen TV hung on one wall. It was muted but turned on, split into four screens: CNN, MSNBC, FOX, and C-SPAN.

Vale's desk was the single smooth, clean surface in the entire room. Anna wondered if the paper chaos everywhere else bothered him.

He stood up from his desk, unfolding his long, lean body when Anna walked in. He wore another perfectly pressed gray suit that matched his silver hair. He was apparently too high up the food chain for snappy-casual. Standing with him was his lawyer, a puffy-eyed Englishman named John Singleton. On Vale's desk was a single legal pad with a long, handwritten list of bullet points in a neat cursive script. When he saw Anna looking at the pad, he flipped it over.

As they shook hands, his pale blue eyes traveled down her body and back up, lingering on her legs a little too long. She wished she'd worn her usual pantsuit.

"I liked your pictures of the Congressman," she said, hoping to build rapport. "Did you ever think of being a professional photographer?"

"No."

So much for rapport. She sat across from his desk.

"How long have you worked for Congressman Lionel?"

She liked to start with simple background questions to which she already knew the answers. The witness would get comfortable, and she would get a baseline for what his truth-telling looked like.

Vale had worked for the Congressman for two years, he said. As LD, he was responsible for advising the Congressman about legislative issues and supervising the Legislative Assistants who conducted much of the research. As he spoke to Anna, he stared at her with an unblinking gaze. She consciously stopped herself from squirming under it. She sat straighter and tried to channel Jack's cool gravitas as she transitioned to more pointed questions.

"Did you ever know Congressman Lionel to hire an escort?"

Vale glanced at his lawyer. Singleton had said nothing so far and said nothing now. Vale turned back to Anna with a pleased little smile. "You're damn right I did. Everyone knew about it."

"Whoa, whoa!" Singleton jolted to life, reaching forward to place a hand on his client's arm. "Let's talk for a minute, okay?" Turning to Anna, he said, "Would you mind excusing us?"

Chester the intern smiled at the MPD detective but rubbed the tinted Clearasil on his neck nervously. He sat next to his assigned attorney in the now-empty reception area.

"Have you ever gone up to the Congressman's hideaway?" the detective asked the intern.

"Sure! We had a Fourth of July party up there just last month."

"Ever go up there without the Congressman?"

"Yeah, once in a while." Chester blushed. "Some of the Legislative Assistants will take the key from Jamiya's desk, bring some beers up, and drink on the balcony. You're not going to tell the Congressman, are you?"

"He doesn't know?"

"No way. He'd kill us!" Chester's hand flew to his mouth. "That's not what I meant."

Jack made no effort to start his interview of Congressman Lionel with rapport building.

"What's your full name, sir, and your date of birth?" Jack asked.

"Why are you wasting my time with that?" Lionel glared at Jack. "You can get that from the Internet."

"I'm not interviewing the Internet."

"Emmett Douglas Lionel, March fourteenth, 1949."

"How long have you had this office here in the Rayburn Building?"

"Dammit, I'm not answering questions that you can answer on Wikipedia. You want to ask me a real question, go ahead."

"Agent Randazzo," Jack said, "please note that the Congressman refused to answer that question."

Sam smiled down at her legal pad and wrote.

"It's his hour, Lionel," Davenport told his client. "Let him ask what he wants."

Jack could feel Davenport's frustration with his client. Lionel should answer as many innocuous questions as he could and then be able to say he'd been cooperative.

"I've been the District's Congressman for thirty-one years, and I've had this office the whole time."

"And how long have you had the hideaway?"

"This one—two years. I had a smaller one before that."

Jack had learned a lot about hideaways over the last few days. Every senator and a few powerful House members had small offices within the Capitol where they could work without trekking back to their office buildings. For many years, the very existence of the hideaways was secret. They were the back rooms of proverbial backroom deals and the enablers of some infamous congressional womanizers, such as Lyndon Johnson. Each hideaway was unique, carved out of interstitial spaces in the Capitol over the centuries. Some were tiny windowless rooms in the basement; the nicest had views or balconies, like Lionel's. All were assigned by seniority. As one of the longest-serving members of Congress, Lionel had moved into his most recent hideaway when a senator died two years ago.

"Who has access to your hideaway besides you?" Jack asked.

"Anyone could have access."

"Okay, let me put it this way. How many keys are there?"

"Three."

"Who has them?"

"Me, my Chief of Staff, and my scheduler, Jamiya. She keeps her copy in her desk, but she never locks her desk. Anyone could take it out of there."

"Do staffers ever go to the hideaway?"

"I throw a party for them there every Fourth of July. It's the best place in the District to watch the fireworks."

"Are there any other occasions when staffers go into your hideaway?"

"Certainly. I sometimes have meetings with senior staff there. Mostly Stanley and Brett. And I know the LAs and interns drink beer up there sometimes. On the sly."

"Who else goes into your hideaway?"

"All kinds of people—other members, lobbyists, the occasional journalist. I have meetings there all the time."

"Who have you had in your hideaway over the last six months?"

Lionel grumbled as he tried to recall his guests. Jack doubted any of these people would be relevant to the investigation. But Lionel was talking. Now that he was getting warmed up, Jack would start asking him more pointed questions.

Anna and McGee stepped into the reception area.

"Dammit," McGee whispered to Anna. "That lawyer's trying to stop Vale from talking to us."

Anna agreed, but there was little they could do.

"At least he *wants* to talk to us," Anna said. She wondered why.

"To you." McGee chuckled. "When you get back in there, bat your eyelashes at him a little."

Singleton opened the door and gestured for them to come back in. He looked nervous and unhappy. "Brett hadn't shared this information with me before."

Anna and McGee sat down across from Vale again.

"Anna," Vale said, leaning forward as if they were talking over dinner. "Everyone knows that Lionel sees escorts. It's an open secret."

Anna nodded, trying to pretend she wasn't floored.

She glanced at McGee to make sure he was writing it down. He was staring at Vale. When Anna caught his eye, he started scribbling.

"Tell me about it," she prompted.

"It's been going on since I started. Sometimes the women would come to his office here in the Rayburn Building after hours. Usually, he'd meet them at some hotel outside the Beltway. Outside of D.C., nobody recognizes him."

"How did you know he was doing it? Did he talk about it, or did you see him meet these women?"

Vale brushed an invisible speck of dust off his gray jacket. "He never spoke about it, but I saw them. We all did. When they came to the office, they didn't look like constituents, frumpy and dumpy. They looked like swimsuit models in business suits, with their hair pulled back, maybe wearing a fake pair of glasses. If he had a 'constituent meeting' at the Ritz in Pentagon City, he wasn't talking to concerned citizens about potholes."

"Do you know any of the escorts' names?"

"No."

"Who else in the office knew?" Anna asked.

"Stanley. Jamiya. The LAs. We all talked about it."

Anna asked for more details, but Vale said he had no knowledge of the escort agency itself. He was refreshingly forthcoming, which unnerved Anna. She kept trying to figure out his angle. Perhaps she was getting too jaded and couldn't accept that someone would tell her the truth for truth's sake. But something about him was just . . . off. In any event, it was time to ask about the homicide that had brought her there.

● ● ●

Jack was done with background questions. "Have you ever used the services of an escort agency, perhaps one called Discretion?"

Davenport held up his hand to his client. "Let me reiterate my understanding that these interviews are being treated as matters occurring before the grand jury. Any leak of Congressman Lionel's answers to the press would be contempt of court, and I would expect it to be prosecuted."

Jack understood that the Congressman was worried about the upcoming primary election. D.C. was famous for forgiving politicians for their flaws and foibles—Exhibit A was former mayor Marion Barry, who had been caught on video smoking crack with his mistress and now sat on the City Council. But there would be no time for Lionel to put his dirty laundry through the spin cycle if it were aired now, a few weeks before the primary.

"Yes," Jack said. "This is a criminal investigation in the grand jury stage and thus secret. The U.S. Attorney's Office won't release details of it while the investigation is ongoing. Any information we gather would come out only in the course of some future criminal proceeding, if it came to that." He didn't take his eyes off the Congressman. "Do you remember my question?"

"You gonna prosecute me for using prostitutes? Maybe I need immunity."

"There's not gonna be any immunity here, sir. You are presently a subject of my investigation, along with everyone else in your office. But I can tell you this. It's not the policy of the U.S. Attorney's Office to prosecute the johns in escort cases. And it's not what I'm investigating. This is a *homicide* investigation. If you have information that would tend to clear you of homicide, I'd appreciate you sharing it now, *before* an indictment is issued."

"Congressman, we've discussed this." Davenport looked at his client. "You know my advice."

"I know." Lionel shifted his chair sideways, so he could face the window. He looked out at the Capitol dome as he spoke. "I belong to a gentlemen's club. The concierge referred me to Discretion about five years ago. I have occasionally met with the agency's employees over that period."

This was the first time Lionel appeared vulnerable. Jack handed the Congressman a color copy of a DMV photo. "Do you know this woman?"

"Sasha." The Congressman nodded. "Her real name was Caroline McBride."

"How did you know her?"

"Through Discretion. I saw her five or six times over the past couple of years, mostly at hotels. Here at the office once or twice." Lionel nodded toward the couch where Davenport's associate was taking notes. The young man shifted uncomfortably on the leather cushions. "That's how I know her name—a visitor has to be on the Capitol Police list and show ID to get in the building after hours. The agency allowed an exception to their usual policy so I could book appointments here in my office."

"Tell me everything you know about Sasha."

"I don't know anything about her. It's not a date. There's no 'getting to know you' talk. Anything she told me would be a story, anyway. Like the name Sasha."

"Was she engaged?"

"I said, I don't know anything about her."

"Did you arrange to meet Caroline on Sunday night?"

"No, I did not!"

"Tell me what happened that night."

"I had an early dinner at the Monocle with a group of developers who I'm trying to interest in a riverside revitalization project. Stanley Potter was staffing me. We came straight back to the Capitol afterward. There was a stakeholders' meeting for the energy bill in HC-5 starting at seven. Many members of my staff were there."

"What's HC-5?"

"A meeting room in the lower level of the Capitol."

"Were you with Mr. Potter the whole time?" Jack asked skeptically. He knew from police reports that the Congressman had been intercepted coming down the stairwell from the hideaway at eight-fifteen P.M. that night.

"Of course not. We mingled. I don't need to be staffed at a party. Around eight o'clock I saw my intern, Chester. He told me that Caroline McBride was waiting for me in the hideaway. I didn't know what was going on. I had no idea why she was there."

"Why would she come to your hideaway if you didn't make an appointment with her?"

"How the hell would I know? You think I would bring a girl to the Capitol itself? That's insane. It's crawling with reporters, members, and their staff. I might as well hold a press conference."

"Or tweet a picture of her to your constituents," Jack said. "Men have been known to behave recklessly in these circumstances."

"I haven't been reelected fifteen times by being careless. When Chester said she was here, I went upstairs to find out what was going on. The hideaway was unlocked, but no one was inside. I glanced around and didn't see anything. I went back down the stairs, and that's when the Capitol Police officer came running up. He said a woman had fallen from my balcony. That was the first I heard of it."

Jack nodded. The Congressman's story suggested that he was an innocent bystander. But the story was a gold mine for Jack—because he had an e-mail proving it false.

Potter tried to smooth his rumpled blue shirt over his big round belly as he contemplated the question. Although unfailingly loyal, he was also obviously uncomfortable with the position he was in. He shifted his portly body before answering.

"I was still at the reception when I got a call from a friend on the Capitol Police. He said that a woman had fallen from the Congressman's balcony. I called Brett's cell—he was back at the office. He came and met me at the hideaway. Lionel was there with a Capitol Police officer." Potter winced. "I called Lionel's lawyer, and he rushed over. And that's when we met you."

"She looks like you." Brett Vale looked up from the DMV photograph. He slid it back across his desk to Anna. "No, I don't recognize her."

"Do you recognize this?"

Anna handed Vale an evidence bag. His eyebrows went up when he saw the diamond ring inside it. "Where'd you get this?"

"Sorry, we can't answer questions. We just ask them. Do you recognize it?"

"No. Nice, though. Somebody spent a lot of money."

Anna took the ring back. "What were you doing the night the woman fell from your boss's balcony?"

"I was at the energy reception with him for a little bit. But I couldn't stay—so close to the vote on the energy bill, there was a lot of work to do. I came back here. That's where I was when Stanley called me. He told me to come to the hideaway."

"Was the Congressman at the party while you were there?"

"Yes."

"The whole time, or did he leave?"

"I don't know. It wasn't my turn to watch him."

Once Jack had wrung every detail out of Lionel's false story, he signaled to Samantha. She handed Congressman Lionel the printout.

"Sir," Jack said. "Let me show you something we pulled off your computer."

Lionel and Davenport leaned over the desk to read the e-mail.

| | |
|---|---|
| To: | Zachs, Chester |
| From: | Lionel, Emmett |
| Time: | August 29, 2012, 16:17 |
| Subject: | Visitor |

Chester, please escort my guest, Caroline McBride, from the North carriage entrance to my hideaway at eight p.m. tonight.
Thanks.
EDL

There was a second e-mail from Lionel to the Capitol Police, asking them to put Caroline McBride on the list to be admitted to the Senate carriage entrance that night.

"What kind of bullshit is this!" Lionel exploded, rising from his chair.

"Our forensics team found it," Samantha said with clear pride.

"This is a setup!" Lionel shouted. "Youngblood!"

"Sir, this e-mail was sent from your account," Jack said. "Did you send it?"

"Why don't we take a break," Davenport said.

"He has a mole in my office." Lionel looked around, his eyes wide with fear, as if someone might be hiding under his desk. "Daniel, I'm going to—"

"Wait!" Davenport put up a hand and stood. "Lionel, be quiet." The attorney turned to Jack. "If you'll please step outside for a moment, I need to confer with my client."

As they stepped into the reception area, Jack turned to Samantha with a grin.

"We got him."

"Have you discussed the case with Congressman Lionel?" Anna asked Vale.

"Only once, at his house. He talked about the fact that we would all be interviewed."

"What did the Congressman say?"

Vale scrunched up his narrow face into a fierce grimace. "'Tell 'em the damn truth!'" he roared. It was a perfect imitation of his boss.

"Is there anything I didn't ask that you expected me to ask, or anything you haven't told me that I should know?" It was one of her standard closing questions.

Vale paused, then smiled. "One thing. The Congressman said he'd be unavailable that evening; he was meeting with a 'constituent.' He didn't say who it was, and there wasn't anyone on his schedule."

Chester the intern nodded. "Yes, I got this e-mail from the Congressman. I did what he asked. I brought the lady up to the hideaway. A minute or two later, I saw the Congressman at the cocktail party in HC-5 and told him she was upstairs. He went up to see her."

"Have you spoken to Congressman Lionel about it since?" the detective asked.

"No." Chester shrugged. "I'm just an intern. I don't get a lot of face time with the Congressman. I just do what I'm told."

"Did the Congressman talk to you about what you should say or how you should act in this interview?"

"He just said that I shouldn't offer you any coffee," Chester replied sheepishly. "And there was certainly no need to order a tray of Danishes."

Anna stood up, thanked Vale, and shook his hand. It was cool and dry. He held the handshake too long. She pulled her hand back and returned to the reception area. The rest of the team was already assembled there. Jack and Samantha were huddled in quiet conversation. Davenport came out of his client's office just as Anna emerged from Vale's. The defense lawyer held a large envelope.

"Jack, this interview is over."

"I have some more questions."

"I'm sorry, but the Congressman has a very busy day. I hope this has been useful."

"Very."

"One more thing." Davenport handed Jack the envelope. "While we were talking, my firm filed this motion. Your friend Dylan Youngblood is the Congressman's primary challenger. I'm not accusing you of anything, but this entire interview was improper. I'm moving to have all of today's statements suppressed. And to have you and the rest of your office recused from this case."

# 25

Brett Vale stood in the bullpen office, watching out the window. His lawyer had gone to tell on him to Daniel Davenport. "His" lawyer. What a joke. The guy was obviously Lionel's pawn. That lawyer would throw him under the bus in a second if it would help Lionel. Potter didn't see it—he was blindly devoted to Lionel. But Vale knew he could trust only himself.

A moment later, he saw what he had been waiting for. The prosecution team walked down the marble steps of the Rayburn Building toward Independence Avenue. The two lawyers led the way like a pair of ducks leading their ducklings.

There she was, talking to the bald black prosecutor, their heads in tight together. Vale didn't like how close they stood. He'd felt a connection with Anna Curtis from the moment she'd walked in today. She looked just like Sasha—it couldn't be a coincidence that she was investigating the whore's death.

He was sure she felt the connection, too. He could tell by the way she listened to him. More than that; she *understood* him. She was probably talking about him right now, telling that bald guy what a great witness he'd be.

He was going to be a star witness. He would tell her everything she wanted to know about Lionel. He would make the case for her.

And when it was over, she would be grateful.

He lifted his Nikon D90 and pointed it out the

window, using the telephoto lens to bring the prosecutor's pretty face into sharp focus. He snapped a picture of her profile. Taking her picture excited him. He kept his index finger on the button, clicking away until she walked out of his sight.

## 26

The team crammed into a couple of unmarked Crown Vics that the MPD detectives had parked near the Starbucks. Anna hopped in back with Samantha, and Jack rode shotgun next to McGee. They spent the ride to the USAO excitedly sharing stories of their interviews. Anna could see that Jack was exuberant.

"We caught him in a lie," Jack said. "That's almost as good as a confession."

"I dunno," Anna said. "The more I talk to Vale, the more I like him as a suspect."

Jack turned to look back at Anna. "Vale didn't send any e-mails setting up an appointment with our victim that night."

"True." She nodded. Computers didn't lie. "What about Davenport's motion to recuse you?"

"Typical defense garbage."

"A judge might see merit in it."

"I'm not concerned about it, Anna." He glanced back at her. "Enough."

Jack's tone held a pointedness that verged on biting. Sam and McGee both glanced at him, and Anna knew they'd heard it, too. She suppressed her own sharp retort. If she engaged him now, her own tone might edge closer to a lovers' quarrel than a legal debate.

McGee dropped the three of them off at the back entrance to U.S. District Court, then drove away on C Street. He and his team would continue interviewing Caroline's acquaintances.

Anna and Jack went through courthouse security

and waited as Samantha checked her gun in the locker room. When all three of them were through, they headed to the new wing of the courthouse. They went to Judge Redwood's chambers and asked the law clerk whether the judge had signed the immunity order. She had. Jack nodded with relief as the law clerk handed the paper to Anna.

Then they all went to the third floor, where the federal grand juries sat. Inside the grand jury suite, a Court Security officer told them that Madeleine Connor was waiting for them in Witness Room #2. By the time they knocked on the door, it was a little after eleven A.M. They walked into the witness room and found two women. Anna knew that the one in the white linen skirt suit, sitting with perfect posture, had to be Madeleine. She was beautiful in the way of a woman fighting Mother Nature with every possible weapon: hair that must be going gray, colored a rich caramel; Botoxed forehead; big breasts defying gravity; StairMaster-toned, tanned legs. Next to her sat a plainer woman, with silver hair and a brown suit.

Madeleine stood and held up some papers. "I've been waiting for two hours. The subpoena says to come at nine."

"And it requires you to be here all day," Samantha said. "I told you to bring something to do."

Anna didn't think that antagonizing a woman you were hoping to use as a cooperator was useful. She offered her hand. "I'm Anna Curtis, one of the prosecutors. Sorry for your wait. It's been a busy morning."

"You're a lawyer? You look like you could be one of my girls."

Fabulous. She looked like a hooker. Plus, she was twenty-seven—she hadn't been a "girl" for nine years.

"Thanks," Anna said, "but this job has pretty good benefits."

The madam's laughter tinkled through the room. The silver-haired woman introduced herself as Jane Thomasson, Madeleine's attorney. There were handshakes all around. They all sat at the small table in the middle of the room, and Jack handed Thomasson a copy of the immunity order.

"With this order, you're required to testify truthfully in the grand jury," Jack said to Madeleine. "Normally, you'd have a Fifth Amendment privilege not to tell us about anything that might incriminate you, like your escort business. Now you have to answer our questions, but your answers can't be used against you in any prosecution. We can't even follow up on leads based on your answers."

"Fine," said Madeleine. "If no one can prosecute me, I'm happy to testify."

"That's not what I said. You can still be prosecuted. Just not using your testimony."

"What good is that? Then I'm not talking."

"That's not a choice, Ms. Connor. This order compels you to testify. If you don't, you'll be jailed today. No one wants that to happen. What we all want, and what this order compels, is that you testify truthfully."

Madeleine looked at her lawyer, who leaned over and whispered to her. They had been waiting all morning; her counsel should have prepared her for this, Anna thought. Maybe Madeleine hadn't understood her.

"Okay, Ms. Connor," Jack said, standing up. "The grand jury is waiting for us."

Madeleine looked surprised. "Don't you want to hear what I have to say first?"

Anna looked at Jack, wondering whether to take Madeleine up on her offer. If a witness was willing, a prosecutor interviewed her before locking in her testimony in the grand jury. That gave the witness a chance to hear the questions in the comforting presence of her attorney, rather than having to answer them for the first time in the grand jury, alone. And such a preview helped the prosecutor fashion the most effective questions, to make efficient use of limited grand jury time. More important, it revealed any rough patches in the testimony. A witness with something to hide was often not truthful in the first session with law enforcement. If the witness said something that the prosecutor suspected wasn't true, the prosecutor could do more investigation before asking the witness to testify about it under oath. The last thing the prosecutor wanted was to lock in a lie. Talking to Madeleine now would be helpful.

But Anna shook her head. "The immunity order doesn't cover your voluntary statements to us. It only immunizes your compelled grand jury testimony." Anything Madeleine said outside the grand jury was fair game, should the government choose to prosecute her.

Thomasson nodded, agreeing that a witness conference was not the way to go in this case.

Jack and Anna walked into the grand jury, leaving the three other women in the witness room. Only prosecutors and witnesses went into the grand jury—there was no judge or defense counsel. Jack would call Madeleine in momentarily but first had to introduce the case. The jurors looked up from their newspapers, books, and iPads. Anna hadn't been in this grand jury before; she didn't know these jurors. She smiled at them and got a few smiles in return.

The jurors were regular citizens who had been sent a letter saying it was time to do their civic duty. There was a rule saying D.C. residents couldn't be obligated to serve on a jury more often than every two years, but most residents got their jury summons every two years on the dot. There was a lot of crime and not enough citizens to go around. Service on a grand jury was more onerous than a trial jury—its tenure lasted for several months.

Anna looked around, noting the differences between this federal grand jury room and the ones in Superior Court. This room was much nicer, the facilities newer, gleaming with a white-on-white color scheme. The jurors sat at ascending rows of long white Formica tables. The space was similar to a college seminar room except the focal point was not a blackboard but a long white table at the front. It was set up with three chairs. Jack gestured for Anna to sit in the middle seat. Anna took her seat while Jack began his brief opening statement. The court reporter silently depressed the keys on his stenographic machine as Jack spoke.

"Good morning. Today we have the case of *In Re: Caroline McBride*." He read out the case number. "The decedent was a twenty-one-year-old Georgetown student who was pushed from the balcony of the Capitol two nights ago."

A collective gasp went up. They'd all heard of the case in the papers. Jack gave them some of the basic facts about the investigation, then called Madeleine into the room. As she walked in, the jurors made murmuring sounds. She was striking in her white suit. Jack gestured for her to sit in the chair next to Anna. It was probably the most scuffed and dirty thing in the white room, a seat that had been sat in by every conceivable witness: cops, housewives, convicted killers, drug dealers, homeless addicts. Madeleine looked at it with distaste, then sat, gingerly smoothing her white skirt under her thighs before pressing on the dirty white plastic. She minimized her contact with the chair with a pencil-straight spine that didn't touch the seat back.

Jack sat on the other side of Anna. It was an awkward setup. Anna was used to the Superior Court grand jury room, in which the prosecutor stood far away from the witness while conducting questioning. The side-by-side arrangement in this federal court grand jury room gave the impression that they were all collegial participants in a Q&A panel.

The jury foreman stood up and asked Madeleine to raise her right hand. "Do you swear or affirm to tell the truth, the whole truth, and nothing but the truth, so help you God?"

"I do."

"Good morning, ma'am," Jack said. He took his reading glasses out of his suit pocket and slid them on.

"Good morning." Madeleine smiled calmly. She was either incredibly confident or a great actress. Probably a bit of each, Anna thought—both skills would be helpful in her career.

Jack led her through the basic biographical information and told her about her rights for testifying in the grand jury. Then he said, "You're here testifying under court order, which means that you do *not* have a right to remain silent, but nothing you say will be used against you." The jurors leaned forward. They had heard this before and understood that it meant the testimony would be good. "Do you understand that?"

"Yes."

"You must tell the truth. The grand jury can bring perjury charges against anyone who lies in the grand jury. Your immunity does not cover lying here. Do you understand that?"

"Yes."

"How do you feel about testifying here today?"

"I'm not happy to be here. I had hoped that my business would never become the business of the authorities. I don't want to get anyone into trouble. But I also want to protect my girls, and I want to help you find who did this."

"What is Discretion?"

"Discretion is my company. It's an escort service."

"What do you mean by 'escort service'?"

"I match lovely young women with well-established gentlemen who are looking for companionship."

"How much do you charge for this companionship?"

"It depends on the girls. Rates start at a thousand dollars for a two-hour-minimum session. For girls who are in particular demand, the rates can go up to five thousand a session."

"To cut to the chase—your customers are paying to have sex with your escorts, right?"

"No. The man is paying for her time and company. If, in the course of their time together, she chooses to have sex with him, that is between consenting adults."

"Ma'am." Jack looked at her sternly over his reading glasses. "These men aren't paying a thousand dollars just to have someone to talk to over dinner. They expect the women will have sex with them, right?"

"In my experience, most men expect that the woman they take to dinner will have sex with them. But I don't dispute your point."

"Is that a yes?"

"Yes."

"And your escorts also expect to have sex with these men, correct?"

"It's always the girl's choice whether to become intimate or not. But my girls are professionals. They are generally open-minded, and they know that their job is to please their customer. And they're the best in the city."

"Who are your typical clients?"

"My motto is 'For the man who can afford anything but publicity.' That tends to include CEOs, politicians, and diplomats. My clients have the means and the incentives to pay a premium to be sure that their hobby is kept secret."

"Where do these appointments take place?"

"Wherever the man prefers. Most single men in the city prefer their homes. Married men and out-of-towners prefer hotels. Some men like to take a girl with them on a trip. The fee for trips ranges from five thousand to ten thousand per day. We've had girls flown to the Caribbean, Europe, L.A. Travel expenses are covered by the client, of course. There's also a monthly option, where a girl is exclusively yours for thirty days. She'll drop anything to be with you at a moment's notice. It's used mostly by Saudi princes."

"How long have you operated Discretion?"

"About twelve years."

"How did you get into the business?"

"I worked as an escort myself. But escorting is a young woman's job. The business side suits me better now."

"Where is your office?"

"I do everything from my home. Meet the girls, give

etiquette lessons, receive the money, keep the books, and so on."

She seemed proud. Anna imagined the Internet pop-up advertisement: *Local woman makes millions working from home! You can, too!*

"How many escorts do you employ?" Jack asked.

"Thirty to thirty-five, at any given time."

"Do your escorts all know each other?"

"No. I don't throw an annual Christmas party. I'm the only one who knows all the girls. Of course, some girls refer their friends to me, and sometimes they work together. But the fewer girls who know each other, the less gossip there can be about the clients." She smiled. "And it's harder for the girls to get together and form their own competing agency."

"How do you get your clients?"

"I used to advertise, first in newspapers and then online. Now I only take referrals from existing clients. It's safer that way. No unexpected law enforcement." She sighed ruefully.

"Are you familiar with an individual named Brian Stringer?"

"I don't want to get him in trouble."

"It's too late for that. And there's no privilege for incriminating your friends. You can confer with your lawyer, if you'd like."

Madeleine shook her head. "No, I believe you." She then explained how Brian had been a client when she was an escort, and now served as her tester. To Anna's relief, Madeleine corroborated much of what the concierge had already told them. When witnesses corroborated each other, it was like mortar to the bricks of an investigation.

"How did you set up appointments?" Jack asked.

Madeleine said that she used the same paper system from when she started the business. She didn't trust computers or her own ability to keep the information away from hackers. So she kept track of the appointments and schedules of all the escorts in binders. Men who wanted a date called her—sometimes weeks in advance but often a few hours before they wanted an appointment. She called the women and told them where to go. The escorts took only cash, which helped keep them off the authorities' radar screen. After a date, the woman would bring the cash to Madeleine's home. The escort kept 50 percent plus any tip; Madeleine kept the rest.

Jack pushed a button in the wall, and a screen descended from the ceiling. He placed Caroline McBride's DMV photograph on an Elmo projector, and it was beamed onto the screen. "I'd like to show you a document labeled Grand Jury Exhibit Number One. Do you recognize the woman in this photograph?"

"Yes." Madeleine's face lost all hint of a smile, and her voice grew soft. "Sasha. Her real name was Caroline McBride. She was my top escort. A beautiful girl, smart, well mannered, warm. No hang-ups. Perfect."

"When did she start working for you?"

"About three years ago."

"How did you come to hire her?"

"She was referred by one of my other escorts, a young woman named Nicole Palowski. They were roommates."

Jack had her explain TrickAdviser and Caroline's climb through the online ratings. Then he turned to the day of her death. "Did Ms. McBride have an appointment the night she died?"

Madeleine paused, seeming to steel herself. Then

she gave the answer she'd come to give. "Yes. Congressman Emmett Lionel called me early that afternoon to set up an appointment with her."

A female juror exclaimed, "Lord have mercy!" Others murmured and shifted.

Jack waited for the room to settle down. "How do you know it was Congressman Lionel who set up the appointment?"

"He was a regular client. He's called me many times, enough that I recognize his voice. I also recognized the phone he was calling from."

"What was that number?"

"On my caller ID, it shows up as 'U.S. House of Representatives.'"

"Is there any actual number that comes up?"

"No. Nor the name of the representative. I think the politicians know that. It makes them perhaps a bit less cautious about calling from their offices."

"Had Congressman Lionel had appointments with Ms. McBride before?"

"Yes. He liked variety, but Sasha was special. The Congressman had four previous dates with her. Twice at a hotel and twice at his office in the Rayburn Building. This time he wanted to meet her in his hideaway at the Capitol. That made me nervous—but for some men, the risk *is* the turn-on. I called Sasha that afternoon and told her where and when to go. That was the last time I spoke to her."

"Have you had any further conversations with the Congressman since then?"

"No."

"Had you ever known the Congressman to be violent with any of your escorts?"

"He had quite a temper, but nothing like this."

"What do you mean by a temper?"

"He could get belligerent if he thought a service wasn't up to snuff. He yelled at a few of the girls. They brushed it off as harmless posturing, but now I see that behavior in a different light."

"The subpoena requires you to bring any documents related to the night in question, or your business in general. Did you bring these documents?"

"I did." Madeleine pulled a single sheet of paper from her Louis Vuitton bag. "This is the booking sheet. You can see the time the Congressman called and what he asked for."

Jack marked the paper with a sticker as Grand Jury Exhibit #2. The sheet had one line across the middle of the page: *E. Lionel, Sasha, U.S. Capitol Senate Carriage Entrance, 8 p.m.* The remainder was blank. Jack put the page on the Elmo.

Anna motioned to Jack. "May I ask a question?" she said. He was the lead lawyer, but she could jump in. He nodded. Anna turned to Madeleine. "Is this all that was written on the page originally?"

"No, I covered over the other entries when I copied this. You don't need those."

"The subpoena requires you to produce the entire document, not a redacted page," Anna said. "What other paperwork do you keep?"

"I keep a client information sheet for every client, listing his information and preferences, the escorts he's used and the dates he used them, and other details. It helps me match my clients with the experience they're looking for. I also keep a sheet like that for each of my girls. And then I have a master calendar for all the dates."

"Did you bring any of those documents?"

Madeleine shook her head firmly. "No. This page is all you need. The rest of my records mention a lot of good people who have nothing to do with this."

"Ma'am, the subpoena tells you what we need," Anna said. "It requires you to produce *all* documents mentioning or related to Ms. McBride or the Congressman. We need to know who else made appointments with her, what her schedule was like. Had anyone ever given her problems before? We have a right to see all of your records. You can't pick one page, redact it, and be done."

Madeleine glared at Anna. "I can't turn over my books to you. I promised my clients—and my girls—*discretion*. I won't do that to them."

"I understand your feelings, but you have no choice in the matter. Please bring all of those documents tomorrow."

"Do you have any idea what you're doing?" A note of desperation crept into Madeleine's voice. "How many lives you'll destroy? Powerful men will lose their careers. For the women, it will be even worse. I've been in this business for over a decade. Most of my girls have gone on with their lives, gotten married—sometimes to men who don't know they were escorts. How will they bounce back from the public humiliation of a sex scandal? It's always harder on the women. What man would bring home Monica Lewinsky to meet his family? Eliot Spitzer got his own TV show, but where is Ashley Dupré?"

"Ashley Dupré is a sex columnist for the *New York Post*," Jack said. His voice held no sympathy for Madeleine's associates. "Your escorts and your clients knew their activities were illegal. They decided to take the risk."

Anna felt some sympathy for the people whose lives

would be affected. But a young woman was dead, and Anna's main concern was finding who had killed her. "Bring your business documents here tomorrow," Anna said. "*All* of them."

Madeleine stood up. "I need to consult with my lawyer."

Jack nodded. "We'll take a fifteen-minute break, folks."

The jurors got up, stretched, and headed to the bathrooms and vending machines. Jack, Anna, and Madeleine filed into the witness room. Samantha and Thomasson were standing by the CSO's desk.

Madeleine grabbed her attorney's arm and pulled her to a corner. "They want me to turn over my books!" She was obviously trying to keep her voice low but was so upset that everyone could hear.

Anna could see the jurors watching the whole scene. They should only see the evidence presented in the grand jury room itself.

"Why don't you talk in the witness room?" Anna suggested to Thomasson.

Madeleine and her attorney went into the room and conferred with the door closed. After a few minutes, Thomasson opened the door and gestured for them to come into the room. Madeleine was sitting with her arms crossed over her chest. Anna closed the door behind them.

"Is all of this really necessary?" Thomasson asked.

"It is," Jack said. "You don't have any basis to withhold the records."

Anna was glad Jack agreed with her about this.

"She won't do it," Thomasson said.

"We can get a search warrant right now," Sam said. "We'll just go to her house and take the records."

"Not based on her immunized testimony," Thomasson countered. "Look, she's not going to destroy the papers, I guarantee it. She understands that would be felony obstruction of justice. But she won't just hand them over to you."

"We'll ask the judge to compel her," Anna said.

"Fair enough. But she wants to fight it."

"All right." Jack sighed. "Let's call the judge."

Jack rang the judge from the witness room's telephone. A law clerk put him through.

"Mr. Bailey?" Judge Redwood's voice came through the speaker.

"Good afternoon, Your Honor. I have defense attorney Jane Thomasson here, as well as her client, Madeleine Connor. We have a matter that requires your intervention. We hope to schedule a hearing as soon as possible."

Jack briefed the judge on what was happening. "The government is going to move to compel Ms. Connor's records. We can have the motion to compel filed with the court by . . ."

He looked at Anna. "By this afternoon," she mouthed.

"By this afternoon," he said.

"Can you respond before midnight tonight, Ms. Thomasson?" asked the judge.

The lawyer didn't look happy about it, but she agreed.

"Okay. I'm putting you down for a hearing tomorrow at eleven A.M.," said the judge. "And I want both sides coming prepared. Ms. Connor, bring your records to court tomorrow. If I do rule in the government's favor, I will order that the documents be turned over straightaway."

Unlike the hearing about the congressional videotapes, this time Anna was happy with the judge's
signal.

"What if I don't turn them over?" Madeleine asked
her lawyer.

Her lawyer shushed her—bad strategy to let the
judge know you were already thinking about violating
an order. But the judge had heard.

"Then I'll hold you in contempt, Ms. Connor."
Judge Redwood's voice dropped an octave. "And
you'll go to the D.C. Jail, where you'll be held until
you comply with the Court's order."

Madeleine's eyes got wide. "What about my clients?" she asked. "And my girls? They'll be exposed if
I turn those books over."

"An unfortunate consequence of engaging in illegal
activity."

"Can I at least warn them?" Madeleine asked.

"Ma'am, you should talk to your lawyer." The
judge's disapproval rang through the speakerphone.
"But I expect she'll advise you not to have any
off-the-record conversations with your clients or
the women you employ as escorts—that is, your
co-conspirators—telling them about this investigation. Should it be interpreted as dissuading them from
testifying, or encouraging them to destroy evidence,
your conversation would constitute obstruction of
justice."

"Which your immunity doesn't cover," Jack added.

Madeleine looked at her lawyer, who nodded. The
madam's arrogance had transformed into fear. Anna
had seen this transformation many times before, at the
moment a person realized it was not a game, that they
were actually in trouble. Madeleine wanted to fight to

protect her escorts and her clients. But would she sacrifice her own liberty for their privacy?

"I can't go to jail again," Madeleine said to her lawyer. "I won't."

"Shh," said the lawyer.

"Then you will obey my order tomorrow," the
judge said, and hung up.

# 27

Anna, Jack, and Samantha emerged from the courthouse into John Marshall Place Park. The park provided a shady green spot between the federal courthouse and the Canadian embassy. Anna wasn't surprised to see a bunch of journalists set up there, with their cameras pointed to the courthouse's side door. Reporters often lingered near the courthouse when they heard that something big was going on.

Anna was surprised to see Madeleine standing calmly in the plaza, with her lawyer looking uncomfortable at her side. Journalists pressed around the two women, shouting questions at the madam.

"Madeleine! Do you think Congressman Lionel killed your escort?"

"Are you cooperating with the prosecution?"

"Who are your other clients?"

News vans sat on the C Street curb, their raised poles snaking with red wires. They were broadcasting live. Someone must have tipped them off that the madam had come in to testify—perhaps a grand juror, or someone who worked at the courthouse, or even someone in Anna's own office.

"No comment, no comment!" said Thomasson, tugging at her client's arm.

Anna felt a wave of sympathy for the madam, as well as a twinge of guilt for putting her in this position. Anna knew what it was like to be caught in a media stampede—although at the moment, she seemed invisible to the reporters.

But Madeleine didn't look unhappy. She was standing still and smiling at the crowd. A fresh coat of pink gloss glimmered on her lips. She put up her hands, shushing the reporters so she could speak. Anna suddenly realized who had alerted the press. "I think Madeleine called the reporters herself," she whispered to Jack.

He nodded. "She's ready for her close-up."

The rules prohibited grand jurors and government agents from talking to anyone about an ongoing grand jury investigation, but those rules didn't apply to Madeleine or her attorney. A witness could hold a press conference if she wanted—and it looked like that was exactly what Madeleine was doing.

Madeleine spoke slowly but forcefully. "For many years, I ran an agency called Discretion. Caroline McBride was working for me when she was killed. I've been ordered by the government to turn over my agency's books and records. I'm fighting like hell not to! But I've been warned that if I don't turn them over, I'll be put in prison."

Anna looked at Jack. "She's clever. This is her way of getting around Judge Redwood's instruction without having any off-the-record conversations."

Madeleine looked straight into a camera. "I promised my clients discretion, and my girls, too. But I'm afraid I won't be able to keep that promise. I'm sorry. The hearing is tomorrow morning. Before I turn over my records, I'd like to warn my clients and my girls that their names may be exposed."

"What will you do to warn them?" asked a reporter.

"That was it," Madeleine said. She pushed her way through the crowd.

# 28

Nicole curled on a corner of the filthy mattress, trying to stay on the parts that were unstained. It was impossible. The entire mattress was covered in mysterious blotches, one bleeding into the other. They could be blood, or piss, or a spot of mumbo sauce. Nicole shuddered and pulled her knees closer to her chest, squeezing herself into an even smaller ball.

She hadn't slept all night. She was terrified, shaking and sweating, in desperate need of coke. The rest of the basement offered no escape. There were no windows. The only door, at the top of the dilapidated steps, was locked. The cement walls were streaked with rusty stains; the floor was partially covered with a balding brown carpet that looked and smelled like it had been reclaimed from a dump; the whole moldy cellar was lit by a single bare bulb in the middle. She wasn't sure if it was day or night. There was *stuff* everywhere: furniture, boxes, crates, garbage bags overflowing with clothes and stuffed animals. It looked like an episode of *Hoarders*.

Who were her captors? Two guys had driven her here last night, making no attempt to prevent her from seeing the rowhouse into which she'd been dragged. Then they'd thrown her into the cellar without giving her a clue as to why this was happening. They could be Madeleine's enforcers cracking down on her freelancing. Or political operatives trying to shut her up for what she knew. Maybe someone she owed money. She'd made so many enemies lately, it was hard to keep track.

The door at the top of the stairs creaked open. It was T-Rex. Nicole's fear instantly turned to relief—a Pavlovian response to the sight of her drug dealer. She hurried to meet him as he came down the stairs. He was tall, white, and muscular, with a shaved head and tattoos covering every inch of his neck, arms, and chest. She'd slept with him a few times, first for fun and later to cover her debt. Although he was wearing a black T-shirt and jeans now, she knew his tattoos stopped at his groin in a tangle of thick barbed-wire designs. He was the closest thing she had to a friend now.

"T-Rex!" She held her arms out to embrace him.

His huge palm was like a padded club, hitting her jaw with a loud thwack. Pain exploded across her face, and she fell to the floor.

"Fuck you, Nicole. Where's my money?"

She looked up at him, shocked and then furious—at herself for her stupidity. Of course, T-Rex hadn't come to rescue her. He must be the reason she was here in the first place.

"Hey, hey, that ain't the way it's done!" an unfamiliar voice called from the top of the stairs. "You gonna bruise that beautiful face."

A man with smooth brown skin and short black hair trotted down into the basement. He was as tall as T-Rex, but thin rather than muscular. His perfectly symmetrical features and bright white teeth gave him a leonine beauty. The man smiled and offered a hand down to Nicole.

She hesitated, shaking off her pain, then took his hand and let him help her to her feet.

"You okay, baby?" He gently put his hand on the cheek where T-Rex had hit her. His thumb brushed away a tear.

Nicole didn't know what to say. She wasn't okay. Her jaw hurt, and she was terrified. T-Rex crossed his arms over his chest and glared at her. But this man's touch was soothing; his brown eyes looked concerned for her. She nodded at him, gulping back her tears.

"Everybody calls me Pleazy," he said. "How about you?"

"Nicole."

"Okay, Nikki, let's talk. You and T-Rex got a problem. I got a solution."

She didn't like being called Nikki, but she wasn't about to say that now. She looked him over. He wore Rocawear jeans and a button-down shirt. She was surprised to see the hip, expensive clothes in this basement. Something about the fact that he'd spent hundreds of dollars on his outfit made her feel like he was more trustworthy.

"I hear you been dabbling in the business," Pleazy said. "That's good, that's fine, I respect that. Girl like you got obvious talent. But you need a manager. For your safety. And to protect your earnings."

"I don't want a pimp!"

T-Rex took a step toward her, hand raised. "Dammit, Nicole! You got no choice."

She cringed and covered her face with her arms. Pleazy stepped smoothly between them. "Chill, man. I got this covered."

T-Rex glared but lowered his hand. "She's been jerking me around for months. Promising to pay, running when I come. She owes me enough to make a down payment on a house. I'm done fucking around."

"See, Nikki, the man is upset. And I gotta tell you, he's not inclined to let you walk outta here. He wants to make an example of you." Pleazy's voice was soothing, but a chill crept down her back. "I told him, Give her a chance. So that's why you're here. To work off your debt through me."

Nicole stared at Pleazy. The man was proposing some sort of indentured servitude. She shook her head.

"Now, wait up before you say no, just hear me out. You keep a third of what you make. I take another third. The rest goes to T-Rex. I run a good stable. Got four good girls upstairs. They make, average, five hundred a night. You'll be all paid up in a couple months. Free to go do whatever you like. You could go, you could stay. You might find you like my way. Maybe you even learn something. Meanwhile, I keep you safe, give you a roof over your head. I set up the appointments, I take care of the business. All you gotta do is what you're already so good at. It could be good for you, Nikki. You could stop running."

There was something seductive about his voice and about what he was proposing. The idea of relinquishing control was incredibly tempting. Stop running. Stop struggling to make things work. Stop being surrounded by alien pimps taunting and hitting her. She wasn't equipped to deal with the world she'd gotten into. He would take care of her, protect her, run the business. She could just lie back and let the world spin underneath her without constantly trying to stay upright.

A tiny part of her old self shook its head. She'd never wanted this.

"Oh, and Nikki." Pleazy's voice was like honey, so sweet that even the nickname sounded smooth on it. "There's one more thing."

He took his hand off her cheek, and she backed up, thinking he might hit her. But he reached into his pocket and pulled out a small cylindrical glass tube and a tiny Ziploc bag with a waxy yellow-white rock in it. It was what she'd craved every minute of the last few days.

He took out the rock and placed it in the glass pipe in front of a steel wool filter, then pulled out a lighter and held it out like a prince offering the keys to his kingdom. She reached for the pipe, but he held it away from her. "Mm-mm. What do you think, Nikki? Have we got a deal?"

Her jaw throbbed, making it hard to think, but that was the least of it. She had to have that pipe. She would do anything for it.

"Okay," she said. "Okay."

"That's my good girl."

He handed her the pipe. She flicked on the lighter, held the flame to the glass, and inhaled. The fire incinerated the rock, and smoke poured into her lungs. Finally: relief and release and sweet annihilation. She closed her eyes and basked in the chemicals coursing through her body, delivering pleasure to every nerve. Everything was gonna be okay.

She opened her eyes to find Pleazy smiling at her with great tenderness. His face was the most beautiful thing she'd ever seen. He leaned down and kissed her, ever so gently.

"We're gonna make a fine team, Nikki. I've got big plans for us."

He took her hand and led her up the stairs.

# 29

The newspapers fell for Madeleine Connor, and they fell hard, like a tweenage boy with his first crush. Anna sat at a computer in the war room and scanned through the Google hits. The Capitol murder investigation was the top story on the home page of every newspaper she clicked to. The story had the perfect dynamic: Murder and sex drew in the readers, and the political element meant even the most respectable journalists could talk about it.

By now all the papers had pictures of Caroline. There was a photo from her high-school yearbook, with her blue eyes radiating innocence, and a more recent picture from Facebook, where her smile had an inscrutable quality that hinted at something darker. The papers also ran photos of Madeleine Connor with the courthouse behind her. The madam was photogenic—the Botox and plastic surgery looked odd in person but made for a glamorous head shot. Bloggers were raving about her beautiful white linen suit, the particular pink of her lipstick, where she might have bought her shoes. In the most popular photo, she smiled with her eyes averted from the camera, pushing aside a strand of caramel hair that the wind had blown into her face. She looked sexy and mysterious and just vulnerable enough to elicit sympathy for the woman who was being forced to disclose the dirty secrets of powerful men.

With the coverage came criticism of the government's work. Why hadn't they arrested Lionel yet, some bloggers asked. Few of the friends Lionel had made in over thirty years on Capitol Hill would go on the record in his defense. There were odds posted on when he would resign. Many people were betting on, and clamoring for, a quick arrest.

Anna wasn't bothered by that criticism. The nation could jump to conclusions—and they might be right—but an important part of her job was not bringing charges against an individual until she was sure. "Beyond a reasonable doubt" was a heavy burden, and for good reason.

One criticism did bother her, however: the assertion that by forcing the madam to turn over her entire client records, the government was needlessly humiliating people, clients and escorts alike. Many assumed Congressman Lionel was the culprit and thought that the prosecutors were fishing for other politicians to target for visiting prostitutes, or that they were motivated by prurient interests. These were activities between consenting adults, the writers said, so why should a puritanical government snoop into them?

"It's like we're Big Brother in a pilgrim's hat." Anna looked up from her computer to Jack, who was typing away on the other side of the conference table.

"Don't worry about it." He didn't look up from his laptop. He was deep into his work, editing the motion she'd written to compel Madeleine's documents.

Anna kept reading and stewing. She needed a fuller picture of the business—especially of Caroline's johns—before she would feel confident that they had the right guy. She wasn't about to let Madeleine decide which lines in her record books were relevant and which could be redacted.

"It's ridiculous," she said. "This is a murder investigation."

Jack looked up. "Anna, what have I been telling you from the beginning? Don't worry about what people are saying. It'll always be something. You just do the right thing. Keep your head down, ignore the hype, do your job."

She nodded, admiring his steadiness. He was so much better than she was at focusing on what was really important. But his advice was easier to follow if you were already a legal star. Unlike Jack, she was still building her reputation. It mattered what people said about her.

She pushed herself away from the computer and rolled her chair to the conference table. As she flipped through her legal pad, a small flower fell out. A sprig of lavender had been pressed between the pages. She appreciated both Jack's gesture and the fact that he'd done it discreetly.

"Thank you," she said quietly to him.

He smiled at her. His smile still had the ability to make her heart do a little flip-flop.

Jack e-filed the motion to compel Madeleine's records. After he pressed *send,* he turned to her again. She expected him to head home. It was a little after six P.M., and he usually tried to be home by seven to eat dinner and spend time with Olivia before the little girl went to bed.

Instead, he said, "McGee's bringing the ring to the Tiny Jewel Box tonight. Want to meet him there?"

"What about that whole 'let the cops do their thing, we'll do ours' lecture you gave me?" Anna looked at him curiously.

"We did our thing. Our motion is filed." He smiled at her. "I just thought it would be fun."

She agreed. Her favorite part of the job was going out with the police and talking to witnesses. They gathered their stuff, headed to the elevators, and rode down to the first floor.

As they stepped out of the steel doors and into the USAO lobby, Anna saw Eva Youngblood coming in through security. The self-defense instructor picked up her purse from the X-ray conveyor belt and waved at them.

"Well, hello. It's my two favorite prosecutors," Eva said. "Anna, are you coming to class tonight?"

"I have to miss it again. We're working on a pretty intense investigation."

"That poor girl killed at the Capitol?"

Anna nodded.

Eva turned to Jack. "I'm sorry if our friendship is causing you trouble on this case. Dylan didn't mean to put you in the crosshairs by praising you. He just thinks the world of you, that's all. Now I hear Lionel wants you off the case."

"I'll be fine," Jack said. "It's nothing I haven't handled before."

"Do you think that woman, the madam, will have to give you all her escort agency records?"

"We can't comment," Jack said. "It's a grand jury investigation."

"Of course." Eva pushed the button for the elevator. "I bet there are a lot of nervous heads on Capitol Hill tonight."

The Tiny Jewel Box was D.C.'s iconic jewelry store, where the wealthy and stylish went for baubles. Anna had passed the signature red awnings countless times while walking on Connecticut Avenue. She'd never had a reason to go inside.

The bells tinkled lightly as she and Jack stepped out of the noisy city heat and into the cool, quiet store. Crystal chandeliers illuminated ivory-and-glass cases full of sparkling jewelry. The salespeople were dressed in suits one notch finer than most lawyers'. Anna watched a salesman hand a velvet tray of David Yurman pendants to an older gentleman who looked vaguely familiar.

"These are the ones on your wife's wish list, Ambassador," the salesman said.

Anna felt intimidated and out of place. Her dad had been an autoworker in Flint before he was laid off and descended into alcohol-fueled tirades; her mom became a medical assistant after she finally left him. The fanciest place Anna had shopped growing up was Meijer, a downmarket version of Target. When she went to law school, she kept herself reined to a tight student budget. Here in D.C., she lived modestly on the salary of a government worker who was paying back law-school loans. She'd graduated from Meijer to Ann Taylor, but her specialty was scouring the sales racks for suits marked down from $299 to $59.99.

Jack seemed perfectly comfortable in the fancy store. He waved Anna over to a jewelry case and pointed to a display of engagement rings setting off a blaze of glitters. She looked for ones that were similar to the ring McGee had found on Lionel's balcony. But Jack pointed to a completely different model. "Do you like this one?" he asked her.

She looked at him, first puzzled, then panicked. Had he initiated this outing as part of the case development

or to gauge her reaction to different styles of engagement rings? Suddenly, the room felt too hot.

A grandmotherly saleswoman came over. "May I
help you?"

"Can we see this ring?" Jack asked.

"A wonderful choice," the saleswoman said. "As
soon as you came in, I could tell you were a couple in
love."

"We're actually here from the U.S. Attorney's Of-
fice," Anna said quickly. "Part of an investigation.
We have an appointment with the owner, Matthew
Rosenheim."

"Ah. I'll get Mr. Rosenheim for you."

The saleswoman hurried off. Anna could sense
Jack's disappointment. She continued to look down
at the jewelry, now to avoid making eye contact with
him. The last thing she wanted to do was talk about
the style of engagement ring she liked.

The grandmotherly woman returned. "Come right
this way," she said. "Mr. Rosenheim will see you in the
Red Room."

Anna noticed the other customers watching them
walk through the store. An old lady looking at
brooches gave them the stink-eye; Anna occasionally got these looks of disapproval as one half of a
mixed-race couple. A middle-aged woman smiled at
them and whispered to her friend, "Beautiful couple."
That was slightly better, but Anna didn't want to hear
*any* comments, positive or negative, on how she and
Jack appeared together. *We're prosecutors, people,* she
thought. *Here on a very important case.* Jack seemed
amused by the attention.

The Red Room was a romantic room with red walls
and another crystal chandelier. She and Jack waited in

carved chairs before a cherrywood table. Sitting there, she found it hard not to feel like they were a couple about to embark on a romantic journey together. She looked everywhere but at Jack's face.

Detective McGee came into the room with the store owner. Matthew Rosenheim was a smiling, elegant man who looked like he'd be comfortable showing earbobs to the Duchess of Cambridge. He greeted them cordially and took a seat. Jack explained that they'd found a ring in the course of a homicide investigation.

"It appears to be from your store," Jack said. "We're hoping you might be able to tell us who bought it."

McGee took out the plastic evidence bag and handed it to Matthew. The store owner looked at the ring through the clear plastic.

"Yes, that certainly looks like one of our rings. The TJB stamp is right here."

"Can you tell who bought this particular ring?"

"It's quite possible. But we are committed to the privacy of our customers. If we're given a subpoena, we will of course comply with it, but without that, I'm afraid I can't divulge personal information about our clients."

Anna had anticipated that. She handed him the subpoena she'd typed for this purpose. The store owner looked at it and nodded. "Very well. May we take the ring out of the bag?"

McGee sliced the bag open, made a quick note on the chain-of-custody log stapled to it, then handed the ring to Matthew. It had already been dusted for fingerprints.

Matthew took the ring like a nurse in the delivery

ward of a hospital, with great care and expert handling. "May I keep it overnight for analysis?"

"'Fraid not," McGee said. "Gotta keep the chain of custody. Can you do it while I watch?"

Matthew nodded and took out a jeweler's loupe. "Every stone has unique features," he said as he examined the ring. "Like fingerprints." He jotted some notes on a paper. "I'll run this information through the Gemological Institute of America database. We should be able to identify the stone and the buyer."

"How long will that take?" Anna asked.

"Twenty-four hours."

They thanked the owner and left. The whole conversation took less than fifteen minutes. She and Jack didn't have to go to the jewelry store, Anna thought. McGee could have easily handled this on his own. Jack had just wanted to show her the engagement rings.

# 30

When they got back to the office, Anna fled to her own floor instead of going to the war room with Jack. She needed some time to herself.

It was seven-thirty at night, and the U.S. Attorney's Office was quiet. She was the only lawyer left on the Sex Crimes floor, and was glad for the solitude. She could bury her personal issues in work. There was plenty of it. She prepared for tomorrow's hearing about Madeleine's books, then continued to look for legal authority to compel the congressional videotapes. Jack still had to respond to Davenport's motion to disqualify him from the case.

It was hard to keep up with Davenport's army of lawyers. At least they had Sam and her FBI analysts combing through phone records and credit reports. Anna and Sam might have their differences, but the woman was a worker. Anna looked out her window to the FBI's Washington Field Office next door. It was a big square building of concrete and glass. Rumor had it that the WFO was shockproof, so if someone set off a bomb, the FBI building would simply bounce the shock waves back, turning the U.S. Attorney's Office into a heap of rubble. The USAO had no such protections. Anna had seen bullet holes in the windows on the lower floors.

As Anna gazed out the darkened window, she saw a figure appear behind her, mirrored in the glass. She turned to find Jack in her doorway.

"Hey," Anna greeted him with surprise. "I thought you'd be home by now."

"Too much to do. Luisa agreed to stay with Olivia as long as I need." He handed her his draft response to Davenport's motion.

Jack looked exhausted. Davenport's motion had clearly gotten to him. Like most AUSAs, Jack believed in the honor and importance of being a prosecutor. They weren't just advocating for a client; they were fighting for justice, wearing the white hat. There was nothing more upsetting to a prosecutor than a personal attack on his integrity. Despite his advice to ignore criticism, Anna could see that Jack was taking this motion personally.

She felt sorry for purposely distancing herself when he was having a hard time. She stood and went to him. "Hang in there," she murmured.

She wrapped her hands around his neck, stood on her tiptoes, and kissed him. He pulled her toward him, pressing her body against his.

There was movement in her peripheral vision. Anna pulled her mouth from Jack's and looked over. Her boss, Carla Martinez, stood in the doorway. Anna jumped away from Jack as if she'd been electric shocked. How could she have been so careless? To be kissing Jack in the office, with her door open!

Carla looked as surprised as Anna felt. "Oh my goodness, I'm sorry," Carla began. "I didn't think—"

"No, no, I'm sorry," Anna interrupted. "I didn't mean to be, um . . ." She couldn't come up with anything coherent to say.

Jack cleared his throat. "Welcome back, Carla. How was the National Advocacy Center?"

"Thanks, my course at the NAC went well. I just got in, came here right from the airport. I saw the light on in here and thought I'd get an update on the case, but . . . I'll catch up with you two tomorrow, okay?"

Before Anna could speak, Carla turned and hurried back down the hall.

"It's a total disaster." Anna paced the length of Jack's kitchen an hour later, wondering whether there was any way to minimize the damage she'd just done to her career and her relationship with Carla. Raffles sat by his food dish, his orange eyes following Anna as she paced.

"Come on. It's not that bad." Jack leaned against the kitchen counter, nursing a bottle of Dogfish Head India pale ale. They were using the loud whisper adults employ when they're fighting but don't want to disturb sleeping children.

"Jack, she's my boss. She's probably the one person in the world I most want to impress."

"You don't think dating me is impressive?"

She was too upset to laugh. "Not for someone in my position. That's why we agreed to keep our relationship private."

"Look, I haven't told anyone. But something like this was bound to happen." Jack took a swig of his beer. "Life's gonna be a lot easier if we just give in to the inevitable and stop hiding."

"Were you *trying* to out us?" Her voice was getting louder.

So was his. "Anna. I came to discuss the case. *You* kissed *me*."

Anna knew that part of her anger at Jack was misdirected anger at herself. She sat at the kitchen table. "I'm sorry. I just—I can't stand the idea of another office sex scandal."

"Don't worry about Carla." Jack set down his beer and put his hands on Anna's shoulders. He began to knead her tense muscles. "She's not going to go gossiping about us."

"How can you know that?"

"Carla knows how to keep a secret."

"What does that mean?" She ducked her shoulders away from his hands and turned to look at him, trying to imagine what kind of secret the two rivals would keep for each other.

"Nothing." He put up his hands in a gesture of surrender. "Look, I've been in this office for twelve years, and I've seen some real sex scandals. This is pretty mild. We're both single adults. It's not like we're on opposite sides of a case."

"Ouch," she said at his reference to her relationship with a public defender last year.

"Look, this isn't a problem." Jack sat down next to her. "As far as I'm concerned, it could've come out months ago. Anna, I'm in for the long haul. We're going to get married one of these days. And we'll invite our colleagues to the wedding. It doesn't seem worth the struggle to keep it secret for a few extra months."

Anna's stomach somersaulted. She wasn't ready to be married or even to talk about being married. The only marriage she'd ever seen up close was her parents'. They'd been madly in love at first, according to family lore. But most of Anna's early memories ended with her father, drunk and screaming, taking a swing at her mother. Later, when her father was passed out on the couch, her mother would try to explain: *Your father loves us, he just has trouble showing it sometimes.* That was the kind of love Anna never wanted to see again. It was why she became a sex-crimes and domestic-violence prosecutor in the first place.

Even if she got over her general qualms about marriage, she wasn't sure she was ready to marry Jack. She loved him. But marrying him meant jumping ahead ten years, giving up parts of her life that she'd always hoped for. There'd be no traveling around the world. No happy hours with her girlfriends. Just the life of a middle-aged mom, hurrying home from work in time to take care of Olivia, who didn't want her there. Anna wasn't sure she could do it.

"We've only been dating for six months," she said at last.

"We've known each other for a year and a half. I'm thirty-seven. I don't need the two-year courtship. I know what's out there, and I know a good thing when I've found it."

"I'm only twenty-seven."

It sounded weak even to her ears. Most of her high-school friends were married, many with kids. Even her law-school friends, who'd postponed coupling in favor of professional goals, were getting engaged and married. Twenty-seven was a perfectly appropriate age to settle down.

"We're not your parents," Jack said softly. "I won't turn into your father if we say 'I do.'"

She looked down at her hands. Jack was a good man, gentle and generous. With him, she would never have to fear what her mother had. But Jack was also set in his ways, demanding, and stubborn. She could see her life being consumed by his—to the extent that it hadn't been already.

"I assumed we were both in this for good," Jack

said. "I wouldn't have involved Olivia if that weren't so. But now it seems that I need to ask. What's *your* plan for us, Anna?"

"I don't have a plan." Her voice rose in pitch. "And I don't want one."

Jack cleared his throat and looked away from her. This was the first time he'd ever mentioned marriage. He'd probably expected a more enthusiastic response.

"Then what are you doing here?" he said.

"I care about you a lot, Jack." As soon as she said it, she knew it was a mistake.

"Oh, you 'care about' me? That's good to know."

"No, I mean I love you. But marriage is something I need to think about, that's all."

"Fine."

Jack turned and went upstairs. Anna sank back in her chair. She had hurt him, deeply. But she didn't know what else to say.

A shuffling noise came from the living room. Two big green eyes peeked up from behind the couch. With her black hair in two high pigtails, Olivia looked like a frightened Muppet.

"Olivia?" Anna called quietly.

The little girl shuffled into the kitchen. She wore purple pajamas with footies. She looked worried.

"What's wrong, sweetie?" Anna knelt down so her head was level with Olivia's. "Did we wake you up?"

The little girl nodded.

"I'm sorry," Anna said. "We should have been quieter."

"Can I have a glass of milk?"

Jack had a no-drinks-after-bedtime policy to avoid bed-wetting. But this seemed like a good time for an exception. Anna filled a plastic *Princess and the Frog* cup with milk and handed it to the little girl. Olivia took a long gulp. Raffles meowed, so Anna poured some milk into a saucer for the cat.

"Are you mad at Daddy?" Olivia asked.

"No, sweetie."

"Are you going to leave us now?"

"No." Anna was surprised by Olivia's concern. She used a napkin to wipe the milk mustache off the girl's upper lip. "Sometimes grown-ups have disagreements. But they're still friends, and they still love each other. They just have to figure things out."

Anna felt a weight of responsibility as she said these things to Olivia. Any fight she had with Jack would affect more than the two of them.

"Mommy and Daddy were fighting like that right before she left and went to heaven."

Anna tried not to show her surprise. Olivia had been two years old when her mother died. That must be one of her earliest memories. What had her parents been fighting about? Did it have something to do with why Jack wouldn't talk about Nina's death? Anna brushed the thoughts aside to give her full attention to the little girl. She tentatively put her hands under Olivia's arms. Feeling no resistance, she lifted the child onto her lap.

"No one's leaving," Anna said.

The warm little body felt comforting on her lap. When Olivia finished her milk, she let Anna lead her to her bedroom. Anna tucked her in, then got suckered into a round of flashlight tag, then a telling of *Little Red Riding Hood*. Olivia didn't seem to want to let Anna go. But by the time the wolf was wearing Grandma's bonnet, Olivia had fallen asleep. Anna looked at the little girl and wondered if they'd just broken through a wall. She kissed Olivia's forehead and tiptoed out of the room.

She went into Jack's room. When her eyes adjusted to the dark, she saw that he was already lying on his side of the bed, facing the wall. She washed up and changed into cotton shorts and a tank top.

When she slid under the blanket, he didn't move. If he were really asleep, he would stir when she got in. She rolled over and lay on her side, facing the opposite wall. The room was painfully silent. They stayed like that for a long time, awake but not speaking, side by side but with their backs turned to each other.

# Wednesday

# 31

It wasn't her alarm clock but the quiet of the house that roused Anna from sleep. She opened her eyes and looked around Jack's bedroom, flooded with sunlight from the stained-glass arch above the curtained window. Jack wasn't there.

She glanced at the clock: seven o'clock. Jack and Olivia should be puttering around downstairs, eating breakfast, negotiating how much TV Olivia could watch that day. The quiet was eerie.

Anna slid out of bed and padded downstairs. She looked by the front door and saw that Olivia's backpack and Crocs were gone. Olivia sometimes went to the park with Luisa on summer mornings, and Jack had been having the nanny come earlier than usual since the Capitol case started. But where was Jack? A note by the coffeepot answered her question. *Went in early,* Jack's handwriting said.

Anna tried not to feel stung. He could go in to the office early if he needed to. Still, with their fight the night before, his early departure had a distinctly chilly feel.

She showered and dressed in the quiet house. The coffeepot held some lukewarm coffee, which she poured into a mug and drank down to the bitter dregs. She grabbed a granola bar, locked up the house, and walked to the Takoma Metro station alone. Though the morning was already hot, the day hadn't yet reached unbearable levels. It was a beautiful walk, through shady streets of colorful Victorians and adorable bungalows. She often smiled at the fleets of Priuses parked in the famously liberal neighborhood. Normally, she would enjoy the walk, the most peaceful part of her day.

But Anna was still upset about the argument with Jack. She hated to hurt him, although she seemed to be doing a fair amount of that lately. On the other hand, how could he expect them to get married when he still wouldn't talk to her about his late wife? Olivia's comment about her parents fighting made Anna realize how little she knew about Jack's prior marriage. Ideas and suspicions had tumbled through her head last night, as she tangled up the sheets with her insomnia. Now she was so tired, she felt like she was moving through water.

When she got off the Metro at Judiciary Square, she went directly to the Firehook for more coffee.

"Where's Mr. Jack?" asked the barista as he handed her the cup. With his Jamaican accent, he sounded like he was asking for Meesta Shock.

"I don't know." Anna managed a smile as she paid. "I haven't been to the office yet." Who was she kidding? Even the barista could guess they were dating.

When she got to her office, a note in Vanetta's handwriting was scrawled on the wipe-off board on her door: *Marty wants to see you.* Suddenly, she was awake with a nervous energy more powerful than any caffeinated beverage. Being summoned to the front office meant trouble. Five minutes later, Anna sat anxiously in the anteroom outside the office of Marty Zinn, the acting U.S. Attorney.

"Ah, Anna, glad I caught you," Marty said, emerging from his office. He was a slim white man with a graying beard and intelligent brown eyes. The few hairs that remained in his male pattern baldness were cropped short. "Main Justice wants to see us about the Capitol murder case. We'll take a cab. Jack's already on his way."

Her stomach performed a back handspring. She'd been nervous to be summoned by the acting U.S. Attorney—and he was being summoned by his bosses at the Department of Justice. The political appointees at DOJ usually limited themselves to setting budgets and policies, letting the U.S. Attorneys prosecute cases autonomously. There were only two reasons the politicals would call a local AUSA into the Main Justice Building—if she were receiving an award, or if something were going very wrong with her case. She knew she wasn't getting an award.

The Department of Justice occupied a full block on Pennsylvania Avenue, halfway between the Capitol and the White House. Built during the Depression, it was a hulk of gray limestone decorated with geometric metal art deco accents and a handful of the requisite columns. Inscribed into a wall of limestone were the words: "The Place of Justice Is a Hallowed Place."

Inside, the building seemed less a temple to justice than a poster child for post-9/11 security precautions. There was an ID check, then a line, then another ID check. Anna walked into a small glass compartment, and the doors closed her in with a swoosh. Machinery beeped and hissed around her while cheerful Muzak played through the speakers. She wondered if the music was supposed to ward off claustrophobia while visitors were scanned. She didn't know what the security officers were learning from their bank of computers, but she imagined the machines were bomb-sniffing, metal-detecting, and imaging what her body looked like under her black pantsuit.

Finally, the glass doors slid open, and she stepped into the historic lobby. This part of the building felt more like a Hallowed Place, with its soaring ceiling and sober stone walls covered in murals illustrating the redemptive power of justice. Her favorite mural was *Contemporary Justice and Women*. It depicted Justice as a female figure with a sword, cutting the chains of tradition that held back a young woman; the freed woman then walked toward the light of her new position in the world. When Anna had come here for her credentials two years ago, she'd been inspired by the mural, imagining herself wielding the sword. Today she thought of her argument with Jack about marriage and touched her wrists on the spot where the painted chains had held the young woman. She realized what she was doing and stopped.

Jack was already there, waiting for them. He looked handsome and all-American in a navy suit, white shirt, and red tie. He nodded hello, appearing neither upset nor particularly happy to see her. He'd always had a good poker face. A file folder was clasped in his hand; it held Lionel's motion to disqualify him from the case, his own response, and the case law backing him up. "In case the Director wants to tell me what a good job I've done," Jack deadpanned.

The three of them went up two flights, then walked through hallways big enough to drive a fire truck through. At the suite of the Executive Office for U.S. Attorneys, they were shown into the Director's conference room. The room had coffered ceilings, a deep green carpet, and oak-paneled walls covered in oil paintings of EOUSA Directors going back to 1953.

In the center of the room was a conference table long enough to seat forty people.

Two DOJ officials waited for them.

At the head of the table was EOUSA Director Tommy McIntyre, a trim and neatly dressed African-American man. McIntyre's office oversaw all ninety-four U.S. Attorney's Offices across the country. It was his job to supervise and coordinate the vast majority of federal criminal prosecutions. It was McIntyre who had chosen Marty Zinn as D.C.'s acting U.S. Attorney, to serve until the President nominated and the Senate confirmed a replacement. That meant McIntyre could remove Marty at any time. McIntyre's beaming face was on all the e-mails and flyers that EOUSA periodically sent out to AUSAs throughout the country. He was not smiling now.

Seated next to McIntyre was Melissa Rohrbach, an Associate Deputy Attorney General and the longest-serving DOJ employee. She was legendary as the institutional memory and the conscience of the Department. The names "associate" and "deputy" in her title were misleadingly modest. She was the eyes and ears of the Deputy Attorney General, who oversaw every division of the Department of Justice, including the U.S. Attorney's Offices, the FBI, and over a hundred thousand employees. Her presence meant that the case was being watched at the highest levels. Anna, Jack, and Marty sat down across from the DOJ officials.

"Thanks for coming down on short notice," McIntyre said. "I hate to drag you away from your work. But with allegations this serious in a case this consequential, we have to make sure we're dotting all our I's and crossing our T's."

"Of course, Tommy," Marty said. "It's always a pleasure to see you, whatever the occasion." Anna could tell from the obsequiousness that he was nervous.

"Tell me about this motion Congressman Lionel filed to take Jack and your office off the case. He sent me a letter asking me to reassign the case even if the judge doesn't. Now, I don't know if there's an actual conflict, but he suggests a real appearances problem. What are you thinking?"

Marty looked flustered. He was usually the chief of the Civil Division of the U.S. Attorney's Office, a hardworking career government employee with no criminal law experience and no ambitions to move past his current post. Whenever there was a shift between U.S. Attorneys, he was happy to serve as the acting head of the office—not to change anything but to make sure the gears kept turning smoothly until the next U.S. Attorney was appointed. Jack, on the other hand, was often talked about as a potential U.S. Attorney. In that position, he would become Marty's boss. Even as Homicide chief, Jack had more juice around the office than Marty did, regardless of who was the acting U.S. Attorney.

"I defer to Jack," Marty said.

McIntyre looked to the Homicide chief.

"There's no merit to Lionel's claim," Jack said, his voice deep and steady. "It's become fashionable for defense attorneys to attack the prosecutors personally. We'll continue to give this case our best work despite it."

McIntyre nodded—everyone knew that the practice of criminal law had become less cordial. "But is it true that you have a personal relationship with Lionel's opponent, Dylan Youngblood?"

"I know him. He was a year ahead of me at Georgetown Law. We served on some bar committees together when he was in private practice. We both work out at the Y across from the MLK Library, so we're occasionally on the same court for a pickup basketball game. I gave two hundred dollars to his campaign."

McIntyre looked troubled. "And he's indicated that if he wins this election, he'll recommend you as U.S. Attorney."

"Look, he knows my work, and he knows my vision for the office. He was on the interviewing committee when I put in for it the last time around. But I don't owe him anything. I would never slant a homicide investigation for any reason. It doesn't make sense to take me off a difficult case just because my name has been floated around. Anyway, whoever wins the election doesn't get to pick the U.S. Attorney. He can make a recommendation, but it's the President's choice."

Rohrbach had been listening quietly. She spoke up. "No one here doubts your integrity or skill, Jack. But you can see the problem with the public perception, right?"

Anna watched Jack's face. *She* saw the problem, but she could tell that Jack rejected the suggestion that he would be anything less than perfectly ethical.

"No, I don't see a problem," he said.

Rohrbach turned to McIntyre. "Are any other offices prepared to handle this case if D.C. is recused?"

"Maryland could do it," McIntyre said. "Rod's got a great team of lawyers up there."

"They're not homicide prosecutors," Jack countered. "They get some murders in their RICO cases,

but my office investigates hundreds of homicides a
year. I know the detectives to rely on and the ones to
avoid. I know how to put a homicide case together
and how to present it to a D.C. jury. This is what I do.
That's why Lionel wants to get rid of me."

Jack's Homicide section was unique. Most U.S.
Attorney's Offices had jurisdiction to prosecute only
federal crimes, such as bank robberies, large-scale
drug trafficking, or frauds that crossed state lines. The
vast majority of street crimes, such as rape or homicide, were handled by state or local prosecutors. Because D.C. was a federal city, the federal prosecutors
handled all the crimes. The combination of federal
resources and Jack's expertise with homicide cases was
unmatched by any other prosecutor in America.

McIntyre turned to Anna. "You've been quiet. What
do you think?"

Anna sat up, surprised to have the question posed
to her so directly.

She thought Jack shouldn't be prosecuting this case.
She knew he was scrupulously honest and wouldn't
sacrifice the integrity of the case for his own personal
gain. But someone who didn't know Jack might not
see that. An outside observer might think he would
skew the case to help his friend win the election. It
was crucial not only that the justice system be fair but
that it be perceived as fair in order for people to have
confidence in the system. And the whole case could
be overturned on appeal if a judge found that Jack
shouldn't have been at the helm.

Anna was also worried about Jack personally.
However much he didn't want to withdraw from the
case, things could get much worse if he stayed on.
Davenport would continue to file motions challenging

his impartiality. If a judge ordered Jack to be recused for having a conflict of interest, DOJ would be obligated to launch an ethics inquiry about his handling of the case. If Jack weren't recused and there was a trial, Davenport would try to distract the jury with arguments about the government's bias—and Jack's friendship with Youngblood would be Exhibit A. In the last big case Davenport tried, his client was acquitted, and the judge ordered an investigation of the prosecution team's tactics. A few years later, that investigation of the prosecutors was still ongoing.

It would be better for Jack if he stepped off the case now. No one would think twice if the Homicide chief assigned the case to one of his seasoned prosecutors. Though Jack usually had excellent judgment, Anna suspected he was too close to the subject here. Certain of his own ethics, he couldn't see how others might perceive a bias. He couldn't see that he was going down a path that could destroy him.

"Jack's a great lawyer," Anna said, "who's got a team of great lawyers working for him. I think it would be better to reassign the case to someone who isn't friends with the Youngbloods."

"I agree," McIntyre said. "Jack, you've got to come off the case. We won't make a big deal of it. Just file a line striking your appearance."

Anna hadn't expected her opinion to be the deciding factor. She looked at Jack, who was glaring at a spot in the middle of McIntyre's tie. The muscle in Jack's jaw throbbed. He was furious. She braced herself for the fight they would have after the meeting was over.

"But Melissa," McIntyre continued, "do you think the entire D.C. office needs to be recused?"

Rohrbach shook her head. "Jack can be walled off. Whoever works on the case can report to someone else."

Marty nodded in agreement. "Anna has her own supervisor, the head of the Sex Crimes section. We'll assign another Homicide prosecutor who can report directly to me."

"It's a mistake to put the B team on this matter," Jack said.

"Anna's not the B team." Marty laughed nervously. "And we've got a very deep bench in the Homicide section."

"Good. Then that's the plan." McIntyre smiled at Jack. "You've done a great job on the case, and we thank you for that. Of course, we know you've got no actual conflict of interest. But we've got to think about how it looks to the outside. It'll be better for everyone this way."

McIntyre stood up. The meeting was over.

Jack shook McIntyre's hand and walked out of the conference room. Marty stayed to make small talk with the DOJ officials. Anna excused herself and hurried down the hallway.

She quickly caught up to Jack and walked beside him in silence. They went down a curving flight of stairs, which deposited them in the center of the second floor in the Great Hall. At the front of the huge ceremonial room was the *Spirit of Justice*, a ten-foot-tall cast-aluminum statue of a woman whose bare breasts had provoked controversy for decades. Reporters made a sport of photographing the Attorney General announcing pornography prosecutions with the semi-nude *Spirit* in the background. The statue had been famously covered with a velvet modesty drape

during John Ashcroft's reign. Now she was uncovered
again, her burnished breasts gleaming triumphantly.

"Jack." Anna put a hand on his arm. "This is for
the best."

He stopped walking and pivoted toward her, re-
moving his arm from her grasp. "It's ridiculous, Anna.
Davenport files a bullshit motion smearing me, and I
just withdraw?"

"It looks like you're taking the high road. If you
stayed on the case, the attacks weren't going to stop."

"They're *still* not gonna stop. You think Davenport's gonna give you a pass? He'll pull the same crap
with you that he's pulling with me. This just encour-
ages him."

"I'll handle it."

Their voices echoed off the cavernous stone walls
of the Great Hall.

"I see." Jack put his hands on his hips. "This works
out perfectly for you, doesn't it? You've got your big
case. Now you can go 'prove yourself.'"

"That's not what this is about, and you know it. If
you stayed on, it would have hurt the case. It would
have hurt *you* in the end. I was trying to protect
you."

"By stabbing me in the back?" Jack's green eyes
glowed with anger. "You basically told them that even
my teammates don't believe in me."

"I thought I was the B team," Anna snapped.
"Come on, you know I believe in you. But it looks like
you have a conflict. It's a problem, whether you want
to admit it or not."

"If you thought there was a problem, you should
have told *me*, not Tommy McIntyre."

"I *did* tell you! You ignored me. Dammit, Jack, if

Tommy McIntyre asks for my legal opinion, I'm gonna give it."

"I'm not talking about your legal opinion. He asked your opinion of *me*. If somebody asks me, 'Is Anna the best lawyer for this case?,' I don't say, 'No, I've got more experienced prosecutors, but I love her and want to work with her.' I say, 'Yes, she's the best.' Because I'm loyal."

Anna cringed. It was what she'd feared from the beginning. He'd put her on the case because of their relationship, not because he thought she was a good lawyer.

"That's why you didn't take my opinion seriously," Anna said. "Because you don't really respect it."

"That's not what I'm saying. I'm talking about loyalty. I agreed to pretend that we're not together, but the fact is, we *are* together. If you love somebody, you support them."

"I *was* supporting you."

"The hell you were. You were showing off. You saw which way the room was going, and you jumped on board."

"You're so wrong. It's like we were in different meetings."

A couple of lawyers came into the room and looked at them curiously. Jack turned and walked out of the Great Hall; Anna followed. They went down the last flight of stairs and out of the building onto the sidewalk in front of the Justice Department. The traffic on Pennsylvania Avenue was heavy, the tail end of the morning rush. The air was so muggy that the honking of horns seemed to reverberate, held aloft by the humidity.

He faced her on the sidewalk, seeming to wait for something. She held out her hands—what?

"I don't know what you want me to say, Jack."

"How about 'sorry' for stabbing me in the back?"

"I didn't stab you in the back. I wasn't being disloyal, just honest. Loyalty doesn't mean you always agree with somebody."

"Oh yeah? What do you think loyalty means?" His voice was low and furious.

"It means I tell you what you *need* to hear, not only what you want to hear."

"Well, that's big of you. Thanks for those words I needed to hear. You know what you need to hear? Fuck you."

"Oh, that's a brilliant argument," she said. "Well put, Clarence Darrow."

As she said it, she realized this was more than an argument. He had never spoken to her that way. Jack's BlackBerry rang, but he ignored it.

"No, you know what?" he said. "I should be the one apologizing to you. I'm sorry that I thought you knew how to have a real relationship. I should've known you weren't ready for a commitment when you wouldn't admit that we were dating. That should've been clue number one."

"Jack, let's talk about this when we both calm down." Anna nodded at the buttoned-down men and women passing them to go into the Justice Building. "Later tonight."

"No, let's not. We've talked enough. I think it's best if you don't come by tonight." He took a deep breath. "Or any night."

She blinked with surprise. He was breaking up with her? "All my clothes are at your house," she said.

"I'll have them shipped."

"What about my cat?"

He turned and strode off. Broiling with anger herself, Anna made no attempt to go after him. It was ridiculous. He had such a need to be in control of everything that he couldn't handle her speaking her own opinion. At that moment, she was glad to see his back.

Her BlackBerry rang. Anna brought the phone to her ear.

"Hey," Samantha's voice greeted her. "Why isn't Jack picking up?"

"He just got taken off the case."

"Jesus. Not *now*."

"Would there be a better time?"

"Hard to imagine a worse one. Madeleine Connor is dead. She killed herself."

# 32

Anna's first instinct was to call out for Jack to come back. The Homicide chief was only half a block away, striding east on Pennsylvania Avenue. But he was off the case. And, apparently, out of her life. She watched him disappear into a crowd of pedestrians and brought her mind back to the phone call. She would have to handle this on her own.

"How did she do it?" Anna asked.

"Shot herself in the head," Samantha said. "The cleaning lady found her this morning."

Anna pictured Madeleine's beautiful white suit spattered with crimson. "Oh, man." She fought down a bubble of nausea. "Why? Did she leave a note?"

"No note. I guess she couldn't face being a witness," Sam said. "She didn't want to have to turn over her books."

Anna's chest tightened with guilt—had she been too zealous in trying to get Madeleine's records? Had she driven the woman to suicide? The traffic swooshed around her, oblivious to the fact that her case had just veered off a cliff. She'd come to the U.S. Attorney's Office to save lives, not destroy them. Somewhere along the way, she must have taken a serious wrong turn.

Anna had never imagined that her witness would kill herself. She remembered the way Madeleine had brushed aside her own lawyer outside the courthouse, walking confidently up to the reporters' microphones. The woman was a fighter.

In fact, Anna had never heard of a witness killing

herself. What prosecutors worried about was a witness being killed by a defendant or his crew. Witness intimidation was a serious problem in D.C. Witnesses didn't want to come forward, or they recanted their testimony, because they were afraid of being murdered.

Anna remembered Madeleine's warning in the grand jury—that if she turned over her records, powerful men would lose their careers. She looked up. The Capitol loomed at the end of Pennsylvania Avenue. Heat radiating off the asphalt made the white dome seem to shimmer and wave.

"How confident are we that it was a suicide?" Anna asked.

"I'm told she was clutching the gun in her hand. I haven't been to the scene yet."

"When you get there, poke around a bit, will you? Look for signs of forced entry, that sort of thing. Don't let the ME jump to any conclusions."

"Will do," Samantha said. Then she added with a tone of grudging respect, "I was thinking about that myself."

They hung up. Anna plodded down Pennsylvania Avenue. She was reeling with the double whammy of Jack's breakup and Madeleine Connor's death. Madeleine had either killed herself or been killed because of the investigation. Either way, Anna carried the responsibility for the woman's death. Meanwhile, she was seething at Jack, the one person from whom she'd normally seek comfort. She felt impotent and furious and sick.

Anna reached the brick patio outside the U.S. Attorney's Office. Now, she realized, she had to face Carla, who'd walked in on her kissing Jack last night. Great.

Like taking off a Band-Aid, she should get it over with as quickly as possible. Anna went inside, took the elevator to the tenth floor, and knocked on her boss's open door.

"Come in," Carla said, turning from the computer. She acknowledged Anna with a nod, as if she had been expecting her.

"I'm sorry about last night," Anna said. She sat in the chair across from Carla's desk. A bright quilt hung on the wall next to the Sex Crimes chief; a candy bowl sat on the edge of her desk, brimming with miniature Snickers bars. Anna's stomach roiled at the prospect of eating anything.

"I was surprised," Carla said mildly.

"So was I. I thought no one was on the floor. Even so, it was stupid."

Anna found it easier to talk about than she'd expected. What she'd considered a major catastrophe last night seemed pale and puny compared to everything that had happened this morning.

"Oh, Anna, I'm not worried about you sneaking a kiss in the office after hours. I'm worried for your sake. He's going to break your heart."

Anna gave a short laugh. She had expected a lecture about professionalism or the dangers of dating a supervisor.

"He kind of already did. We broke up this morning."

"Because of me?" Carla asked.

Anna couldn't interpret the other woman's expression. "No." She told Carla about the DOJ meeting and its aftermath. "You must be wondering how I always get in these situations where my personal life and my work life are so intertwined, huh?"

"When you spend most of your waking hours in the office, your personal life *is* your professional life," Carla said. "So, I'm supervising you on the Capitol case. How's it going?"

"Not well," Anna said. She told Carla about Madeleine's death.

"Goodness, you've had quite a morning," Carla said with real sympathy. "First, Anna, this woman's death wasn't your fault. There's nothing you should have done differently. As for Jack—" She paused, carefully considering her words. "How much has he told you about his past relationships?"

Anna shook her head. "Remarkably little. I know he loved his wife. I know she was an MPD officer. I know she was killed in some random street crime."

Carla let out a breath. "Jack is a good man, but he's terrible at relationships. He doesn't know what he wants, and he sure doesn't know how to hold on when he's got someone good. You're better off without him."

Anna studied Carla's face while trying to keep her own blank. Carla knew something about Jack that she wasn't revealing—about his relationship with his wife, perhaps, or the circumstances of her death. Anna remembered Jack's statement that Carla was good at keeping secrets. What secret did he share with his fiercest rival in the office—but which he would never share with Anna?

Whatever it was, it didn't concern Anna anymore—although it would take all her self-control not to speculate. For now she needed to get out of here. She thanked Carla and left the office.

# 33

The upstairs floors of the rowhouse were better than the basement where Nicole had been trapped. There was little clutter, at least not in the rooms used for business, and efforts had been made to keep the grime to a minimum. Still, the rooms had seen better days, and even those days hadn't been so great. The furniture was cheap and old; the walls were scarred; the discolored carpet looked like it had a case of mange. The place smelled of fried food and cigarette smoke, poorly masked with passion-fruit air freshener.

Unlike the mattress in the basement, this one sat on a bed frame and wore a fraying olive-colored sheet. The single window was covered with a dark blanket tacked up around the frame. Day or night, the room was lit only by the floor lamp standing in the corner. A brown dresser with a large mirror next to a closet. The closet door had a dead bolt on the outside. Nicole tried not to think about why the lock was on that side of the door.

She lay on the mattress and watched her client get dressed. She hadn't done much for him, just lay there, feeling the relief of the crack Pleazy had given her, letting this guy do what he wanted. Nothing more seemed to be expected of her.

This was her fourth incall of the day. Pleazy had set everything up. He'd come in here before the first client, put his arm around her shoulder, and given her another hit from the glass pipe. She'd allowed the comforting haze to envelop her as the series of tricks paraded through the bedroom, through the bed, and through her body.

They said 90 percent of success was showing up, right? For this gig, it was 100 percent. All she needed to do was lie here. There was nothing funny about it, but she giggled.

At the sound, her client turned around and glanced at her. He was pulling on a RadioShack shirt, probably here on his lunch break. His name was embroidered on his shirt: Armanio. He looked at her with sympathy as he tied his shoelaces.

What was he pitying her for? She was fine. Guy worked at RadioShack.

"Fuck you, Armanio."

She turned to her side and studied her fingernails. Only fragments of the red polish remained. The nails themselves were torn and filthy. She closed her eyes until she heard the guy leave the room. Even then she didn't move.

The first time she had sex, she was thirteen years old. It was after school, and she was watching TV in the rec room in the basement. A rerun of *Saved by the Bell*. Larry had come downstairs. He worked Thursday through Monday as the floor manager at Macy's, so he was home every Tuesday and Wednesday. Her mother was at work. He sat next to Nicole on the couch. "Good show?" he asked.

She didn't answer, just stared at the TV and waited for him to start touching her.

She knew what he did to her was wrong. He was a grown-up, her mother's husband. He shouldn't do this, and she shouldn't let him. But she was supposed to do what he said. And he was nice to her. He was the only person who gave her gifts, who took her to the movies. She was grateful for the attention. He always gave her something afterward: the latest Britney Spears CD, candy, the new pair of Guess jeans she'd begged for. She didn't know the term "grooming" then, but now she understood it. Getting her used to accepting rewards in return for letting him touch her, getting her ready for the next step.

She was too ashamed to tell her mother.

"The boys in your class are gonna want something from you," Larry said as Mario Lopez flirted with Elizabeth Berkley on-screen. "You gotta learn what it is so you know what to stay away from."

It didn't make sense, did it? But she wanted him to be happy with her, to keep loving her. She let him do what he wanted.

It hurt, a bright searing pain that tore through the center of her body. He grunted in her ear and then lay on top of her, crushing the air from her chest. The sound of canned laughter filled her ears as the scent of Larry's sour musk filled her nose. When he finally let her up, she went to the bathroom, cried, and cleaned up the blood. "Don't tell your mother," he said after she came out of the bathroom. "This is our special secret." He gave her a pair of Ray-Bans. She didn't tell her mother.

He kept doing it, most Tuesdays and Wednesdays. She got pregnant when she was fifteen. Looking back, it was a miracle it hadn't happened sooner. She told her mother the pregnancy was from a boy in school. The abortion was more painful than she'd expected. She lay in agony afterward, her stomach cramping, wringing her out. She was sure she would die. She wished she would die.

A few weeks later, Larry came down to the rec

room and put his hand on her thigh again. But she was done. She pushed his hand away and stood up. "I can't do this anymore," she said. She turned and went upstairs. He didn't touch her again.

She didn't tell anyone until a few years later, during her freshman year at college. In English class, she read *The Color Purple*. Celie's experience with incest and sexual abuse resonated with her. Nicole walked into the Georgetown police station to make a report. They sent her away. Since it had happened in Pittsburgh, they said, she had to report it to the Pittsburgh police.

Instead, she worked up the courage to tell her mother. Her mother said she didn't believe her—and at the same time, that it was Nicole's fault. That Nicole was a slut. Her mother loved Larry; she'd always had mixed feelings about her daughter. And Nicole knew her mother was right. It was her fault. She was a slut.

Nicole stopped talking to her mother and stepfather, and they stopped paying her tuition.

A friend had introduced her to Madeleine soon after the fight. Being an escort seemed like the answer to all of Nicole's problems. Fun and harmless, and she made enough money to pay her tuition and then some. She could live like the Georgetown rich kids lived.

Now Nicole sat up in the olive-colored bed and looked around the dark bedroom. She was so thirsty. She couldn't remember the last time she'd had anything to eat or drink. She wondered if anyone would bring her something. Ridiculous. Where did she think she was, the Willard?

She put on the only clothing she had here, the zippered leather dress. It was starting to smell. She padded down the hall barefoot. The door to another bedroom was cracked open, and she could hear panting noises from within. Through the crack, Nicole could see a dark-haired woman sitting astride a man, both naked, rocking. Nicole kept walking.

She went downstairs and found the kitchen at the back of the house. There was nothing in the fridge but a couple of Coors Lights, some half-empty Styrofoam carry-out containers, and the sticky residue from past generations of takeout. Dirty dishes filled the sink and covered the counters. Those must be all of their dishes, Nicole thought when she opened the cabinets—the shelves inside were almost entirely empty. A large cup sat alone on the top shelf. It was a giant goblet made of thick green glass and encrusted with fake precious stones. "King Pleazy" scrolled across the rim in rhinestones and peeling fake gold.

Nicole took down the heavy goblet—it had to weigh at least three pounds—and filled it with water from the faucet. Holding it with two hands, she took a single blissful gulp.

"Oh my God!" a female voice exclaimed from behind her.

Nicole turned to find a chubby black woman standing in the doorway and staring at her with horror.

"What?" Nicole asked, looking around for a spider or rat on the floor.

"You can't drink from his Pimp Cup! Put it back, quick, before Layla sees you!"

Nicole had no idea what the woman was talking about but felt the urgency in her voice. She dumped the water and set the goblet back up on the shelf, although she was still thirsty.

"Who are you?" Nicole asked.

"Peaches. One of Pleazy's girls."

"And who's Layla?"

"Pleazy's bottom."

"What?"

"His bottom bitch. The most trusted girl. Layla's been with him so long, she's practically his partner."

As if on cue, a pockmarked white woman with brassy blond hair and dark roots came into the kitchen. She wore turquoise eyeliner that mismatched her mean little gray eyes. *Pleazy* was tattooed across her fat pink arm. She eyed Nicole up and down.

"So you're the new girl," Layla said.

"Nicole," she replied, extending her hand. Layla ignored it. After a moment, Nicole let it drop to her side. "Where can I get something to eat?"

"You'll eat when I say you eat. There ain't nothing for you now."

"Then I'll go pick something up. How do I get the money I earned tonight?"

Layla looked at her for a moment, then bellowed, "Pleazy!"

The pimp appeared in the dirty little kitchen, which was starting to get crowded. He held a cell phone in one hand and a pen in the other.

"This bitch wants her money!" Layla said with a snicker that sent flecks of spit onto Nicole's cheek.

"I'm hungry and thirsty, and I want a break." Nicole wiped Layla's saliva off her face. Peaches slowly backed out of the kitchen.

"Okay, girl, I understand," Pleazy said. "But we got two more tricks set up for you. They almost here. Take care a them. Then we get you something to eat."

Nicole didn't like being told when she could eat. "Just give me my share, and I'll get myself something. Then I'll do the next two guys."

"Your share?" Layla laughed. "You don't get no

share. Your share is a roof over your head and not getting your ass whupped."

Nicole looked to Pleazy, who shrugged. "That wasn't our deal," she said. "I keep a third."

"Sure, baby, sure." Pleazy nodded. "But I keep it safe for you. What would you do with that money anyway? Waste it on shoes and shit." He laughed and took the glass pipe and a tiny Ziploc bag from his pocket. He held it up, tantalizing her. "*I* take care of you now."

Nicole stared at the pipe and understood she would never see any money from Pleazy. Charlie Sheen himself could come in here and have a go at her, but she wouldn't get a dime. She'd get paid in drugs.

She'd fallen far, but she wasn't a crack whore.

"You know what?" she said. "It was nice meeting you all. It's been an education. But I'm going home."

As she headed to the front door, she felt empowered. This was one of the few times she could actually walk away from someone offering her cocaine. Her last hit had been half an hour ago. The high had worn off, leaving her with a relatively clear head. Soon she'd feel desperate enough to do anything for another hit—but she'd worry about that after she got the hell out of here.

Her hand was on the chain at the front door when Pleazy's arm went around her neck.

"Oh, no, you don't," he said. His elbow locked around her throat. Nicole thrashed and struggled but couldn't break away. "Nikki, Nikki, Nikki. Why you got to make me do this?"

He spun her around, then punched her in the stomach.

Nicole collapsed to the ground, doubled over in

pain. Pleazy pulled her up by the hair. He pulled back his fist; she winced and closed her eyes, but he was careful not to hit her in the face. Instead, he punched her in the stomach again, then dropped her to the floor.

She spasmed in pain, and her empty stomach dry-heaved. She looked up, wiping spittle from her lips and tears from her eyes. As she rose to her knees, a hard kick sent her rolling across the floor into the wall.

"Stop," she tried to plead between gasps, but little sound came out.

Pleazy grabbed her by the hair one more time. "What's that?" he asked. "I thought you were gonna apologize, but I'm having trouble hearing you."

He yanked her by the hair, pulling her up the stairs. The two other women laughed as Nicole scrambled up the stairs after him, trying to stay on her feet so he didn't rip the hair out of her head.

"I'm sorry," she tried to say. Pleazy dragged her back to the bedroom with the olive sheets. He threw her onto the floor. She tried to curl up into a ball. "I'm sorry!"

"I'm disappointed in you, Nikki. Now get the fuck up. *Up!*"

She hauled herself to her feet, hyperventilating. Her scalp was on fire, her stomach throbbed, and her legs were shaky from the adrenaline. He blocked the doorway, staring at her with a cold fury.

"Turn around, bitch," he said softly. He grabbed the leather shoulders of her dress and pushed her face-first down onto the bed. "I don't think you're ready for any more appointments tonight. First there's something you got to learn."

He held her down on the bed with one arm, hiking up her skirt with the other. She wasn't wearing any panties. He smacked her hard across her bare bottom. Then he unbuckled his pants and let them drop to the floor. She panicked, realizing what he was about to do. She kicked back, spun around, and bit his forearm. He recoiled, screeching in pain.

Her triumph was short-lived. He punched her in the face. It was like a sledgehammer to the skull. For an instant everything went black, and the only sound was a ringing in her ears. She stopped struggling.

He pushed her onto her back and put a forearm across her throat, pinning her down by the trachea. She gasped for air she couldn't take in. Through the fog of pain and terror, somewhere far away, she heard him saying, "Goddammit, Nikki! Look what you made me do." But he didn't stop. He was on top of her, grinding, pumping, doing what all the other johns had done to her tonight. But this was different. It wasn't about pleasure or release for him. It was about power and control and showing her who had it. She went numb. If she didn't, she might go insane.

He took his arm off her throat. She sucked in a painful rush of oxygen. When he was done, he lay on top of her, crushing her, like so many men before. For an instant, she thought she smelled Larry's old musky smell.

Pleazy finally grunted, stood, and pulled his pants back up. When he was all refastened, he reached down to touch her cheekbone, where he'd hit her. She flinched—but his fingers stroked her cheek softly.

"Damn, girl. I didn't mean to fuck you up like that." He grasped her elbow and pulled her to standing. She pushed her skirt back down, realizing as she did that the act was a useless remnant of modesty from a different world. But, she thought, at least the worst was over.

She was wrong.

He opened the closet door. "You gotta learn obedience, Nikki."

He put his shod foot on the small of her back and heaved. She flew and crashed into the closet wall, then crumpled to the cluttered floor. She was in pain everywhere at once. She wondered what parts of her were broken. She wondered if any parts of her *weren't* broken. He gazed down at her with sadness, as if truly sorry that he had to do this to her.

"You understand who's in charge, Nikki, we'll get along just fine."

He slammed the door shut. Inside the closet, it was black. Through the ringing in her ears, she heard the dead bolt slide into place.

# 34

Samantha had never worked a homicide in this part of the city. When she responded to a typical shooting, she would pass drug boys ready to bolt in the other direction, or law-abiding neighbors armed with machetes, the weapon of choice after D.C. banned handguns. But as she turned her Durango onto Kalorama Circle at eleven A.M., she passed Lululemon-clad women with yoga mats slung over their shoulders and Hispanic nannies pushing thousand-dollar Bugaboo strollers. It was a world unaccustomed to the violence that Sam saw every day.

Madeleine's stone mansion was surrounded by yellow police tape. Sam recalled the last time she'd been here, only two nights ago. She'd felt a certain affinity for the single woman, living alone, working long hours to be successful at her chosen business. Now Sam felt a twinge of regret—then brushed it away. Anna might feel guilty, but Sam would not. She hadn't killed Madeleine. She wouldn't allow herself to feel like the villain for investigating someone else's bad deeds.

Samantha was sorry to hear that Jack was off the investigation. He was a pro who knew how to build a case like this. Anna was sharp, but too cautious for Sam's tastes.

Inside Madeleine's house, a team of MPD crime-scene techs were at work, fingerprinting, searching, and cataloging what they found. Samantha made her way past the living room where she'd talked with Madeleine two nights ago, and into a study at the back. Like the rest of the house, it was furnished in antiques and delicate floral prints. A picture window overlooked a neatly landscaped side yard. The room was a pretty oasis from the rigors of urban life and was obviously where the madam had spent much of her time. And it was where she died.

Madeleine Connor's body slumped forward in a high-backed wooden chair. Her head lay on an antique writing desk, her face twisted to the side. A stain of deep red surrounded her head. She was wearing black silk pajamas with a black silk robe; the color of the robe made it hard to see the bloodstains on the collar. Blood spatter covered the chair, a desk lamp, and the raspberry-colored wall behind the desk, centered at about three to four feet high. A bullet was lodged in the wall, in the middle of the spatter. It looked like Madeleine had been sitting at the desk when the single shot went through her skull.

Sam glanced at the entry wound in Madeleine's right temple. Even with the naked eye, Samantha could see the blackish circle of seared skin surrounding the wound. Rounds were heated to over 1,600 degrees Fahrenheit when expelled from a gun. Seared flesh was a classic sign of suicide, when the gun was placed directly on the skin. Samantha took a step closer to see the madam's right hand resting on the desk, still clutching a .380 Beretta.

"Some folks'll do anything to avoid that grand jury, huh?" McGee's deep voice rumbled behind her.

"You think this was really a suicide?" Samantha asked.

"Gun in the decedent's hand. No signs of forced entry. No one else in the house. Even the FBI should be able to solve this one."

"That part I agree with."

Sam looked back at the corpse, the blood-spattered desk and walls. In nine years, Samantha had been at the scene of dozens of deaths. Something about this one wasn't right. She couldn't quite put her finger on it yet.

She'd had doubts from the moment she heard how Madeleine died. Women didn't often kill themselves with a bullet to the head. They liked to look nice when they died, often putting on makeup beforehand and using methods that wouldn't mess up their face. A bullet to the brain was a messier and more masculine suicide method.

"No note?" Sam asked.

"I'm thinking that press conference yesterday was her note. She didn't want to turn over her records, but she wasn't going to jail."

"Was there a box for the gun or a box of ammunition?"

"Hm. Not that we've found."

"Any sign of the agency's records here in the house?"

McGee shook his head.

"Check the garbage, look for a shredder, ashes in the fireplace, something like that," Sam suggested. "And don't let the cleaning lady leave before I speak to her. I'm gonna look around."

"Suit yourself," McGee said. "But my men have been through the house. There's nothing in it."

That itself was suspicious. Madeleine was dead, her books detailing the workings of her escort agency gone. Dozens, perhaps hundreds, of D.C.'s most powerful men had a motive to kill her.

Sam walked through the house slowly, like a real

estate agent making an appraisal. It was the home of
a woman who liked beautiful things. The decor was
coordinated throughout in shades of raspberry, cream,
and chocolate. Antique furniture filled the rooms
except the kitchen, which had the stainless-steel appli-
ances and granite countertops necessary in any pricey
renovation of a historic home. Sketchings and floral
artwork covered the walls.

Upstairs was more of the same. A tech was dust-
ing the hallway for prints, but otherwise, it was de-
serted. Madeleine's large master bedroom was at the
back of the house. A raspberry and gold comforter
covered the neatly made bed. Raspberry curtains
were held back with gold tassels. The white linen
suit that Madeleine had worn to court yesterday was
draped over a brown velvet chair. On a dresser was
a photograph of Madeleine with a gray-haired man.
A boyfriend or family member? Samantha took the
photograph.

She headed to the master bathroom, the reposi-
tory of secrets in any woman's home. Madeleine's
big bathroom was larger than the bedroom Sam had
as a kid. Marble countertops and bath, ornate gold
mirror. Counter covered with expensive lotions and
serums with words like "anti-aging" and "rejuvenat-
ing." Sam could relate. She shook off the urge to try
the creams. She snapped on a pair of latex gloves
and opened the drawers in the vanity: a floral case
with high-end makeup, a hair dryer that looked like
it could take out a SWAT team, a variety of brushes
and curlers.

Sam felt empathy for the woman who'd died alone
in her house. In many ways, they were alike. Samantha
was thirty-four, single, and very aware of her ticking

biological clock. If she died tomorrow, she would leave behind a similar collection of lotions and hair products in an empty house.

In the cabinet under the bathroom sink was a curious item. Next to household cleaners and hand-soap refills was a large safe bolted to the floor. The door to the safe was cracked. Samantha pulled it completely open. The black felt-lined interior was empty.

Sam went downstairs to find McGee. An officer pointed her through the door at the back of the kitchen. McGee was surveying the fence in the small backyard. It was made of thick wooden slats and was over eight feet high.

"No climbing over that without a ladder," Sam said.

McGee turned to her. "Yeah. And the back door was locked with dead bolt and chain. Windows latched. Front door locked."

"Just the lock in the door handle? Or also the chain and the dead bolt?"

"Just the door handle, so the cleaning lady could get in with her key."

"Someone could lock that from the inside, go out, and close the door behind them."

"True."

"Background check on the maid?"

"Clean."

Samantha handed McGee the photograph of Madeleine with the gray-haired man. "We can ask if she knows this guy. Neighbors hear anything, see anything, last night?"

"Nothing yet. And no papers in the garbage, no ashes, no shreddings, no books."

That comment triggered a flash of recognition.

"Come with me," Samantha said, heading back into the house.

In the sitting room, a tech was shooting photographs of the madam at her desk. Samantha leaned over the corpse to turn on the blood-spattered lamp.

"That's not how she was found," the photographer protested. "Don't touch anything!"

Sam peered closely at the corner of the desk where it touched the wall. "Look at this," she said to McGee.

McGee squinted at the desk. It was hard to catch, because the desk was a dark brown and the walls raspberry. The blood spatter covered the dark pink wall in a typical pattern, denser by the bullet, with the flecks more spaced out toward the edges—except for a small spot on the wall near the desk. There was a clean patch, rectangular and a few inches square, in the area where the spatter started to peter out. Samantha pointed to the antique desk. There, too, was a clean patch.

"Something was on this table when that bullet went through her skull," Sam said.

"Oh, shit."

"I doubt it."

"Very funny." McGee frowned. He preferred to be the one making the jokes—and the evidentiary discoveries. "What, then?"

"Based on the size and shape"—Sam pointed at the straight edge that delineated the stain on the desk—"I'd guess a small notebook or something like that."

McGee whistled through the gap in his teeth. Then he called to one of his technicians. "Bag her hands," he directed, pointing to the corpse. "Let's see if there's any gunshot residue."

# 35

Anna managed to keep it together as she walked from Carla's office. As a prosecutor, she was used to things breaking badly. It wasn't unusual to be yelled at by unsympathetic judges or cursed at by hostile family members of the defendant. The ability not to cry in public was a key skill learned early on. She kept a pleasant face as she greeted people in the hallway. Until she got to her own office, shut the door, and sat down at her desk.

Then she let her face crumple, as it had been threatening to do since she stood in front of the Main Justice Building. She cried for the woman who had been in her office a day ago and now was dead; for the end of her relationship with Jack, which, despite its complications, had brought her much happiness; and for the fact that Caroline's killer was still out there somewhere. She cried until she ran out of tissues, then jotted a note to buy another box, and cried a little more.

She thought about calling her sister, Jody, for advice. But she wasn't ready to admit to Jody that her relationship—and her case—were failures. She knew what Jody would do in this situation: wipe her face and get back to work.

Anna took a deep breath, found a Starbucks napkin in her drawer, and wiped her cheeks. She took out a compact of powder and dabbed at her splotchy face. Her blue eyes were rimmed with red, but that would pass in a few minutes. She tucked a strand of hair behind her ear and decided she looked respectable enough for anyone who might come into her office. She snapped the compact shut, then swiveled her chair so she was looking out the window at the homeless shelter and the Capitol behind it.

Jack wasn't on the case anymore. But she'd been around him long enough that she should be able to guess his strategy. What would he do?

She considered the facts—and the numbers. In four days, two women from Discretion had been killed. She didn't think Madeleine's death was a suicide. Whoever had killed Caroline might be covering his tracks. She had to consider the real possibility that more Discretion women might be targeted.

The killer had known where Madeleine lived, and he might know how to find the other escorts. How could Anna find them? All she knew about the other escorts was their working names from TrickAdviser.

The madam's lawyer might know more. Anna called Jane Thomasson. She offered her condolences, which Thomasson accepted graciously.

Anna asked, "Did Madeleine say anything about suicide yesterday?"

"No. She knew this was the end of Discretion, and she was mourning that. But overall, she was optimistic. We talked about the fact that it might be the start of something better. She mentioned the Mayflower Madam, book deals, movie rights, even joked that she wanted a spot on *Dancing with the Stars*."

That sounded more like the reaction Anna had expected from the madam. "Do you know whether she had plans to meet anyone last night?"

"Not that I know of."

"Do you happen to have Madeleine's records or a copy of them?"

"No. They should be in her home. We were going to go over them this morning before the hearing."

"What about the other escorts who worked for her? Do you know their names or have any idea how I can get in touch with them?"

"No, I'm sorry. She deliberately kept their identities secret."

Anna thanked the attorney, and they hung up.

Where else could she find out information about the other escorts? She needed an unrestricted computer. She considered going to the war room but didn't want to run into Jack and risk continuing their fight. Instead, she went down to the library and logged on to TrickAdviser. She called up the profile of every escort who worked for Discretion and printed out their screen pages. But there was no way to contact them. Their profiles didn't include photos. Without Madeleine or her books, Anna had no idea who these escort avatars really were, where they lived, or what their phone numbers were.

She brought the printouts to her office and studied them, hoping to find some pattern or clue. Nothing popped out immediately, but she was glad, at least, to lose herself in work for a bit.

An hour later, Samantha was in Anna's office with a box of items seized from Madeleine's house. She confirmed what Anna had suspected.

"The Medical Examiner found no gunshot residue on her hands," Sam said. "Which means she wasn't holding the gun when it fired."

"Someone else shot her," Anna murmured. She needed a moment to process the information, but Sam had already digested it. She barreled ahead.

"She had two cell phones. This one looks to be

personal." Sam pulled up a dual-screen Android phone from the box. "But this one is a burner." She handed Anna a basic LG cell phone. "Pay as you go, no subscriber information. And it's the same number that was on the back of the card we took from the concierge."

"If I subpoena the records, can you have your analysts schedule out the call records from these phones? Maybe we can figure out who the johns or escorts are that way."

"Sure, they can try. It might take a while. I spun through the call logs and contact lists on both cell phones. There's one number that appears in them both, listed as Morris. And it was the last number she called last night. Might be a boyfriend."

Anna dialed the number on speakerphone, so Samantha could hear. It went to voice mail. A man's deep voice said, "You've reached Morris Peal at Dewey and Simon . . ."

Anna knew the law firm of Dewey & Simon. She'd interviewed there during her last year of law school before landing her dream job with the U.S. Attorney's Office. The firm had two hundred lawyers in D.C., over a thousand worldwide, and offices across the globe.

"Should we leave him a message?" Anna said.

Sam shook her head. "I think I'll pay Mr. Peal a visit."

"You mean we'll pay him a visit."

Sam sighed as she stood up. "Let's go."

# 36

Dewey & Simon was located in a glass office building on the same section of K Street where Anna and McGee had questioned prostitutes plying their trade in the dark of night. Now early-afternoon sunlight shone on lunch-bound lawyers and lobbyists as they walked to upscale sandwich spots, pricey restaurants, and food trucks tweeting out their locations through the neighborhood.

Anna and Samantha walked into a large, airy lobby overlooking a tree-filled inner courtyard. A uniformed security guard ignored them as they breezed confidently to the elevator banks. They rode to the twelfth floor, the highest in the building. In a city without Washington's height restriction, the downtown would be a canyon of skyscrapers like New York. But D.C.'s height limit, which originally mandated that no building be higher than the Capitol, kept the skyline low.

The elevators opened onto Dewey & Simon's sleek white reception area. A pretty young woman sat at a long, curving glass reception desk.

"We're here to see Mr. Peal," Anna said.

"I'm so sorry." The receptionist smiled sadly at them. "He's canceled all his appointments today."

"He'll want to see us," Samantha said, flashing her FBI credentials.

The receptionist's eyes widened. She picked up the phone and spoke softly behind a cupped hand. When she hung up, she led Anna and Samantha down a wide hallway hung with huge panels of cubist paintings.

They stopped in front of a closed door. The receptionist seemed to muster up all her courage, then knocked.

"What is it?" barked a voice inside.

The receptionist opened the door and peeked inside. She signaled for Anna and Sam to enter, then
scurried away.

Morris Peal sat tall, hands folded together calmly
on the desk in front of him. He was a large man with
close-cropped gray hair and a square chin battling the
forces of jowliness. His pink-rimmed eyes were the
only visible sign of anything amiss in his otherwise
formidable figure. Anna assumed he'd heard about
Madeleine's death on the news. It was being widely
reported. Between police scanners and leaks within
MPD, there was no keeping it a secret.

Anna had read Peal's online résumé. He was a partner in Dewey & Simon's government-affairs practice
group, which everyone outside the practice called lobbying. He was senior enough that he didn't have to
spend his days writing the research papers or Power-
Point slide shows that were the grunt work of younger
lobbyists. Peal had never been a young lobbyist. He'd
come to Washington right out of college, forty years
ago, to work as a legislative correspondent for his
local congressman—the equivalent of working in the
office mail room. He stayed on the Hill for almost
thirty years, eventually becoming the Chief of Staff for
his state's senior Senator, a powerhouse on the Senate
Appropriations Committee. When his Senator became
chairman of the committee, Peal left the modest life
of a public servant for a seven-figure salary in Dewey
& Simon's lobbying shop. The key value to his clients
was the close relationship he had with that powerful
Senator. Now his job was to nurture the friendships

he'd developed in Congress for the rest of his life.
Anna guessed he spent his days at restaurants, golf
courses, and on the telephone. As a result, when his
clients needed a favor, they got one.

Peal sat behind a huge black desk with nothing
on it but a sleek telephone and an iPad. His floor-to-
ceiling windows overlooked the trees of Franklin Park.
Next to him, the requisite ego wall was practically
wallpapered in photos of Peal with gray-haired men,
differentiated only by their varying degrees of baldness
and paunch. Anna recognized both Emmett Lionel and
Dylan Youngblood in the photos.

A single photo sat on the credenza behind Peal.
He and Madeleine, smiling, cheeks pressed together.
Madeleine wore a sapphire-blue evening gown, Peal a
tuxedo.

"We're sorry to bother you, but we're here about
Madeleine," Anna said. "I understand the two of you
were close."

"You could say that." Peal gestured for them to sit
in the black leather guest chairs. "We were together
for eight years."

"We're very sorry for your loss," Samantha said to
Peal. "When was the last time you spoke to her?"

"Last night."

"Do you mind telling us what she said?"

He shook his head. "She had been torn—earlier—
between going to jail or keeping her promise of discretion. But she made her decision when she spoke
to the press. She didn't need the business anymore. I
could support her." Peal waved his hand at the wall of
photographs and gave an ironic grunt. "Frankly, I was
more worried about her client list getting out than she
was."

"So you were familiar with her business?" Samantha asked.

"She killed herself thanks to you people! And you're still investigating her escort service? Unbelievable."

"No," Samantha said. "We're not investigating Madeleine's business. We're investigating her possible homicide."

His eyebrows went up, and his hostility dialed down. "You think Madeleine might have been murdered?"

"We're looking into all the possibilities," Anna said. She wished Samantha hadn't been that direct yet; when a woman was killed, the most likely killer was her husband or lover. If Peal realized that he was a potential suspect, he didn't show it. His demeanor softened, and he leaned in toward the investigators.

"What can I do to help you?"

"Do you know if she had any enemies?" Anna asked.

"Sure. If you're a successful businesswoman, you have enemies. There are bad clients, and bad employees, and rival businesses." His eyes narrowed. "Belinda."

"Who's Belinda?"

"She was an escort who left Discretion to start her own service. She was poaching girls from Madeleine. She wanted to *be* Madeleine."

"Have you met Belinda?" Anna asked.

"A handful of times, I—" Peal stopped, as if considering whether he should speak openly to law enforcement. "Back when she worked for Madeleine, Belinda occasionally, uh, entertained some friends of mine. After she quit to start her own business a couple months ago, Madeleine and I drove past her house a few times to see what she was up to. Madeleine was furious. She wasn't going to have it. But it's not like she could make employees sign a non-compete agreement."

"So what did Madeleine do?" Samantha asked.

"Madeleine wanted to destroy Belinda, and Belinda knew it. Dispute resolution can get messy when your whole business is illegal. I don't know exactly what Madeleine did, but I'm sure it wasn't pretty."

Anna doubted Peal was as naive about Madeleine's actions as he claimed. If Anna were a small-business owner contemplating a competition problem, the first person she would turn to was Jack. Or rather, she would have turned to him. She had to get used to the past tense, she realized with a pang.

Now wasn't the time to press Peal about Madeleine's methods. But they'd follow the lead. A dispute between two rival madams was fertile ground to investigate. Anna asked Peal for Belinda's address, and he gave her a location on O Street in Georgetown. Samantha jotted it in her notebook.

"Did you know Caroline McBride?" Anna asked. "Also known as Sasha."

He shook his head. "I might have seen her around, but all I know is what was on the news."

"Do you know the names or contact information for any of Madeleine's other employees? Or anyone else involved in her business who might shed some light on this?"

"No, I just know some of the girls by their business names." He shrugged. "Their real names might be in Madeleine's record books. She kept them in a safe in her bathroom."

"One more question, sir," Samantha said. "Where were you around ten P.M. last night?"

His red-rimmed eyes lasered to the agent. "What, am I a suspect?"

"We're just doing our job."

"I was at home, alone. I don't think there's anything else I can add to your investigation." Peal stood up. "Now please excuse me."

He gestured to the door. As Samantha and Anna left his office, Anna decided against serving him with a subpoena. That would guarantee his hostility. If they needed to talk to him again, they knew where to find him.

Walking back down the hall with Sam, Anna whispered, "To Belinda's house?"

"Absolutely," Sam whispered back. "Let's find out what madams consider alternative dispute resolution."

# 37

Belinda's house was a posh brick rowhouse on one of Georgetown's prettiest cobblestone streets. A beautiful redhead answered Samantha's knock at the front door. Anna assumed that she was an escort. The woman was in her early twenties, beautiful, and meticulously groomed. Her long red hair had been blown out then curled into a cascade of waves, the kind of glossy, natural 'do that took ninety minutes to achieve. She wore a green camisole and tight jeans that were so distressed, they had to cost a fortune.

"Belinda?" Samantha asked.

"No, I'm Randi." The redhead looked Samantha and Anna over, then stepped aside. "Come in, everyone's inside already. You're from Discretion, too?"

Samantha stepped into the foyer. "No, dearie," she said, showing her credentials. "FBI. We're here to see Belinda."

The woman's eyes widened. "Oh my God . . ."

Sam pulled Anna into the house behind her, then walked confidently toward the sound of feminine voices. She whispered to Anna, "That was consent, right?"

They entered a living room decorated with lavender walls, a white couch, and zebra-skin chairs. The air was heavy with the scent of perfume and the sounds of feminine chatter. Every seat was occupied by a young woman, eleven in all, each as beautiful and highly produced as the one who'd greeted them at the door. Most of them wore similarly distressed jeans and silky blouses. Designer purses sat at their feet like expensive, well-trained puppies. It looked like a photo shoot for Urban Chic.

Anna guessed these women were all Discretion escorts, here to commiserate with one another over the madam's death. Or perhaps Belinda was taking the opportunity to recruit them to her own business.

The redhead trotted in behind Anna and Samantha. "Belinda! It's the FBI!"

The chatter stopped abruptly. In the silence, an Asian woman stood up from the couch. She wore a belted silver tank top, black leather boots, and dark jeans that clung to her legs like tights. The other women looked up to her like students to a professor. She was clearly the alpha escort.

"Can I help you?" she asked.

"We hope so. I'm Special Agent Samantha Randazzo from the FBI. Are you Belinda?"

"Yes."

"May we speak to you privately? We're investigating Madeleine Connor's death."

"I thought Madeleine committed suicide."

"Can we ask you a few questions about her?" Samantha said.

"No, I'm sorry. Why don't you leave me your card. You've interrupted me with my friends."

"Was Madeleine a friend of yours as well?"

"As I said, this really isn't a good time."

The rest of the women watched in silence. Samantha turned and faced the crowd.

"Two women from Discretion have died," Samantha said. "You all might be in danger, too. We'd appreciate if anyone would be willing to talk to us."

"We can offer you protection," Anna added.

"What danger?" asked Randi. "You want to put us in the Witness Protection Program?"

"No," Anna answered. "There's no reason to think any of you need to be permanently relocated with a new identity. But we can put you up in a hotel for a while under assumed names."

"Hell, I do that every night anyhow," a leggy brunette laughed. "At nicer hotels than the government can afford."

"Stop!" Belinda's voice was loud and authoritative. She looked around the room slowly, making stern eye contact with each of the women. "No one says anything else." The escorts quieted in their seats. Anna could see that none of them would talk as long as they were here in Belinda's house. Belinda turned to Samantha. "I'm really going to have to insist that you leave my home. Now."

Anna and Samantha sighed in unison. They had no authority to stay. Belinda walked them back into the foyer. Anna could hear the chatter start up as soon as they were out of the living room.

At the front door, Samantha handed Belinda her card and said, "You know, you and all of those women could be in danger."

"We always are. That's part of the business." Belinda glanced at the card. "But we don't run to the police."

"When was the last time you saw Madeleine?"

"Madeleine herself or one of her thugs? I assume somebody told you about Madeleine and me or you wouldn't be here, right?" Neither Sam nor Anna answered her. Belinda shrugged. "No matter. It's no secret that we didn't get along. She didn't treat people very well. She acted like she was all concerned about her clients and 'her girls.' That was just for show. The only thing she really cared about was herself."

"I see." Sam nodded. "Can you tell me where you were last night around ten P.M.?"

"I was with a gentleman friend."

"Would he be willing to corroborate your story?"

"Of course not. You know what I do." Belinda opened her front door, letting in a wave of hot air. "Good night."

She shut the door firmly as soon as they were outside. Sam and Anna walked to the Durango, which seemed enormous parked on the narrow historic street. The SUV had heated up like a greenhouse while they were gone. Sam turned on the ignition and blasted the air-conditioning but kept the truck parked.

"Those women have to come out of there at some point," Anna said. "We can try to talk to them without Belinda running interference."

"We'll need more than the two of us. Let's see if McGee can come or scare up a few detectives."

Anna called and told him what was going on.

"Wait," he said. "You're telling me there are a dozen beautiful escorts sitting in a house in George-town and you need someone to talk to all of them?"

"Right."

"This is a real sacrifice you're asking of me."

Fifteen minutes later, two maroon Crown Vics pulled up behind the Durango. Anna saw McGee and four more homicide detectives crammed into the first one; the second car held another four burly detectives.

She and Samantha met McGee on the sidewalk. Anna raised her eyebrows at the cars. "I take it there weren't any other homicides to investigate today."

"C'mon," McGee chuckled, "you think anyone's

gonna turn down this assignment? I got a few more guys on their way!"

Anna had to laugh.

"You ladies can go," McGee said. "We got this under control."

Anna was anxious to get back to the office; she and Sam had a pile of subpoenas and document requests to get out the door—things like subscriber information for the phone numbers in Madeleine's phone records, and the phone records and criminal history of Belinda and Peal.

She handed McGee a stack of Victim/Witness Assistance brochures. "Make sure you tell them we can put them up for the night. At a hotel, not at your house."

He laughed. "I'll work my charms, but not that well."

Sam and Anna drove back to the office. They had gone only a few blocks when Anna's BlackBerry buzzed with a new text message. She glanced at it, then rocked back with surprise. She wondered if it was some kind of sick prank.

# 38

Nicole huddled in a corner of the closet, aching, scared, and all cried out. She'd seen just enough before Pleazy locked her in the darkness to know that the closet was full of foul junk she didn't want to be touching: dirty socks, a stained bra, something that might've been a used condom. The floor felt sticky under her left thigh. Her whole body throbbed.

She kept closing her eyes and reopening them, sure that one of these times she would find herself back in her own soft bed in her apartment overlooking the National Cathedral. This couldn't be happening to her. She was supposed to be a senior at Georgetown. Not a drug addict. Not a crack whore. Nicole had friends—once. She had money and men and glamour. She had a future. This was not her life. She wasn't here.

But each time she opened her eyes, she was in the closet in the dark.

She heard creaking—someone walking up the stairs. Was it Pleazy coming to let her free? The thought filled her not with hope but terror. He was too strong, mentally and physically, for her to fight. She couldn't beat him. Once he opened the closet door, she would never stop being his bitch.

She still had one lifeline. She unzipped a pocket of her leather dress and pulled out her cell phone. She was too scared to make a phone call, in case Pleazy heard her talking. But she could text. Her thumb traced the edge of the smooth touch-screen, relishing the feel of something familiar. In vain, she tried to think of a friend she hadn't alienated—a teacher who cared about her—someone to turn to for help. Even if there were anyone, she couldn't let anyone from her old life see her like this. If she had any remaining glimmer of dignity, that would extinguish it.

From another zippered pocket, she pulled out the business cards Capri had handed her last night. Using the light of the phone screen, she looked at the cards. There was handwriting on the back of the one from Anna Curtis. *I can help you. Call me.*

Bullshit. This Anna chick didn't want to help Nicole. She wanted Nicole to help *her*. Prosecutors didn't give out their business cards so they could provide charity to street prostitutes. They gave out their cards when they were building a case.

So here was her choice. Call Anna Curtis. Answer the prosecutor's questions. Tell her what happened to Caroline—what she, Nicole, had done to make it happen.

What would go down then? Perhaps they would lock her in jail immediately. Worse, she would have to face Caroline's family and all of their shared friends at Georgetown and Discretion. The newspapers would learn the truth. The world would know what she'd done. Everyone would despise her. It made life with Pleazy seem almost appealing.

No. It didn't.

Through a blur of tears, Nicole tapped out a text message on the cell phone.

## 39

The text message was from a number Anna didn't recognize. It read:

> Help! Ur looking 4 me. Im trapped 1923 2 st nw 2d
> flr bedrm closet. 2 women 1 man he raped me.
> nicole

Nicole, Caroline's mysterious vanishing roommate? Anna wondered how long it would take to get to 2nd Street.

"Hey, Sam," Anna said, "take a look at this."

Sam stopped at a red light, and Anna showed her the text message.

"You know that phone number?" Sam asked.

"Nope."

"The address mean anything to you?"

"Nope."

"Pretty thin."

"I know. Can't get a warrant. Should we call 911? Or McGee?"

"MPD? No, I'll check it out myself." Samantha gave Anna a grudging smile. "*We'll* check it out."

Sam swung the Durango onto Rhode Island Avenue. Anna held tight to the handle, glad to have such an aggressive agent. Some officers had to be begged just to do their jobs, and you could forget asking them to do anything unusual. It was better to work with an agent she occasionally had to hold back than one she constantly had to prod.

Jack would say it was too dangerous for Anna to go along. But he didn't have a vote anymore. She was her own woman. She didn't have to report to her boyfriend about where she was going or who she was going with. She could do what she wanted to do, and no one would worry about her.

The neighborhood of Bloomingdale was in transition. The addict-to-architect ratio was about even, but the architects had the momentum. The shops on the corner of Rhode Island and 1st Street, Northwest, reflected the mixed demographics. There was Windows Café, a coffee shop with purple awnings, smoothies, and free Wi-Fi. Next door was the Chinese Dragon carryout, a Chinese/subs/burgers/fried-chicken joint with scuffed bulletproof glass protecting the proprietors from their customers. The clientele of the two adjacent restaurants were self-selecting and rarely overlapped.

Second Street was lined with narrow rowhouses ranging from shambles to chic. There were three for-sale signs on the block. White carpenters' vans and green renovators' porta-potties dotted the rapidly gentrifying street. Though it was a bit too early for commuters to be returning from work, there were a few people hanging around outside. Many of the homes had no air-conditioning, so residents without steady work gathered on the stoops and street corners.

The address in the text was an end unit that hadn't experienced any renovations. Its few remaining shutters clung to scarred brick walls at chaotic angles; the tiny yard was trash-strewn and overgrown with weeds; metal bars covered the lower windows, which were streaked with dirt. Boxy old air-conditioning units sprouted from the upstairs windows. The house was dark and silent. Samantha parked at the curb in front, blocking off a fire hydrant.

"Stay in the car," she said as she hopped out of the Durango.

"Why? If it's Nicole, I want to talk to her."

"You're not armed."

"Then shouldn't you at least call for backup?" Anna said to Sam's retreating back. The agent ignored her. As Samantha strode up the sidewalk, Anna reconsidered the benefits of having such an aggressive agent.

Sam went to the first-floor window. She cupped her hands against the glass and peered in. Then she marched up the steps and buzzed at the front door. A minute later, the door opened. A thick white woman with bottle-blond hair stood in the doorway, hands on her hips. Anna could see Samantha and the woman having a short conversation. After a minute, the woman stepped aside to let Samantha into the house.

Anna climbed out of the car and jogged up to the front door. She didn't know what assistance she could provide, but she wasn't letting Samantha go in there alone. The agent scowled at her, but before Samantha could tell her to get back into the car, Anna introduced herself to the woman.

"Hi, I'm Anna. I'm working with Agent Randazzo. What's your name?"

"Layla."

The woman wore a sleeveless white T-shirt revealing a tattoo on her fat pink arm: *Pleazy.* Anna tried to gauge Layla's age but could only tell that she'd lived a hard life. Layla could be anywhere from mid-thirties to early fifties. Her cheeks were deeply pockmarked, her face was jowly and lined, and her brassy hair had dark, greasy roots. She had sneaky gray eyes.

Layla stared at Anna suspiciously but stepped back and allowed her to step in with Samantha. Anna ignored the nervous feeling in her belly.

The entranceway was a narrow hall with wooden stairs going up. To the right of the entry hall was a shabby but uncluttered living room. It was much neater than some witnesses' homes, although it held the unmistakable smell of poverty, a mixture of cigarette smoke, weed, stale sweat, and fried food. At the back of the house, Anna could see a portion of a grimy kitchen with a sink full of unwashed cups and dishes. All of the rooms appeared empty.

"We're looking for someone named Nicole," Samantha said. "Do you know her?"

Layla folded her hands across her bosom. "No."

"We got a report that Nicole might be here in this house," Samantha said. "You know anything about that?"

"Sorry."

"So you don't mind if we take a look around?"

Anna could see the calculations going through the woman's head. If she refused, it would raise the alarm bells. The police might search anyway, and if they found anything, she would look guilty for trying to hide it. But if she said the officers could search, she would seem innocent. The officers would think she had nothing to hide, and they might go away. Anna had seen dozens of cases in which guilty people, with incriminating evidence in their cars or homes or on their persons, consented to a police search based on this miscalculation.

Finally, Layla nodded. "Okay."

"Great. Thanks."

Sam headed straight toward the stairs. Layla's face twisted with rage and fear. Her bluff had been called.

"Pleazy!" she screamed. "Pleazy! Po-po coming!"

A slim, good-looking African-American man appeared at the top of the stairs. He held a dull black 9-millimeter Luger in his right hand, pointed at the floor.

"Gun!" Anna shouted. She glanced at Samantha, who already had her Glock pointed at the man at the top of the stairs.

"Police! Put your gun down!" Samantha barked in the Voice of Authority. "Now!"

"Okay! Don't shoot!" Pleazy's voice was an octave higher than Anna had anticipated. He was either a tenor or terrified. He held his left hand up, bent down, and placed his gun on the floor with his right hand. He stood, holding both hands up.

"Come down the stairs!" Samantha instructed. "Keep those hands up. No sudden moves."

He raised his palms and slowly came down the steps.

Anna should have known what would happen next. She'd dealt with enough domestic-violence cases to know that you could never turn your back on the woman. But she was so transfixed by the immediate threat of the man with the gun that she'd let Layla slip out of her vision.

The burly woman crept up behind Samantha and slammed a thick green glass goblet down on the agent's head.

# 40

Sam's gun fired as she staggered to her knees. Anna jumped at the sound—gunfire in an empty room was thunderous. Her ears rang. Layla, too, stumbled backward, covering her ears. The rowhouse acquired a new bullet hole, this one in the drywall at the top of the steps. Before Anna could do anything else, an arm clamped around her neck from behind.

"Go, Pleazy, go!" Layla yelled. "We got these bitches!"

Pleazy flew down the stairs, stumbled through the foyer, and fled out the front door. Anna clawed at the arm around her neck. Her fingers were ineffectual against the strong elbow cutting off the air from her lungs and the blood to her brain. She experienced raw, unreasoning panic. Then she started to see red. Oh God. What was it Eva had said? It took six seconds for you to lose consciousness when the blood flow to your head was cut off. What was the move, what was the move?

Anna turned her shoulder into her attacker's chest and yanked the arm down. She didn't get out, but she got enough breathing space that the red faded from her vision. Anna rammed her shoulder into her attacker's chest. She pulled the arm down a little farther and jammed her fingers over her shoulders, toward her assailant's eyes. She wasn't sure she was doing anything right. Actual fighting was way more chaotic and scrappy than a controlled drill in the gym. But something worked. Her fingers sank into soft tissue—she hoped an eyeball—and her assailant screamed, loosening the grip.

Anna ducked her head out of the elbow and took a step back, ready to deliver the groin kick. She was shocked to see that her attacker was a woman, about her age and maybe forty pounds heavier. Anna didn't think a groin kick would be much use. Instead, she lashed out with the heel of her palm, rotating her waist for torque and punching through her target, like she'd practiced in class. The meaty part of her hand barreled into the woman's nose.

There was a crunch, and the woman staggered back into the living room with a shriek. She fell down, clutching her face. Blood trickled between her fingers. Anna had never punched anyone before. She stared at the bleeding woman before shaking herself out of shock and turning to Samantha.

The agent was on her knees, her head bleeding and her face scrunched into an expression of pain. In her right hand she clutched her weapon, pressing it to the floor. She was trying to get up but couldn't seem to get her bearings. Layla looked at Anna, then at Sam's gun. Layla dove forward and grabbed the agent's right arm, trying to wrestle away the weapon.

Anna charged toward her. "No!" she yelled. She drove her knee squarely into the side of Layla's head. It hurt her knee but seemed to hurt the woman even more. Layla fell to the side, and the gun went skittering across the bare floor. Layla lay in a heap, moaning.

Anna turned to face Samantha. The agent rose to one knee with a grimace. "Are you okay?" Anna asked. Her voice was raspy from having been choked.

Sam nodded silently. Anna darted across the room to retrieve the gun. It trembled violently, although she held it in both hands. She'd held a gun only once before, when Jack took her to a firing range with McGee and insisted that she learn how to handle a weapon. Anna sent up a thanks for his insistence. She kept her index finger off the trigger and along the side of the barrel so that, shaking like she was, she didn't accidentally shoot someone.

Layla kept her eyes on the weapon in Anna's hand but didn't move. The nose-bleeding woman glared at Anna, but sat against the couch and showed no interest in renewing her attack. No one else appeared in the rooms.

"You got a registration for that firearm?" Samantha straightened up. She held out her hand for Anna to give back the gun. Anna hesitated. Samantha had taken a significant blow to the head. Was she in any state to have a gun? Anna fell back on what she'd seen on *Grey's Anatomy.* "Who's the President?" she asked. "What's the date?"

"It's the date I arrest you for carrying a pistol without a license if you don't give me back my gun, Annie Oakley."

Anna turned the weapon muzzle-down and handed it to Samantha, who seemed to feel better as her hand closed around the black steel.

"Thank you," Samantha said.

"It's your gun."

"No. I mean thank you. You saved my ass."

"Tony never would've given me another eggplant patty if I hadn't."

Sam's eyes kept skimming around the house as she pulled out her cell phone and hit something on speed dial.

"Calling for backup?" Anna asked. Samantha nodded.

"What a fabulous idea. I wish someone had thought of that before."

Jack's worries about Anna going out to crime scenes no longer seemed so excessive. Now they seemed pretty wise. Maybe it wasn't so bad to have someone worrying about her.

Within minutes, the house was covered in law-enforcement officers, both uniformed MPD and FBI agents. Layla and the other woman were cuffed and led to an ambulance.

An emergency medical technician tried to examine Samantha, but she shook him off, insisting she was fine. "I've had worse bumps on the head from roller-blading," she said.

Law-enforcement officers spread out through the house, securing the first-floor rooms and heading down to the basement and up to the second floor. Samantha went upstairs with her fellow officers. Anna followed right behind.

At the top of the stairs, Anna could see four small bedrooms, each decorated sparsely with a queen-size bed dominating the space. The beds had sheets but no blankets. She realized this wasn't a family home. It was a business. They were running incalls out of here, probably advertising online. With the explosion of the Internet, that was a popular business model, perhaps even more popular than the track.

The bedrooms all appeared empty. One had an open window leading to a fire escape. Anyone else who'd been in the house during the scuffle had fled.

In a bedroom with olive sheets, an MPD officer opened the closet door. He kept his gun trained on something inside. "Sam!" he called. Anna followed Sam into the bedroom. She peered over Sam's shoulder into the dark closet where the officer was pointing his gun.

Cowering on the floor was a skinny woman in a ruined leather dress, holding up a hand to shield her eyes from the light. Anna recognized her from the DMV photo, although it looked like the woman had survived a nuclear holocaust since she'd gotten her driver's license. Nicole Palowski stared up at Anna with hollow, haunted eyes.

The nurse removed the deflated bag of saline and attached a new one to the top of the IV pole. A clear tube ran from the bag into Nicole's arm. The woman sat in the hospital bed propped up with pillows, wearing a hospital gown that kept slipping off her bony shoulders. The room was super-air-conditioned, raising goosebumps on her arms. Nicole was so thin, Anna thought, she looked like a famine victim or a supermodel.

A tray of hospital food sat in front of her, untouched. The only thing she'd been able to get down was a small portion of a milk shake. Monitors beeped and whirred around them.

Anna and Samantha had been sitting with her for half an hour. Mostly, the nurses had been talking to the patient. Samantha hadn't said much. Anna suspected the agent was still shaky from being hit, although she insisted she was fine.

Anna expected the nurse to chastise them that the patient needed rest. But the nurse barely glanced at the visitors. After she was done with the IV, she made a few notes on a chart and turned to walk out. Anna asked if she could get an extra blanket for Nicole. The nurse returned with a warm blanket, which she draped around the patient's shoulders. Nicole smiled at Anna.

The doctors at George Washington University Hospital had handed down their diagnosis. Nicole was suffering from internal bleeding and malnutrition. Most dangerously, she was dehydrated; hence the IV.

It was amazing, Anna thought, how the woman's face had filled out in the two hours since she'd been admitted, diminishing the skeletal look of her sunken eye sockets. She was far too thin, but the saline drip had plumped up her desiccated skin like an air pump filling a deflated ball.

The first thing Nicole wanted to know was what had happened to Pleazy. Anna told her that the police had caught the pimp—whose real name was Lorenzo V. James—on Rhode Island Avenue around the same time they found Nicole in the closet. Pleazy was likely going to jail for a long time. He had enough prior felony drug convictions that he was looking at a fifteen-year mandatory minimum sentence for possession of a firearm. There were a variety of other charges they could bring against him and the two women who had attacked Samantha and Anna.

"We might ask you to testify against him at trial," Anna said.

"Good," Nicole said, chin up, eyes hard.

Anna could see Nicole meant it, which was huge. Getting a prostitute to testify against her pimp was often impossible, even when he had beaten the woman bloody. Studies estimated that over 80 percent of prostitutes were raped by their pimps, though the crime was rarely reported to law enforcement. Pimps were famous for their ability to command loyalty while wielding extreme cruelty. It was like a domestic-violence relationship in that the victim was deeply in love with her abuser. But Anna could see that wasn't the dynamic here. Nicole wasn't in love with Pleazy. She wasn't going to cover for him.

"So where have you been the last few days?" Anna asked gently. "We've been looking for you."

"I know." Nicole chewed her lip guiltily. And then she talked. Once she started, she couldn't seem to stop. Her voice was weak, and she was obviously in pain, but she needed to speak. Anna guessed she'd been on her own a lot lately. She was dying to be heard, to be known—maybe more than she'd been dying of dehydration.

They learned that Nicole was from Butler, a small town north of Pittsburgh. She'd started at Georgetown University four years ago and had been majoring in psychology. She liked D.C. and the college but had a hard time affording the lifestyle after her parents stopped paying for things. She was currently taking a "break" from classes. She lived in Alban Towers, right where McGee had gone to look for her.

"Did you know the police were trying to find you?" Anna asked.

"Yes," Nicole said. "I didn't want you to find me."

"We kind of guessed that. Why?"

Nicole didn't respond at first. Anna could sense her struggling with whether to open up. They couldn't make Nicole talk to them; she was in no shape to be hauled in front of the grand jury. And Anna knew that Nicole wouldn't open up unless she wanted to. Unless she decided that Anna could be trusted.

Nicole opened her mouth, but instead of speaking, she began to sob. Her cries were soft, but her whole body shook with them. Anna handed her a tissue and waited. When Nicole finally quieted, she took a deep breath and met Anna's eyes.

"I'm responsible for what happened to Caroline McBride."

Anna kept a neutral expression. "How so?"

"I set up her appointment that night."

"Wasn't Madeleine responsible for all the appointments?"

"Madeleine didn't know what was going on with this one. Caroline had met with Congressman Lionel before. I guess he was pretty bold about having escorts come to his office. So one night maybe four or five months ago, this staffer saw Caroline in the office, and he fell for her. Men did that all the time. She just had this pull.

"It was hard for him to get the appointment. You can't look up 'Sasha' or 'Discretion' in the phone book. He must've gotten it from the Congressman's cell phone or something. So he called up, told Madeleine that the Congressman had referred him, and booked an appointment with Sasha. Once he'd been with her, that was it. He was convinced he was in love with her. Kept booking appointments. At Caroline's rates, he must've bankrupted himself. But he was crazy about her. Like *crazy* crazy. In a weird, meticulous way. Once he fixated on something, he was obsessed.

"To her, he was just another john. Not even one she particularly liked. To him, she was his destiny, *the one*. So he started trying to see her outside of appointments. For free, like they were really dating. He followed her home one time, left notes and gifts at our door. He was like, 'I can take you away from all this,' blah blah blah. He wanted to marry her. He didn't even know her real name, but he wanted to 'make an honest woman' out of her.

"Caroline didn't want him. She was the top escort in the city. She asked him to chill, but she was too sweet and polite. He didn't get the message.

"He started getting jealous about her clients. One time he waited outside our building all night with that camera he was always carrying. It was stalkerish, but Madeleine wouldn't let Caroline call the police. Finally, he interrupted one of Caroline's other appointments. That's when Madeleine finally put a stop to it. She banned him from the agency and sent some big guy to 'have a talk' with him. Scared the crap out of him."

"Do you know the staffer's name?" Anna asked, although she could make a pretty good guess.

"Brett Vale."

Anna nodded, picturing the lean silver-haired staffer with the translucent blue eyes. She remembered those strange eyes skimming up her own bare legs.

"I'm not understanding something," Anna said. "How is any of this *your* fault?"

Nicole looked out the window and spoke to the hazy blue sky. "Caroline and I were fighting a lot at this point. I racked up a ton of debt. Credit cards, borrowing from my friends and from . . . my dealer."

"And from Caroline?"

Nicole nodded and looked down. "By the end, she was paying all the rent. Food, too. We fought about every fucking thing. If I borrowed her lip gloss or a purse, if I left dishes in the sink, if I partied a little too hard some night. I didn't need that shit from her. Then Madeleine fired me. I had all these debts and no income.

"Brett came up to me one day, said he wanted to make a private arrangement. I knew he was trouble, but I needed the work. I met him at his place. It was weird. There were pictures of Caroline all over his walls. And he didn't want to have sex with me. He just wanted to talk about her and get information from me. He ended up crying on my shoulder, telling me how much he loved her, how he couldn't live without her, that sort of thing. It was insulting. I mean, *I* was an escort first. I got her into the business.

"Anyway, Brett gave me a thousand dollars' cash to help him set up one more meeting with Caroline. He wanted a last shot at winning her over. Thought if he had the face time, he could convince her to be with him. He was all romantic about it.

"I knew there was no chance. But I needed the money. And fuck Madeleine. And—God help me—I was mad at Caroline. I was jealous of her. Her success. Everything."

Her long brown hair covered her face as she bowed her head and choked back a sob. "So I did it." She looked back up at Anna, her fingers twisting the hospital gown. "I told him how to meet her. He called Madeleine and booked Caroline as if he were the Congressman. He knew the Congressman's computer password—said he kept it taped to a note under his keyboard. Brett just needed to know her real name to get her through security. We never told clients our real names, but Madeleine made an exception for congressmen. So I told him it was Caroline McBride. I think he was gonna propose to her."

Anna tried to tally it all up, as she nodded calmly. Did the story match up with the other known facts? It did. Did Vale seem like he could do this sort of thing? He did.

"I watched her get ready that night," Nicole said, using a corner of the bedsheet to wipe a tear running down her cheek. "So excited to have an appointment at the Capitol. Putting on her new suit. I knew who was waiting for her. And I didn't tell her. I just watched."

"You didn't know he was going to kill her," Anna said.

"Have you talked to Brett Vale since that night?" Samantha asked.

"No way."

"Do you know if he had anything to do with Madeleine's death?" Samantha asked.

Nicole's eyes widened. Locked in the closet, she hadn't heard that Madeleine was dead. "Oh God, what happened?" She started sobbing again. "I don't know why I'm crying. I didn't even like her."

Anna put a hand on Nicole's arm and patted it. Nicole leaned over and pressed her face into Anna's shoulder. She cried in great heaving gulps. Anna held her without speaking. Eventually, Nicole's sobs shifted down to whimpers, then sniffles. She sat back and used a napkin to blow her nose.

"Do you know whether Vale keeps any weapons in the house?" Samantha asked. That was one of the first things a police officer wanted to know when preparing a search warrant. Samantha was ready to go bust down Vale's door.

"I didn't see any, but I wouldn't be surprised," Nicole said. "He's crazy."

Anna took Nicole's hand. "What happened to Caroline wasn't your fault. And your information today has been really helpful. Can we return the favor? Do you want some help getting out of this life?"

Nicole nodded.

"I made some calls while the doctors were looking at you," Anna said. "I got you into a residential drug-treatment program. They'll take you tomorrow, when the hospital releases you. And then I want you to meet some folks from Polaris. It's a great organization that helps sex workers find the courage and resources to leave the business. They have some ex-prostitutes working there. They're amazing. And they're really looking forward to talking to you. We might even be able to get you into transitional housing, if you're interested."

There was no one like an ex-prostitute to help a current one get out of the business. Anna could do only so much as a prosecutor. The best luck she'd had in helping women escape prostitution was to introduce them to other women who'd managed to get out.

Anna gauged Nicole's reaction. If she didn't want to leave the life, any help Anna could offer would be worthless.

Nicole's expression was something Anna didn't see often enough. It was the rare and priceless look of a woman who was ready to get clean.

Anna might actually be able to help her.

"Thank you," Nicole said.

Anna and Samantha had a lot of work ahead of them tonight, but for a moment, Anna allowed herself the thrill of satisfaction. Bringing someone back from the brink was the best part of her job.

# 42

Anna and Samantha spent the rest of the night in the war room, corroborating everything they could about Nicole's story. Mostly, Anna lost herself in the work. But at one point she looked up at the clock and saw it was eight-thirty P.M.—Olivia's bedtime. She pictured Jack sitting on Olivia's bed as the little girl slowly read aloud from *James and the Giant Peach*. Anna remembered how Olivia had cuddled with her last night, the way the little girl had seemed not only to want but to need Anna's presence. For a second Anna wished she were sitting on the foot of the bed, patting Olivia's foot and smiling encouragingly as she read. Anna felt a warm wistfulness in her chest. Was she feeling . . . could she be . . . motherly?

She shook it off. It was too late for her to feel all lovey and maternal toward Olivia. She refocused herself on the case.

By ten P.M., she and Samantha had covered every angle they could think of, and they couldn't find anything wrong with Nicole's story. The Tiny Jewel Box sent Anna a fax confirming that Brett Vale had bought the engagement ring found in the hideaway. Anna subpoenaed the three major credit-rating agencies, with Samantha working her contacts to get an expedited response: Vale had maxed out six credit cards in the last six months.

McGee arrived at the office with a Georgetown Cupcakes box that held eleven cupcakes—"I couldn't wait!"—and a sugary grin. After Anna filled him in,

McGee wanted to get a warrant to arrest Vale immediately.

They had probable cause to arrest Vale. He had lied to them about the engagement ring, at the very least, and that was a federal offense. If Nicole were telling the truth, Vale had lied to them about almost everything else as well.

But it was possible that Nicole's story wasn't true. The last thing they wanted to do was arrest the wrong guy. Just being arrested on a charge like this could ruin someone's reputation and career. And if further investigation eventually concluded that someone else had killed Caroline, the wrongful arrest of Vale would be Exhibit A in a "police rushed to judgment" defense. Or the eventual defendant could claim Vale *was* the real killer, to create a reasonable doubt.

Anna found herself wishing she could talk to Jack about it. Not only because he was the prosecutor whose judgment she most trusted. She instinctively wanted his input on all of her most important decisions. She would have to figure this out herself. She was determined to prove she could do it without him.

Anna called Carla, who listened carefully and gave her sound advice. Ultimately, they decided to search Vale's house first. If that provided enough corroboration of Nicole's story—if they found photos of Caroline tacked up all over his walls, for example—they would arrest him.

Sam made a series of phone calls to her FBI supervisors, hashing out an Operations Plan and getting a SWAT team pulled together. By twelve-thirty A.M., Anna had finished writing the affidavit in support of the warrant to search Brett Vale's home. She called the duty judge, apologized for waking him up, and

told him that Samantha would come over to swear
out the warrant. By 1:45 A.M., Samantha had returned
from the judge's home with a signed search warrant.
By two-thirty, a team of MPD officers and FBI agents
had assembled in the war room. The officers planned
the execution of the warrant and finished off the cupcakes.

Brett Vale rented an apartment on the top floor of
a converted three-story rowhouse near Eastern Market. Officers called up floor plans of Vale's building
and records of everyone who lived there. Each floor
constituted its own one-bedroom unit. The lower
two condos were also rented by Capitol Hill staffers.
There'd been no 911 calls to the building over the
last ten years, and none of the residents had a police
record. People who worked in political jobs were
always thinking of the Senate confirmation hearings
they hoped to have someday and keeping their records
clean for that golden moment. Anna hoped the atmosphere would make the search less dangerous for the
team.

Still, they would go prepared. The SWAT team
would carry Heckler & Koch MP5 submachine guns;
Sam's search team would carry their sidearms. It
sounded like a lot of firepower to search the home of
one Capitol Hill staffer. But after Pleazy's house, Samantha was taking no chances.

By five-fifteen A.M., Samantha, McGee, and the
other officers headed down the elevators, out the front
doors, and to the curb. The eastern horizon was just
starting to turn from black to gray. They would raid
Vale's house at precisely six A.M.—the earliest moment
allowable under the terms of the standard "daylight
hours" search warrant. Most of the officers piled into

a couple of unmarked white vans parked in front of the FBI's Washington Field Office, across the street from the Building Museum. McGee unlocked his Crown Vic, and Anna started to climb in when Samantha put a hand on her shoulder.

"I can't let you come," Samantha said. "I'm sorry."

Anna stood up with surprise. She'd figured she was part of the team. "I won't get in your way."

"I know. You're an asset. Truly." That was the most effusive Anna had ever heard Sam. "But I have to do this one by the book, no frills and no extras."

"Even after everything yesterday?"

"Especially after everything yesterday." Samantha smiled and lowered her voice. "I have to get my mojo back."

"I won't touch your mojo."

"Look, I need these guys to respect me. Not be thinking of me getting my ass saved by a lawyer. Anyway, we need you by a computer, ready to look up anything if a legal issue comes up, ready to whip up that arrest warrant if we find enough at his house. I'm counting on you to make those lightning-quick ninja-lawyer moves." Sam smiled at her. "Okay?"

"Okay." Anna sighed. She could see Sam's point. It would be good to have someone in the office on standby.

"Get a little rest," Samantha added. "I guarantee I'll call if we need you."

Anna nodded. But she didn't head off right away. She stood for a few minutes in the warm night air, watching as the officers drove north on 4th Street. It wasn't because she really wanted to go with them on the search warrant.

What she wanted was to go back to Jack's house,

curl up next to him, and go to sleep. She wanted to tell him what had happened and hear his reaction. She even wanted to have him scold her for taking another dangerous field trip.

No. She tried to restoke the righteous anger she'd felt earlier, when Jack was being so stubborn and blind at Main Justice. But all she felt was a bone-deep exhaustion and the creeping fear that, maybe, she had also been in the wrong.

Brett Vale peered around his Smart car. It was parked on F Street, across from the Building Museum and spitting distance from the FBI's Washington Field Office. Through the lens of his Canon EOS 40D, the camera he preferred for shooting at night, he watched the officers drive away on 4th Street. He briefly wondered where the group was heading so early in the morning. But that wasn't what interested him. What really interested him was that Anna Curtis now stood on the empty street corner, alone. He turned the lens back to her slim, solitary figure. She looked so lonely and vulnerable, standing in the yellowish glow of the streetlight. He had to suppress a giggle. It was perfect.

# Thursday

# 43

The sky was the medium shade of gray that meant the sun would peek over the horizon any minute. It was 5:59 A.M., and except for a lone jogger, this residential street on Capitol Hill was quiet. The sidewalks were lined with well-maintained red-brick rowhouses, many of which were divided into two- or three-unit condos. Residents here were highly educated and house proud but, as congressional staffers, not affluent.

The SWAT team trotted toward Vale's rowhouse, through the front door, and up the steps to the third floor. Sam followed them. Four additional officers guarded the perimeter of the building. The SWAT team would enter and clear the place; then a separate team led by Samantha would do the search. Usually SWAT wouldn't let the case agent enter with them. But Sam had insisted.

They stood in front of Vale's door and waited for their watches to read six o'clock. Then they knocked. Announced, "FBI! We have a warrant! Open up!" Counted to thirty. No answer. Took the battering ram to the door. Flooded into the apartment, guns drawn, high-beam flashlights shining around, shouting for anyone inside to come out. Samantha strode in behind them.

As soon as she entered, she flinched at the sight of a blond woman sitting on the couch. The SWAT members saw it, too. Beams from half a dozen flashlights flicked over and settled on the back of the blonde's head.

"Stand up! Hands up!" a SWAT guy shouted at the blonde. The woman didn't move. "Dammit, hands up!"

The woman was perfectly still. The SWAT officer swung around and pointed his submachine gun at her face.

"Holy fuck," he said.

Sam strode over and followed the beam of his flashlight. The blonde on the couch was not a person but a full-sized mannequin wearing a blond wig. She was dressed in an ivory skirt suit similar to the one Caroline wore when she was killed. Her blue eyes stared blankly ahead. The mannequin's vacant gaze made Samantha shiver.

From the other rooms, guys were shouting, "Clear." A couple minutes later, the SWAT leader pronounced, "All clear." No one was home. Samantha snapped on the panel of lights at the front door.

The SWAT leader pointed her to the bedroom. Another blond mannequin, this one in a lacy black teddy, lay in the bed. In the dining room, a third dummy in jeans and a white sweater sat at the table. The doll's hands had been carefully positioned around a mug and her head slightly tilted to one side, as if she were listening intently to someone on the other side of the table. Sam guessed that was where Vale sat.

But where was he?

Not SWAT's problem. Their job was to clear the apartment. The mannequins did not constitute a threat. The SWAT team bade their goodbyes and took off. Sam's own team would do the search. She radioed them in. Then she walked around the apartment, soaking it all up.

The bachelor pad was stark and neat. The walls

were white; the couch beneath the first mannequin was black leather. A sleek black Polk entertainment system dominated one side of the room. Abstract black-and-white photos hung on the walls. The living room had a cathedral ceiling that must have been a bump up from the original rowhouse's. Sam's heels clacked on the polished wood floors as she looked around. The overall impression was an exhibit in a modern art museum.

Sam cursed when she saw that there weren't pictures of Caroline pasted all over the place. When Nicole had mentioned that, Samantha recalled the homes of a few stalkers she'd investigated before: photos haphazardly tacked up over a desk in a chaotic shrine. That wasn't the case here. And if Nicole was wrong about that, what else had she gotten wrong? There would be major problems if the witness who was the basis for their warrant proved unreliable.

Sam chewed her lip and gazed at the arty picture hanging over the fireplace. It was an enormous black-and-white photograph of a smooth white hillside in front of a black sky—artistic, sensual, and abstract. On closer inspection, she saw it wasn't a hillside. It was the curve of a woman's hip contrasted against dark sheets.

Sam looked more closely at the other matted, framed photos. One was a woman's mouth, full and sensual, gleaming with shimmery lipstick. Samantha recognized the mouth. It was Caroline McBride's. She glanced back at the other pictures and realized they were all Caroline. Here was an artful section of her calf; here was the back of her neck; here were her hands. Farther down the hallway, the images were less abstract, more recognizable. In a series of three framed prints in the hallway, Caroline window-shopped through Georgetown, apparently unaware that she was being followed.

As an evidentiary matter, it was a bonanza. Vale had not only been stalking her, he'd been photographing it. Samantha directed a tech to photograph all the pictures as they were hung on the walls, then seize them as evidence. Nicole had been right. Samantha exhaled a breath she hadn't realized she'd been holding.

Where was the guy's camera? Samantha directed all of the officers to look out for one. As her team searched room by room, she simply browsed, getting a feel for the obsessively neat man who lived here. His closet was hung with neatly pressed and starched clothes. Even his underwear was folded into perfect tighty-whitey squares.

A small leather tray on his dresser held change but no wallet. Wherever he was, he had his wallet with him. In his medicine cabinet were bottles of Xanax and some herbal energy mega-supplements from a sketchy-sounding website.

If the apartment were a treasure map, the kitchen was where the X would go. Samantha opened the oven and found what would be the center of her homicide case against Brett Vale: A Fendi purse sat on the top oven rack.

Sam signaled the tech to take a photograph. Then, with gloved hands, she took out the purse and opened it up. There was a matching wallet. Inside was Caroline McBride's Georgetown ID. Vale must have picked up the purse as he ran away. And then he hadn't been able to bring himself to throw it out.

Sam looked at the picture of the pretty student whose life had ended at the Capitol. Before she was a homicide victim—before she was Washington's most expensive escort—Caroline McBride had been a smiling, hopeful girl on her first day of college.

A voice interrupted her thoughts. "We got it."

Sam looked up from the wallet. Steve Quisenberry was holding up a fancy black camera with a big telephoto lens.

"Where was it?" she asked, setting down the wallet and taking the camera.

"Front hall closet. There are a few more and a bunch of memory cards. Guy likes cameras."

Sam didn't know much about photography, but this Nikon looked expensive. It was large and black, with a lens big enough to wrap your hand around and a screen on the back for viewing pictures. Samantha flicked it on. She scrolled through the pictures on the screen going backward, through the date stamps, seeing the older ones first.

The first photographs were of a stone mansion surrounded by a garden of flowers. The sky was dark, but the lights blazed in the first-floor windows. Samantha recognized the house.

"That's Madeleine Connor's place," Quisenberry said.

"Yeah." Samantha nodded. "And look at the time stamp."

The orange text on the corner read 8/7/12. The night the madam had been killed.

"He killed Madeleine Connor so we wouldn't learn about his relationship with Caroline." Samantha said the words slowly, trying out the theory. "But what did he do with her record books? Are they here?"

"Haven't found 'em."

Sam kept flipping through the pictures on the

Nikon. Now there were photographs of a young blond woman on the street. At first Samantha thought they were more pictures of Caroline. They had the same far-off voyeuristic feel as the ones Vale had mounted on his walls. But the woman's hair was slightly different, the features distinct. By the third photo, Samantha realized that these were not pictures of the dead escort—the subject of these photos was Anna Curtis.

One after the other, Samantha paged through shots of the pretty prosecutor: getting into the Dodge Durango with Samantha, walking alone on Pennsylvania Avenue, standing outside the main Justice Building with Jack. *Yesterday.* Vale must have staked out the U.S. Attorney's Office, photographing and following Anna as she came and went.

"Oh, shit," Samantha said.

She unclipped her phone and called Anna. There was no answer.

# 44

Jack walked down the hall in his pajama bottoms and poked his head into Olivia's room. "Morning, kiddo. Time to get dressed."

Olivia was playing with Kara and Darren, her favorite African-American Barbie dolls, by her Dream House in the corner. The dolls were having an argument about whether or not to get married. Olivia looked up at him and nodded somberly. "Can Anna help me get dressed today, Daddy?"

"I'm sorry, baby. She's not here this morning."

Olivia was quiet, and Jack could see the fear rounding her big green eyes. She was wearing the *Princess and the Frog* barrettes Anna had gotten her. He cursed to himself. Why did Olivia suddenly have to warm up to Anna just when things fell apart between them? Perhaps the two events were not unrelated. What were the lyrics to that old song? "Don't know what you've got till it's gone." He wasn't ready to tell his daughter that Anna wasn't coming back.

Instead, he tried a straight bribe. "You can wear your new sundress."

"Okay," Olivia said quietly. She usually loved to break out a new outfit.

Jack sighed and headed to the kitchen. He'd make blueberry pancakes for breakfast, try to cheer her up. Now that he'd been kicked off the Lionel case, it wasn't like he had to rush into work.

His BlackBerry rang as he pulled the Hungry Jack mix from the cupboard. A call from Samantha.

"I can't talk about the investigation," Jack answered. "In case you hadn't heard."

"I heard, and I'm sorry, but that's not why I'm calling. Do you know where Anna is?"

Jack glanced at the clock on his microwave. "I'm sure she's at her home, asleep. It's six-fifteen A.M. How would I know where she is?"

"Oh, come off it, Bailey. I'm a federal agent. I can tell you two are together."

"I'll plead the Fifth on that one. Have you tried her office?"

"I called, but she isn't there. She's supposed to be at home resting by her phone, but I can't reach her. And she has a stalker."

A tight ball of fear condensed inside his rib cage. "Talk."

"You're recused from the case."

"Talk, Sam."

Sam told him what they'd found. Jack thanked her, hung up, and tried each of Anna's numbers. No answer anywhere. He called Olivia's nanny and tried not to let her hear the panic in his voice. But she must have; Luisa said she could be at his house in fifteen minutes. He strode back to his bedroom and threw on jeans and a T-shirt.

Twenty minutes later, Jack pulled his Volvo station wagon onto Wyoming Avenue and parallel-parked at the curb in front of Anna's place. She rented a basement apartment in one of the elegant town homes lining this shady street. Jack had been here only a few times; Anna spent most of her time at his place. In retrospect, that was similar to the rest of their relationship. He had absorbed Anna into *his* life and made little effort to try to work himself into hers.

Not that she'd ever asked him to join her at happy hours with her friends. She was the one who'd wanted to keep things hidden. But if she'd asked him, would he have gone? Probably not. It would be awkward to be the homicide chief hanging out with the young prosecutors. He was happy for her to leave her youth behind and sit at his elbow, his partner in a decidedly grown-up life. That was probably part of what scared her about marrying him.

Jack set aside thoughts that had stopped being relevant as of yesterday. He just needed to make sure she was safe. Then they could proceed with their regularly scheduled breakup.

He strode up the walk and down the three concrete steps to her front door. The small, high window next to the door was dark. He pounded on the door and rang the doorbell. "Anna!" No one answered. She had offered him a key, but he hadn't taken it. He never slept at her apartment.

He turned back the way he'd come. On the side of each step leading down to her apartment was a small potted plant. Or, rather, pots holding the dried husks of former plants. Anna hadn't been home enough this summer to care for them. He knew she kept a house key in one of these pots. He lifted each one out of its saucer and finally found the key in the third pot.

As he straightened up, he saw a gray-haired lady peering down from the next townhouse. He raised a hand in greeting, but that just made her scowl deepen. He shrugged and let himself into Anna's apartment.

It was dark and quiet inside. "Anna!" he called. No reply. He walked through the living room. It had all the signs of a place that wasn't in use. The plant in her high basement window was wilted and on the brink of extinction. The bookshelves on either side of her red couch were covered in dust. He walked past the galley kitchen and the little bathroom, both dark and empty. He hoped he'd find her in bed, sound asleep. Perhaps she'd slept right through her phones ringing. He pushed the door into her bedroom. Her bed was made, and everything was neat and untouched. He ran a finger over the striped comforter. It, too, was covered in dust. She hadn't slept here.

The ball of fear bounced painfully around his chest.

A single picture frame sat on the nightstand next to her bed. He picked it up. A rare photo of Anna and him taken earlier this summer. Olivia had grabbed the camera and surprised them by taking a good shot. Jack and Anna sat on a park bench at the zoo, his arm around her shoulders. He was pointing to the camera and smiling, and Anna was beaming up at his face with pure adoration.

He wondered if he'd ever see that look on Anna's face again. He wondered how he'd make it through the months and years ahead if he didn't.

He had been too harsh with her at Main Justice. She had been wrong, but his reaction hadn't been fair. However much it upset him to be contradicted in front of the DOJ officials, Jack knew that there was something that was bothering him more.

He'd been upset about Anna's reaction when he mentioned marriage. He had known for the better part of a year that he wanted to marry her. But could he blame her for not wanting to become a wife and step-mother after six months of dating? It was a huge step. If she needed time, he should've given it to her.

He went into the kitchen, scribbled a note on a Post-it, and stuck it on her dusty coffee machine.

Pictures of Anna and her friends adorned the face of the refrigerator. Jack's eye fell on a picture of Anna, her friend Grace, and some other young AUSAs goofing off at Poste, drinks in hand. The last time Anna had gone to one of those happy hours, Jack had given her a hard time for coming home late and had lectured her against drinking with work colleagues. He knew firsthand the direction that could go.

Thinking back on it now, he felt somewhat ashamed of his reaction. Of course young AUSAs were going to go to happy hours after work. He'd done the same thing when he was younger. What had really bothered Jack—although he'd never mentioned it—was the fear that Anna would end up flirting with some other guy. Jack was too old to go out like that anymore; he had Olivia and too many other responsibilities. But that didn't mean Anna should miss this part of the bonding between young prosecutors.

As Jack stepped into the living room, he was greeted by an unfamiliar voice.

"Sir, raise your hands where I can see them!"

A uniformed MPD officer stood in the doorway. He looked to be about twenty years old, blond hair in a buzz cut, nervous sweat on his forehead. He had one hand on the front doorknob as the other unsnapped the holster on his Glock.

"It's okay, Officer," Jack said, walking toward the policeman. "My girlfriend—that is, my ex-girlfriend— lives here."

"Stop where you are!" the officer shouted, fumbling to draw his weapon.

The cop looked terrified. Hands trembling, he pointed the gun at Jack's heart.

# 45

Lost in thought, Anna barely noticed the man coming up behind her on the sidewalk. She was preoccupied with the search warrant and her breakup with Jack. And so she committed Eva Youngblood's cardinal sin: She let her guard down.

The morning was hot already, but Anna's hair was pulled back into a wet ponytail, which helped stave off the heat. She hadn't gone home to sleep in the two hours since Samantha and the team had driven off. Instead, she'd gone back to the U.S. Attorney's Office and showered in the gym. She was wearing the same suit, but at least she was clean underneath. After another night without sleeping, she needed caffeine.

She was headed to the Building Museum, which sat kitty-corner to the U.S. Attorney's Office. The giant redbrick structure was one of the most beautiful and underappreciated museums in the District. Although its exterior was modeled after a sixteenth-century Roman palazzo, American Civil War soldiers marched across a stone frieze. Inside, the atrium courtyard was the size of a football field, five stories high, with open arcaded galleries all around. The tall ceiling sat atop colossal yellow Corinthian columns delineating a huge carpet patterned with red and gold designs. A fountain sprayed in the middle. There were exhibits hidden in rooms lining the outside of the atrium.

But no one went to the Building Museum at seven A.M. for its exhibits on architecture. They went for the coffee shop tucked into a corner of the atrium. The space provided a beautiful respite from an otherwise gray neighborhood.

Anna nodded to an obese, sleepy security guard sitting inside the front door. His eyes were at half-mast, and he barely seemed to notice her. She headed across the atrium to the coffee shop, debating whether she'd spring for a latte.

When Anna got inside the little coffee shop, frugality won its usual victory over taste, and she ordered a plain coffee. After she poured in a dollop of milk, she turned and walked back toward the atrium, where a few tables were set up outside the coffee shop. She almost ran into Brett Vale. She stifled a scream.

What was the LD doing here? While a search warrant was being executed on his home twenty blocks away?

The man had disintegrated significantly since she'd interviewed him in the Rayburn Building two days ago. His slicked-back silver hair had broken free from the constraints of hair gel and was sticking out in multiple cowlicks around his head. Stubble dotted his jaw. His white button-down shirt had sweat stains under the armpits.

Vale smiled at her. It was a faraway smile, as if he saw something the rest of the world couldn't and was proud of this ability. Anna found it disturbing. She took a step back.

"Hi, Anna," he said, stepping forward to close the distance she'd created.

"Ms. Curtis," she corrected. She stood her ground. "What are you doing here?"

"Just getting a cup of coffee. Like you."

She knew he didn't work or live anywhere nearby. She glanced across the long lobby to where the sleepy guard sat at his desk. There wasn't a metal detector or X-ray machine at the entrance, as there were at many museums. Vale could have brought anything in. She tried to catch the guard's eye, but his face drooped toward his chest. He was sleeping.

"I'm sorry," Anna said. "But I can't talk to you. You're represented, so we can only talk with your lawyer present."

"You mean Singleton? Lionel's pawn? What a joke. I fired him."

She wasn't sure she believed him. More important, she didn't like the vibe she was getting off him. He wouldn't do anything crazy in a public place, right? Except he'd killed Caroline McBride at the Capitol. Anna had no idea how crazy he could be.

Her purse vibrated with a series of short bursts. Her BlackBerry was probably the most diplomatic way out of this uncomfortable situation. She would fake an emergency and hightail it out of here. "Please excuse me," she said. She brushed past him and went to one of the tables and set down her coffee. While she dug through her purse, Vale stood exactly where she'd left him, watching her intently.

Anna pulled out her BlackBerry and saw that the buzz was from voice messages landing in her in-box. The calls must have been made while she was in the gym shower, blocked by the lead walls of the National Security section. She scrolled through her call log: two from Samantha and one from Jack, but just one message, from Sam. Was Jack calling because he missed her? She would deal with her personal life later. She checked Sam's message.

"Anna, this is Samantha. You're not going to

believe this. Vale was stalking Caroline, just like we thought. Now he's stalking *you*. Call me right away."

A shot of adrenaline sparked through her gut. She turned around to see where Vale was—as he slid up next to her. He smiled at her.

"So," he said. "You guys find the killer yet?"

Anna jumped back. "We're following all available leads." She swallowed back a lump of fear. "I'm sorry, but like I said, I can't talk about it."

"I can help you, you know." Vale again walked into the space she'd vacated. "I have more information you'll want to hear."

"Uh-huh." Anna abandoned her coffee and walked toward the entrance of the museum. She shot a glance at the guard, fifty yards away across the open courtyard. Still sleeping. Should she run or shout? She didn't think she could outrun Vale.

"About Madeleine Connor," Vale continued. "It wasn't a suicide. She was murdered."

Anna wanted to get away from him, but she wished she could record what he was saying. Her BlackBerry was in her hand. Keeping Vale's pale blue eyes fixed with hers, she fumbled with the keypad, trying to call back Samantha.

"What makes you say Madeleine Connor was murdered?" she asked. She tried to compose her face into an innocent, interested expression.

"I saw it. Not the murder, but right before. I have proof."

Anna hit the green *send* button on the BlackBerry.

"We're a good team," Vale said, smiling. His breath smelled stale. She wondered when was the last time he'd brushed his teeth. "We get each other. I'll be your source, like Deep Throat. Solving crimes by day, doing . . . other things by night."

He reached out and lightly stroked Anna's shoulder. She flinched, pulling her shoulder away from his touch. She could hear the BlackBerry down by her waist as her phone call rang to Sam's cell. She walked a little faster. She and Vale were halfway to the museum entrance.

"Who are you calling?" Vale asked, looking down at the BlackBerry in her hand. His voice grew suspicious. "You're not calling my lawyer, are you?"

Anna heard Sam's tinny voice pick up on the other end of the line.

"Anna? Are you okay?"

Anna drew the phone to her ear and spoke with fake cheer. "Hi, Agent Randazzo, it's Anna. I'm at the Building Museum, and Brett Vale is here. You remember Brett, right? From Congressman Lionel's office?" She forced a smile at Vale.

"What the fuck!" Vale smacked the BlackBerry to the ground. It thunked on the carpet. "Are you even listening to me? I don't want to talk to the FBI! I want to talk to you."

"Calm down," Anna said. She reached down for the BlackBerry, but Vale kicked it away. As she stood up, he was in her face.

"You calm down, you bitch! Don't you tell me what to do!" Spittle flecked her face as he shouted. "I try to help you, and you call the FBI? Un-fucking-believable! You're just like Sasha!"

"Hey, there, kids, there's no call for that!"

The deep baritone of the museum guard came from behind Anna. Vale's eyes went wildly from the big guard to her.

"She's my girlfriend," Vale told the guard. "It's okay."

He clamped a hand on Anna's wrist and pulled her toward the front door. The guard seemed confused.

"I'm not your girlfriend, you crazy asshole." She twisted her wrist out of his grasp.

She ran to the guard, who looked bewildered. She stood behind his bulk and wondered if he was armed.

Vale stared at her, his eyes furious and manic. She could tell he was contemplating another swipe at her, even with the guard between them. He was unhinged.

"You bitch," Vale said in a low voice. "This is not done. This is so not done between us."

He spun around and ran out of the museum.

"You okay, miss?" The guard looked more frightened than she felt, and that was saying a lot.

"I'm fine." Anna nodded, although her hands were trembling. She pointed a shaky finger. "He's getting away." The guard made no effort to follow him.

Through the glass door, Anna saw Vale throw himself into a tiny silver Smart car parked at the curb. As he sped off, she ran outside and tried to note his license number.

Then she ran back into the atrium and found where her BlackBerry had been kicked. She picked it up. "Sam?"

"Yes, I'm still here! Are you all right?"

"Yeah. Vale's in a silver Smart car, heading west on F Street."

# 46

Jack rubbed his wrists where the handcuffs had pinched, while the officer apologized for the third time. "I'm so sorry, Mr. Bailey! We got a call for an intruder here."

"It's okay." Jack forgave him for the third time. "We won't need a beer summit."

It wasn't this kid's fault. Jack blamed the nosy neighbor next door. Even she wasn't so unreasonable. Jack didn't live here. Wearing jeans and an old T-shirt, digging through Anna's potted plants, he must've looked fairly suspicious.

The patrol officer held out his cell phone. "Detective McGee wants to talk to you, okay?"

"Sure." Jack took the phone from the rookie. He'd suggested that the kid call McGee to confirm his identity. "Bailey."

"Hey, Chief, you want me to work on expunging that arrest?" McGee chuckled. "Maybe I can call in a favor, get you community service. You'd look good in an orange vest, picking up trash on the Beltway."

This was just the beginning of the ribbing Jack would take for the incident. He sighed. "Luckily, it was just a stop-and-frisk, but I appreciate the gesture. Is there any word on Anna?"

"She's fine. I'm walking her into the office right now, matter of fact. You wanna talk to her?" He heard McGee's muffled voice saying, "It's Jack."

"No, that's okay," Jack said. "Just tell her—"

"Tell me what?" Anna asked from the other side of the line.

"Ah, hi, Anna." He paused, sorting out his thoughts. "I'm glad to hear you're okay. I was worried about you. I mean, everyone was worried."

"Thanks, I'm fine," Anna said. She was silent long enough that Jack thought she might have hung up. "How's Olivia?"

"Okay. She misses you."

"Now I know you're lying."

There was much more he wanted to say to her. He wanted to tell her what he'd realized as he walked through her empty apartment, wondering if he'd see her again. How much he loved her and needed her. But he couldn't make the words come together. He stood there, holding the officer's cell phone to his ear, listening to Anna's silence on the other end.

"Well, it's been good talking to you," Anna said.

"Right. You, too."

Jack hung up. He shepherded the rookie cop out of Anna's basement apartment. Then he filled up a glass to water her plants.

Anna handed the cell phone back to McGee and tried not to let the wistfulness show on her face. But McGee was too good at reading body language.

"You know," the big detective said softly, "he doesn't go running like that for anybody else."

"I know."

She realized McGee had intuited just about everything there was to know about her and Jack's relationship. She tried not to let him see her blush. He smiled, clamped a big hand on her shoulder, and escorted her through the lobby, up the elevator, and to her office. He held out the chair for her to sit.

"I should make a habit of this," Anna said. "I feel like a princess."

"Wait till you see all the paperwork this morning is gonna cost you. That'll make you feel like a frog again."

Before she did anything else, she needed to call Caroline's mother. Donna McBride had the right to know what was happening before it hit the news. With McGee sitting in her office, Anna dialed the McBrides' number.

Donna McBride answered the phone. Anna told her that she had some new information and asked if she wanted to meet in person.

"Please tell me now," Donna said. "I don't want to spend half the day wondering."

So Anna told her what they'd found out about how Caroline was killed: how Caroline believed she was going to meet a congressman that night, how Vale had been stalking her, the fact that he'd bought her a ring and was planning to propose. As Anna spoke, Donna McBride cried softly into the phone.

But it was a different kind of crying than three days ago. There was relief in it. Hard as it was to hear what happened, there was a comfort that could only come from knowing. When Donna stopped crying, she said simply, "Thank you."

# 47

Sam sped the Durango south on 14th Street, lights and sirens going. Morning rush-hour traffic clogged the street. Although some cars pulled aside to let her through, many sat in her way. Samantha honked and veered around a minivan. "Tell 'em we'll be there in under a minute," she said to Quisenberry, keeping her eyes on the road.

Quisenberry nodded and repeated the information to the Metropolitan Police Department.

The BOLO had quickly gotten a hit. An MPD officer driving around the Capitol had seen the silver Smart car heading west on Independence Avenue by the Botanical Gardens. The officer was following the Smart car with lights and sirens. But Vale wasn't pulling over; he had sped up. And the officer was losing him. MPD officers were prohibited from engaging in high-speed chases.

Sam turned onto Independence Avenue and headed east. She would intercept Vale. The Smithsonian Castle was coming up on the left when Samantha spotted the silver Smart car—with the MPD cruiser following—heading toward her. Blaring her horn, she swung the Durango across the two left lanes, so its big black body blocked the oncoming traffic.

Vale had no intention of stopping. He swerved the Smart car around the Durango onto the sidewalk. A family of tourists screamed and dove out of the way. Samantha cursed. This was tourist central. The Castle was the information center for all the other Smithsonian museums on the Mall.

A black iron fence surrounded the Castle, with a stone gate providing an opening to the brick walkway and gardens. The gate's opening was about the size of a man's wingspan. Vale zipped his little Smart car right through the gate and kept going, out of sight.

"Fuck!" Samantha hit the steering wheel in frustration. The Durango wouldn't fit there. Neither would the MPD cruiser. "Get the helicopter," she said to Steve.

"On it." He spoke quietly into his cell phone.

Sam straightened the SUV and sped down to 7th Street, hooked a left, then turned left onto Jefferson Drive, which ran parallel to Independence Avenue, on the other side of the Castle. There was the Smart car, speeding west. Sam sped after him. The long grassy expanse of the National Mall was on their right.

As she drove after him, she could hear other sirens approaching. Two marked MPD cruisers came toward them from the west. They parked in the middle of Jefferson Drive, blocking the street. That hadn't stopped Vale before, and it didn't stop him now. The Smart car hopped the sidewalk again, sending sparks flying as the bumper hit the concrete. Then it drove north across the Mall.

"Lunatic," Samantha said. She steered the SUV up the sidewalk and followed the Smart car onto the grass. She had to swerve around a pair of joggers on a gravel path.

"This seem like a good idea to you?" Quisenberry asked, holding the door handle as the SUV bounced and swerved.

"Of course not," Samantha said, and pressed harder on the accelerator.

Vale's Smart car had nothing on the Durango when

it came to driving on grass. The SUV gained on the Smart car as it cut across the park. Another broad gravel sidewalk sliced through the north side of the park. Accelerating, Vale tried to turn on the gravel. His tiny car skidded sideways. Samantha could see the wheels turning back and forth as Vale struggled for control. He never got it. His car plowed through a park bench, splintering the wooden slats and sending pigeons flying in every direction. Then it lodged itself into a hundred-year-old elm.

Sam parked on the grass a few feet away.

"That is why we don't do car chases," Quisenberry said, unbuckling his seat belt.

"What?" Samantha said innocently, climbing out of the truck. "No one was sitting on the bench."

A silver door flashed open, and Vale's long, lean figure shot out of the car. He ran north, cut across Madison Drive, and sprinted up the sidewalk in front of the Natural History Museum. He merged into the crowd of tourists going up the museum's steps.

"You take the car," Samantha shouted to Quisenberry. She took off running. "Police, stop!"

They couldn't shoot at Vale, not when he was in a crowd of civilians, not when he wasn't an imminent threat to anyone. She had to catch him. Her high heels were Rockports for exactly this purpose. Sexy on the outside, running shoes on the inside.

Vale sprinted up the steps to the Natural History Museum. He was fast, but Samantha was a trained FBI agent. She was faster. She closed the distance between them and caught up to him in the domed lobby, where a mounted elephant held its trunk jubilantly in the air.

She tackled Vale. He was tall but light and not used

to physical combat. Samantha easily brought him to the ground. She stuck a knee in his back and cuffed his hands behind him while dozens of astonished tourists gaped.

"Your tax dollars at work!" Samantha smiled at a tour group of old ladies as she hauled Vale to his feet and led him out of the museum.

# 48

ongratulations!" Grace yelled over the din of the restaurant.

A dozen pomegranate margaritas were raised over the white tablecloths and clinked together; some pink liquid splashed into candles glowing inside rose-petal globes. The drinkers laughed and shouted. Anna tipped her glass back and let the tart icy drink go down her throat.

They were in the bar of Rosa Mexicano. Thousands of rose petals were pressed between glass panels covering the walls and ceiling, illuminated from behind. Handsome Latin waiters crushed avocados into fresh guacamole in stone bowls. A wall of windows overlooked the flashing lights of Chinatown. Grace had pushed four tall, round tables into a line, and Anna and Samantha sat at the head, surrounded by sex-offense prosecutors and FBI agents. Grace had herded the AUSAs here; Samantha had brought the agents. It was a good mix. Most sex-crime prosecutors were female, and most FBI agents were male. It made for some fun interagency flirting, which Anna watched with amusement.

The bar kept filling up. McGee brought a loud contingent of MPD detectives. Tony Randazzo arrived and gave Anna a quick congratulatory hug. He sat next to his sister and immediately began razzing her about a picture of her being shown on TV. Anna smiled at the siblings, who were obviously close despite their teasing. She wished Jody could be here, too. In fact, Jody and Tony might hit it off.

As word of the happy hour got out, more lawyers, officers, and agents piled in. Each stopped over to congratulate them. Typical for lawyers, everyone wanted to hear—and opine on—every detail of the case.

"Tell ya the truth, I'm glad it wasn't Lionel." McGee came over with a beer in his hand. "The Lion's been standing up for this city since I was a boy." He slapped Anna on the back and chuckled. "Now I owe you two drinks! You cleared two of my homicides with one arrest."

"Don't chalk up the second stat yet," Anna said, finishing the last sip of her first margarita. Grace immediately set another in front of her. "We don't know that Vale killed the madam."

"Are you kidding me?" McGee hooted. "He had the motive—the madam would have told us he was stalking Caroline. He had the opportunity—he was at her house. The proof's on his own camera."

The TV above the bar played the news. It showed a photo from some tourist's cell phone of Samantha leading Vale down the steps of the museum. The agent looked gorgeous and fierce, her dark curls windblown, her cheeks flushed from the chase. Vale's face was contorted in rage.

Tony nudged his sister and pointed at the TV. "See, you look like a badass."

"I'm amazed you can run in those heels," Anna said.

"Running was the easy part," Samantha said, scooping guacamole on a chip. "Quisenberry's never gonna let me drive again."

"Wise man." Tony turned to Anna. "Congratulations on making it through your first case with my sister. That alone is a major accomplishment."

"She's great." Anna smiled at Samantha. "Once you get past the rough edges."

"Rough edges is right," Tony said. "Sam once dumped a plate of linguine on a customer who pinched her ass."

Anna covered her mouth so she didn't splutter margarita as she laughed.

"That's why I had to go into law enforcement," Sam said. "Mom fired me."

Soon Tony and Anna were engrossed in an animated conversation. He was easy to talk to and easy to look at. She leaned back and tried to soak it all in: Here she was, a victorious lawyer, a free woman, out with friends and flirting with a cute guy.

Somehow, though, it felt like she was trying to convince herself what a great time she was having instead of actually having it.

She really did like Tony. He had recently bought Sergio's from his parents, he told her. He described his plans for renovating the restaurant and modernizing the menu. She was impressed.

"But you've gotta keep those eggplant patties!" she said. "They're the best."

"Tell you what," Tony replied. "Come over Saturday night. I'll whip up some of my new creations for you. You can be my menu consultant."

Samantha interrupted. "Are you asking my lawyer out on a date?"

"It's not a date," Tony said. "It's just an opportunity for us to get to know each other a little better in a private, romantic setting."

Anna laughed. He really was a great-looking guy, with thick dark hair and liquid black eyes shining with humor. And he was a good cook—she was sure his new dishes would be terrific. At some other point in her life, she would have loved to go out with him.

It didn't feel right now. She knew it didn't make any sense, but—it felt like she'd be cheating on Jack.

"That sounds delicious," she said. "But I'm just getting out of a relationship. I'm not in the right place now."

"I understand. Things like that take time." He glanced at his watch. "I'll ask you again in a few minutes."

Samantha gave Tony a shove toward the bar. "Go get us some drinks, Romeo."

The TV by the bar switched to a shot of the prosecution team leaving the federal courthouse three days earlier, after the Speech or Debate Clause hearing. There were Jack and Anna towing their wheeled briefcases behind them. Jack looked professional and intimidating as he no-commented his way past the reporters. Anna walked next to him, occasionally glancing at his face. Watching her image on TV now, it was obvious that she was in love with him. How could she have thought she could hide it from their colleagues? She remembered what she'd felt when they walked out that day—overwhelmed by the reporters but knowing that whatever else happened, she and Jack were a team facing the world together.

The newscasters praised the investigators on how quickly they'd found the alleged killer. For Anna, it was a professional dream. She was getting the respect she'd craved from her fellow prosecutors. She was a hero in a very public way. And here she was, out with her friends at Rosa Mexicano, drinking the pomegranate margaritas she'd missed when she spent her nights at Jack's house. It was exactly what she'd wanted a few days ago.

She didn't feel the glow of satisfaction that she'd expected. She felt oddly empty.

"Something's bothering you." Samantha broke in on her reverie. "What is it? This is our night."

"I was thinking Jack should be here."

"Did you guys break up?"

"What makes you think we were dating?"

"Give me a little credit."

Anna nodded. Even the barista had guessed.

"You want to tell me what happened?" Samantha asked, with uncharacteristic softness.

Anna didn't often talk about her personal life with her colleagues, but she found herself telling Samantha about Jack. Maybe it was the margaritas, or the camaraderie they'd built up over the last few days. Samantha was a good listener. Anna found it a relief to finally tell the agent. She wondered how much easier her whole relationship with Jack would've been if she'd been open about it from the beginning—if she'd shared and celebrated it with her friends instead of hiding it from them. When Anna finished, Samantha put a hand on her arm.

"I've known Jack for a while," Samantha said. "He has a bear of a temper. But he'll eventually admit when he's wrong. Sometimes it just takes him a while to figure it out."

Anna nodded. When Jack first broke up with her, she'd thought he would come to realize his mistake. Now she felt a growing fear that *she* had been wrong. She had been wrong to contradict him in front of the DOJ bigwigs. Sure, she could hold her own opinion, but she should have expressed it more forcefully to him in private. In public, she should have had his back.

She was also starting to think she was wrong to conceal their relationship. The Discretion escorts concealed their liaisons because they were paid to do it. Why had Anna treated her relationship with Jack the same way? At the time, she thought it was helping her career, helping her get the respect of her colleagues and peers. Now that she had the respect of her colleagues and peers, she realized that she wanted something more.

She wanted *Jack's* respect. She wasn't sure whether she'd had it before, but she was sure she had lost it now.

Tony returned to the table with another round of pomegranate margaritas. Anna thanked him but took just one sip. She'd fall asleep right here if she had a third drink.

"Hey," Samantha said. "Have you seen Vale's photos of you yet?"

"No." Though everyone had been talking about them, she hadn't laid eyes on them herself. "The idea makes my skin crawl."

"So you don't want to see them?" Samantha took out her BlackBerry and scrolled to a file. "I had the tech-support folks e-mail them to me."

"Am I going to have nightmares after this? You should be shouting, 'Shut your eyes, Anna, don't look at it no matter what happens.'"

The two women leaned their heads together to look at the photos one by one. There was Anna, walking all around the city, oblivious to the fact that a man was watching her, following her, photographing her. She shuddered at the thought of Vale so close yet hidden from her sight, clicking away.

Although his demeanor at the interview had been strange, she'd never contemplated that she could be personally at risk. She knew that one in twelve American women would be stalked in their lifetime. Somehow, as a prosecutor, she'd felt immune. She'd taken this job in part to escape the violence of her childhood, and now she expected to be on the other side of it. It was a painful reminder that anyone, including her, could be a target.

Sam opened another photo, but it was a picture of Madeleine's house, not Anna.

"Wait." Anna put her hand on Sam's BlackBerry.

Something about the mansion lit up at night caught her attention. She studied it. Zooming in on the high-resolution image, she could see a lot of detail. She could read the license plates of cars parked at the curb in front of Madeleine's townhouse. She saw a gray cat slipping through the bushes. And there, through a first-floor window on the side of the house, she could see a glimpse of the brightly lit sitting room. Anna could make out the madam's figure sitting at the desk where she'd been shot.

There was something more. On the wall was a dark shadow of a person that didn't match up to Madeleine's seated figure. Someone had been standing in the room with her. While Vale was outside taking pictures.

Anna remembered one of the cryptic things Vale had said at the Building Museum. *I saw it . . . I have proof.* He had seen someone else in the house with Madeleine.

Anna told Samantha about Vale's words as they looked at the shadow in the photograph. They zoomed in on the sitting-room window.

There, on Madeleine's desk, sat a little greenish-gray

block. Right where the blood spatter had been absent. Anna couldn't make it out, but that was the beauty of digital photos. "Keep zooming," she said. Sam enlarged that part of the picture until just the top of Madeleine's desk filled the screen.

The hair on the back of Anna's neck seemed to become electrified.

"Holy shit," Sam said.

The item on Madeleine's desk was unmistakably a brick of cash. Five little bundles stacked on top of one another, each with a mustard-colored currency strap.

"Mustard straps mean hundred-dollar bills," Samantha murmured. "A hundred of them."

Fifty thousand dollars had been sitting on the desk when Madeleine was shot. The money wasn't there when the police processed the crime scene. It hadn't been at Vale's house or in his car.

Anna and Sam looked at each other and pushed their margaritas away at the same time. They were celebrating too soon.

Through the haze of tequila, Anna tried to puzzle it out, like a difficult logic game. Why did Madeleine have a huge chunk of cash on her desk right before she died? Where was the money now? And who was the unseen person casting the shadow on Madeleine's wall?

She wasn't sure she would like the answers.

# Friday

# 49

Waking up in her basement apartment, Anna didn't feel at home anymore. The water pressure in her shower was weaker than she remembered, and she didn't have any shampoo. She washed her face with a dried sliver of soap she pried off the shower caddy and hoped that the tiny glob of conditioner she coaxed out of an old bottle would be enough to clean her hair. Most of her toiletries were at Jack's house. Even her cat was there. She hadn't realized the full extent to which she'd abandoned her single life until she found herself single again.

She dried herself with a crunchy towel and stepped into the steamy windowless bathroom. The only noise in the apartment was the muffled banter between Matt Lauer and Ann Curry. She'd turned on the TV to have background noise in the uncomfortably quiet apartment. She missed the cheerful patter of Jack getting his daughter ready in the morning. She missed the glow of morning sunshine through the Victorian's stained-glass windows. She even missed Olivia's pranks. Had her basement apartment always been this dark and lonely? She supposed so. She just hadn't had anything to compare it with. Now she knew what she was missing.

As she wrapped her wet hair in a towel turban, she heard NBC4, the local station, interrupting the *Today* show for some breaking news: Congressman Emmett Lionel was holding a press conference. Anna threw on a bathrobe and hurried to the TV in the living room.

She got there in time to watch Lionel take the

stage with Betty at his side. It was the same setting as his press conference a few days ago. But it was a totally different atmosphere. Gone were Lionel's angry posturing and blazing eyes, replaced with a defeated slump. Betty maintained a placid expression but with a new sag to her chin; she seemed to have aged a few years in the past few days.

"Good morning," Lionel said. Though his face was solemn, his deep voice quavered. "I would like to thank everyone who has supported me over the years and especially during the last difficult week. It has meant the world to Betty and me. So it is with regret that I announce I will not seek another term in office. As you all know, I have been completely cleared in the recent investigation. But I exercised poor judgment in my associations."

Anna wasn't sure whether he was referring to hiring Vale or his own affairs with escorts. He didn't elaborate.

"The investigation has taken a toll on me and on my family. My first duty must be to my family now, to help them heal after this very difficult time. I will step down at the end of this term."

Reporters shouted, but Lionel waved them off. He wasn't taking questions. He held Betty's hand, and they walked off the stage together.

Now that the case against Lionel was over, Anna had expected celebration from the Congressman's camp, maybe even some gloating. Davenport had graciously issued a public statement praising the USAO for clearing his client, and he had withdrawn all of his motions. She hadn't expected another tearful press conference or for Lionel to step down.

The talking heads chewed over the announcement

with relish. No one believed the Congressman's bromide about wanting to spend more time with his family. But the stories about his affairs were continuing to emerge. His trusted adviser was practically a serial killer. The consensus was that Lionel's reputation was too stained for him to ride out the scandal. The only way to avoid further humiliation was to step down.

Lionel's resignation left one serious candidate in the Democratic primary, which was only five weeks away: Dylan Youngblood. In a town as Democratic as Washington, D.C., that meant Youngblood would be the next congressman. And Jack was the presumptive next U.S. Attorney.

Just in time for Anna to move her things out of his house.

Anna sighed and went to the kitchen. There was nothing to eat. She smiled, imagining the concoctions Olivia might be making from the full cabinets at Jack's house. Anna realized that she would rather be helping the little girl than puttering around her own empty apartment. After all those mornings of missing the peace and quiet of her place, it was a surprising discovery. She fished in her cabinet until she found an unopened bag of Mayorga espresso. When she turned to the coffeemaker, she saw the yellow Post-it note with Jack's handwriting.

She plucked the note off the glass pot and read it several times. *Anna, I love you. I'm sorry. Call me.* He must have left it there when he came here yesterday. It wasn't the first time he'd dropped everything to run to her aid. She sat down at the kitchen table and looked at the note for a long time.

She wanted to call him. No, she wanted to go to his house. At this time of morning, he was usually in the shower. She imagined letting herself into the bathroom, taking off her clothes, and climbing into the steam. She smiled and ached, thinking about the look on his face as she pressed her breasts against his soapy back and said hello. She still loved him.

But if she went back to him, it would have to be for good. He didn't want a girlfriend to play around with; he wanted a wife and a mother for his daughter. She had no idea how to be a good wife or mother. She didn't know how to keep her own identity while being a supportive partner and parent. She might never be like Eva Youngblood, able to throw fund-raisers for Dylan one day while throwing down mock attackers on another.

She couldn't reconcile with Jack unless she was ready to marry him. And she didn't know if she ever would be.

She stuck the note on the fridge. Then she went to the bedroom and pulled out the best suit still hanging in her closet, a black sheath dress with a matching jacket. She put it on, then made herself look as nice as possible with the limited toiletries remaining in her apartment. It was going to be a big day.

Samantha was waiting for Anna in the war room, surrounded by stacks of papers and to-go coffee cups. When Anna walked in, Samantha pushed one of the coffee cups toward her. "Latte for you."

"Thanks!" Anna was touched by the gesture from an agent who hadn't even wanted her on the case a few days ago. "How long have you been here?"

"Awhile. I ran all the license plates from the cars on Madeleine's street in Vale's photo." Samantha thumped a stack of papers. "They're all just neighbors.

And I went through Vale's bank records. There's no sign of the fifty thousand."

"Like Jack would say, nothing in a homicide case is going to be that easy."

"Any other ideas?"

"Yeah, I was thinking about this all night. Maybe Vale was telling the truth—maybe whoever he saw in the house killed Madeleine and took the money. Could be they stuck it in a mattress. But they also might've deposited it in a bank. Is there a way to run a records check on local banks and see if anyone deposited fifty thousand dollars or so in the last few days?"

A smile grew on Sam's face. "We can pull the CTRs."

"Walk me through that."

"Currency Transaction Reports. Banks are required to file a report for all cash transactions over ten thousand dollars. Deposits, withdrawals, cashing checks, whatever."

"Can we get the CTRs for the last two days?"

"Probably. By law, the bank has to file a CTR within thirty days of the transaction. But these days banks usually file electronically as soon as the transaction is made."

"Let's try it."

Sam pulled up a database run by the Treasury Department's Financial Crimes Enforcement Network. "FinCEN received more than fourteen million CTRs last year. That's about forty thousand a day. But if we limit it to the D.C. region, we're talking about—" Samantha typed a couple of keystrokes. "Ugh. About five thousand CTRs for the past two days."

"Too many."

"It's a lot. But doable. I've had a team of analysts

going through the calls to Madeleine's burner phone, identifying the callers. I'll have them turn to this instead. But what are we looking for, exactly?"

"I don't know. Deposits of fifty thousand or so, I guess. By people with a motive to kill Madeleine. Peal, Belinda, whatever johns your analysts have identified. Is there a computer program that can cross-reference Madeleine's phone records against the CTR database?"

"Ha. Design that program, and you can retire a millionaire. No, the analysts have to do it one by one. But that's what they do. When you see my SAC, thank him profusely for all the resources he's put into this case."

Anna nodded. She knew that the "vast resources of the federal government" often meant a couple of underpaid analysts toiling for long hours in a cubicle. This was the part of a criminal investigation that was quietly heroic and not amenable to TV depictions like on *Law & Order*. It was slow, unglamorous, meticulous work. But agents like Samantha and her team, toiling painstakingly over pages of fine print, were the ones who made the big breaks in cases like this.

At nine-fifteen that morning, Anna sat in the front row of a magistrate's courtroom in U.S. District Court. At the prosecution's table was Harold Schwarzendruber, the veteran homicide prosecutor who'd been assigned to take Jack's place on the team. Anna was no longer a prosecutor on Vale's case, since he had attacked her. But she wasn't going to miss his arraignment.

Vale stood with his public defender but craned his neck to stare balefully at Anna. His hands were cuffed in front of him, and he wore an orange prison uniform. He had a newly black eye, and his pale hands clawed at the cuffs. Prison didn't agree with him. But he would be there for the foreseeable future. The fact that he was arrested after leading the police on a high-speed chase branded him a risk of flight. The court-room clerk read the charges against him: The lead charge was the murder of Caroline McBride.

The former LD opened his mouth to say something to Anna, but his lawyer was on top of things. The lawyer clamped a hand on Vale's arm and whispered forcefully in his ear. Vale shook his head, seeming to disagree, but he stayed quiet, just glaring back at Anna periodically.

The public defender announced that his client pleaded not guilty to all charges. He might change his plea later, but it was unlikely. He had too much to lose.

*You were right,* Anna thought as she met Vale's eyes. *This isn't done between us. Not by a long shot.* She would testify against him at trial.

Harold suggested that Vale be given a psychological evaluation at the jail, and the judge ordered it. The judge also wanted to know whether the prosecution would bring further charges against Vale, for killing Madeleine Connor. Harold turned back to Anna. She whispered to him that they were still working on the question of who had killed Madeleine Connor. Harold stood back up and said, "It's an ongoing investigation."

The judge set a trial date, and the arraignment was over. Vale's lawyer followed him through a side door to the cell behind the courtroom, and Anna headed out the traditional doors into the wide hallways of U.S. District Court. Harold stayed behind—he had another appearance in the courtroom this morning.

As Anna walked to the curving stairs, a bunch of reporters surrounded her. They asked questions in low, subdued voices. Federal court had that effect on people.

"Can you tell us how the investigation led to Brett Vale?" one reporter asked.

She wasn't supposed to say anything to the press about a pending case. But Anna stopped when she got to the edge of the marble atrium. She decided to give one quote.

"We had a great team from the FBI and MPD, including Special Agent Samantha Randazzo and Detective Tavon McGee," Anna said. "They're tireless and talented investigators. And the credit for the legal work should go to Jack Bailey. He's a fair and honest prosecutor."

She walked on.

By the time she got back to her office, there was a voice mail waiting for her from acting U.S. Attorney Marty Zinn. "Anna, please come to my office as soon as possible."

She'd known she would get into trouble when she made the statement to the press; she'd just wondered how much. She headed down to the fifth floor like a woman heading to her execution. But Marty greeted her with a big smile as he pointed for her to sit in one of his guest chairs.

"Congratulations on the arrest," he said. "You must be delighted."

"Thanks," she said cautiously. "I am."

"We've all been impressed with how you handled the case."

Anna nodded, waiting for the "but."

"And I'd like to offer you a promotion," Marty said. "There's an opening in the Homicide section doing cold cases. As you know, it's a specialty position, usually reserved for a senior prosecutor. But I think you'd be a great fit."

"Wow, I'm flattered." Anna paused, considering how to handle the offer.

Marty took it as a cue to keep persuading her. "I spoke to Jack yesterday. He's looking to get more female prosecutors in the section. Offering more flexible hours, part-time options, that sort of thing."

Anna raised her eyebrows with surprise. Jack hadn't told her about the changes. But he had taken her suggestion after all.

"That's wonderful," she said. "I'm happy to hear that Jack's going to be more flexible."

"So will you take the cold-case position?"

It was one of the most prestigious positions in the Superior Court section of her office. The woman who'd held it before was a highly respected older attorney who'd left to become a judge. Marty's offer was a major vote of confidence. Everyone would take her seriously if she were the cold-case prosecutor.

"Who would be my supervisor?" Anna asked.

"Jack."

"Then I'm sorry, but I can't do it."

"Why? I thought you two got along well."

"We do. Problem is . . ." She considered the implications of what she was about to say. "I'm in love with him."

Marty squirmed and looked away. Although discussions about romance had to come up periodically in an office of five hundred employees, he clearly had not anticipated one now.

"Er, I see. Does Jack—um—reciprocate your feelings?"

A nervous bubble of laughter rose in her throat. She swallowed it back down. "I really don't know at this point. But I know I can't be supervised by him."

"Okay. Well. Thanks for letting me know. I'm sure Carla will be happy to keep you in the Sex Crimes unit."

The meeting came to a quick close after that. Her statement to the press never came up.

It was almost the end of the day when Samantha walked into Anna's office with some papers and a grin. "We got a hit!" she announced. "The analysts are still working, but there's one CTR by someone whose phone called the madam. You'll never guess who it is."

"Belinda?"

Sam shook her head and handed Anna a printout from the database. The transaction was a withdrawal of fifty thousand dollars on Tuesday from a Bank of America on Wisconsin Avenue. Anna had been expecting a deposit, not a withdrawal. But she was more surprised by the bank account from which the withdrawal had been made. It was Dylan Youngblood's family checking account.

"How many times did Youngblood call the madam?" Anna asked.

"Dozens. From his home and his personal cell phone. He was a regular customer of Discretion."

Anna rubbed her temples. The Youngbloods seemed to have such a perfect marriage. She wanted to believe that was real, although she'd seen signs that it was under strain. Poor Eva.

"We need more female politicians," Anna said.

"Amen."

Anna gazed out the window at the abstract globe rotating on the roof of the National Academy of Sciences building. She imagined herself in Dylan Youngblood's shoes—a rising-star politician in a hotly contested election with a madam about to disclose records showing all the illegal extramarital sex he'd had. Dylan could have tried to bribe the madam to keep her quiet. Or killed her. Or both.

"Can we find out more about the transaction?" Anna asked. "Maybe he talked to somebody at the bank?"

One subpoena and ninety minutes of wrangling later, Bank of America gave them one more piece of information. The day after the cash was withdrawn, Eva went to the bank and accessed her safe-deposit box.

Anna mulled that over. Why was Eva going to the safe-deposit box? Anna wanted to see what was in there. She weighed whether they had enough evidence to get a search warrant for the box.

"I don't think we have enough for probable cause yet," she concluded with disappointment.

"No," Samantha agreed. "But we definitely have enough to have a little talk with the Youngbloods."

Sam reached for the phone. Anna put her hand over Sam's, keeping the phone in its cradle.

"Wait," she said.

She had an idea.

# 50

Eva looked around the house, her hostess radar on high alert for anything out of place. This was the biggest fund-raiser they'd throw all season, and everything had to be perfect. But it wasn't. Everywhere she looked, something was out of place, or smudged, or just wrong.

Their house was an airy contemporary with walls of glass on the perimeter of every room. It wasn't huge, but everyone in D.C. knew how much a home on Military Road—walking distance to the Friendship Heights Metro—was worth. The white-on-white decor was accented with stark contemporary art; the modern furniture was from Room & Board; the overall look was clean, dramatic, and bold. But the maid had left the accent pillows on the couches, despite Eva's specific instructions. Did she have to do everything herself? She stuffed the offending pillows into the hall closet.

A steel table in the foyer held a large clear vase of white calla lilies that were starting to wilt. That's what she got for ordering the cheapest thing in stock. Eva tried to arrange them so the browner ones were in back. Small Japanese ceramic plates held the smoked almonds that Eva put out at every party. Salt made people drink, which loosened their wallets. The caterer would pass equally salty hors d'oeuvres during the cocktail hour. Nothing too fancy—the goal of the affair was to raise money, not spend it.

Eva walked to the wall of sliding-glass windows at

the back of the house and scowled at the white tent that covered the yard. The laborers hadn't finished putting together the dance floor. She wished they'd hurry. She'd arranged for three rented chandeliers to hang from the three peaks inside the tent, which lent the tent an extravagant air at a slight cost. Dozens of dinner tables were covered with white tablecloths, votive candles, more calla lilies, and four hundred settings with Styrofoam plates and plastic cutlery. At five hundred dollars a head, they would raise a mint.

They needed it. Dylan had exhausted the funds in his campaign account a month ago. For the past month, the Youngbloods had been lending their own money to his campaign. And Dylan had to spend twice as much as Lionel just to be competitive with the veteran politician.

After the fortune spent on television ads, radio spots, polling, lawn signs, bus placards, flyers, and other chum, Dylan had begun to poll within striking distance. But it was not until Lionel's scandal that Dylan had pulled ahead. Now that Lionel had dropped out of the race, donors were practically lining up to give money to the presumptive next congressman from the District of Columbia. People wanted to give to the winner. Dylan had raised more in the past eight hours than during the last month. After tonight, Eva hoped, the campaign would be back in the black. She felt an electric bolt of pride at her contribution to her husband's success.

Eva glanced at her watch: five-fifteen P.M. The caterers were late. The valet parking service and the band were supposed to arrive in thirty minutes, the guests in an hour and fifteen. Time to get dressed.

As she climbed the steps, she could hear her

husband talking on the phone in the second bedroom, his home office. A political campaign required 100 percent of the politician's effort, much of it devoted to raising money. Dylan spent hours in that little room, calling friends, family, acquaintances, anyone he'd ever met, and asking for checks up to twenty-five hundred, the maximum allowable by law.

"Of course," he said. His voice sounded puzzled and uncertain, not the tone he usually used to make his political pitch. "Yes. I mean no, I can't do it tonight. We're having a fund-raiser at our house."

Eva stopped in his doorway. Dylan sat at the steel and glass desk in his usual position, phone to ear. With his sandy hair going gray at the temples and the light tan acquired from picnic fund-raisers, he was better-looking than when they'd met eleven years ago. He was staring down at a legal pad. She knocked on the doorframe to get his attention. He looked up, and she impatiently pointed to her watch: Time to get dressed. The party was black-tie-optional; Dylan would trade his suit for a tux. He nodded and looked back down at his pad.

In the master bedroom, she took off her Diesel jeans and button-down shirt and threw them on a chair. She'd specifically worn this shirt to the hairdresser so that she wouldn't ruin her sleek updo when she undressed. She'd also had her makeup professionally done at the salon. She didn't like the smoky eyes and full red lips they'd painted on her, but it was too late to change it now.

She admired her semi-nude figure as she walked past the full-length mirror. Daily workouts and teaching self-defense classes made her petite body more buff than most political wives'. She had well-defined muscles on her arms and legs, a flat stomach, and a toned butt. She walked into the large walk-in closet attached to the master bedroom. When they'd bought the house, they'd thought this room would be a nursery. Now she had no baby, just a walk-in closet, her figure, and the time to focus on her career—Dylan's career, really.

Eva tried to appreciate the silver linings, although they felt thinner these days. As she'd tried to find the elusive problem behind their inability to have a baby, several doctors mentioned her "advanced maternal age"—as if being thirty-seven were some kind of disease. And Dylan was working later and later more nights a week.

Six months ago, Eva had suspected an affair with someone at the office. She'd hired a private detective. When he told her the truth, it was worse. She was wounded but not surprised.

After all, she'd met Dylan while working as an escort at Discretion herself. She had been twenty-six years old, working for Madeleine to pay for grad school. Dylan was a young corporate lawyer and a big client of Discretion. He soon became one of her regulars.

He was engaged to someone else at the time—some rich girl from a rich family. His own rich family approved. Although his family loved the fiancée, he didn't. He was bored. He broke off his engagement and asked Eva to marry him. She was the girl in a fairy tale. It was what all the escorts hoped for. A perfect life awaited.

After they got married, she'd assumed he stopped seeing other women. But six months ago, her investigator had found that he was back using Discretion—a regular customer again. She confronted him, furious, and he swore to put an end to it.

Eva took down the hanger holding tonight's outfit and peeled off the Nordstrom garment bag. Underneath was a scarlet cocktail dress. She stepped into it, zipping up the back herself. She looked in the mirror approvingly. The one-shouldered red sheath showed off her muscular arms and set off the dark upsweep of her hair. The hem, just above the knee, highlighted her tanned legs while covering enough thigh to be sufficiently demure for a political function. She'd calibrated the precise balance between sexy and appropriate. She put on diamond earrings and a pair of crystal-encrusted silver heels in which she would still be six inches shorter than her husband.

Dylan came into the bedroom, pulling off his tie. She waited for him to appreciate her in all her styled, lipsticked, red silken glory. But he looked at her with a troubled expression.

"That was the police on the phone. They wanted to know where I was Tuesday night."

Eva froze. "What did you tell them?"

"I was at that meeting you set up with the church group. Then they asked if I'd taken out any money from our bank account recently, and if we had a safe-deposit box, could they look in it."

"No!"

Dylan pulled off his shirt, tossed it into the laundry hamper, and shook his head. "I can't say no. I raked Lionel over the coals for not cooperating with the police. And why shouldn't I let them? I said they could look in the box tomorrow morning."

"Dylan! Call them back right away. Tell them you can't see them until Monday."

"Why?" He frowned at her, then slowly turned to face her full-on. "Dammit, Eva! Is there something in the safe-deposit box I should know about? The fucking police are calling."

"Don't speak to me in that tone! If you need to know something, I'll tell you."

"It's my bank account, too."

"I'm the one who handles everything around here. Look at the house downstairs. Who do you think did that? The tent, the crystal, the flowers? Practically for free! I do everything for you."

"You get a pretty good deal out of it." He gestured around their large master suite.

"I deserve it. I could have had anyone. I gave up my life for you. I gave up having a baby for you! While you were running around, fucking those whores!"

Dylan sighed. "Oh, Eva. I've said I was sorry."

"If you're sorry, call back the police and cancel. Tell them they can't see the safe-deposit box, and you're not answering any questions."

"God, Eva. What's in the box?"

"You don't want to know."

"I'm going to see it for myself. With the police."

It might've been a bluff, but her rage was faster than her intellect at that moment.

"You ungrateful bastard! Do you want to go to jail as an accessory to murder?"

Dylan took a step back. "What are you talking about?"

"It was all going to come out! Madeleine was going to turn over a book full of details of every night you spent with those girls. They would know I was an escort, that we met because you hired me."

"It was a grand jury investigation. Those are secret."

"Oh, come on. There are always leaks. That bitch Madeleine could write some tell-all book, and we'd be chapter one! We would have been destroyed. What were you doing about it? Nothing. Well, I wasn't going to let that happen."

"What did you do, Eva?"

"I gave up everything for you. I put off having a baby for your career. And now I can't. The only thing we have left is your political star. I'm not letting that burn out."

Dylan sank down on the bed. His voice was a whisper. "What did you do?"

"I went to her house, and I made her an offer. Fifty thousand for her books. She wouldn't take it. She was going to tell them about you. About me. About the money I offered her, about everything. You have to go *through* your opponents. So I shot her." Eva smiled. "Which was a brilliant move, I have to say. I saved our money and got the books. Don't worry, I burned the records. But the cash is in our safe-deposit box. I have to figure out how to launder it. Literally. It's all bloody."

"Are you crazy?" Dylan looked like he would vomit. "Have you fucking lost your mind? How could you?"

"How could *I*? You were going to do nothing. You weak, incompetent ass. I gave you an alibi, and I fixed the problem. You ought to be thanking me."

Dylan stood, strode over, and slapped her flat across the cheek with more speed and power than she would've thought possible from her politician husband. Her head snapped back. She collapsed into a white leather chair.

When she'd learned that he was still hiring Discretion girls, she'd contemplated a divorce. But she had too much invested in his success. She was too old to start over. Now she buried her face in her knees and let one small sob escape.

"Eva." His voice was softer. He had never hit her before. "I'm sorry. Come here."

She looked up at his outstretched hand. She took it. He helped her to her feet. She let her husband pull her in to him. Then she went through him.

Eva pistoned her knee between his legs, her signature move. Dylan grunted and folded into himself. She grabbed his head and slammed his face down on her knee. She felt the cartilage in his nose collapse, saw the blood streak across their plush white carpeting.

"It's too late for sorry," she said. "Now I have to go and fix it."

She left him bleeding on the floor.

# 51

As Sam pulled the Durango into the Youngbloods' driveway, Anna could see a portion of a large white tent out back. A blue van was parked in front of them, and men in tuxedos were unloading sound equipment and brass instruments. Anna knew the fund-raiser was due to start in about an hour. But this couldn't wait.

When they'd called him, Dylan had been so accommodating on the telephone, answering their questions so easily—he sounded like a man who had nothing to hide. He claimed that fifty churchgoers could swear to his whereabouts the night Madeleine Connor was murdered, and he seemed to know nothing about any recent activity in his bank account. It was Eva they wanted to talk to now.

They were stopping by unannounced to do the interview with no advance notice. They wanted to give Eva as little time as possible to think about what to say, to prepare any fake stories, or to consult with anyone. They had finished their phone call with Dylan less than fifteen minutes ago. This was as good as they were going to get.

Anna and Samantha walked up the stone path to the boxy white contemporary. The walls were sheer glass. It seemed rather exposed for a house on a main artery, Anna thought, but to each her own.

Samantha rang the doorbell. When no one answered, Anna peered in the floor-to-ceiling window next to the bleached white wooden door. The foyer

was all white, with a brushed metal table holding a
vase of big white flowers. No one was there. Sam rang
the doorbell again.

Finally, Dylan Youngblood descended the staircase.
He stopped on the landing as if uncertain whether
to come to the door. Anna was stunned by the City
Councilman's appearance. He wore gray pin-striped
pants and a white undershirt spattered with bright red
blood. One of his eyes was swollen shut and his nose
canted in a sickening C shape. He held a blood-soaked
Kleenex under his nostrils. The wounds were fresh. He
swayed dizzily.

Samantha pushed open the door and rushed to
Dylan's side. She flashed her badge, keeping her other
hand on her gun. "Sir, I'm Samantha Randazzo, FBI.
We just spoke a moment ago. What's going on?"

"Eva! She just did this to me!"

He made a vague pointing gesture, then stumbled
and grabbed the banister for support.

Anna stared at him in horror. Eva had battered her
husband? The ground seemed to shift beneath her feet.
Anna had worked on hundreds of domestic-violence
cases and knew that violence happened between all
kinds of people: rich and poor, old and young, to male
and female victims. But Eva and Dylan? They were
supposed to have the perfect marriage. Eva was supposed to be the perfect wife. And yet here was Dylan,
clutching a Kleenex so soaked with blood that red
rivulets streamed down his forearm and dripped onto
the white marble floor.

Anna expected he would react to this assault like
any other domestic-violence victim. He would tell
them the truth now, while he was shocked and upset
by what had happened. By the time of the trial, he

would probably be reconciled with Eva and would re-
fuse to testify against her. But what he said now would
be admissible in court.

"What happened, sir?" Anna asked. She took a
pack of tissues from her purse.

"She killed Madeleine Connor." He sat on the
stairs. "Dear God."

Anna handed him a fresh tissue. He told them everything that had happened.

The Friendship Heights branch of Bank of America
stayed open until six P.M. on Fridays. Eva could just
make it under the wire. Although her instinct was
to speed over there, she deliberately drove the speed
limit. No time to get pulled over.

Inside the branch, the male teller gave Eva's red
cocktail dress a curious once-over. "Just remembered a
brooch I want to wear at my party," she told him. He
smiled and led her to the vault. He put his key in the
lock next to Eva's, and they unlocked the little steel door
together.

Eva took the metal box to the privacy cubby. There
was the stack of money, now brown and wavy with
dried blood. She tucked the brick of cash into her
purse. Amazing how small fifty grand was in denomi-
nations of a hundred.

When she was done, Eva walked out of the bank's
glass doors and exhaled with relief. She'd take the
money, tie a rock to it, and throw it into the Potomac.
It was a shame to throw away the cash, but it was the
only safe thing to do now. She'd been willing to spend
the money for peace of mind, anyway.

Then there would be nothing tying them to the
crime. She'd bought the Beretta at a Virginia gun show

many years ago. The seller had taken cash and kept no record of the sale. Since her days at Discretion, Eva had never felt entirely safe. Having an untraceable weapon had helped give her a feeling of security. On Tuesday night, she'd been careful to wear gloves while loading the gun, so there would be no prints on the cartridges. She'd wiped the gun clean before putting it in the madam's hands. She hadn't touched anything in Madeleine's house.

She and Dylan would figure out how to approach things tomorrow, after they both calmed down. Eva smiled grimly as she walked down Wisconsin Avenue. With luck, by the time she got home, the caterers would've set up their warming dishes, the band would've set up their instruments, and the valet parkers would've set up their sign on the front lawn. She would glide through tonight's fund-raiser on autopilot. Her hostess instincts had allowed her to do that many times, when inside she felt like killing someone. She wasn't sure Dylan had the same talent, but she expected his sense of self-preservation would kick in. He could say he got his black eye from a thrown elbow during a basketball game.

A big African-American man in an off-white suit blocked her path on the sidewalk. She smiled and tried to step around him. He moved over to block her way.

"Excuse me," she said testily.

"No, ma'am, excuse me." He held up a police badge. "Tavon McGee, MPD, detective first grade. Ms. Eva Youngblood, you're under arrest."

Two police cruisers pulled out of an alleyway and parked at the curb next to Eva.

Her heart expanded to fill her rib cage, then contracted to the size of a lima bean. The detective took the purse off her shoulder, turned her around, and handcuffed her behind her back. She could see the glass doors of the Bank of America, where the teller was standing. He held up a cell phone, taking pictures of her in her red dress and handcuffs, being led to an MPD cruiser. Eva briefly wondered how much money the teller would make for those photos.

"Thanks for your help," Detective McGee said as he opened the police car's back door. "We didn't have enough evidence to get into that safe-deposit box— until you went there in response to the FBI's phone call. Prosecutor got an anticipatory search warrant. We could search the box and arrest you or Dylan only if you went to the box."

He put a hand on her head and lowered her into the backseat. Her first thought was that he was ruining her updo.

The detective shut the door, closing her into the smelly backseat. She watched him through the mesh wire that separated the back from the front. He put her purse on the front seat, snapped on a pair of rubber gloves, and pawed through her stuff. It took him less than five seconds to pull out the dirty brick of cash.

"Mm, mm, mm." He smiled at Eva as he held up the money, which was covered with the dried blood of Madeleine Connor. "I hope you got a lot more of this, 'cause you're gonna need a good lawyer."

Sunday

## 52

The pedicure room at Bliss, the spa in the W Hotel, was beautiful and serene, done in shades of light blue and filled with vases of hydrangeas. New-age music played softly from hidden speakers, and the air was lightly scented with eucalyptus and rosemary. Everything was designed to soothe and relax, and that was exactly how Anna felt. She reclined in the cushy white chair and watched the man painting her toenails a cheerful pink. Just looking at the color made her happy. She glanced over at Grace's feet. Grace had chosen a metallic white polish, which looked great on her dark brown toes.

"Nice choice," Anna said.

"You, too." Grace smiled and raised her mimosa. "Thanks for the pedicure."

They clinked and sipped. Anna had planned the day out for the two of them. She owed her friend some quality time.

"I'm sorry I've been out of the loop lately," she said.

"Life of the prosecutor. Happens to all of us."

Anna nodded, although they both knew it wasn't just the usual work demands that had stolen time from their friendship. True, she'd been caught up in a big case. But she had been absent for longer than the Capitol investigation. She had been too absorbed by her relationship with Jack. That wouldn't happen again, Anna promised herself. In the future, she would strike a better balance.

"What's been going on with you?" Anna asked.

"Not much." But then Grace launched into a story about a witness who'd pulled down his pants and mooned her because he didn't want to testify. Anna and Grace laughed so hard that the guys painting their toes had to stop and wait for them to stop shaking.

When their pedicures were done, they went up to the P.O.V. rooftop bar at the top of the hotel. It had famous views of the White House, the Mall, and the monuments. They ate brunch, gossiped, and watched hip young Washingtonians flit about. After their plates had been cleared, Grace leaned forward and whispered, "I want to hear about the Youngbloods."

Anna glanced around them. It was after three P.M., and the place had started to clear out. They were alone in their corner. Still, she kept her voice soft as she described the scene at the Youngbloods' house.

"It was so disturbing. I mean, we've seen worse injuries and more sympathetic victims. But it was like watching an idol fall off her pedestal. I thought Eva had it all figured out. But she's even more messed up than most of us."

"Everyone's got something," Grace said. "No one's as clean as she looks from the outside."

"You know, I grew up in this messed-up house. I wasn't sure I knew how to make a marriage work. But now I figure, hell, I have as good a shot as anybody else. Maybe better."

"Of course you do!" Grace met her eyes sternly. "So what are you thinking?"

"I miss Jack. And every night at eight-thirty, I've been wishing to be in Olivia's bedroom, kissing her goodnight. I want to be with them. I'm ready for it."

"Oh, girl." Grace smiled sadly. "Just when I thought I was getting you back."

"No, no," Anna said. "I'm gonna do it better this time. I can be a good partner and also have a life of my own. I think Jack's figured out how to be more flexible, too."

"Have you talked to him about this yet?"

"No. But I'm going to."

The waiter came over with the bill. Grace tried to pay, but Anna was too quick. "You got all the margaritas at Rosa," Anna argued as the waiter took her credit card.

They went downstairs and emerged onto 15th Street. The humidity had finally let up, and it was a clear, beautiful summer day. They walked past the White House, around a group of kids playing roller hockey in the paved park that used to be Pennsylvania Avenue. They strolled through Lafayette Park and then headed up Connecticut Avenue.

"So I was hoping you could help me," Anna said.

"How so?"

"I want to show Jack how much he means to me. How ready I am to be with him and Olivia."

"Are you?" Grace asked. "Ready?"

"I am."

Anna said it with confidence, knowing neither of them was perfect, but also knowing they belonged together. He had some secrets, she realized that. Something with his wife, something with Carla, maybe more. Whatever they were, she would deal with them. They had problems to overcome, but she was ready to take them on. He was a good man, and she loved him, and the more she saw of the world, the more she understood what precious things those were. She wanted him back. If she could convince him to take her.

They reached the red awnings of the Tiny Jewel

Box. Grace kept walking, but Anna put a hand on her friend's arm. "Actually, I was hoping you could help me pick out a watch for Jack."

"Wow, from the Tiny Jewel Box? Fancy."

"Yeah. I'm not sure how this is done, reverse-gender-wise. But I think I need a token to show Jack how serious I am." Anna smiled and breathed in the clean summer air. "I'm going to ask him to marry me."

# ACKNOWLEDGMENTS

I'm thankful to all the police officers, agents, and victims' advocates with whom I've worked on cases similar to those in this novel; their dedication has improved the lives of countless girls and women in D.C.

In researching *Discretion*, I relied on many professionals who took time from busy lives to speak with me about their work. I'm very grateful for this generosity, from which I gleaned fascinating true stories and details for this book. Any errors are my own. Thanks to: Kate Connelly, for her thoughtful insights into prosecuting escort cases; Mike Ferrara, for his expertise on the Speech or Debate Clause; Zulima Espinel, Missy Rohrbach, Moira McConaghy, and Dayle Cristinzio, for guiding me through the procedural machinations and actual hallways of Congress; Kelly Higashi, for her encyclopedic knowledge and all her support and friendship over the years; Glenn Kirschner, who is both an incredible crime fighter and an incredible resource for a crime novelist; Michelle Zamarin, Tejpal Chawla, Eric Gallun, Lou Ramos, and Ed, for their knowledge of specialized areas of law enforcement; Kristen Brewer, for her expertise on human trafficking; Detectives Bill Xanten and Carter Adams, for their insights into the lives of MPD homicide detectives; Detective John Marsh, for his knowledge of computer forensics; Detective Steve Schwalm, for his expertise on matters ranging from gorilla pimps to john jams; Matthew Rosenheim, who taught me about diamond identification; Dr. Mauricio Cortina, who helped me explore psychological angles for some of my characters; the instructors of IMPACT-DC, for their excellent self-defense course; and FBI Special Agent Steve Quisenberry (after whom Samantha's fictional partner is named), for his incredible eye for detail and for helping me keep Samantha in line.

I'm indebted to many people who shared their stories and insights but did not wish to be publicly acknowledged. Thank you for your time, honesty, and trust.

In some ways, a great literary agent is like a great lawyer, equal parts professional ally, personal confidante, tireless advocate, marketing guru, critic, psychologist, and magician. My deepest gratitude goes to my incredible agent, Amy Berkower, who is all of that and more.

I am thrilled to continue working with my editor, Lauren Spiegel. Sharp, ever cheerful, and shockingly wise beneath her beautiful exterior, Lauren amazes me with her ability to make a story better, and to make that wrenching process feel like a fun gossipfest about the characters.

Thanks to the wonderful team at Simon & Schuster, especially Stacy Creamer, Marcia Burch, David Falk, Shida Carr, Sally Kim, Marie Florio, Abby Zidle, Emily Remes, Josh Karpf, Ashley Hewlett, Meredith Vilarello, Cherlynne Li, MacKenzie Fraser-Bub, Parisa Zolfaghari, and Beth Thomas. I truly appreciate all the opportunities you've created for me.

I am grateful to Barbara Delinsky and George Pelecanos, two exceptional writers whose work I have admired for years, and who have been remarkably generous with their time, advice, and guidance through the publishing world.

A big thank-you goes to my good friends and

earliest readers: Lynn Haaland, Jenny McIntyre, Jeff Cook, Missy Rorhbach, Jen Wofford, and Jessica Mikuliak, for their flashes of brilliance, their bluntness when necessary, and their provision of stiff drinks after the aforementioned bluntness. I might have completed this book without their help, but it wouldn't have been nearly as good, or as much fun.

My family has supported me in a thousand ways, with encouragement and love. Thank you to my mom, Diane Harnisch; my sisters, Kerry Hughes and Tracey Fitzgerald; my father and stepmother, Alan and Laurie Harnisch; and my in-laws, John, Carol, and Barbara Leotta. Special thanks are due to my cousins, Marilyn Reis and Jack Small, for all of their support and assistance as I've transitioned from prosecutor to writer. I am filled with love and amazement for my two little boys, who have been so sweet and patient as I wrote this book (although I hope they won't read it until they are much, much older).

Thanks most of all to Mike, my fun, adorable, scorchingly intelligent husband, without whom none of this would have been possible.

Keep reading for a sneak peek of
the next Anna Curtis novel from
Allison Leotta

## A GOOD KILLING

COMING SPRING 2015!

# 1

When I was fifteen, my favorite place in the world was the high-jump setup at the school track. The bar provided a simple obstacle with a certain solution. You either cleared it or you didn't. In a world of tangled problems with knotty answers, that was bliss.

I guess it all started out on that field, the summer before my sophomore year. That's when I fell in love with Owen Fowler. I never could hide how much I wanted that man.

That's why everyone immediately thought I murdered him. Watch any TV crime show, and the person who says "I couldn't have killed him—I loved him!" is the one who did it. Nothing fuels hate like love gone wrong. So when the coach went up in flames, people naturally looked to see if I was holding the match. But I swear: I didn't kill him.

You don't believe me, Annie, I can see it in your eyes. But I'll tell you everything, exactly how it went down. You probably won't agree with what I did. You definitely would've done things differently. But by the end, I hope you'll at least understand.

So—ten years ago. The athletic field was the most beautiful place in Holly Grove. A girl could feel like she was part of something good on that rectangle of perfect grass, surrounded by bleachers shining silver in the sun. Come fall, the football players would own the field, and the stands would hold ten thousand screaming fans. But in July, the stadium was empty, and the kids who went to Coach Fowler's sports camp got to use the spongy red track that circled the field. The air smelled of fresh-cut grass, the clean sweat of a good workout, and the occasional whiff of Icy Hot. To this day, I still love the smell of Icy Hot.

And I loved the feel of the high jump itself. That moment at the peak, as my back sailed over the bar and I looked straight up at the sky—suspended above the earth, touching nothing but air. Like I could detach from the physical world with all its problems. For a second, at least. I was free. It was my little piece of heaven.

You know what I mean, right? You were a pretty good sprinter yourself. What'd you place in the two hundred meter? Eighth in the state? But track didn't mean the same to you. You'd found another way out. By the time I turned fifteen, you'd already accepted that scholarship to U of M. That summer, you were just killing time before college, hanging out at the track a lot. You told Mom you went to watch me, but you were really there to flirt with Rob. Don't fuss, you know it's true. He was a hottie. And not just because he'd been starting quarterback that year—king of the town! He was objectively hot. Guess he peaked early.

You know why he suddenly got interested your senior year, right? After all those years of not knowing your name? No offense, but. You finally grew some boobs. My own chest didn't show signs of catching up any time soon. The high jump was the one place where my resemblance to a wall was still an advantage.

I was aiming to break your school record for high jumping. Six feet, one inch. I thought if I broke it, people would finally start calling me "Jody" instead of "Anna Curtis's little sister." I remember the day I first believed I could do it: July 15, 2004.

I was trying to figure out why my jump had stalled. I was doing everything right, but it just wasn't taking. I tried again: stood at my starting place and sprinted toward the bar. I hit my mark and rounded the turn toward the mat: five strides, pivot, jump! I flew backward, arched my spine, and kicked my feet up. But something was off, I knew it even before my butt knocked down the pole. As my back hit the mat, I heard the bar clatter to the ground, and Rob laughing in the distance.

I said, "Fuck."

"Watch your language, young lady."

Coach Fowler stood next to the mat, which was a surprise. He was the head of the whole camp and mostly stayed with the football team, leaving the lesser athletes to the lesser coaches. The thrill of him noticing me was canceled by the fact that it was when I'd messed up.

"Sorry, Coach!"

I jumped off the mat and fetched the pole. We set it on the risers together. He was tan and tall, with an athletic build and that aura of authority. The sun threw golden glints off his blond hair. He must've been forty at that point, but he was way cuter than the teenage boys he coached.

"You're a good jumper," Coach said. "You could be great—but you have to really want it. Do you really want it?"

I looked over where you and Rob were sitting. Rob was tugging on the tie of your hoodie. The coach followed my gaze.

"Your sister's a good runner. Fast, determined, scrappy," he said. "Jody—you're better."

I blinked with surprise. He knew my name. And . . . not many people thought I was better than you at anything. He reached over and pulled my hand away from my cheek. I hadn't even realized I was touching my scar.

"It's barely noticeable," he said. He cleared his throat and pointed to my pink chalk mark on the ground. "The problem is your approach. Your mark is too close. You shot up this spring, so your stride is longer. You need room to stretch out those long legs."

I tried not to blush at the implication that he'd noticed my legs. Coach took a piece of blue chalk out of his pocket and drew a line on the ground, about three feet behind my pink mark. He also moved back my starting mark. "Try that."

I trotted to the new starting place, feeling the blue nylon of my team shorts brushing against my glamorously long legs. I looked at the coach's marks and wasn't sure I could do it. I glanced at him, and he nodded. You and Rob stopped talking to watch me. I took a deep breath, squinted at the high-jump bar, and sprinted toward it. I reached the coach's mark and counted off my curve, demanding my legs cover as much ground as they could with each stride: one, two, three, four, five. Pivot. Go!

I jumped. And I flew.

I knew it was perfect the moment I took off. I felt it in my legs, my hips, my spine. I soared back over the pole with inches to spare. Suspended in the air, I looked at the bright blue sky and the soft white clouds and felt a moment of perfection.

I landed on my shoulder blades and let myself somersault backward. A few runners broke out into applause. You yelled, "Go, Jody!"

I jumped on the mat. "Yes!"

"There it is!" Coach yelled. "Good girl! Do that at a meet, and we'll be putting your name up in the gym."

I bounced to the edge of the mat, and Coach met me with a high five. Then he held out his hand to help me down. I took it, feeling honored, shy, and electrically happy. His grip was steady and strong. Dad had never held my hand like that. Coach's fingers tightened around mine as I stepped down, then opened to release me. But I didn't want to break the connection. I kept holding on to his hand for a few seconds after he let go.

# 2

Anna felt a gentle nudge on her shoulder but kept her eyes closed. Another nudge followed, more insistently. She smelled fresh-brewed coffee and heard morning birds chattering, but all she wanted was to stay curled in warm oblivion. She closed her eyes tighter, determined to hold on to her sleep. It was like trying to hold on to water; the harder she squeezed, the faster it slipped away. She cracked an eye.

The unfamiliar bedroom was bright and lovely, decorated in expensive neutrals. Her black pantsuit was draped neatly over an ivory chair. She glanced down and saw that she was wearing only her bra and panties from the night before. She became aware of a dull headache, throbbing with each beat of her heart. Blinking, she pulled the blanket to her chest, sat up, and tried to remember how she'd gotten here.

A pair of warm brown hands handed her a steaming mug of coffee. Anna looked up at the hands' owner. Her friend Grace smiled down at her.

"You look like your hair got caught in a blender," Grace said.

"I feel like it was my whole head."

At least she understood where she was: Grace's guest room. The night before came back in a series of images that grew blurrier toward the end: placing her engagement ring on the table at the Tabard Inn; walking through Dupont Circle with tears streaming down her face; meeting Grace, Samantha, and the detectives at Sergio's restaurant to toast the jury's verdict in the

MS-13 case. And wine. Endless glasses of wine, which, despite Anna's wholehearted efforts, had succeeded in blotting everything out for only a few short hours.

And left her with a massive hangover. She groaned and rubbed her temples. Grace handed her two Advil, which she gratefully swallowed down with coffee. It was sweet and milky, which coaxed a smile through the blur. Her life was a mess, but at least she had a good friend who knew how she took her coffee.

Anna spotted her cell phone on the nightstand. She had two "unknown" calls from a Michigan area code, and a string of worried texts and calls from her fiancé. Correction: her ex-fiancé. She let the phone thump back down.

"I would've let you sleep longer," Grace said, "but you have a phone call."

"Jack?"

"Who else?"

Anna shook her head, which was a mistake. She wondered how long it would take for the caffeine and ibuprofen to kick in. "We're done."

"He tracked you down here," Grace said. "That doesn't sound 'done.' That sounds kind of romantic."

"He's the Homicide chief. If he can't locate his ex-fiancé, he should resign."

"I didn't want to hit you with this, but . . . he's distraught. And you know he's not the distraught type."

Anna plucked unhappily at the blanket. She wanted to talk to him—she wanted it like a dieter wants cupcakes. But there was nothing left to say. She knew Jack loved her. He loved another woman, too.

"Please tell him I'm fine, and I'm sorry, and I can't talk to him now."

"Okay, sweetie."

Grace handed her a box of Kleenex and left. Anna

banished a rogue tear, as her phone buzzed from the nightstand. It was the "unknown" caller from Michigan again, the same 313 area code as her sister. She blew her nose and picked up.

"Hello."

"Hi, Anna? It's Kathy Mack. From Holly Grove High School?"

That was another world, and Anna needed a moment to get there. She stared at the ceiling until her memory caught up with the conversation: Kathy was an old friend of her sister's. Anna saw her occasionally, when she went home to visit Jody in Michigan. They'd never traded phone calls.

"Kathy—hi! Is everything okay?"

"Actually . . . no. There's a lot going on here. I don't know where to start. I guess I should start with this: Coach Fowler died. He— Some people are saying he was killed."

"Oh—that's terrible."

Anna sat back against the pillows. Since she was a kid, Coach Fowler had been a major figure in her hometown, leading Holly Grove's football team to the state championship several times. He was the most successful member of their community, and one who gave back. His recommendation helped Anna get a college scholarship and out of their small, rusting town.

"It is terrible," Kathy said, "but that's not exactly why I'm calling. See, the police want to question Jody."

"What? Why?" The coach had mentored Jody in high school, but that was ten years ago. As far as Anna knew, they hadn't been in touch since then.

"I have no idea," Kathy said. "And no one can find her. The police went to her house, but she's not answering her door. I've tried her number; she's not picking up."

"Thanks for calling me," Anna said. "I'll try her now."

They hung up and Anna dialed her sister's number. She got an automated message she'd never heard on Jody's phone before: "The person you're trying to reach is no longer available." It didn't let her leave a voice mail.

Anna's chest tightened. She was always vaguely worried about her little sister. For the last few months, they hadn't spoken as often as usual. If Jody were in trouble, Anna might not even know.

She welcomed a reason to get out of town for a while. Get away from Jack, D.C. Superior Court, and the inevitable sympathy from everyone she'd have to uninvite from her wedding. She could take a couple days off. Prosecutors often did after a big trial.

She swiped through her phone, tapped the Expedia app, and clicked on a last-minute deal to Detroit. Then she called Kathy back. "Thanks for calling, Kathy. I'm flying to Michigan this afternoon."

# 3

As soon as the airplane screeched to a halt on the runway of Detroit Metro Airport, Anna powered up her phone and tried to call her sister again. No luck. Her headache was receding, but the worry in her stomach grew.

She got off the plane and hurried past a wine bar, golf shop, and day spa—besides the casinos, the airport housed the most sophisticated commerce in Detroit—and took the escalators down to baggage claim, where she looked for Cooper Bolden. Kathy had arranged for Cooper to pick Anna up. He'd been a friend in high school, a sunny, bookish kid whose family owned a farm on the outskirts of the county. She hadn't spoken to him in ages. Last she heard, he'd become an Army Ranger and gone to Afghanistan. She scanned the area for him now, looking for a tall, skinny boy with knobby knees and flapping elbows.

Standing against a pillar, scrolling through his phone, was a man with a chest like a Ford 350. He wasn't wearing glasses, and his black hair was shorter, but under a couple days' worth of stubble was a familiar lopsided grin.

"Cooper?"

He looked up and she could see his eyes: light blue rimmed with indigo. She rushed forward to hug him. He stumbled, laughed, and hugged her back.

"Anna. Hi! Easy."

"Easy? You're three times as big as you were in high school."

Cooper laughed. "Maybe only twice as big." He pulled up the jeans on his left leg, lifting the hem. Below was a silver prosthetic limb. "Compliments of the Taliban."

"Oh, Coop. I'm sorry."

"It's okay. They didn't get the best part of me."

"Your spleen?"

"No. My enormous"—he held his hands two feet apart—"intellect."

"Of course."

"You look great," Cooper said. "Just like I remember you. Except more . . ."

"Weary?"

"No. Grown-up."

Anna grabbed her suitcase off the conveyor belt. When she packed it, two days earlier, she thought she'd spend a few nights at Grace's house, in the process of moving out of Jack's. Now she had the dizzying sensation of being a nomad, with no true home anywhere on earth. For the last year, she'd lived with Jack and his six-year-old daughter in their pretty yellow Victorian. After their engagement, Anna started calling it "our house." At Jack's urging, she'd begun to make it her own: rearranging where the mugs were kept, registering for silverware. But now she'd have to find her own apartment. She had to go to that pretty yellow Victorian and pack everything up, deciding which things to take and which to leave forever. She'd see all Olivia's toys and first-grade artwork and know that she had no claim to them. Because, much as she wanted to be—as often as she'd gone to parent-teacher conferences, braided the girl's hair, pored over parenting books trying to figure out the right answer to every six-year-old question— she wasn't Olivia's mother. Without Jack, she was nothing to Olivia. She was just a woman with a suit-case and a hangover.

Cooper took the bag from her hands. "I got it," he said.

She came back to the present and glanced at his leg. "But—"

"Can't stop me from being chivalrous."

She'd had a hard breakup, but he'd lost a limb for his country. It put things in perspective. Normally, she'd insist on carrying her own luggage, but now she just said, "Thanks."

As they walked toward the parking lot, she saw that Cooper's gait had changed too. It used to be a long, loping bounce, like a frisky colt finding his bal-ance. Now his stride was shorter, more deliberate, and with a little hitch that could be interpreted as a swag-ger if you didn't know better.

"Have you heard from Jody?" Anna asked. "I still can't get ahold of her."

He shook his head. "All I know is the police want to interview her."

"I wish she'd called me. I'm a lawyer."

"I expect she knows that," Cooper said with a smile. "And she doesn't need a lawyer. She'll be glad to see her sister, though."

"I hope so. Can we go right to her house?"

"Sure."

In the parking garage, she followed him to a handi-capped parking space and reached for the door to a gray sedan. He shook his head. "That's not mine." He walked to the other side of the sedan, where a huge black Harley-Davidson sat in a motorcycle spot. She glanced at the bike and then at Cooper's prosthetic leg.

"Don't worry. There's a double amputee riding across America." He strapped her bag to a luggage rack and handed her a helmet. "He was fine when he started, but he lost both legs in a motorcycle accident."

She laughed, weighing the risk to her life versus the risk of hurting his feelings. She'd never ridden a motorcycle before and was mildly terrified. She reached for the helmet. Cooper opened a saddlebag and pulled out a black leather jacket, similar to the one he was wearing, and held it out to her. But it was mid-June, warm and balmy.

"No thanks," she said.

"It's to protect your skin if we have a crash."

"Oh, that's reassuring."

She put on the leather jacket. It smelled of cedar, cherries, and the faint hint of another woman's perfume. Cooper straddled the front seat. She climbed onto the seat behind him and grabbed the metal handles on the sides of the seat, leaving a wide berth between their bodies.

Cooper glanced back. "Don't be shy. Scooch up nice and close and hold on to my waist."

She hesitated, suddenly wary. Who picks someone up from the airport on a motorcycle? What if she'd had more luggage? She met his clear blue eyes and found only earnestness there. She slid forward and put her arms around him.

He started the engine and pulled forward. As the motorcycle drove past the parked cars, her heartbeat quickened. She was very aware that she had a large man between her legs, her breasts pressed against his back, and a giant engine humming beneath her. She could feel Cooper's lean muscles beneath his leather jacket. She wasn't cheating on Jack, she reasoned. First: she was just getting a ride. Second: she and Jack were done. Third: she hoped she didn't die.

Anna tried to pay for parking, but Cooper beat her

to it. He pulled out of the parking structure and onto the service road. Anna could reach out and touch the car in the next lane—which would take her arm off. As he pulled onto the highway's on-ramp, Cooper yelled, "Ready?"

"Yeah," she lied.

The bike roared up to Michigan's 70 mph speed limit. She held tight to Cooper's waist. The motor filled her ears and the pavement flew under her feet. She wondered how it would feel if her body hit it. The bike angled low into a curve, and Cooper swung between her thighs. Her adrenaline surged. She was scared and thrilled and very aware of being alive.

Halfway between Detroit and Flint, Cooper slowed the bike and took the exit ramp marked "Holly Grove." Anna's grip relaxed, but her chest tightened. She'd been relieved when she left this town, and she never liked coming back. The only thing she really loved here was her sister.

Cooper passed through the historic downtown. It must have been charming once, but it wasn't used for much these days. The courthouse and city hall still looked respectable enough, but the storefronts in between were mostly vacant and dilapidated. With each auto factory that closed, the town took a hit. And the commerce that still remained in Holly Grove was in the suburbs. Cooper continued out there, passing subdivisions anchored with strip malls, big-box stores, and massive parking lots. He turned onto a smaller cross street, leaving the commercial strip behind.

As they came up to the curve before Holly Grove High School, Anna noticed an acrid smell, growing stronger. The football stadium came into sight, and she stared at it in shock.

A burned-out car was smashed into the center of

a blackened circle at the bottom of the stadium's cement wall. The ground beneath it was an oily scab of scorched earth. The top of the stadium appeared unscathed, with the word *BULLDOGS* still gleaming in blue and silver. The charred smell was so strong it was like sticking her head into a recently used barbecue grill. Yellow crime-scene tape surrounded the area. A few police officers lingered around the perimeter.

Cooper pulled the bike to the shoulder, put down the kickstand, and took off his helmet. The roar of the engine was replaced with the chirping of insects. She took off her helmet, too, smelling fresh-cut grass, ashes, and gasoline.

"What happened?" she asked.

"This is where Coach Fowler died," Cooper said.

"How?"

"He came around this turn. Guess his car was going pretty fast. Crashed right into the stadium. His car went up in flames. He didn't make it out."

She climbed off the bike and walked to the edge of the yellow tape. A cop on the other side glanced over but didn't shoo her away. She guessed the crime-scene work was done and they were just waiting for a tow. Cooper stood next to her.

The car was a classic Corvette. A few spots of blue paint were still visible, but most of the outside was burned black. The hood was smashed in so far, the car looked like a pug. A circular web cracked the windshield in front of the driver's seat.

Anna looked at the ground between the road and the stadium. There was a dirt shoulder, a section of grass, and then a cement apron abutting the concrete wall. There were no skid marks.

"You know what's weird?" Cooper said.

"Other than Coach Fowler crashing right into his

stadium, without making any apparent attempt to stop?"

"Cars don't generally explode on impact. I mean, it happens sometimes, but it's not like the movies. It's rare. And when cars do catch fire from a crash, there's usually a more heavily burned area where the fire started, like around the battery or gas tank, and then some less burned parts. But the coach's car is blackened all around. To me, cars look like this when someone has taken serious steps to make it happen."

"How do you know so much about burning cars?"

"I saw a lot of them in Afghanistan." Cooper ran a hand through his short black hair. "I was in one."

Anna glanced up at his face. He was looking at the stadium, but seeing something else. Before she could respond, a police officer came up to them. "Help you?"

"Actually, yes, sir." Cooper straightened and put a hand on Anna's shoulder. "We're looking for my friend's sister, Jody Curtis. I understand you are, too. Do you know if she's been located?"

"She's at the station now."

"Is she okay?" Anna said.

"Seems so."

"Thank God." She was flooded with relief. "What's she doing at the station?"

"Being interrogated," the officer said. "In connection with Coach Fowler's death."

That made Anna pause. *Questioned* was one thing. *Interrogated* sounded a lot more adversarial.

"Thanks, Officer." She turned to Cooper. "Can we head to the station?"

"Let's go."

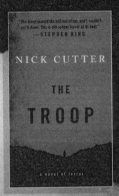
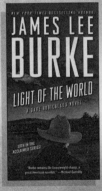

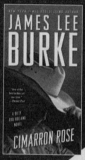